Stuart White has lived in London, Hong Kong and Los Angeles.

As a journalist he has travelled widely in Europe, Africa, Asia, North and South America.

He covered the conflict in Bosnia, the drug wars in Colombia, the Iraqi Scud attacks on Israel, and the Rwandan refugee crisis.

This is his sixth book.

Kiss Of
The Angel

Also by Stuart White

FICTION
Death Game
Operation Raven
'Til The Fat Lady Sings
The Shamrock Boy

NON-FICTION
Zeebrugge: A Hero's Story (with Stephen Homewood)

Kiss Of The Angel

STUART WHITE

BLAKE

Published by Blake Publishing Ltd,
3 Bramber Court, 2 Bramber Road, London W14 9PB, England

First published in Great Britain in 1995

ISBN 1 85782 102 5

British Library Cataloguing-in-Publication Data: A catalogue
record for this book is available from the British Library.

Typeset by MC Typeset Ltd, Wouldham, Rochester, Kent

Printed in Finland by WSOY

1 3 5 7 9 10 8 6 4 2

– Angels are spirits, but it is not because they are spirits that they are angels. They become Angels when they are sent. For the name Angel refers to their office, not their nature.

You ask the name of this nature, it is spirit; you ask its office, it is that of an Angel, which is a messenger.

SAINT AUGUSTINE

Every angel is terrifying.

RAINER MARIA RILKE, Duino Elegies, 2

AN AGE FOR ANGELS: Spiritual, commercial interest in Heavenly beings on the rise.

Los Angeles Times, 1992

To
Carol Clewlow

PROLOGUE

Hand in hand, fearfully, down into the dark basement, into the place of this child's torturing dreams, the place of her dread and her terrified awakenings.

This is where the monsters live, the ill-defined shapes who climb these stairs in the night, who creep through the village, into her home, and up into her room where they mingle with the shadows and the moonlight, leaning, leering and threatening untold fates.

So she is cold, rigid with fear, and only the large rough hand closed on hers gives a vestige of strength and protection. The voice is strong and sure, inspiring fear but also a pathetic trust. It has said the monsters and the demons can be banished by the strength of light and of his presence.

His probing torch beam advances like a challenging lance, and she imagines she hears the monsters scuttle deeper into the blackness. Then he flicks a switch and the harsh light of the naked bulb floods the basement.

And the voice that, in dread, she believes, says, look, no monsters and no demons now, all gone. And the little girl feels gratitude like a rush of blood to her skin, and she clings to her unlikely saviour. She feels the comforting harshness of the stubble, the now reassuring man smell of sweat and tobacco and whiskey.

So she sits on the bare and dusty ex-Army cot beneath the wooden stair, just as the man tells her to. And she does as he directs her, puts her hands where he says. Then blinks as the flashes – one, two, three – blind her momentarily.

And she knows – doesn't she? – that this is the small price of gratitude, the price she must pay, the cost of which she is too young to understand, but which is surely worth paying to banish the demons that hover above her bed at night.

And yet, and yet.

There is a germ of thought in her childish unconsciousness, in the as yet unformed mind, and it forces its way to the surface like an unseen air bubble on a vast ocean of ignorance.

And the thought asks: Are there other demons too? Demons that come with the light, on rough, trusted hands?

Off Catalina Island, California, 1966.

The boat rocks them like an expensive cradle fit for the rich and the pampered, the famous and the soon-to-be-so, soothing them with the soft swell and the gentle slap of waves like a mother's caring caress.

The sigh of the wind sings like a deceptive lullaby that drifts in through the open cabin window as the man stirs and stretches a hand to the smooth, naked thigh squashed against him in the bunk.

Rising desire competes with curiosity at the sounds that have plucked him from the shallow trough of slumber. Art Helm presses his hand, more urgently now, against the firm young flesh.

"Did you hear that?"

His voice is a low and hoarse whisper next to the soft pink ear, but the rhythmic breathing continues undisturbed.

For a moment he studies the fleshy, almost cruelly sensuous lips painted with silver lipstick by the moonlight that pours liquid over their bunk, over the mouth that never fails to excite him.

He leans down, face on face, and feels the rough rasp of the youth's unshaven skin against his own, and marvels at his own perversion. Loves it, hates it, realises that it is an inevitable, integral part of who he is, has been and will always be.

Art Helm swings off the bunk, feeling the wet suck of their parting flesh, then slips into his Bermuda shorts and pads barefoot across the planked floor.

Picking his way through the few hasty and lust-discarded clothes he goes up the three wooden steps, quietly pushing aside the narrow swing doors, stepping out onto the small aft-deck.

Sea-quiet, with just the night's oceanic song of wind in the rigging, the bass creak of timber and the irregular percussion of the sea's chop against the hull.

The stern-tied dinghy bobs this way and that to the push

of the swell and wind, and the frayed edges of the waves spark and twinkle with phosphorescence.

He begins to believe he has imagined the cries that woke him, that perhaps they were something he projected himself into the half-world between sleep and waking.

So he sits, back propped against the aft cabin, feet over the side, taking a pack of Lucky Strike from his Bermuda shorts, lighting one with his gold Ronson, the one inscribed: 'From Mom and Dad on your 21st.' The Mom and Dad who do not know, could never understand, what their son is now.

In the distance Art can see the bulk of Catalina Island, and the twinkle of lights from shore, where tomorrow they will all picnic and bathe.

It has been a wild, abandoned night, free of nosey neighbours and restraints, of unselected gatecrashers, of moralists and Puritans. A boat is a secure world of its own.

Each knew what each risked. Jail, years of disgrace and degradation and confinement. A shudder runs through his body at the thoughts.

He tries to banish them with the reach of the infinitesimal universe above, and the vastness of the ocean below. And he thinks of stardom, of the future house in Bel Air, Beverly Hills, Malibu, perhaps all three.

Of dinner in fine restaurants, of antiques, and fine clothes, a Mercedes Gull-Wing, and of – it was not to be denied – more like the full-lipped youth back in the cabin. Perhaps even of a day when he could live openly the love that still dared not speak its name in America.

He sucks down on the stub of the Lucky, then flicks the butt into the Pacific where it sizzles briefly and disappears like the light of a long-dead star.

And he hears voices.

Low whispers, guttural with fear and effort. The deep bass of a man, the scared falsetto of a girl, both amplified by the water. Art Helm slides slowly into the well of the aft-deck and eases himself around so that he faces towards the bow, and peers along the side of the deck.

He sees a pale ovoid of a face, momentarily illuminated by the moon, sees it looking quickly in the direction of the stern, as though alerted, then sees it disappear into the jumbled bas-relief of mingled shapes. Art ducks down, breathing heavily, terrified of discovery, fearing he may have been seen.

He knows the danger, but senses also, with some inborn instinct, the opportunity and the possibilities this witnessing brings.

He crouches, listens, following the hoarse, whispered commands, the pleas and then the exhaled grunts of effort followed by the short, brutal slap of something heavy hitting the water.

And he risks once more peeping over the deck, sees the two shapes, separate now, defined by their blackness in the shadow of the deck, sees them suddenly half-illuminated by a shaft of moonlight, fused like a statue of conspirators.

And he smiles.

When Art finally climbs back into the bunk the cool of his body wakes the youth. "You're cold."

"I've been on deck."

The youth turns inwards suddenly aware of the palsied hand against him: "Art, you're trembling. Have you seen a ghost or something?"

"Something," Art Helm says, "something like that."

Then he pulls the lithe and muscled body into his, amazed once more at the power of his desire.

The grainy black and white home movie was the only source of illumination in the darkness. Suddenly an arm came up, caught in the branding iron of the projector's beam, casting a shadow across the screen, the finger plunging into the mass of celluloid bodies, singling out one.

"There." The finger jabbed like an accusation.

"Yesss . . ." the voice was like the slither of something primeval.

"Would you like to play with him? Would you like him to

be your friend? To bring him here? Would you?"

And from the blackness the voice gave its wet, sucking reply: "Friend. Play. Yesssss . . ."

CHAPTER ONE

Smog hung like an evil halo over Los Angeles, and the city's poisoned perfume of hot tar and exhaust fumes rose on the late afternoon air.

Off to the West the orange sun began its slow dive over the Malibu mountains and the Pacific.

Looking down from the balcony, Flavor Cartouche could see the vagrants with their sleeping rolls, their possession-loaded wire mesh supermarket trolleys, their dirt'n'sun tans, settling down for the night, gossiping and smoking until the light went.

Below Ocean Boulevard at the foot of the fenced off cliffs, across the traffic-scarred Pacific Coast Highway, past the expensive beach houses and the wide stretch of sand, the surf crashed in on grey breakers.

Across to her left, through the tall palms, she could see the pier jutting out like a finger into the ocean.

She heard the rattle of a china cup behind her, and turned. It was Jack. "Tea?"

1

"Thanks." Flavor took the cup, scenting the pale fragrance of Earl Grey.

"Best time, don't you think?"

Flavor sipped and nodded: "Makes all that seem irrelevant," she inclined her head backwards, back, figuratively over Santa Monica, and the urban sprawl that went under many names, many cities, LA. West Hollywood, Hollywood, Torrance, Brentwood, Inglewood, Watts, East LA, West LA, Redondo Beach, Hermosa Beach, Tarzana, Ventura, Bel Air, Beverly Hills, Holmby Hills, but that the map showed, and the world knew, as Los Angeles, Greater Los Angeles. Probably among the best known initials in the world. L.A.

She looked down at the vagrants – hobos they'd called them in a gentler age – at the men, and increasingly the women, who had lost their jobs, their money, their marriages and families, who through accident, or divorce, or misfortunes of health or finance no longer had a roof over their head.

And who ended up here, at the very edge of their known world, on the lawns above the Pacific Ocean. For here they were tolerated, fed sometimes. Here was where they slept in the shade, hoarded their remaining prized possessions, played chess, read, argued, discussed, panhandled occasionally from the senior citizens who strolled along the clifftop.

Flavor saw one young white man, his hair a thick and matted mass, turn and look up at her and Jack on the balcony. It was too far away to see if the look was wistful, resentful, or just one of longing.

But she knew it was a look from a failed corner of the American dream to the core of its realisation. For long moments each looked at the other from their different worlds, then the man turned away.

As if reading her thoughts, Jack said: "At least they get a square deal here. No-one arrests them for vagrancy or drives them off. Thank God for the Santa Monica City Council."

Flavor shivered: "That's something, I suppose. I'm going inside."

She pulled the balcony door closed behind her and settled on a long, burgundy sofa, knees pulled up to her chin, both hands holding the cup that balanced precariously on her knees.

Made it all seem irrelevant, she had said; well, not all. Not the two bodies, two severed heads now missing, and two carved wooden angels left in their place.

A gay hairdresser and a straight, married bank clerk. Why? And what was the connection, WAS there a connection, or was it copycat? Same modus operandi, no forced entry into the homes where death had occurred, no apparent struggle.

Both had been forced, or persuaded, to kneel, then dispatched with a Samurai-like stroke.

The killings fell into the fragmented LA system of jurisdiction. Flavor and the Los Angeles Police Department got the hairdresser from Brentwood, the cops in the San Fernando Valley got the bank clerk.

Duplication, repetition, two separate investigations into the same (she was certain) killer. Where would the next one be? There would be a next one, she was certain of that too.

Here in Santa Monica, with its own police department, in the LA County Sheriff's area, Orange County? She drank some tea.

Two was not technically a serial killing, and for it to be classified as serial everyone had to be sure it was the same perpetrator – same perp, in cop slang.

Could it be some one-off weirdo, and then a copycat, yet another psychotic rolling loose in this city of crazies like a marble in a box, who had read it all in the LA Times; the decapitation, the missing head, the wooden angel, and decided that was for him too?

Gay was a drawback, too, certainly in Victor Alassio's case. Victor liked cruising, he was into leather, and late-night pick-ups in the bad end of Santa Monica Boulevard. His house was full of E, ice, amyl nitrate poppers, and enough kiddie porn to make the Vice Squad retch.

So it was, hey, you know, one of those faggot love feud murders, everyone knew they were animals when spurned, cutting off the lover's gonads, stuffing them in his mouth, using the guy's cock for a blood paintbrush.

That was how she knew her colleagues felt. And she'd say, well what about the guy in the Valley, Smith, the bank clerk, wife and kids, family values, church on Sunday?

And the other detectives would look at her and mime opening a door and stepping out. The closet, Flave, he just wasn't out of the closet yet, and anyway, it was the Valley, and we have enough problems of our own over here.

Gay murders, not the same; as long as they kept it among their own kind, fine by us, they all have AIDS anyway, probably better off signing out this way.

And she knew, all too well, about keeping murder and violence among own kinds, and how it didn't matter, not as much, not the same as, you know, the same as . . . Yes, she knew about keeping it among their own kind.

She looked up: "Hi."

"More?"

"Thanks." Jack poured out some steaming tea into Flavor's cup.

"Penny for them."

"Nothing, really."

"You're thinking about the case, the hairdresser?"

"How did you know?"

"You've had your nose in the file all day."

Jack picked up the blue folder from the foot of the sofa. Flavor smiled, and took the folder: "It's bugging me."

"The Times believe they're not connected. Three weeks apart, one had time to copy the other."

"Maybe." Flavor opened the file for what seemed like the hundredth time, and looked into the eyes of Victor Alassio.

"But you don't think so."

Jack sat down at Flavor's feet, and their eyes met, Flavor's brown and intense, Jack's piercing and blue.

"I don't think so, I KNOW so."

"Beheading, though, that's weird even for LA."

Flavor took a hot, comforting mouthful of tea, "ONLY in LA."

"And you think – forgive me, KNOW, that it's the same guy, and that he'll do it again."

"Or she, Jack, never forget, death is an equal opportunity employer."

"And it burns you up, because all you can do is wait. You've got nothing, right?"

"Zero."

"The police in the Valley?"

"Zip."

"I'm sorry."

Flavor eased herself off the sofa, went back to the window, looked out at the Pacific, at the sunset, at the sheer beauty and magnificence of it.

And she felt a burn in her gut that was like indigestion. It bothered like constipation, like something in your shoe, or some splinter under your skin. Like when you tried to sleep when you wanted to pee, or felt hungry; it was an irritation that wouldn't let her rest.

She turned:

"And one day, one night, soon, he'll do it to someone else, and we have to wait for that, for a human being to be killed, beheaded. To have their head taken away like a trophy, until we can get somewhere."

"Why next time, why not now?"

"Because next time, God help us, he might leave something, or we might be able to establish a pattern, a link."

Jack gave a sceptical grin: "You're a good cop, Flave, but you can't KNOW."

"I forgot to tell you, I'm also a witch." Flavor laughed, but not much.

"I never know when you're joking. Cop-witch, that's a new concept. Santeria rituals down at the station house."

"You got it."

"Want to fly your broomstick into your room-mate's

bedroom tonight?" Jack gave her what Flavor had come to realise was a come-hither look.

"Much as I like you, as much as I like living at an apartment I could never afford to buy in a zillion years, I really don't think we've reached that stage in our relationship."

"That stage in our relationship . . . YET?"

Flavor laughed.

"Is that a no comment, Lieutenant?"

"No comment."

And Flavor was thinking. He'll do it, he, she, it – the Angel – that's how she thought of the killer – the Angel. Maybe not for a month, maybe not for two, but he'd do it.

If he hadn't taken the heads, maybe he could stop, but when you started collecting – even heads – you didn't stop at two.

CHAPTER TWO

Art Helm had the Beverly Hills house of his dreams, mock-Tudor, half-timbered, three blocks from residential Rodeo Drive. Had the antiques, the Mercedes, a long plural of them, down to the latest metallic silver sports convertible that sat in the gravel driveway.

He sometimes parked it next to Jack Nicholson's at Lakers' games. His 'n' hers, Art called them.

The money too, millions of dollars of it that bought the designer clothes, the vacations in Maui, Aspen, Puerta Vallarta, that bought, throughout the Seventies and Eighties, a rampant fill of sex.

Sex taken all hours, all places, with all types, all ages, from the fumbling rough encounters in bath houses, health clubs, in automobiles, to the paid-for liaisons in poor, foreign lands where sex could be bought for small change.

The love that had once dared not speak its name now shrieked stridently in the name of desire.

He had met Serge before the Great Plague, before the

news that he and all those who had lived as he had lived, dreaded. It was ironic, or perhaps poetic, he would sometimes reflect, that love and the virus had struck him at the same time.

When he read of Victor's death, it was a name from so far back down the list of such names it was almost expunged from memory. But despite everything a shiver of something like fear had passed over Art Helm.

But his life was focused now on survival, on diets, on keeping healthy, on exercise and positive thinking, and on this man whom he had come to love.

So he suspected nothing when the telephone call came, was a little puzzled by it, but no more, was too preoccupied with the spectre that lived within him, that ate at him, that fought for possession of his body.

And now, at this final moment, there was only utter terror and incomprehension and total blackness that came with the swish of a falling blade.

Flavor pulled her Buick Skylark in behind a gaggle of TV wagons, showed her ID to the officer at the barrier and went up the gravel drive.

A man with a clipped-on tag that showed him to be an aide to Mayor Pablo Saldana greeted her: "Lt. Cartouche?" She nodded, showed her ID once more from the palm of her hand, and was led round the curve of the drive to a police trailer.

Inside she saw three men sitting, bulky and awkward, behind a table. A third man stood in the half-light next to a cupboard.

Elsewhere in the trailer, uniformed officers busily installed typewriters and telephones.

The aide said: "Lt. Cartouche, police chief Davis, police chief Andrew Solvang of the Beverly Hills Police Department, Mayor Saldana."

"Sir." She inclined her head to the head of the Los Angeles Police Department, her ultimate boss. "Gentlemen."

Davis remained seated, but the other two rose awkwardly, and put out their hands to be shaken. They knew her reputation.

No-one introduced the third man.

"Please sit down, Lieutenant," the Mayor of Los Angeles invited her. She did, and then said, without preamble: "I presume it's number three."

"Yes," Davis said, "it's number three. Now it's serious, this man is a serial killer, and we must find him." He saw Flavor's eyes raised in query, and answered her before she could frame the question:

"Art Helm."

"THE Art Helm?" But it was reflex, a kind of articulated WOW. This was Beverly Hills, movie-star land, the top brass were out, suddenly it was SERIOUS, so of course it was THE Art Helm.

"Yes. Murdered, decapitated, the severed head taken."

Witch, a voice said in Flavor's ear, her own voice, the inner voice that spoke to her a lot.

She said, looking at her chief: "But this is Beverly Hills sir, not our jurisdiction."

"Which is why I'm here." It was the Mayor speaking, Saldana, a Latino for a rapidly Latinised city. "Chief Davis, Chief Solvang . . ." he inclined his head to both of them, "are in agreement with me that this is too important to be hampered by questions of territory and jurisdiction."

Solvang nodded. It was after all, HE who was essentially conceding, the murder was on his patch. Not often that Bev Hills got high profile killings.

". . . clear now that we have a serial killer loose in the Greater Los Angeles area. I have obtained the permission and co-operation of ALL law enforcement agencies from Santa Monica to San Bernardino, from San Juan Capistrano to Malibu and throughout the San Fernando Valley, to form a special Task Force to find this man."

Flavor risked a glance at the big man, his face still in shadow, still silent, and she desperately tried to place the face she knew she had seen before.

"After your success with Hans Tooter, we felt you were amply qualified to lead this force . . ."

Tooter, Mr. Chocolate Chip. His speciality was kids. Kids walking out of school then disappearing into thin air.

He killed four children before they caught him.

Flavor had been in charge of the Murder Squad team, and they'd staked out schools.

And she had tried to figure how – why? – a kid would, presumably, get in a vehicle with a total stranger, because these kids had walked out of school and just VANISHED off the face of the earth until their pathetic corpses turned up.

Never take candy from a stranger. But kids did. Candy and what else? A super Nintendo game? Was Mr. Stranger Danger a games freak?

She went back over the autopsy reports, and discovered that the contents of the stomach of each kid contained the ingredients that went into ice-cream.

His plan was simple in its grotesque evilness. He would go down to Häagen Daz and buy a quart of chocolate chip ice-cream. Then he'd park his van a quarter of a mile from school.

Sit with the window open, elbow out, spooning in the chocolate chip. He'd wait for a kid, a loner, boy or girl, it didn't matter to Tooter. He'd offer them some ice-cream, suggest there was more in the back of the van, lure the poor kid in, gag them, then take them back to his house in Pasadena, reverse the van up into the garage, and bundle the kid out. The bodies turned up on garbage dumps, violated and strangled.

Not just ice-cream, either. Chocolate chip. And Häagen Daz chocolate chip at that. So they went back to the schools, and checked each location in relation to the local parlour.

They staked out parlours, looking for single guys in closed vehicles, around the times the schools came out. They got him in three days, tailing him from the parlour, to a nearby school where he tried to lure a little freckle-faced kid with a scoop of chocolate chip.

Tooter was a talker. Within ten minutes he'd confessed everything, and at his home they found clothes, schoolbooks, enough evidence to convict him, and for once the courts agreed.

He was up on Death Row in San Quentin now, secretly enjoying his sobriquet, but ever-practical, daubing his cell with excrement, scratching his face, and hearing voices from God, in a bid to avoid meeting Him.

And one of the detectives who'd worked on the case, who had kids himself, and who had seen the violated bodies, made himself a promise.

The day they gassed Tooter he planned to go up to San Quentin, sit in the witness row, and as they strapped Mr. Chocolate Chip in the chair ready for the cyanide pellets, the detective would take the top off a litre of Häagen Daz – chocolate chip, of course – and offer Tooter a spoonful through the glass.

"Thank you sir – "

"I haven't finished, Lt. Sharing command with you will be Lt. McCall here," he pointed at the big man in shadow, ". . . of the Beverly Hills Police Department."

So that's how she knew the face. Redneck Rory McCall, Quick-Draw McCall, Trigger Happy McCall.

". . . you may not know, but Lt. McCall had a similar success with a serial killer when he was working in Michigan. You will be allocated a team of detectives, special resources from city and if possible, state funds. We're talking to Sacramento in the morning. Who knows where this madman might strike next?"

As her eyes gradually adjusted to the light, she saw for the first time the expressions on the faces of the men opposite. They're SCARED, why? And then; of course, this is Tinseltown. He's hit Hollywood. If it had been East LA he could have chopped Gonzalezes and Alemans and Ferreras until the vacas came home.

But Helm was a STAR, was money, was powerful friends,

was connections, was high-profile AIDS charity work. Helm sat next to Elizabeth Taylor at five hundred bucks a pop fund-raising dinners.

When this crazy – the Angel, she thought, the Angel – when he was killing bank clerks in the Valley and has-been hairdresser queens, that was, well, OK. But now he'd come into the very heart of Tinseltown, he'd come into the very soul of the city. Nightmare on Paranoia Street.

If he could reach out and touch the Gods of LA, the gilded, the gifted, the adored and the normally invulnerable, the rich beyond dreaming of it, then what terrible possibilities?

Then fear would run guttering like fire through the streets of every movie enclave in town, through Beverly Hills, and Bel Air, through Holmby Hills and the Malibus, beach and canyons both.

For it was their deepest nightmare, the devil fear that dwelled within them. That despite the riches, the POWER, the beauty, despite everything they could buy – and they could buy everything, ANYTHING – one day someone would come, to their homes, with murder in their hearts, a knife or a bullet for the idols they loved/hated so much.

So things had to happen, MUST happen, because law enforcement careers and the future of politicians were in danger. The re-election of district attorneys was threatened.

People like Helm had money and power and influence, but twelve drive-by shooting victims on a hot Labour Day weekend in the barrios could slide by on twelve paragraphs tucked away in the Metro section of the LA Times.

When someone murdered Art Helm then it was People Magazine, and Entertainment Tonight, 20/20, Hard Copy and A Current Affair.

Add a perfumed whiff of scandal, and you could be sure the supermarket tabloids, the National Enquirer, The Globe, and the Star would crawl and trawl until they found something. And there was ALWAYS something.

Then the dredging up of old stories on star-obsessed fans,

the stalkers, and out it would come, all the Hollywood poop raked steaming and smelling onto the public sidewalk of Main Street, USA.

She felt the first sensation of disgust at the men, at their naked fear of the possible falls from grace, and at their roused-from-sleep smells and the odour of their self-interest.

And then there was McCall. Chief Solvang said: "May I introduce Lt. Rory McCall of the Beverly Hills Police Department."

McCall came out of the half-shadow. He was big and wide, with an open face, sandy hair falling over his forehead, tired-dark eyes that gave little away. He wore a white shirt, green tie, brick coloured sports jacket and dark slacks.

As she took his hand and he leaned towards her she smelled soap and water, shampoo, and a breath of bourbon?

"Ma'am."

"Lt. McCall." And then she couldn't resist it. "Shot anyone lately, Lt?"

There was not a flicker from the eyes: "Not since the last time Lt. Cartouche. That means cartridge in French, doesn't it? Perhaps you're descended from a line of marksmen?"

"Est-ce que vous parle francais?"

"I get by."

Chief Solvang said angrily: "Let's get this straight, Cartouche, right from the beginning. Lt. McCall is a fine officer with a fine record. He was also totally exonerated by Internal Affairs, and by the court of enquiry. You two are to work together, so I suggest you apologise."

Chief Davis added: "I'm amen on that, Lieutenant. I think an apology is appropriate here."

"I'm sure Lt. McCall took it in the spirit it was intended."

"Absolutely, ma'am."

She held his eyes: "But if it makes him feel better, then, of course I apologise."

"Accepted gracefully."

"No problem sharing command with me?"

"Absolutely not. I think women bring a great depth and

13

perspective to police work."

"In which PR handout did you read that?"

He smiled, and she felt the chill as though someone had opened a refrigerator door: "Believe me, I'm a practising non-sexist."

Chief Davis said: "You'll work well together, I'm sure of it." And thought: Creative tension, it'll help. They'll hate each other's guts, they'll be fighting like cat and dog, and they'll each bust a gut to make sure it's THEY who crack the thing.

This was good pairing.

He added: "And with Chief Solvang's agreement, you'll work out of an LAPD office. We'd like to meet with you tomorrow, 2 p.m., and listen to your ideas."

Flavor said: "Sir." McCall looked at Solvang who gave an imperceptible nod, and McCall said: "We'll be there."

Outside, Flavor and McCall stood together watching the gaggle of Pressmen, photographers and TV crews converge on the three officials heading for their cars.

He turned to Flavor, his tone sharp: "OK, now we've stopped performing for the top brass, let's cut the crap. I don't like it any more than you do. I don't recall the LAPD asking for our help when he chopped the fag hairdresser over in Brentwood. I'll work with you, but don't try to push me around. If you do I'll burn your ass."

"I have just one question before we work together. Why'd you shoot him, McCall? Just for me, no witnesses, no court of enquiry. It won't go any further, but I'd like to hear it."

"He was pointing a gun at me from a distance of fifteen feet. It was a three fifty seven Magnum, Smith and Wesson. I told him to put it down, he wouldn't. So I shot him. It was him or me."

"They never found the gun."

"There was a riot on at the time, I just about got out with my life as it was."

"Protecting Rodeo Drive? Personally I would have let

insurance handle it."

A TV light swung, and for a second his face was illuminated in the glare. He looked – naked?

"Fuck Rodeo Drive and fuck YOU. They can burn Ted Lapidus and Armani and the whole shebang, all I care. But I'm a police officer and I swore that I would protect and serve. I meant it. He was pointing a gun at me, and if I hadn't shot him he would have used it. Satisfied?"

"He was fifteen," she paused, "and he was black."

"Nice ring to it, it would have sounded good read over my casket. Another cop down, wasted by a minority minor without a gun."

"Some think you just blew him away because he was a rioter and a jigaboo."

"Some are wrong."

"You did the same in Detroit, so I hear."

"Bank robber with a 12-gauge. I still have some of the pellets in my legs."

"He was black too."

"The city has a high black population." He said it dry, deadpan.

"I know cops who never even DREW their guns in thirty years."

"They're lucky."

"You don't have a reputation as a nigger-lover."

"Tut-TUT, Lt., not the N-word? And from you of all people."

He was trying to smile, and there was just the breath of the Arctic.

She extended a finger, pointing it accusingly. If she had to work with this trigger-happy ape, she had to get on top of it at the start.

"If you work with me you keep your gun in its holster."

In an instant his face was just inches from hers, and the ferocity of his tone stunned her:

"You listen to me, college kid. I was nailing perps before you bought your first Kotex. I shot two people in my life, and

15

both were trying to kill me. I couldn't give a goddamn motherfuck what you think, or THINK you know. You and your kind are so PC you can't see a crime anymore until you've checked your colour chart."

"I've heard rumours about you, McCall. I think something happened to you in Detroit, something bad, or you wouldn't be working with the Mickey Mouse police in Bev Hills."

To her astonishment he seemed to shrink back as though she had struck him, and his tone changed.

"I came to California for the sunshine and the oranges, just like why you left the bayou, I imagine."

"Break the rules, I won't back you."

"The new generation cops with their psychology majors and their love of fair play."

"Believe it."

"You want to catch this guy?"

"More than anything." And she did. More than ANYTHING.

"Well instead of standing around here like two hookers on a street corner, why the hell don't we go talk to someone?"

He turned his back on her and scrunched off up the gravel drive to the pillared porch.

The uniformed policeman consulted his notebook: "His lover discovered the body around midnight, dialled 911, and then went into shock."

"Male lover?"

"Yes ma'am."

Flavor groaned inwardly. This wasn't small fry like Alassio, and it was all too big to dismiss now, but she wished the gay thing wasn't there. She felt there was a danger they'd look in wrong directions. Three victims, two gay. They'd draw the wrong conclusions.

She had that feeling – the witch feeling – that gay had nothing to do with it, and something else did. She saw

McCall raise an eyebrow to her, as in, faggots, what else can you expect? She looked away.

"Time of death?" McCall asked.

"Not definitely established yet, sir. The body is still warm, no rigor mortis. If the lover is speaking the truth, Helm was probably killed somewhere between when the lover went out at eight-thirty, and midnight when he got back."

"Body still here?" Flavor asked.

"Yes, ma'am." The policeman took them from their position near the front door, down a long, dazzlingly mirrored corridor, past the to-ing and fro-ing men and women who attend such violent deaths, and into a long room that glistened white.

White walls, white carpet, white rugs, white sofas, counterpointed with silver and steel objets d'art.

And there, behind one sofa, the relative off-white of a sheet, and a humped thing beneath it, and the big, darkening stain of human blood spread in a semi-circle.

They stood over the corpse, the uniformed policeman knelt down, put a hand on the sheet, looked up at Flavor – not at McCall – and said:

"Ready for this, ma'am?"

Her nostrils flared in anger, and she felt the familiar irritation and frustration. I'm a woman, it's violent death, blood, a gruesome corpse, so I'll faint.

She said tetchily: "I've seen hundreds of these, officer. I was first-on-scene when the Mob threw a guy out of a helicopter from five hundred feet. Just do it!"

He pulled back the sheet. There had been a lot of blood, a deep, glutinous spread of it, soaked deep now into the once expensive, now ruined, carpet.

There was no head, just a severed stump of neck a fraction above the shoulders. Where the blood had coagulated in a mass with severed vein, muscle and tissue, it resembled the butt of a melted red-wax candle.

McCall said: "OK" and the policeman re-covered the corpse.

Flavor said: "I suppose you looked around, gardens, shrubberies, pool, cupboards, you know?"

"Yes ma'am. No sign."

"Did he leave anything?"

She wanted to say – an angel? Did he leave a carved, wooden angel? Because if he had not, then perhaps it was someone else, something different. Not him. Not the Angel.

"I believe so," the officer called to a colleague who came over with a transparent plastic bag. Flavor noticed both officers were wearing rubber gloves. AIDS precautions. There was a lot of blood in this room. The man caught her eye: "Don't worry ma'am, the outside of the bag is clean."

She took it and held it up so that both she and McCall could get a clear look at the contents.

Inside the bag, stained with blood, was the carved figurine of an angel on a plinth. The head was cast down, the palms vertically together against one another as if joined in prayer, wings unswept from the shoulder blade, then furling generously until the tips reached the figure's base.

Without being able to actually touch it, it appeared to have been carved from wood, which had been left unpainted and unvarnished. She and McCall passed it between them, back and forth, turning it, viewing it from all angles.

At last it was returned to the officer. Flavor said: "We want it tested. Fingerprints, fibres, blood, the type of wood, how rare, where you can buy it, stuff like that."

The officer looked at McCall, quizzically. He knew McCall was the officer in charge, and this woman was clearly involved, but she wasn't Beverly Hills PD, he knew that.

"Do it," McCall said, "Lt. Cartouche of the LAPD and I are working together on this." He saw the officer's eyes widen slightly.

"Why Jimmy, don't look so surprised. This murder case is so important it has its own goddamn Task Force now."

The officer looked at Flavor, with what she suspected was hostility: "We'll do it, ma'am."

"Thank you."

Flavor and McCall went outside into the fresher air.

McCall said: "There was one of those in Brentwood, right, at Alassio's house? And over in the Valley?"

"Identical."

"What's it supposed to signify?"

"Search me."

"Could it be a copycat?"

"No. They're identical, and we didn't issue a picture, and we didn't say how big or small it was. Three the same, same size – what looks like the same wood? No way."

"Same guy then."

"Or gal. Any theories?" She knew what his theory would be, wanted to hear him articulate it in its crushing simplicity.

"Top of my head? OK. Three victims, two definitely gays, maybe the other joker too."

"And?"

"I'll bet one of them will be HIV-positive, or the full-blown thing, take my word for it. Some guy has sex with all three, maybe he's a pick-up, some down and out, does it for cash, wildman, maybe a bit queer himself. Whatever. But he's a little disgusted with himself. He's been used by the well-off, in Helm's case, the famous."

"Go on."

"He goes to them for money, semi-blackmail, he'll go to the National Enquirer, that kind of stuff, they tell him to go fuck himself."

"Then?"

"He wakes up one fine morn to the news that he's HIV-positive, and then his head just explodes. Forget money, he wants REVENGE. Maybe he's an ex-felon, can't legally buy a gun, he gets a sword instead. He telephones to ask for a meeting, tells them about the HIV. They're worried now, he's a smoking gun, so they agree to meet him. Whacko, he chops them."

"What about our happily married bank clerk in the Valley?"

"Who knows? A lot of these guys are normal family men during the day, raging queens by night. This is LA, Lieutenant, get real."

Flavor could see the grey of dawn seeping like dye into the dark blanket of the night outside, and felt the chill of sleeplessness, the morgue-like coldness that seemed to invade her in the aftermath of violent death.

She pulled out a pack of Marlboro and lit one, inhaling deeply, pulling the smoke deeply into her lungs. It felt good.

"Hey, I'm sorry," she proffered the pack to McCall.

"The surgeon-general says smoking is hazardous to health," McCall said, straight-faced.

"The surgeon-general should join the LAPD, he'd discover one or two other things. Did you ever?"

"Three packs a day man." He snapped his fingers: "Quit just like that. Cold turkey. And quite a lot of Wild Turkey too."

"Man wins a prize."

"What's your little Sherlock Holmes on this one?"

She shrugged, and drew again on the cigarette.

"Did you ever read a book called The Collector? It's a classic in its way, by an English author called Fowles?"

"Can't say I have." He took something out of his coat pocket. It was a Snickers bar. He peeled the wrapper and bit off a chunk, chewing vigorously.

"You think this guy Fowles did it, this English writer guy?"

"Jesus, McCa – " she suddenly realised her foolishness.

"Anyway, they made this book into a movie. A BAD one incidentally."

"You a movie buff?"

"My roommate is a screenwriter."

"No shit?"

"The guy in The Collector, he collects butterflies, chases them with a net, pins them under display cases. No girlfriend, loner, then he spots this girl and falls in love with her. Wants her."

McCall said: "So he kidnaps her – kind of collects her, right?"

"Right."

"Happy ending?"

"The girl dies. Just like the butterflies."

"And you think this guy is a collector – of heads? Why?"

"I don't know." She threw the half-smoked Marlboro to the ground and drove it into the gravel with the stub of her toe.

"Let's talk to the lover."

Serge had been vomiting continually since he had discovered his lover's headless body, and now his face was the colour of a morning-after camp fire.

He had a thin, delicate face, a bushy scene-type moustache, and his hair was a dark stubble razored close to his scalp. They read him his rights and went through the routine.

What time had he gone out, where to, a health club on La Cienaga, they'd check it. The help was a Filipino couple called the Rosas. According to Serge it was their regular night off – Helm would have known that, maybe planned accordingly – and they'd gone to a cinema in Westwood Village. They'd check that too.

McCall said: "And you found the body around midnight?"

"Yes," Serge nodded, blowing his nose on a sodden white handkerchief.

"How'd you know it was him?" McCall asked abruptly, with what Flavor thought was unnecessary cruelty.

Serge looked up through the tears and the grief: "We've been together for seven years. Do you know the line from the Dory Previn song: 'I've learned his body's line and length?' "

And memorised his grin, thought Flavor, inappropriately.

"I've learned his soul's complete circumference . . ." McCall said, and paused, adding ". . . I know his lies". He didn't look like a man who listened to Dory Previn, Flavor thought, let alone remember the words.

McCall said: "Did you know his lies, Serge? Did he lie to you, did he have secrets, other lovers?"

"Not that I'm aware of."

"Enemies?" Flavor asked.

"Everyone has enemies," he gave her a withering look, "even those who think they don't."

"Are you an American citizen, Serge, green card holder, resident alien, what?"

Flavor rounded on him: "What is this McCall, we're not the INS, who gives a damn?"

"Get over here," McCall pulled her to one side and said in a fierce whisper, "We need to know. It could be relevant. Suppose Serge was being blackmailed as an illegal, about to be deported, ANYTHING?"

"It's not about that you damn fool, it's not Serge."

"We don't know that. Eliminate, accentuate, and don't EVER second guess me in front of someone we're interviewing."

Serge said above their fierce whispers: "You don't need to fight. I've been here ten years, I have a green card."

McCall turned back to him: "Where are you from? You have an accent but your English is perfect."

"Riga."

"Russia?" McCall asked.

"Latvia, Lieutenant, once part of the Soviet Empire, now thankfully free. Before I was allowed to emigrate to the United States I practised for seven years, one on one with a Professor of English."

"Good school."

"Not school, a labour camp in Novaya Zemlya, close to the Arctic Circle. My crime was being a homosexual and an intellectual."

"Did you kill your lover, Serge?"

"No. But if I found the one who killed him I would kill that person."

And Flavor knew that, of course, Serge hadn't killed Helm. No-one who had spent seven years in a Soviet labour

22

camp would risk confinement again, possibly death.

They spoke to the Rosas, an inoffensive couple from Cebu, Philippines, who were frightened, mainly for their futures and their work permits now that their employer was dead. They had the cinema ticket stubs, a valet parking chit. All of it was checkable, and she was sure WOULD check.

Outside, the sky was deep red in the East and the birds were chattering restlessly. She lit a cigarette and he chewed pensively on a thumbnail. He was out of Snickers.

At last he gave her a look, and said: "I can't have you cross me like that, not when I'm questioning. I have my way of doing things, you have yours."

She drew on the Marlboro until it glowed.

He said: "Well?"

"If I said I couldn't work with you, that it was impossible, being who we are, would you volunteer to transfer out?"

"Hell no."

"Then it looks like we're stuck with one another. It was just, I don't know, CRUEL. You know how terrified people get here when you ask about their immigration status. Half the city are illegals."

"Yeah, well maybe it was, but it had a purpose."

"I read you." She paused: "I'm going home. I'll call you at eight and I need a number."

He flipped her a card, she took it and turned to go. She heard him clear his throat, as though nervous or embarrassed.

"Lieutenant." She turned: "You ever had a loaded gun pointed at your head, up close? Ever had one FIRED at you?"

"No," she said evenly, "No, to be honest I haven't."

He jabbed an accusing finger: "Then until it happens – and it will, believe me it will – don't sit in judgement on me. One day you just might need me AND my gun. Then maybe you won't be so squeamish."

"Not another word on the subject, that's a promise."

He turned away and shambled off, almost like a big bear, and Flavor watched him go.

He went three blocks, made a right onto Rodeo Drive, then a left where it joined Santa Monica Boulevard. After two miles he made a left on Havenhurst, and saw the early breakfast patrons parking up outside the Silver Spoon. He slid the MGB roadster into the kerb, fumbled for coins, pushed them into the slot, lifted the glass lid and took out an LA Times.

He pulled out the Metro section, flicked through it, found nothing, and threw it on the passenger bucket seat. Too late for the Times, but the TV would be full of it today.

McCall knew he could have handled it alone, he didn't need the psychology cop and her new ideas.

But it had become political now, and they didn't think Bev Hills could handle it. And in his case anyway, there'd always be a big question mark over him after the kid's shooting.

It didn't matter that he'd been cleared by IA and by the court of inquiry, there was the tribunal of political correctness and that never brought in a verdict, it just let innuendo hang over you like a guillotine blade.

He drove the last hundred yards, swung into the narrow alley next to his apartment block, and slipped the MG into his assigned parking spot.

A trail of soap-suds came from the narrow laundry room that was jammed in next to the under-apartment parking places. It reminded him he had a closet full of dirty laundry.

McCall checked his mailbox, pulled out a few circulars, took a Pizza-to-Go flyer off his doorbell, and let himself into the apartment.

The curtains were still closed tight from the previous night, and he left them.

Madonna came out to greet him.

He picked her up, swung her round, nuzzled her face, then threw her on the sofa and poured himself a large bourbon.

He swallowed half, then joined Madonna on the sofa. She climbed up on his chest and licked his face, so he stroked her for a while, then tried to read the LA Times and failed.

Instead, he got up, went into the bedroom, took out the photographs, looked at them for a long time, then put them back and returned to the sofa.

He thought of his daughter, and his wife, then of the kid he had shot, then of the kid's parents, and what it must have been like when they were told. The deep intoxicating draught of misery felled him, and he wept a little, his face buried deep in his hands.

Madonna watched, slightly puzzled, as cats are wont to be when their owners exhibit unusual emotions, then she settled down into refined uninterest.

And McCall fell into fitful sleep, there on the couch.

Flavor closed the door quietly and tiptoed in, shoes in hand, like a kid late back from a date.

"That you Flave?"

"It's the Boston Strangler, go to sleep."

"You need company, a shoulder to cry on, hot passionate sex, all three?"

"I need sleep is what I need, I have to be up in three hours."

She closed her bedroom door, hesitated, then turned the key in the lock, and lay down fully-clothed on the bed as daylight's fingertips began to probe beneath the tightly-drawn blinds.

Flavor was not frightened of Jack. Jack would not try to come to her like a thief in the night. Flavor was frightened of the remaining fragments of the night.

And she was frightened of the Angel. She was frightened of this monster who chopped off heads, and left his statuette calling card. She was frightened that as she slept the Angel would come, supernaturally, and kill her, taking her bloodied severed head to its lair.

And she knew it was stupid, irrational and childish, that she was a grown-up woman and a police officer, and that such fears were the fears of the childhood bedroom, not the adult one.

At length she fell into a troubled doze, and in it, she dreamed that the Angel was standing over her bed, its hands clasped in prayer, head downcast, white, swan-like swings swept behind it.

And she knew that there was no-one who could banish this particular demon. There were no saviours, she had learnt that. Only she could banish the Angel. And the rest of the demons.

Alone.

It was damp and warm.

"Play," the voice said, from the eerie red glow, into the darkness. "Did you enjoy your play?"

And the reply came hesitantly after long seconds of silence, a sibilant serpent hiss from the blackness:

"Yesss . . . play . . . yesss."

"Soon," said the voice, "soon there will be a new toy. Would you like a new toy?"

A snake slither of tongue in the darkness, a wet sucking sound: "Yes. Yesss . . ."

"Soon there will be more play, and a new toy. Now rest, away from the light."

"Play. Yessss."

Shifting noises in the darkness, like an animal settling in its lair, then only silence.

CHAPTER THREE

They met outside the neat, suburban home in Tarzana. It was
baking hot in the San Fernando Valley, at least ten degrees
hotter than LA, and McCall was flopped back in his
open-topped MG when Flavor pulled up.

When she walked up to the car he had his eyes closed and
appeared to be asleep, but when she said: "I hope you've got
a Factor 30 on, I'd hate my new partner to get skin cancer,"
he said, without opening his eyes, "We don't get skin cancer
in my family. We've always been cholesterol in my family."

He flipped a lever and the back of the seat came up:
"Alassio and Helm were lovers. First link."

It took her aback. It was ten in the morning, and they'd
parted at four. How the hell could he have discovered that
already? Clearly it was a possibility – but how had he
discovered it so soon? She was miffed. She felt as though
she'd made a late start in some race.

"Don't you ever sleep?"

"Not well," he leaned across, and opened the door for her, and she clambered awkwardly into the low-slung car. "I took a walk around my neighbourhood, early. There's a gay bookstore bottom of my street, opens at six – yep, they're buying the stuff at six.

'The word was out about Helm being killed. It didn't take the gay grapevine long to come up with the fact that on his way up, Helm had Alassio as part of his menagerie for a while."

"So he WAS cheating on Serge."

"No. Helm and Alassio were at it twenty-nine years ago."

"What? That's – "

"1966, and Alassio was a minor then. Not that it was allowed then ANYWAY, but he was risking jail."

Flavor took out her Marlboro: "Do you mind?"

"Your lungs."

She lit one, drew on it: "How come anyone remembers 1966?"

"They don't. Most of them weren't even alive then. But Helm is a legend, one of the old queens who was doing it when it wasn't easy to get away with."

"Alassio?"

"After they quit being lovers, Helm got him into hairdressing, funded him, put clients his way. You know the score, the gay Mafia and their fag hags."

Flavor knew what this all meant, certainly in McCall's mind. Two gays, lovers – even if a long time ago – both murdered. It meant she was wrong, and he was right, and it was some gay revenge thing.

It meant something else too. It meant that while she was sleeping, McCall was working. It meant he had contacts she didn't. She didn't believe for a second that he just got up and walked into a gay bookstore, and everyone sort of crowded round him and said, hey, cop, let's give you some background on the Helm killing.

It also meant McCall had managed to get information she hadn't, even if that information was self-serving. And when she'd called him at eight, he either hadn't got the information then, or hadn't bothered to share it with her. She got the distinct impression he'd saved it until they were face to face.

And when they went downtown that afternoon, McCall would have the first breakthrough. She felt — there was no other word for it — jealous and angry. Jealous of him, angry with herself.

Mrs. Smith, the widow, was expecting them, and led them into the living room of the neat, three-bedroomed single-storey house that sat on a suburban street three quarters of a mile from Ventura Boulevard close to Universal Studios in the San Fernando Valley.

Everything about the house, including the location, spoke of normality, of suburban California, of regular values, of dinner at Red Lobster, watching Johnny, and in The Life After Johnny, watching his successor, Jay Leno. There'd be a basketball hoop out back. They'd consider themselves decent Democrats.

The house had an intense, ordered look, like a dam built of fretful housework, unnecessary cleaning; something to hold back a reservoir of sorrow, perhaps even a flood-tide of disintegration.

The woman's face was still etched with lines like the sharp angles of a splintered window. She reminded Flavor of the jagged, fractured woman from the Picasso painting.

The eyes were still red and scratched raw from tears and lack of sleep, and her face had too much make-up, a failed mask against the agony of bereavement.

But her back was straight, her upper-body rigid and unbending, even when she sat. Some residual native pride stiffened her like a ramrod in her spine.

Southern back, Flavor thought, recognising the twang in the woman's greeting. Southern pride, even in grief. She's not from these parts. She had the South stamped on her like an ante-bellum oil portrait.

Flavor had seen the way she looked at her, the questioning look, not insolent, just — slightly puzzled. After the formalities had been dispensed with, McCall said: "Mrs. Smith, some of the questions we're going to ask may offend you. We wouldn't ask them if we didn't feel they were necessary."

"I was questioned quite thoroughly after – " she faltered, "after my husband's death." She said, AH was questioned, MAH husband's death. Georgia, Flavor guessed.

McCall took a breath: "Was it possible that your husband was gay – a homosexual?"

There was a flood of angry red, like paint over the top-coat of grief.

"Richard was a Christian, Lt. He was also a happily married man, with two children. Two children he loved. He would never do anything so –" she sought for the word, found it, and spat it at them, "disgusting."

Family values, Flavor thought. Not good Democrats, good Republicans, pro-Lifers. When Flavor spoke, the woman hesitated a long second before acknowledging her with her look.

"Is it possible your husband had a secret life? Did he . . ." Flavor cast around as though seeking for the right words, "did he go out at night, alone, late at night? Did he ever go on business trips, stay away at night, weekends, that kind of thing?"

The stiffened back was like a rebuke: "My husband was with the Bank of America all his life. He didn't work nights, he didn't go out at nights, 'less he was with us. You could set your clock by him. We ate together most nights. Like a family."

She bit off the last word, leaving it like a snapped-off seal on the document of her faith.

"Did he have any special friends – male friends?"

The disgust was in the woman's throat like a poison now, and it twisted her mouth as she spoke: "He had few friends. His family were his friends. I – I was his friend."

McCall said: "I did say this might be difficult."

She didn't even look at him. "Yes, you did. We'd eat out a

couple of times in the week, nothing fancy, Denny's maybe
..." she hesitated ... "Sambo's sometimes."

Flavor stiffened, feeling the blood rushing to her cheeks.

"...Weekends we'd see a movie, something for the
kids."

The ordered life unrolled before them like a uniformly
coloured carpet.

"We met on vacation in Florida. Fort Lauderdale, the
spring break. We were just college kids."

None of this was necessary now, the woman just wanted
to keep her husband alive with the talking of it, the more the
detail, the broader the portrait, and the more they would
know how ridiculous their theory was.

"I never wanted to live in Southern California, kids doing
drugs, sex and stuff, but this was his home. And WE lived
properly, do you understand?"

"Yes ma'am."

But Flavor plugged doggedly on, sensing the hostility like
a force field: "Did he gamble?"

"No. NEVER, and our financial affairs are in order.
There are no skeletons in our cupboard."

"Alcohol?" McCall asked.

"We are a Temperance family. His father died of drink,
so we knew the misery alcohol causes."

"Enemies?"

"Not that we were aware of."

The woman brought them tea, and as she poured it into
willow-patterned cups, Flavor said: "Where are you from,
Mrs. Smith?"

She turned to Flavor, teapot poised like a weapon:
"Georgia. Monroe, Georgia." She paused: "You?"

"Mississippi."

"What made you want to become a poh-lice officer?"
The accent was even thicker now, and Flavor felt it was for
her benefit.

"Seemed like a good career."

"Y'all need a college degree for that?"

"I have a psychology degree – UCLA."

"Congratulations."

"Thank you, amazing what we can achieve, isn't it."

The hostility was like static in the air.

McCall interjected, and it was like prying two sets of antlers apart: "Mrs. Smith, did your husband have any connection with the movie business, even through his work?"

"No sir. We did the Universal Studios Tour, once. He handled family accounts."

McCall stood up, draining the rest of his tea: "Well, ma'am, thanks for your time. Once again our apologies. We did not mean to cast any imputation on your husband's character."

"I understand. You have a job to do."

Flavor put her cup down on the tray, the tea untouched.

"Actually, I have one more question, if you don't mind."

"Ask it."

"You say your husband led a blameless life."

"Yes."

"Did you?"

"I BEG your pardon?"

"Were YOU sleeping with someone else, Mrs. Smith?"

And even before the woman's eyes could register their anger, their contempt, their history-in-the-veins disdain, Flavor was saying inwardly, This is not personal, not revenge. This is business, just like McCall yesterday, asking Serge did he have a green card.

The cup in the woman's hand fell to the floor and disintegrated with a tiny 'pop'. The tea made a bomb-burst stain on the patterned rug.

"How DARE you! Just because you wear a badge, just because you have some fancy college degree, you –" she bit the rest of the sentence off before it could be spoken. She spluttered, faltered, stopped.

"Uppity nigra, Mrs. Smith? Is that what you were going to say?"

"Flavor," McCall put his hand on her arm, like a warning.

"Was it? Remember the guy in the movie, who was it now, Eddie Murphy? And he's in the redneck bar, and he says, It's your biggest nightmare, a nigger with a badge."

"I treat as I find."

"Then answer my question."

"My upbringing," she was staring straight at Flavor, "was strict. I remained a virgin until my wedding day, and he was the only man with whom I've ever had carnal relations."

"Thank you Mrs. Smith. Good day."

"I shall make an official complaint about your manner."

McCall's face became all farm boy aw-shucks, and he circled, putting himself in between Flavor and the widow.

"Lt. Cartouche didn't mean any disrespect."

"I can speak for myself, McCall." Flavor bought a white business card down among the tea cups. "Please send any complaint to headquarters. The card states my full name and rank."

McCall said, under his breath: "Jesus."

As they left, a tiny object caught Flavor's eye as she passed a shelf. A little enamel brooch, a tricolor, green, white and red with an eagle at the centre. A national flag?

She turned to Mrs. Smith: "That's a flag, isn't it? What is it, France, Ireland?"

"Mexico," the woman said, flatly. "We took our honeymoon in Mexico. My husband – " she faltered. Was that grief, Flavor thought, or was she about to tell a lie, bend the truth a little, and what could it matter, it was a 10 cents enamel lapel brooch of the Mexican flag?

". . . bought it from a street pedlar. I've kept it ever since."

And Flavor looked into her eyes, seeing the hate, seeing the venom, but most of all seeing a lie. And thinking: Why would anyone lie over a 10 cents enamel flag?

McCall almost frog-marched her to his MGB, pushed her in the passenger seat and drove in wordless fury to the nearest Dunkin' Donuts on Ventura.

After his second cinnamon doughnut, half way down his coffee, regular, no sugar, he felt calmed enough to actually speak, and he turned to her.

She was nibbling tentatively on an Old-Fashioned, apparently oblivious to any trouble she may have caused.

McCall said: "I've got news for you, Lieutenant – Southern whites have rights too."

Flavor said through a mouthful of doughnut: "No-one calls me a nigger, especially no-one from Georgia, not even IN Georgia. And that stuff about eating at Sambo's. They know we hate that goddamn place and its name. I grew up with all that, and I'm sure as hell not taking it here."

She flung the remains of the doughnut into the parking lot.

"She didn't call you a ..." he surveyed the Dunkin' Donuts crowd through the glass in front of them, "you know, the N word."

"Near as dammit."

"You upset her, for Chrissake, WE upset her, damn near called her old man a faggot, then asked if she was screwing around, her probably Southern Baptist too."

Flavor took another mouthful of coffee, swallowed it, and said: "Answer me a riddle McCall. What has four eyes but is permanently blind?"

"Spare me riddles."

"MIssIssIppI."

"What?"

"God you're dumb, I,I,I,I . . . four eyes."

"YOU try to remember that Mrs. Smith has just had her old man killed. She's entitled to be a little on the sensitive side so stop trying to be Louis Farrakhan."

"I'll do my level best," she said with as much deliberate insincerity as she could muster.

She dragged a nail down the side of the Styrofoam cup, cutting a deep groove in it, wondering how deep she could go before she'd break the surface and spill coffee all over herself.

McCall took his napkin, took a ballpoint and wrote: "Hairdresser, gay, movie star, gay, bank clerk, straight. Race of all deceased, Caucasian."

He said: "Even Smith waited until the family were out, then INVITED the killer into his own home. He took a day off work, checked when his wife would be shopping, kids at school. Why? How well did he know the caller?"

Flavor said:

"Where could you hide three heads?"

As she said it, it seemed bizarre, unreal. She had the taste of doughnut and coffee in her mouth, the sun was on her skin, she was in the parking lot of a Dunkin' Donuts on Ventura Boulevard, it was 92 degrees.

And she was asking where you could hide three heads.

McCall shrugged and drained the rest of his coffee: "A big deep freeze, a container of formaldehyde?"

"Keep, sure, but HIDE?"

"Yeah, it would be a hell of a shock when you went for the frozen pizza. He could have a cabin out in the woods or the desert, someplace where only he goes. He could have access to a power line, or a generator that powers a freezer."

Flavor finished her coffee, and thrust her nail like a sword through the canal she had gouged in the Styrofoam.

"Simpler than that, he could live alone, or maybe with a batty old Mom or Dad. Maybe he works in a funeral parlour, knows the embalming business, steals formaldehyde and keeps the heads in a jar in the closet.

'He could live next door to either one of us and we wouldn't know. Do you knock on your neighbour's door and ask to check for heads in the closet or freezer?"

McCall turned the key, and the MG's motor coughed into life, the exhaust burbling throatily.

She said, a shade louder over the noise of the tuned engine: "A loner right, no Mom, Dad, no girlfriends, nobody to find his secret?"

"Or maybe he isn't keeping them, maybe they'll turn up on a dump somewhere, or maybe he drove into the desert and left them to the coyotes. I'll run you back to your car."

There was a clunk and grind that set Flavor's teeth on edge as he selected reverse.

"Why'd you buy a stick shift?"

His look was withering: "Is that all this car means to you – that it's a stick shift? You pagan."

He dropped her back at her car, and on the drive downtown she kept thinking about three heads in a freezer; three heads in jars of formaldehyde, three heads in a deep freeze somewhere, hidden among the carcasses. Or three heads out in the desert someplace being eaten by wild animals.

But why the heads in the first place? Why collect HEADS? As trophies like a Borneo headhunter? To prove something? Was there something socially or psychologically significant in severing the heads?

Was the killer an Oriental? Occidentals had a fear of decapitation as a form of death, yet to the Samurai it was regarded as an honour suiting their rank and status.

It wasn't frenzied, no multiple stab wounds, no blood spattered walls, no signs of a death struggle. They died frightened, for what else could have persuaded them to kneel? But there were no marks on the bodies consistent with coercion.

Flavor knew she was going to the first meeting empty-handed. But McCall, three cars ahead now, top down on the MGB, hair blowing in the wind like some insouciant teenager, he wasn't going in empty-handed.

He had the link. That morning McCall, after his initial anger, had been easy-going, doing his Ronnie Reagan aw-shucks act, his friendly boy-next-door thing with his damn fetish of a car.

And she felt he'd been casting glances at her when he thought she wasn't looking. They were all the same, ALL of them, even the dyed-in-the-wool Mississippi racists. They all wanted a piece of black ass at some time in their lives.

McCall no doubt thought he could blow away a black

kid, then make out with a black woman. He'd learn different. She watched the green MGB swing out into the traffic, watched him put his hand up to feel the pressure of the wind blowing over the sports car.

And she vowed. When Hell freezes over, McCall. Not before.

CHAPTER FOUR

Hollywood funeral chic. Black mini-dresses, black rock 'n'roll suits, black stretch limos, black pencil ties and Porsche sunglasses.

Like ebony against the pale blue of an LA dawn breaking on the Hollywood Hills above Forest Lawn.

Famous names in black, household names from movies and sitcoms and sports fields. Old names and new names, and names the public didn't know.

Ironically the very names that decided what the public saw, what they read, what they wore.

Power and money and success in an irresistible trinity. The sleek, the rich, the confident, and all brought now to the one God they could not control, the one idol to whom they all paid obeisance. The dark God of death at whose shrine they now worshipped.

Yet this too was part of the Hollywood success social package. It was like dinner at Ma Maison or Spago, a power breakfast meeting on some Burbank lot, or an eight a.m. story conference.

Like the Christmas break in Maui, the home, the car, the gold-leaf ceilings, the million dollar designer kitchen, the original Matisse, the young, hot mistress, and the snipped, tucked, taut, made-over and tolerated wife.

This morning was noblesse oblige à la Hollywood. To rise at some unearthly hour – and Hollywood rose early by anyone's standards – and have the limo take you out to the Ventura freeway and come off at the Hollywood Hills Forest Lawn exit, or even drive on to the sister cemetery six miles further on at Glendale.

The showbiz funerals were held at dawn to beat the rubberneckers. The day and the time was always kept secret from everyone but the invited. Forest Lawn security was said to be tighter than the CIA's, and yet it always leaked out. Always.

Someone heard someone else discussing it on the telephone, someone's wife told her favourite hairdresser, who rang the Times to make fifty bucks, and someone on the Times rang the Enquirer to make two hundred, and so it went.

But even at a funeral you could network; even at a funeral you could do deals; see who was IN, who was soon to be out. See it by the looks on their faces, by the SMELL of success or the odour of failure.

That is if you could distinguish those aromas from the stench of real fear that dominated such occasions. For it was here that these multi-millionaires realised that not even THEY could beat this. Not forever.

It was here, on occasions like this one they were reminded that one day they wouldn't be the ones sipping pick-me-up Buck's Fizz, snorting coke, or getting daybreak blow jobs from bimbos in the follow-up caravanserai of opaque-windowed Mercedes and Cadillacs.

Instead, they'd be up at the front in the hearse, stretched out in the pointlessly padded casket, powdered and rouged, their dead, blood-emptied veins awash with embalming fluid.

So now they suppressed their shivers in the cool dawn, shook hands, patted padded shoulders, whispered condolences and looked suitably solemn, wondering if it was only THEY who thought these thoughts every time occasion demanded they listen to yet another eulogy to a member of their departed clan.

The Great Plague had increased the frequency of such events, and it was THAT they all feared, gay and straight alike. For who knew how long it had been around, who had it, when it would strike, whether it was already lurking inside like some fifth columnist, *waiting* to strike.

And as if that was not enough, was there a madman loose in Hollywood?

It was four o'clock when Flavor came off the freeway and turned right onto Forest Lawn Drive.

McCall's car was already parked in the lot outside the neo-Georgian building that housed the mortuary and undertaking facility on the public side of the massive iron gates.

He was huddled inside the cockpit of the MGB, both hands cupped around a Thermos cup of steaming coffee.

When she rapped on the window, he flipped the door catch, and let her climb awkwardly into the cramped two seater, before grabbing a spare cup from the ledge behind his seat, and pouring her coffee.

"Thanks." She wiped some condensation from the tiny windshield, and peered at the knot of Press people and sightseers.

"I thought this was supposed to be a secret?"

"It was," he cleared a little circle for himself, "except nothing in this town is ever secret for long."

"How long have you been in LA, McCall?"

"A few years, and call me Rory."

He was looking at her sideways, with his eyes, not his face.

She said: "For the time being, I'll call you McCall. It suits you better."

"Do you think he's here?" He nodded towards the small crowd of Press and sightseers.

"I hope so."

They sat like that for long minutes, drinking the coffee, fighting off the dawn fatigue, then, without warning, without preamble, she turned to him.

"Do you have a family, McCall?" She didn't know why she asked it, the words seemed to come from someone other than her.

His face was like granite. "My private life is my own business."

She put her hands up in mock surrender, and hit the cup on the low canvas hood ceiling, spilling coffee: "OK, no problem. Jesus but these cars are cramped."

She looked back out at the knot of people.

It was one of those never-challenged, never-proved but somehow universally accepted tenets of criminology, that just as the murderer likes to return to the scene of his crime, so also did he like to go along to the funeral for good measure.

Professional interest, morbid fascination, quiet satisfaction at a job well done, a soupçon of remorse perhaps, but most of all EGO.

His presence said, Hey man, that was ME, I did that, LOOK at me, I'm someone, it was ME put that sonofabitch in the casket. All these mourners, cars, flowers, all the black, the widow's weeds, the sorrow, the weeping, all down to ME.

I have taken a human life, and for the first time, I AM somebody.

You could tell the professional vultures, the media people, from the amateurs. They sported finer plumage.

Differently dressed, and oddly; Burberry macintoshes with Nike trainers, scuffed leather jackets from thrift shops with $500 dollar hand-stitched English brogues. Because it was, like, who gives a fuck what you wear to a funeral, to

ANYTHING? We're Press, man, we can do ANYTHING.

They smiled and joked a lot in bunches as small and tight as their lying smiles. This is a funeral, a guy is dead, viciously murdered, and it has absolutely nothing to do with us, not the occasion, none of it.

They won't even let us in, so who cares? They gave off an aura of angry energy directed at, well – anybody. This feeling of you've-kept-us-up-all-night-and-we-don't-even-get-to-the-graveside-so-fuck-you belligerence.

Then the rubberneckers, and sightseers with their Kodaks, Canons, Sony Camcorders and autograph books too.

And did they REALLY think the multi-million dollar mourners in their designer frocks and Armani suits, whose dentistry alone was worth more than the autograph seekers could ever muster, would step out from behind the bullet-proofed, smoked-glass windows and sign AUTOGRAPHS?

"Who is this for? Your daughter, Mary-Ann? OK, With love from Elizabeth Taylor, on the occasion of the funeral of Art Helm?"

But people still went to Lourdes, didn't they? Still bought a sliver of that munificent piece of timber, the original (guaranteed) cross on which Christ was crucified.

This was no different. It was an act of faith. Gotta be in it to win it. So they kept themselves apart from the Press and TV, except when they were wanted for interviews, for human interest colour.

They huddled together in the dawn's chill, these minor incarnate monuments to inadequacy, loud in their inarticulacy, the fat and the small, the prematurely old and the eternally juvenile.

Was one of them the Angel? Perhaps the man over there with the obese hips and the special Big Person tailored jeans? Or maybe the squat, almost Neanderthal, woman who ate mechanically from a vast bag of popcorn?

Or the twin sisters, it was obvious they were twins even from that distance, who wore identical clothes, and as Flavor would learn later, were both spinsters.

With their bare white heads, washed-out faces and Freddie Kreuger nails that clutched, and unknowingly tore into, publicity photographs of Art Helm.

Who completed each other's sentences with telepathic accuracy. Were they the composite that made the Angel?

Wearily, Flavor and McCall climbed out of the cramped sports car, and began to work, moving among the media and the rubberneckers, chatting, joking, gaining confidences, looking into eyes, looking for something that would cry ME! ME!

When they finally got back in the car it was a relief when McCall saw the first distant glimpse in his rear view mirror, and said: "Cortège is coming. Let's get in."

They showed their badges to the Mexican woman at the booth before the gates and were directed up Memorial Drive. They were told to keep right where the drive divided, to go past the Murmuring Trees plot where Helm would actually be buried, then to turn left onto Magnolia Drive.

There, she told them, they would be assigned parking spaces by attendants waiting outside the Old North church.

At the press of a switch the great iron gates swung back and they drove into the Hollywood Hills Forest Lawn cemetery.

Flavor said: "We have a list of everyone allowed in for this, right?"

"Right. Bona fide mourners, our people, Forest Lawn staff, flower deliverers. That's it."

"No Joe Public?"

"No way. Anyway, officially they don't open until ten, so no-one can complain, or lie that they've come to visit Dad's grave or something."

"Press and TV got any helicopters up?"

"Forest Lawn have threatened to sue if they do. Frankly I don't think they'll use choppers. There's places all around these hills a guy can just sit with a telephoto lens or a video camera, no problem. It'll make the six o'clock bulletins."

Shrouds of low mist still hung on the wild and untamed scrub of the Hollywood Hills that rolled almost threateningly to the very edge of the neatly-manicured world of Forest Lawn.

"Why here, why not Glendale? I thought they had a higher star quotient there."

She laughed, despite herself: "If I tell you will you promise not to laugh?"

"Sure," he said, beginning to laugh already. "Don't tell me he'd bought a plot here. I know they do a lay away plan."

"Well he HAD booked a plot, but it's down to Lucille Ball and Humphrey Bogart."

"They here?"

"Yes sir, and it seems Art Helm liked nothing better than running Casablanca on his VCR or watching I Love Lucy."

"Bizarre!"

"I'm with you on Lucy, but Casablanca showed taste."

"Aha – your room-mate the screenwriter."

Her face closed like a shutter.

"My private life is like yours – private."

"The subject shall never more pass my lips, by the way, you and he just roommates, or . . .?"

He let it trail off, deliberately and provocatively. She knew she was being teased and toyed with. She knew McCall didn't respect her, or any cops of her colour, generation or education.

She knew he was trying to keep her off-balance. And if he did that it meant he was in charge, and he clearly wanted that. It couldn't be a partnership for McCall. She was a woman, and a black woman at that, so it was beyond McCall, beyond any of his type to share command with someone like that.

And because of that she hated herself for being manoeuvered into a situation where she was at a disadvantage. But where Jack was concerned she was, and she knew it. She just hoped McCall didn't realise that, or for that matter anyone at the department.

"Hey, McCall, I'll do a deal. I'll give you my blood group and all the rest of it, you know, all the considerable dirt on my murky private life if you give me yours. You start – with Detroit."

She saw the face hardening again, like cement, knew she had pulled a point back. Whatever it was in his private life, she didn't really care or ever want to know. But it was good to see him disconcerted for a change.

And maybe it would stop him asking too many questions about Jack.

He said, icily: "I was out of line. Forget it."

"You got it, McCall."

All Flavor could think of right now was, morbidly, dead people. Hundreds, thousands of dead people. A place of carefully cultivated repose above, of decomposing, rotted corpses or skeletons beneath.

It was like the sea, whose deceptive surface hid its secret, dangerous world beneath. She shivered.

After the church and the hymns, after scanning the faces of the celebrity mourners for – what, a clue? it seemed so naive – they went to the graveside.

The plot had been dug with mathematical precision by the Mexican driver with his purpose-built digger, and even the pile of earth next to the empty grave was covered by what appeared to be the kind of artificial turf sheeting on which indoor football was played.

The dazzlingly white casket – as in life, Helm had wanted his favourite colour – rested on its platform, and as black veils and black hats bowed, the contrast was like a chess board.

". . . Ashes to ashes, dust to dust, in sure and certain hope of the Resurrection. . ."

Ravens, thought Flavor. They all remind me of a flock of ravens, with heads and beaks dipped, ready to peck the heart out of some dead thing.

She saw Serge, poor once-confined Serge, who had now lost the thing he had loved. He had his hands clasped together, and they moved back and forward as though he was – Flavor thought of that old phrase – as though he was wringing his hands, like some aged Greek woman wailing in tragedy.

But no sound came from Serge's mouth. His face was a silent portrait of loss.

She said in a soft voice to McCall: "Does everyone tally with the list?" He confirmed it with a nod: "They're all clean. Everyone invited, all present and correct."

He had cupped his hands and spoken into her ear, and she was faintly irritated that he had come so close, and for the second time she smelled his smell; soap, shampoo, bourbon?

And unknown to her, he in turn, took an accidental draught of her muskiness, and it unsettled and confused him without him having the faintest idea at that moment, why.

She said: "Which doesn't mean it ISN'T one of those s.o.bs."

He muttered quickly: 'Wouldn't rule it out for a second. I'd say this is the most likely bunch, not the bozos outside."

McCall leaned back, feeling slightly dizzy. Which, he concluded, was hardly surprising. The previous night he had deliberately drunk himself into a stupor. His body, which was screaming for rest, had welcomed the oblivion. Then, like a cruel torturer, the booze had woken him after less than an hour, so he could throw up.

He felt sick and exhausted.

The sun was well up now, over the hills, striking like a golden sword onto the mourners and the shiny handles of the casket, reflecting the light, causing some of the mourners to shield their eyes to avoid being dazzled.

When the graveside ceremony ended the two officers returned to McCall's car and drove back to the entrance before the rest of the mourners.

The sun was now glinting off the spear-like peaks of the massive gate irons, and as they drove through, the cry went up: "Here they are."

And eventually the crawl of black limousines appeared

like a giant centipede from Memorial Drive, and once again the gates swept back like arms to allow them egress.

Flavor and McCall watched a uniformed motor-cycle patrolman kick his Yamaha into life, switch on his twin flashing lights, and pull into the road to stop the traffic so the cortège could come out as one continuous stream.

The media and the fans swept in like a sea on the lead limo, and were as quickly parted by the long black hood that curved through them slowly and persistently, and miraculously without touching a soul. Once clear, it swung right onto the road leading to the freeway.

When the last car had gone, the traffic cop kicked his bike off the stand and waved on the lines of impatient, waiting motorists.

The media rushed off to the cars and TV trucks. The fans watched the disappearing tail of the cortège, as though unable to accept it was no longer there, then glanced wistfully up at Forest Lawn.

At last they trudged away, feet dragging in the dust like dispirited survivors of a failed cavalry charge.

Flavor said: "I'm going to check the flower dedications, see if there's anything interesting." She got out of his MGB and into her own car, showed her ID to the woman on the gate, and went back into the cemetery.

Once again she drove past the burial plots with their Elysian and comforting names; Sheltering Hills, Enduring Faith, Loving Kindness, up to Murmuring Trees, where Helm's casket still rested on its platform prior to burial.

She checked each floral tribute, aware that each had to be sent through only five appointed florists or through Forest Lawn itself.

She was looking for something in the words, something that would alert her, something that would scream out – THIS, this is the one.

But it was all on a theme of sadly missed, in loving memory, the earth is a sadder place, you were a one in a million, always remembered. And showbizzy, the final curtain, you were a trouper, a star among stars.

Way off across Evergreen Drive, near the fence that marked the Forest Lawn boundary, she heard shouts from two Mexican workers who were trimming grass.

They seemed agitated, and quickly walked away across the lawns. As they came near her she shouted: "Something wrong over there?"

One clearly had limited English, and just gestured helplessly, but the other said: "We saw a rattlesnake. A beeg one – there . ." He pointed to the spot they had just quickly vacated.

She could see nothing, clearly the snake had gone, but later she told McCall, and he said:

"Sure, the hills around here are full of them, especially now. I wouldn't personally want to sit up there with a camera."

Flavor grimaced: "It gives me the creeps."

"I thought you'd be used to snakes, coming from Mississippi."

"It's not so much the snake, it's that it's a snake in HERE, you know, a graveyard. I find that spooky."

He laughed: "It probably poked its head out, sniffed the Hollywood crowd, knew when it was beaten in the poison fangs stakes, and took off for Sacramento."

"This place is creepy enough without rattlesnakes."

"They're the natives, we're the intruders. They were around here before we were."

She was aware that McCall was speaking, but she was inside her head, thinking what she thought of as the witch thoughts. They sometimes came, uncanny, supernatural thoughts that popped up in her head. Thoughts that disturbed her, that made her doubt the rational and the reasoned.

Snakes in a graveyard. Snakes lying on tombstones, snakes in caskets slithering out of the eye sockets of bleached skulls.

Snakes and death. Omens and portents and messages.

She knew with the rational portion of her mind that it was superstitious backwoods garbage, the residue of tall tales at her grandmother's knee, of overhearing old women's gossip, of listening to the folklore of the frightened and the uneducated.

Yet. When it was the darkest, deepest hour of the night, when rationality fled like a terrified onlooker, then these thoughts came.

It was then that the darkness had power, and the witch in her told her things; things about her past, and perhaps her future, things that her consciousness would not release, things her mind kept locked in some vault into which it seemed she would never be able to break.

But the wicked witch in her stole things from the vault, trinkets of thought, baubles of memory, and dangled them in front of her, taunting her, daring her to remember.

"... Somebody called LA a desert at the edge of the ocean, and believe me, the desert and all its wonderful life forms is just waiting for LA to fuck up, and then it's going to come marching back in here and take over as if we'd never been here."

She came out of her reverie: "We're helping."

McCall said: "And hey, this is California, this is LA, Paradise on earth. And in every Paradise there's a serpent."

At noon, when the sun was at its fiercest, the sky was a cobalt blue, and heat shimmered over the brown, parched scrub and the neat, green, well-watered lawns.

Flavor and McCall had been gone three hours when the black, Econoline van pulled into Forest Lawn.

It went up Memorial Drive, took the first right into Evergreen, swept right in a loop that took it past the statue of Moses, then back on itself, and right into Celestial Drive, a half circle that encompassed the plot of Golden Dawn, that had the Sherry Knoll at its opposite edge.

And there it stopped.

The two occupants did not leave their air-conditioned

sanctuary. Inside it was chilled, like a morgue, and the glare of the harsh sunlight was muted by the smoked glass.

Instead the driver stared out at the name on the plinth, stared as only obsessives will, as if just BY looking, again and again, the truth could somehow be altered.

The words on the plinth read: "Kathleen O'Malley, 1944–1966. God took her in His arms and sat her alongside His angels."

And the eyes of the driver moved up to the statue that stood guard over the plinth. Up to the towering angel, wings upswept, head downcast, its hands clasped together in prayer.

The driver turned and peered into the dark, cold recesses of the vehicle, gazing now at this memory of the past made hideous flesh.

And said, in a voice almost a whisper:

"Come. Come look at the angel."

CHAPTER FIVE

The woman's haunted eyes looked through them, beyond them, back into the terrible past.

Flavor said: "Take it slowly, there's no rush. When you called us, you said you thought you'd seen the killer we're looking for."

"Yes, I've seen your killer, I KNOW I have."

There was just the hum of the air conditioner competing with the dry desert heat, and the sound of their breathing, until the woman spoke again.

"It was out in the desert, about 12 miles from here. We used to go there – John and me. I'd been seeing him for about five months. I knew it was wrong, but I was a kid, and I loved him. He said – " she paused, gave a smile that took her, for a moment, back over the chasm that separated middle age from youth – "he said he'd leave his wife. Do you understand?"

McCall nodded, as if to say, it's the story of the world, honey, don't worry.

"But Palm Desert is a small town, so we had to be, you know, careful, because if anyone had seen us . . ." The woman shook her head, eyes still in the past, remembering.

"So I used to drive into the desert a pre-arranged number of miles, and he'd come out. He'd park off the highway then get in my car. We'd drive another ten, fifteen maybe – like, who else is going to drive out into the desert, middle of the night . . .?"

Flavor said: "But that night . . ?"

The woman lit a cigarette, drew on it heavily, and blew it out, dragon-like through her nostrils: "That night, it was just like normal. At first. We drove out, pulled off the highway, switched off the lights, started to kiss and things, you know . . ." she pulled on the cigarette.

Flavor said: "Sure."

"Then we just lay there and talked, kind of what we'd do in the future, the house we'd have, whether we'd move to another state. I actually believed it would happen," she smiled and shook her head at her own naïvety.

They nodded, inside, burning TELL US, TELL US! And knowing it would have to be slow, that like so many people, she had to tell it her way, this fact before that, that before this. And they would have to be patient.

She had telephoned the task force, asked to speak to Flavor, whom she'd seen interviewed on the TV.

Had said she had important information about the Angel – that was the killer's sobriquet from the moment the news of the carved wooden angels leaked out.

Hers was one of a thousand calls offering perceived help, or information. But this was the first apparently sane person who said she'd SEEN the killer up close. And she would only speak to Flavor; to another woman.

And even then, on the telephone, she had to be coaxed to give her name and address. Had to be persuaded that what she said would remain confidential. No Press, nothing given to the local law enforcement authorities that might lead them to identify her.

That had puzzled Flavor – but the reason became all too abundantly clear by the time the woman, Anne-Marie Fullerton, had finished her tale.

And there had been something, too, in the woman's demeanour, even down a telephone line, something that convinced Flavor it was worth the long trip to Palm Desert in the burning heat of the summer.

McCall had insisted on coming, only a fool would have missed out on this possibility, but it had taken Flavor thirty minutes to convince the woman to let a man sit in on the interview.

Anne-Marie was late-Forties with a given-up, seedy, overweight look, her face coarsened from smoking and too much exposure to the desert sun.

Throughout the interview she kept the TV switched on, but with the volume turned right down, as though she needed the reassurance of the flickering images.

She was a mother, there were two framed pictures of young teenaged boys on the mantleshelf above the unused fireplace. Her husband, judging by the portrait, had more weight than was good for him.

Flavor had an instinct the second she had walked into the living room. It said: She's settled for this. This is her compromise with life, this is her refuge from some kind of fear.

Anne-Marie continued:

"It was after about, oh, I don't know, fifteen minutes maybe." The eyes bored back to the past, back to the horror.

"I heard a noise, like something had touched the car, a scraping kind of noise."

"Did John hear it?"

"No. He had a little deafness on his right side, but then it happened again, and we both heard it."

"Did you look out of the windows?" McCall asked.

"Sure. It was moonlight, you could see as though it was day. There was nothing, and the sound didn't happen again. We thought it could be an animal, a prairie dog, maybe. We talked some more, dozed off."

It was building in her like an explosion, her whole body was tensed like an athlete waiting to leave the starter's blocks, they could see the knotting of her veins and muscles.

She drew heavily on the burning palliative between her fingers and the tip glowed like a coal.

"I woke up. Suddenly, no reason. And it was there outside the window, in the moonlight, looking in." A shudder wracked her body.

Flavor said, gently: "What was there?"

Flavor had that witch feeling, of terrible knowledge, a smell of something from this woman, a smell of fear and death, of hidden agony. And Flavor thought, she knows — something.

The woman shook her head, desperately, like a child that knows in advance it will be called a liar.

"You won't believe me, I know you won't believe me."

"Try us," McCall said, "we didn't drive 120 miles to dismiss what you have to say. What did you see? A man?"

"It wasn't a man."

The woman closed her eyes, and rocked, back and forwards, arms around herself, hugging herself, like a mental patient. Without a word Flavor went across and sat next to her on the patterned sofa.

Putting an arm around the distressed woman, she said: 'It's OK honey, we have all the time in the world. Just tell us what you saw. It wasn't a man, it was a woman, right? We've never said it couldn't be a woman. What did she look like?"

"No . . . No . ." the woman was shaking her head, "You don't understand."

McCall said, evenly: "Just tell us what you saw."

The woman opened her eyes, looked from one to the other, looking for the belief she felt could never come, looking for belief other than her own, in the nightmare she had never before shared. The nightmare she had kept within her like some festering sore for 21 years.

"It was an angel." She said it slowly.

McCall said: "What?"

"I saw an angel."

They lay like silver fish in an Oriental pond, their bodies dappled by the moonlight that fell rippling over them. Anne-Marie luxuriated in it, she loved the lustrous sheen it gave to their skin, and she could feel her man's warmth next to her on the reclined seats, where the thin car blanket had been tossed aside.

His thigh was glued to hers with the sweat of love, joining them like Siamese twins.

She was relaxed and content. Her last conscious thought before sleep was: how easy it is to be happy. Then when she awoke the angel was standing by the car, far enough away so that she could see it was an angel, not a person.

At first, of course, she thought – for a microsecond – that she was still dreaming. That it was one of those dreams that occur in the habitat of first awakening, in your home, your bedroom, around your bed, and all the more real and horrible for that, until you finally, truly, awake.

And then she knew, with dawning horror, that she was not asleep and that this was worse than any awakening nightmare, that this angel was real, not an apparition, not something of imagination.

It was real, it had wings, and it stood by the car as though guarding it.

It was silvery, almost blue in the moonlight, and it stood like a statue, its wings sweeping up from the shoulder and out, then disappearing from view behind the still figure.

The face was indistinguishable at that distance, but the head was cast down, and the palms of the hands were vertical, as though pressed together in prayer.

The girl screamed.

Her lover was awake in an instant, scrabbling at the blanket, eyes gummed with sleep. He was confused and scared.

"John!" She pointed, aware that she was cold as ice now,

the sweat drying on her like a fever victim.

"My God."

She could tell he was scared too. She could feel the contraction of his muscles, the tensing against her.

For long seconds they sat up, arms around each other, looking out into the moonlit desert at this ghostly spectre. Her whole body was trembling: "What is it?"

"Some joker." She felt him fumble for his clothes, and all the while she stared, transfixed, at the motionless angel that glowed – she was aware now, it wasn't just the moonlight – as though luminous.

She heard the rustle of clothes, the murmur of frightened bravado threats. "It's a peeping Tom." And she saw the gun shape appear in his hand, and heard the snap of the door catch.

And she called out: "John, no!"

But he was out of the door, and she saw him clearly in the moonlight, heard him shout something, heard the noise but not the words, and then flinched at the crack of the pistol shot, saw the statue thing come alive, saw it move with ferocious speed, as though it was on wheels.

But it was not running away from the gun, from John. Instead, to her horror, she realised that it was moving towards him like a blur.

And she saw the flash of steel in the moonlight, heard John's cry of fear, heard the cry cut off abruptly, saw John crumple, a silver falling shadow in the moonlight.

The angel walked forwards, knelt stiffly, lifted something that was partially hidden from her, and held it by – a chord? – turned, and walked off into the desert.

And then there was nothing, just the silence and the moonlight. But she knew she was not dreaming. She knew that this was happening, the angel, the shot, John falling, it was all real.

For a while, and to her shame, she did nothing. She would never know how long she waited, hiding like a child beneath blankets, waiting for the bogeyman to go away.

But her bogeyman was real, her terror a living thing.

Yet at last she stirred, wrapped the thin blanket around her, opened the door, put her bare feet to the ground, and stood, shivering in the chill desert air.

She called, hesitantly, just a quaver of sound, but was instantly terrified of her own voice that seemed to boom like a trumpet in the silent void: "John?"

She imagined that something moved in the brush, an animal perhaps, but the noise shocked her, and she started back against the door, closing it. That noise alarmed her too and she began to shake so that her hand beat a tattoo on the metal.

Silence flooded back like a tide, and at last she drew up the courage to call again, this time modulating her voice, as though she might wake up the desert, might bring back the terrifying spectre of the angel.

"John, are you OK?"

And she knew utterly, knew it in her heart, that John was not OK, that something had happened, something sinister and bad and awful and evil, and that she was in the middle of it.

But she also believed with inherited instinct, like a child who knows that Santa is fake but wishes it didn't, that if she called and if John answered, and said he was OK, shocked but OK, then they could get back in the car, drive away, shaken, and talk about it, about the angel.

And then anonymously they could tell the sheriff, and they'd find a new place for their lovers' trysts.

But John, the huddled, strangely-shaped form of John that now lay half in moonlight, half in the shadow of the car, did not reply. So she called again. "John, are you OK? What happened? Did you shoot it? Did it hurt you?"

No sound came from the different John-shape, and she knew there could only be silence from John. She knew with absolute certainty that something terrible had happened. She couldn't mouth the words, but she knew John was dead.

And the finality of that somehow strengthened her, and

she went forward and touched the inert bundle that had, less than 30 minutes before, been this vibrant living thing that she loved, that had entered her, brought her to climax, that had spoken its love for her.

At last she found courage and turned John over, and as he rolled fully into the moonlight, his torso shining naked and silver, she saw at last the horrible reality . . .

She screamed, her mouth a howling O in the moonlight, until the screams peaked and died into a choking, disbelieving sob.

She brought her hands up to her face, and felt with horror for the first time the sticky blood and the fibrous human debris on her face and in her eyes.

She felt it run warm and salty and vile into her mouth. And at first the horror of that robbed her of sound, but then the screams came back like the end of a temporary lull in a storm, and this time she screamed from the depths of her lungs, terrible wolf-like howls of mortal terror and pain and loss.

Because John had no head.

And she carried on screaming, like a mad woman, rending the desert air, tearing it like calico, until her lungs ached and her throat was raw, and then she gagged and retched, and clawed at her mouth, wiping at it with the back of her hands.

All she could taste was blood.

Then slowly she backed away from this frightening thing that was her dead lover. And to her shame, all she could think of was flight, to get away from there, from the headless corpse, from the angel, from the nightmare into which she had been thrust.

She went around the hood of the car, fearful, clutching to it, because it meant normality, and sanity, and she found the driver's door with her scrabbling hands, never taking her eyes off the fearful desert that surrounded her with such menace.

The keys were in the ignition where she had left them, the

engine fired, and by mistake she put the gear shift into Drive, instead of Reverse.

The car lurched forward into the scrub and as she jammed her foot against the brake, the car jolted to a halt so suddenly and with such force, she went forward painfully into the steering wheel.

She pushed the gear into Reverse, and screamed the car backwards all fifty yards to the highway, oblivious to the bumps and scrapes and the squeals of anguish from tyres and bodywork.

And she drove, eyes fixed on the moonlit strip of highway that unrolled like a black ribbon before the car headlights. She almost gasped with relief when she saw the first gas station and adjoining convenience store on the outskirts of Palm Desert.

She pulled over and parked before she realised she was still naked. She scrabbled into her clothes, took a tissue from the glove compartment and tried to wipe some of the blood off her face.

Then she climbed shakily out and went to the rest room. There she stared into into the rust-pocked, dirt-streaked mirror at her bloodied, ashen face. She sluiced herself in cold water, and watched the water darken.

Then she wiped herself clean on paper towels, cleaned the thin, diluted bloodstains off the sink, and flushed away the soiled towels.

She left the rest room, went into the 7–11, bought a pack of cigarettes and a bottle of Scotch, returned to her car, took three calming snorts of Scotch, and smoked a cigarette.

Ignoring the telephones near to the car, she drove several blocks until she saw a telephone on the street. She leafed through the directory, hands shaking, tearing at the flimsy pages, ripping them in her haste, until eventually she found the number for which she was searching . . .

Fumbling for change, dropping dimes on the sidewalk, she eventually managed to dial the County Sheriff's office.

She told the bored and sleepy voice what had happened,

gave directions as best she could, then when the man asked her name and address, she hung up.

She went back to her apartment, drank the rest of the Scotch and passed out. And never told another living soul about what happened until this day.

The deputy was a bored man of forty-five with a paunch, and he clearly resented their presence, casting glances at Flavor, then back to McCall, as if to say, what is all this, and who's in charge, this good old boy or the – coloured lady?

He pulled the file.

"I remember it. I was new on the department. We got a call from some hysterical female. Sent a couple of cars out to the location she gave us. We didn't find anything and there was a wind getting up, it was difficult to see, what with the dark and the sand.

'The next day we got a call from a woman about her husband who hadn't come home the night before. We figured maybe the two were connected.

'So we went back out in daylight, when the wind had dropped. We found tyre tracks on the road like someone had took off in a big hurry. Broken cactus and stuff, so we had a look around, and found a body."

The deputy opened the file, scanned it, squinted: "John Donnell. Decapitated. We never did find the head."

"You ever trace the female?" Flavor asked.

"No – " he hesitated, "ma'am. And he was a married man, actually he was a pastor." The deputy shook his head, "It looked to us as though he was up to no good out there with a girl, and she didn't want anyone to know who she was. The family didn't want any mud stirring, him being a preacher. And he had kids too, he was respected around these parts." He squinted again at the file: "Church of the Holy Saviour, Sycamore Drive. It's all in there."

Flavor said: "Was it very publicised at the time?"

"Not really." The deputy paused, "Look, to be frank, I don't think we said anything to the Press about the head. I mean, it wasn't relevant to anything, and it would have been distressing to the family."

"They were never told?"

"The wife — well, she had to ID the body, and someone had to know why they couldn't have the casket lid open for a viewing. But with her agreement, that was as far as it went. The kids, you know . . ."

The man handed the file to McCall, who tossed it on a chair without even opening it.

The overweight deputy followed the path of the file with his eyes, then looked back at McCall, puzzled. "I thought you wanted that."

McCall said: "You watch television, deputy?"

The man gave a half-shrug: "Sure I watch television, what — "

He stopped in mid-sentence, because McCall had stepped forward, and everything about his stance, the posture, legs apart, arms hanging loose, spelt trouble.

"You been following the news?"

"Listen, mister, you have no jurisdiction here, just remem — "

McCall leapt, grabbing the man by the shoulder, crashing him back into the filing cabinets, his snarling face an inch from that of the deputy.

Flavor watched. Waited.

"You stupid bovine sonofabitch. You been hibernating for a month, asshole? Don't you know what's going down in LA, for Christ's sake? The Angel? A movie star with his fucking HEAD chopped off? Don't you?"

The deputy was red in the face: "You got no right."

"And you sit on THIS? A man decapitated just outside your town, the perp steals his fucking HEAD? Just like up in LA? Jesus Christ man, what are you, a moron?"

Flavor said softly: "Put him down, McCall."

The deputy's bulging eyes turned to her, and she saw they were pleading. Help me. She hated herself for it, but she liked that.

"Put him down, you'll ruin his shirt." McCall relaxed his grip, dusted the deputy down, pretended to help him re-arrange the shirt.

"I could lock you up for that, ASSHOLE," the deputy said with mock bravado. "Like I said, you've got no jurisdiction here."

McCall said: "The way things are going up in LA, by the time this thing is over we'll have jurisdiction over pretty much the whole of the fucking state, you scumbag. As it is I reckon your sheriff isn't going to be pleased when he learns you sat on this."

"Jesus Christ, it was twenty-one years ago. Who says there's a connection? LA's a hundred and twenty miles away."

"No-one," Flavor interjected, "no-one says there's a connection. Hey, McCall," he looked her way, "let's borrow the file and come back another day."

"Sure," he said with an ease he didn't feel, "sure, why not. OK if we borrow this, deputy?"

The man nodded: "Under the circumstances, I suppose. Return it tomorrow."

"We will," Flavor picked up the file, "and thanks."

Outside, the sun was like a branding iron, and Flavor said: "Let's get out of this before we fry." She saw the quizzical, slightly puzzled look that was not unfamiliar to her.

She said: "Black people burn too, McCall, you sure as hell have a lot to learn."

Inside the car she looked straight ahead through the windshield, because she did not want to face him.

"One day, just one fine, sweet day you are going to do that to the wrong person. And that deputy, or cop, or hillbilly sheriff, or whomever, is going to throw you in jail and keep you there 'till you rot. Can't you understand that?"

"Don't fucking lecture me."

She turned to him, furious:

"I am sick and tired of you saying FUCK to me, you

FUCK! We need their co-operation, not their antagonism. He's a goddamned deputy in Palm Desert, for Chrissakes, not the Director of the CIA. It happened TWENTY-ONE years ago, why the hell SHOULD he make a connection?"

McCall threw his head back, and snorted with disgust.

"He doesn't have to be the Director of the CIA or the goddamn FBI to see the connection between a guy who got his head chopped off, and what's going down in LA."

"Jesus," she shook her head, "you just don't get it, do you, you moron? You can't treat people like that. And we HAVE the information, the girl told us. But maybe – just maybe – that hick deputy can help us somewhere else down the line on this. Except now he won't. In fact, he'll make damn sure to fuck over anything connected with this AND us if he gets half the chance."

"Yes, ma'am, thank you for the lecture, I'll recommend him for a citation, now will you please put the air-conditioning on? I'm about ready to be taken out of the oven."

She started the Skylark, put the air on full, and they felt the cold blast like a balm.

They drove back to Anne-Marie Fullerton's house in a silence that McCall eventually broke. He said, sullenly: "You don't believe all that shit about her seeing an angel, not really I mean?"

Flavor shrugged, jumped a red light said: "Shit!", then, "I don't know, she seemed convinced."

"But not convincing. It's a hell of a coincidence, right? Her lover gets wasted TWENTY-ONE years ago, OK, his head is chopped off. But it's 1995 when she comes forward, and hey – what a surprise – it's AFTER all the papers come out with this angel stuff. The kiss of the angel, the angel's revenge, the angel of the lord, have you read that shit?"

"Sure, I've read it. You think that's what made her tell us this stuff about seeing an angel?"

"What else? Half of California is seeing angels. There's an angel revival. This guy will have his own movie soon."

Flavor pulled up outside the house: "But why should she risk telling it all now? He was a married man, a pastor. There could still be a scandal."

He scratched his nose, pretending to be bored:

"Conscience. She was with him when he was killed, I believe her on that. But seeing an angel, nah, I think for that she gets a co-credit with the National Enquirer. She's been waiting twenty-one years to clear her conscience, and she thinks now is the time."

Flavor switched off the engine and with it the air-conditioning and within seconds the car felt warm.

She persisted: "The guy was decapitated, THAT is on the record. And what if she DID see an angel, or what she thought was an angel? And what if that – thing – is the same person who killed the people in LA?"

"What? OK, WHAT if?"

"Then we have our first description of the killer."

"I don't believe I'm hearing this. We put out an APB, for one luminous angel, with wings, probably to be seen at prayer? Give me a break, Flavor."

"It's a start. Find someone with an angel costume, something, Jeez . . ." her voice tailed off, "I don't know."

"It's a start, and it's also a finish. Like, for example, where has our angel been for twenty-one years? He pops one in 1974 – this is your scenario – and steals the head as Numero Uno for his collection. He's so hooked that he disappears for twenty-one years."

He lowered the window, but that just made it hotter: "It doesn't make sense. And the deputies found NOTHING, no tyre tracks, nothing." He wiped his forehead, "God, it's like an inferno out here. How do people live in this?"

"I thought you liked the sun, you sure as hell are always lying in the stuff trying to get your white bread face all browned. Look, McCall, a wind got up that night, the deputy told us that, footprints wouldn't last long in that."

"It's like I said, we don't get skin cancer in my family. But this? Shit, you could fry bacon on the sidewalk. OK, he

RIDES off on a horse, flies off, whatever, and we don't hear from him until 1995. It doesn't fit. If it's the same guy, there has to be a motive, something that links them all."

"Well I don't know the answer, but I know it's the same guy."

He flipped the door handle: "First thing I learned about detective work is that the moment you think you KNOW, the moment you think you have it all figured, that's the moment you don't know shit."

She met his eyes, and for a second there was a strange feeling of intimacy. "You forgot something McCall. I'm a witch, remember?"

"And if I don't get out of this heat my brains are going to turn into tortilla."

"Go easy on her McCall, she's speaking the truth."

He squinted against the fierce light: "Oh, she'd just better be. Or she's going to need a damn good lawyer."

CHAPTER SIX

Victoria Astaire was that lyricised woman of a certain age, and British in the Hollywood sense.

Which was to say she spoke in the formal, artificial English way Tinseltown believed bespoke blue-blooded Olde Worlde aristocracy, although she had spent most of her adult life in America.

She drank tea from Royal Doulton cups, affected an upper-class lisp and stammer, was usually seen clutching a duo of pale Pekinese to her ample if now sagging bosom, and favoured chintzy furniture and heirloom-like antiques in her Pacific Palisades home.

Victoria was the grande dame of Pacific Coast, the hour-long drama cum soap series that had done for the golden state what Dallas and JR had for Texas.

As Martha van Bulen, matriarch of the cathode-fiction TV empire Van Bulen Productions, Victoria presided over a squabbling, fratricidal family that made the Borgias look like the Waltons.

Pacific Coast had propelled her from the lowlands of bit-part, low-budget movies, into the multi-millionaire star stratosphere.

As well as the antique-stuffed mansion in Pacific Palisades, she now owned a duplex in Manhattan and a converted farmhouse in Tuscany, Italy. Which wasn't bad for a girl born illegitimate Elsie Mumford in Clapton, East London on August 31st, 1928, to a parlourmaid, who, in the parlance of the day, had 'got into trouble.'

Not that it was possible to discover that fact any more, since Victoria had done a good job in muddying her trail.

Publicly the star graciously confessed to being in her middle Fifties, but the make-up girls at Burbank who had to do more and more reconstruction work on the valiant but crumbling face, before Victoria could go on camera, knew better.

Elsie Mumford's illegitimacy haunted her long after she had ceased to use that name, and at the same time the knowledge of it, and the poverty of her background, drove her on when it had seemed, in the past, that she must be swamped by despair at her failing career.

She'd been adopted by poor, puritanical parents, and had rebelled at sixteen into a rushed wartime marriage with forged parental consent papers to a soldier ten years older.

He was killed in Germany two months later, and for the next three years Elsie worked as a 'maid' – that was the euphemism – to a prostitute in London's Mayfair.

In the final three months before she left England forever Elsie actually slept with clients herself, saved every penny she made, and in 1949 sailed for Canada with the then small fortune of £350, worth, at that time, 1,400 US dollars.

After a spell shifting scenery and painting props with a Toronto repertory company in return for hot food and a shared room, she was invited to take part in the play. At first it was walk-on, or third spear carrier parts. But later she graduated to real roles in everything from Trilby to Blithe Spirit, King Lear to Midsummer Night's Dream.

In 1954, with just a couple of years' acting experience, Elsie Mumford caught a Greyhound bus for Hollywood, lopped six years off her age, and re-invented herself as Victoria Astaire, actress.

Victoria was a stunner. She was gypsy-dark, ample-bosomed, long-legged, and with a look that could turn men into guacamole. She hung around studio commissaries and Hollywood nightclubs, until she entranced a young producer named Arnie Rosenberg. They were married in 1955.

She became pregnant twice – had abortions twice – and started to appear in Rosenberg-produced, low-budget TV cowboy serials, sometimes as the saloon bar good-time gal, sometimes as the prissy schoolmarm.

In 1959 she divorced Rosenberg, and met Kirk Nielsen, though not in that order. She had a brief but torrid affair with Nielsen, and wisely agreed to part as friends when he tired of her sexually.

Their friendship endured. In part because there were things Nielsen needed that she could not provide, their affair had shown that, but she knew from whence she could.

He in turn needed a woman he could trust, who could advise him, someone with whom he was not sexually or romantically involved, but someone who knew his favourite predilection and could make sure it was catered for.

And he in turn knew hers, had introduced her to it, and helped her satisfy her desire for it.

Nielsen was on the brink of stardom when he met Victoria Astaire, and achieved it in the early Sixties. He was a sure-fire box office king, the big name over the marquee until the mid-Seventies. Then he realised the younger names were taking over, and wisely got out, first into directing, then into production.

In 1980 he started Nielsen Productions, churning out TV movies and series – of which Pacific Coast became the jewel. For his matriarch he chose Victoria Astaire. It was her reward, and they both knew it.

And in the eighth year of Pacific Coast, with absolutely

no end in sight, Victoria had earned around $10 million. She was rich now, rich and successful and assured. Apart from her upbringing as a bastard, she had only two big secrets in her life.

And both were inextricably linked with Kirk Nielsen.

She knew his secrets, and he knew hers, and it bound them, this terrible shared and secret knowledge, like the bonds of old love or old hate.

Victoria Astaire was at first stunned that she should be blackmailed after so long a time.

She replaced the receiver with a sense of shock. It was as though a cold hand had reached out over the years and chilled her like the touch of a ghost.

She realised she was shaking, the now age-mottled hands trembling. Her first instinct was to call Nielsen, but then she realised the caller had made no mention of him. Only her.

Perhaps this was a blackmailer who could be appeased. It was a ludicrously small sum of money – $10,000 – an amateur, not a professional. Perhaps the blackmailer only had a suspicion, no real proof, not after all these years. But Victoria did not want, nor could she afford, even the faintest whiff of scandal.

Victoria Astaire shivered. It was something she would have to handle alone. She would take the money and hand it over. If more calls came, if the blackmailer upped the ante, then she would have to review the situation.

If it COULD be made to go away for $10,000, then everyone got off lightly. If it couldn't, then she would speak to Nielsen. At that point, she was sure, the blackmailer would have to be murdered.

For if the blackmailer knew the secret, had PROOF of the secret, they could all go to jail, even now.

That afternoon, Victoria Astaire drew $10,000 from the Wells Fargo bank in Santa Monica, and that evening asked the chauffeur to ready the Rolls-Royce for her to drive.

And she waited for the night.

At eleven she eased the Rolls onto the Pacific Coast high-way, and drove towards Malibu. She went on, past the pier, past Alice's Restaurant and the Malibu Colony, on past Pepperdine University and onto the coast road in the direction of Oxnard.

She passed Point Dume and when she reached the vast stretch of the Leo Carrillo State Beach she began to count, one, two, and at the third pull-off she made a U-turn across the carriageway and sighed the Rolls to a stop at the pull-in.

There was just a sliver of moon, and soon that was hidden behind rolling sea mist. The only other light came from passing headlights and the white of the curling surf.

The dashboard clock had just tipped the hand down into the new hour and new day when she saw headlights in the rear view mirror. Saw them turned off, flashed on, off, on, and off again. The signal.

She felt absurd, melodramatic. It reminded her of a scene from one of those despised TV movies she had done in the early Seventies when her career was at its nadir.

Victoria Astaire got out of the Rolls-Royce, the brown paper bag of money clutched in one hand, her handbag containing the snub-nosed thirty-eight Colt Python in the other.

She could see a high-profile vehicle in the gloom, and a figure standing by it. A voice called: "Walk down the pathway to the water's edge."

Victoria hesitated.

"Do it!"

Treading carefully, she sought out the pathway between the rocks, eventually felt her feet sink into the soft sand and then she laboured the thirty yards to the water's edge, where the sand became firmer.

She saw the ink-stain fingers of the advancing tide, and the moustache of curling foam out on the breaking waves.

The voice said: "Turn." She did.

"Kneel." She hesitated. "Kneel!" Victoria lowered herself to her knees, clumsily, and with the difficulty of age.

"Did you bring the money?"

She held out the paper bag with her left hand, and at the same time she slid her right hand into the handbag that lay now on the sand. Slowly, carefully, like a blind person, she curled her fingers around the butt of the small revolver.

"Do you have it all?"

"Ten thousand dollars. That's what you asked for."

The figure came forward in the gloom, close enough for Victoria Astaire to see the face. Shock rippled down her spine like electricity.

She said: "Are you out of your mind?"

"No, I'm not out of my mind Victoria."

"How can YOU possibly blackmail ME? You're crazy." And as Victoria said the words, still kneeling, her fingers closed on the revolver, and she slipped the gun out of the handbag.

"But as you see – I'm not."

She dropped the bag of money and put both hands on the gun, pointing the barrel upwards, thumbing back the hammer:

"I can use this, and there's a notch in each bullet. It'll blow your stomach out through your spine."

"Tut, tut, such vulgarity. And I do believe your Queen Elizabeth accent is slipping – Elsie."

"Ruin me and you ruin yourself. Why?" Victoria was genuinely baffled, astonished. "Why do this?"

There was no reply. And too late, above the crash of the surf, and the hiss of the encroaching tide, she heard the soft footfalls in the sand behind her.

She tried to turn, twisting awkwardly with age, trying to bring the gun to bear.

And Victoria Astaire saw, for a brief second, without time even for the scream that was forming in her throat, the angel of death.

Flavor lay back, eyes closed, luxuriating in the hot, green foamy water, a warm, wet flannel draped over her eyes and forehead. She drifted in the shallows of sleep, sensing her body's slow breathing, and the relaxing of her muscles in the gentle caress of the water.

The apartment door opened, closed, with barely a click.

Flavor sat bolt upright in the water, sending a mini tidal wave down to the foot of the tub. She ripped the flannel off her face. Her heart was pounding. She waited, but heard nothing more. She called gently, aware of the quaver in her voice.

"Is that you Jack?"

Through the half-open bathroom door she heard the slow, measured footsteps coming down the pine floorboards of the corridor.

"Jack?"

Flavor reached down to her shoulder holster on the floor beside the bath, and her fingertips caressed the leather.

The footsteps stopped, and there was a clink as something clashed. Glass on glass? Glass on metal? Flavor held her breath, slid out the Smith and Wesson, brought it up and levelled it at the gap between door and jamb.

A deep voice said: "Bearing gifts," and a hand came out holding a wine bottle. A head and face followed, the piercing blue eyes fixed on Flavor.

"It's only Jack."

Flavor put the gun back into its holster, and slid into the visually protective cover of the green foam.

She looked straight ahead, at the mosaic tiles, and said, as evenly as she could: "I nearly shot you then, Jack. And you have my solemn promise that unless you get out of this bathroom NOW, I WILL shoot you."

Her heart was pounding like a jack-hammer, and she realised that she'd been scared. Very scared. Being angry now was compensation.

"Yes, ma'am." The bathroom door closed.

Flavor closed her eyes again. It was the first time that had ever happened, the first time Jack had ever intruded. But it had been brewing, she knew that.

And she asked herself, as she had so many times before. Is that what you want, Flavor? And if you DON'T, what the hell are you going to do about it? Like, find a new apartment and a new room-mate?

She remembered her grandmother saying, "Where you at Flave? Where are you at girl?" So where AM I at, grandma? If only you were alive and here to tell me just where the hell I'm at.

Later, over the trout and the Sancerre, Jack said, by way of apology: "The intention was to surprise you."

"And see me naked? Well, you surprised me too. Congratulations."

"Jesus, it was for a second, I didn't know you were in the bath. The door was open."

"And what did you think I was doing in there, practising the clarinet?"

Jack laughed, mischievously: "Who'd you think I was – the Angel?"

Flavor looked up from examining the crystal of the wine glass, and the meniscus of liquid, that was like a floating disc on the surface.

"Do you think this is some kind of a joke? Huh? A plot for one of your movies? Do you? Don't think I don't know why you've been asking me all these questions, these weeks. Why you've been so interested in this case. I'll just bitty bet that when you boot up that Apple word processor down at Fox every day, up pops a screenplay on this, right or wrong?"

Jack shrugged: "It's a legitimate subject for drama."

"What're you calling it, Angel's Revenge? Think there'll be an Angel 2? You pitched it yet? Made the all-important deal?" The sarcasm was like curdled milk.

Jack had the decency to look embarrassed: "The working title is Angel. And yes, I've taken a few meetings."

"Oh I'll just bet you have, honey. Well remember, at the moment it is still a legitimate – " she bit into the word, "subject of a police enquiry. And I AM heading that enquiry.

And it's not celluloid, Jack, it's not – what did you once call the movies, oh yeah, 'reel life'. Well, it's not 'reel life'; it's REAL life."

She paused: "And it's real death too, I know, I've seen the cadavers. I've smelled them, I – "

"Hey, come on – "

"Don't hey come on me. As a matter of fact the Angel is EXACTLY who I thought you might be."

"Isn't that a mite paranoid?"

"No, it's not paranoid. McCall and I are high-profile, what with television and everything. Who knows with this crazy bastard? Who knows who he might kill next?"

Jack's hand came around the dark green of the wine bottle, skirted a glass, fingertips reaching for Flavor's like emissaries.

Flavor said, harshly: "Don't."

"I'm sorry about the bathroom."

Flavor met eyes that were like chipped ice-blue diamonds:

"And the movie, are you sorry about that?"

"You're a cop, I write movies. End of story."

Flavor drank some wine. It was warming now and she tasted it like the flavour of humiliation: "Well, did you like what you saw in the bathroom, Jack?"

"If you wish me to be honest, I did like what I saw. But it didn't need that. I've always liked what I've seen, from the moment we met. You know that."

"And I also know you said I could room here, and there would be no strings attached."

"Have there been any?"

"Not up until now. But tonight was strings. All this," Flavor waved a hand, encompassing the apartment, "all this belongs to you. Everything that one mill spec screenplays and writer-for-hire money can buy."

Jack downed some wine with a kind of vicious formality, and pointed the empty glass at Flavor like an accusation: "Oh, sure. But I just happened to wait tables for eight years, writing at night and getting ripped off by crooked agents, before I sold that one mill spec screenplay.

'Even then I damn near got cheated out of a screen credit on my OWN movie.'

"Yeah, you earned it, that's not my point. It's just that now, you assume – in time, of course – I'll belong to you too, just like all this."

Jack put head in hands in despair: "Not BELONG to me, dammit, be PART of me. My lover, my partner, my friend."

"And suppose I did want it. Do you realise the harm it could do my career?"

"You could be a consultant on the movie. You could get into Hollywood this way."

"I want to be a police officer, it's what I am."

"So don't worry about it. Anyway, this is a free society. You want what you want, you are what you are. And it's LA, not Boise, Idaho or Selma, Alabama. Forget the bigots."

"It's my choice then?"

"Your choice. We're not all monsters."

"I've never thought that."

"But I'm white and you're black. I'm rich, you're a cop. And I'm writing a movie about a murder YOU'RE investigating. You've thought that, maybe?"

"I've thought about it, but you KNOW what bothers me." Flavor put out her hand and found Jack's.

"Listen to me, baby. Your friendship means everything to me. I don't want to destroy it or lose it. You're the only person who's ever really understood me."

Jack smiled: "We're the same, you and I. I feel it."

Flavor laughed: "You really are sure of that, aren't you?"

"Ninety-nine per cent. So come in from the cold. Know the truth, and the truth shall set you free."

"Very Biblical."

"Very true. We simply have to know who we are, and what we want." Jack paused. "And WHO we want."

Flavor drank some more wine: "You'll get my answer."

"When?"

"When this is over. Until the . . ." she faltered.

Jack shrugged: "A cop's gotta do what a cop's gotta do?"

"I hope you'll never write THAT line."

"No way. But is that a promise?"

"It's a promise."

"OK. I can wait. And how was dinner?"

"Great." Flavor grinned: "Yup, dinner was just great. You're a little treasure in the kitchen." They both laughed.

Jack got up and pirouetted around the table in a mincing, effeminate impression of a woman: "I'm going to make someone a wonderful wife. Hey, do you think I should wear a dress from time to time?"

Flavor laughed: "Come to think of it, it might just suit you at that. That and a little make-up. At the moment you make a LOUSY woman."

The dog found it first, sniffing and yapping at the lifeless thing that swung and swirled on the extreme edges of the tide.

Then the jogger, lagging a hundred yards behind his pet, slowing, advancing hesitantly until he was close enough to see that this thing was – had been – human, and could not possibly be alive.

Then he turned, frightened by death, calling over his shoulder to the dog in a high-pitched, panicky voice. It raced to his side, excited, barking and yelping, and followed him as he ran now, not jogged, up the beach.

It scurried at his heels, as he clambered over the rocks, and sped, breathlessly, along the hard dirt side of the road until he reached a telephone.

McCall put the receiver down: "They've ID'd it. It IS Victoria Astaire."

"Jesus H. Christ."

"You said it."

"We're very deeply in the crap, McCall. Very, very deeply in the crap."

The Mayor swung backwards and forwards, left and right, up and down in his multi-directional leather chair. He was agitated and angry.

He said: "Six weeks, four victims. Goddamn it, this is an epidemic. The media are after MY head, the DA's, the Chief's, ours AND yours in Beverly Hills. This is bringing law enforcement into disrespect. What the hell are you people doing? And where IS Lt. Cartouche?"

"She's on her way sir, she's getting the autopsy results."

McCall was trying to keep his eyes fixed on the Mayor's portrait on the wall. The artist was smart because he'd done what the Mayor's dietician had failed to, and shed at least 20lbs off the Mayor's massive frame.

"Sir, so far we have done everything we can, all the usual checks, forensic and otherwise, no witnesses – "

"Correction. This woman down in Palm Desert?"

"You read the report sir."

The Mayor lifted the folder off his desk, and dropped it again, dramatically enough for the slap to register.

"Yes I read it, and if this ever gets out we'll be the laughing stock. An angel? Do you think we can go to the Press with that – a goddamned angel!? They'd crucify us. You've seen how things are. The whole city has gone angel crazy."

It was true. The murders had now been invested with near-religious significance. It was God's revenge on the Sodom and Gomorrah by the Sea. He had sent His guardian angels to extirpate the sinners and the sinning.

LA's ritzier areas had gone security crazy, if it was possible to be more security conscious in this land of gated compounds, floodlit homes, armed response units, Rottweiler kill-dogs and enough personal firearms to equip a small army.

Bodyguards were working double-shifts and naming their own price. Alarm systems had their OWN alarm systems.

Anyone and everyone in the movie and TV business had started to stay at home nights, behind the guards, the fences and the floodlights.

Some who had no business commitments, and who had, ironically, cancelled European vacations during the Gulf War because of terrorist threats, now busily rented houses in England, France and Spain.

Paranoia was rife. A gardener working on the Bel Air mansion of a retired movie star forgot some tools one evening, went back for them, and was promptly shot by the maid who thought he was a stalking killer.

A fancy dress party goer dressed as an angel, and headed for 1401 Bundy in West Los Angeles, by mistake knocked instead on the door of 1410, and was killed by a single shot fired through the door.

The terrified spinster had seen an angel. It was enough. The police did not press charges.

"Sir, we can't work miracles."

"I'm not asking for miracles, dammit, I'm asking for you to ARREST somebody. I'm asking you to look as though you're actually doing something."

"When we arrest somebody, it'll be the perp, believe me."

"Then WHY? Why, can't you find this person?"

The Mayor's hands were spread, dramatically: "Elections in three months time, and you can take it from me if we haven't got somebody before then, I, the DA, and the chiefs of police can all kiss our jobs goodbye."

McCall looked at him, thinking. How do you explain to people like this? Fat pols who get their criminal knowledge from LA Law and re-runs of Perry Mason.

He said: "Sir. The fact about most murderers is that they're the guy or gal next door. One day the boss chews their ass too much, and they flip.

'One minute they're Jack and Jill Blow from Peoria who wouldn't hurt a fly, the next minute they're in the back of a black and white, facing twenty years in jail, weeping, and wondering how they did it."

"Go on."

"Or they're guys with a record as long as a tailback on

the Golden State Freeway. We know their M.O., we know their haunts."

"But?" the Mayor asked. "I see a big 'But' written all over your face."

"But then there's the guy – or gal – who isn't Joe Blow. He doesn't kill his wife, husband, the guy next door, or the creep who cuts him up in traffic. He's not The Mob, and he's clean. Now HE is the difficult one."

"OK," the Mayor swivelled for effect, "how do you find HIM?"

"We sent a 15 page report to VICAP – nothing." He saw the Mayor's look of incomprehension. "Violent Crime Apprehension Programme, sir. They profile killers, they see if ours matches any other crimes or known perps around the nation."

"So we're left with motive, forensic, circumstantial. Someone sees a red-haired guy leave the scene, or nearby, hanging around. They spot a white Buick, maybe, or a little Mazda with a rust streak. A car that doesn't normally park around there. Or the perp leaves something at the scene, blood, hairs, clothing, a print. Or maybe the victim recently split up with her boyfriend and told friends he'd threatened her. And they tell us."

The Mayor was nodding, Go on.

"Maybe the deceased owed money, or he was in some crazy get-rich-quick scheme that went wrong. Then you've got motive. Who benefits? Who gains by the death? Who wants him out of the way? Is there a will, and who is the beneficiary? Greedy relatives, a wife with an insurance policy?"

"The way the victim is killed, does that have a bearing?"

McCall thought: He reads Detective magazine and watches murder movies. The worst kind.

"Sure it does. Professional or amateur, gun or knife. How many shots? What weapon? Was it a casual intruder, what? If it's a female, has she been raped, before or after?"

"And nothing in your usual pattern is emerging from

these killings? That's what you're saying?"

"I don't know what Flavor has on Astaire. But up to now, no forensic, nothing at the scenes, no witnesses — yes, sir, I know — I mean no witnesses that give us anything we can go on. No connections between the victims."

"Two of them were gay, that's a connection."

"No connection that at this moment means anything. No apparent financial gain for anyone. The same M.O. but nothing that fits any killer we've ever seen. He's known to the victim, he either goes to their home or lures them somewhere. He uses a sword, or an axe, some sharp-bladed instrument. Death comes from one stroke."

McCall exhaled: "Then he takes the heads."

"And no apparent motive?"

"None that we can establish up to now. None of the victims had anything stolen. It was not apparent that anyone had a grudge against any of them. Their financial affairs were in order. OK, maybe revenge for something, but for what? At present sir, we have nothing."

A voice said: "We have now."

McCall turned. Flavor was standing in the doorway, a look approaching triumph on her face.

The Mayor said sourly: "It's customary to be announced, Lt."

"Your receptionist was on the telephone. I thought you'd like the information sooner than later." McCall thought: Blacks and Latinos. Oil and water.

"Victoria Astaire was a heroin addict. I think she was being blackmailed. She went to meet her blackmailer with $10,000 she withdrew that day from the Santa Monica branch of the Wells Fargo bank. It seems almost certain that the person she agreed to meet that night — I'd say her blackmailer — killed her."

McCall said: "Victoria Astaire, a heroin addict? Flavor, are you sure? Heroin?"

It was hardly believable.

Heroin was junkies and burned-out rock stars, it was

ghetto bums on welfare. It was pock-marked, wasted arms, shared needles and AIDS.

Booze or marijuana could be dealt with by a spell in Betty Ford or the Sierra Tucson. Then, if you were famous enough, you could talk about it on TV to Barbara Walters, Oprah or Connie Chung.

But heroin? And heroin and Victoria Astaire? It was almost unthinkable. She was too refined, too old, too genteel, too – British? Was Miss Marple a shoplifter, did Princess Di go with Hell's Angels?

"According to the coroner she could have been snorting the stuff for thirty years."

The Mayor said, almost plaintively: "I watch that show. I actually have her autograph."

McCall said to Flavor: "Did she take it the night she died?"

"There was heroin in her bloodstream."

"She was being blackmailed, she turns up armed – remember the gun they found? This time she's going to end the blackmail the hard way. But it goes wrong, the guy chops her."

Flavor glanced up at him: "She asked her chauffeur to gas up the car and bring it to the front of her house. Then she gave him the night off."

The Mayor said: "She'd want to be alone. She'd hardly go to meet a blackmailer with a driver."

She'd been addressing McCall, and looked at the Mayor as though he was an irrelevant interruption. Which was exactly how she felt about him.

"Right. Except Victoria Astaire has not held a California Driver's Licence since 1982. She was not qualified to drive. That invalidated her insurance. Anyone she hit that night could have taken her for MILLIONS in personal injury compensation, especially being who she was. In addition she could have gone to jail."

McCall said; "She WAS desperate."

"Enough to drive a very big car down a very busy road, at

night, when she probably hadn't driven herself for thirteen years. And do it with enough heroin in her system to give a heavy metal rock star a buzz."

The Mayor scratched the lowest of his three chins: "How come no-one knew? Why were there no whispers? Hollywood is the most gossipy town in the world!"

Flavor answered: "Who knows? She was considered clean. I rang some showbiz journalists. They said she was whiter than white. Her favourite drink, according to the newspaper files, was Earl Grey."

McCall saw the look of incomprehension on the Mayor's face: "It's tea, Mr. Mayor. Kind of an aristocratic English blend."

The Mayor swivelled away from them, and McCall noted that the dark hair was thin, the strands arranged to cover a bald spot. The Mayor swivelled back.

"I'm not a policeman . ." he paused, and gave them the kind of look amateurs reserve for professionals. Kind of, I'm not a policeman/artist/football player/writer – BUT in my heart I know I could do a damn sight better than the pros.

". . . But why kill her? She brings the money – ten grand is not a lot, I mean, Victoria Astaire is worth MILLIONS. Why kill the goose that could lay a lot of golden eggs?"

Flavor shrugged: "Maybe it was just another instalment." She looked at McCall, thinking aloud: "She produces the gun, and things start to go wrong. Remember, there was no money found at the scene – "

" – If the killer TOOK the money, and if the bank had the serial numbers," Flavor saw hope gleam like uncovered gold in McCall's eyes.

"No money found at the SCENE. The California Parks and Recreation people report $20 and $50 bills turning up from Point Dume to Malibu. He didn't take the money. This guy isn't stupid."

The Mayor said: "DID the bank take the numbers, and do they tally?"

"They did, and that's being checked as we speak," Flavor

told him, "but you can bet it's the same stash."

McCall thought about what he had said to the Mayor. Motive. Who gains? What the hell was the motive? Did the deceased KNOW the blackmailer, perhaps intimately? Threaten to expose him? Threaten to go to the police? Simply refuse to pay any more money?

The Mayor said it triumphantly: "So this, this BLACK-MAILER, doesn't even take the money? Isn't that kind of odd?"

"He could have been disturbed and had to flee." The insincerity in Flavor's voice rang hollowly like a tin drum.

"But you don't believe that – " the Mayor looked at them both, deliberately, separately, first at Flavor, then at McCall, somehow dividing them, isolating them "– either of you."

They stayed silent.

"Do you? Lt. McCall?"

He looked up at Flavor, trying to read her mind.

Her look said: Do what you want.

"No, Mr. Mayor, I don't believe that. And I don't think my colleague does either. I believe she was lured there. Almost certainly her addiction to narcotics is a factor."

"Lt. Cartouche?"

"I agree. Mr. Mayor, we have good news – kind of – as well. This morning we got a call from a freshman at Pepperdine. He was out at Leo Carrillo last night, with a girl. They parked near a Rolls-Royce."

McCall said: "Astaire's?"

"Likely. He didn't look at the plates, but the locations seem to check. He remembers another vehicle. Thinks it was a truck, van maybe. Possibly a pick-up."

"He doesn't know the difference between a truck, a van and a pick-up?"

Flavor said evenly: "It was dark, remember, no moon. He was parked some way behind the Rolls, and the – vehicle – was beyond the Rolls. He said it 'seemed' like it was a van or a truck or a pick-up."

McCall said: "He saw it move?"

"He and his girl had been there about ten minutes when the vehicle's lights came on, and it moved off."

McCall's neck muscles bulged with excitement: "So if it passed him, he must have seen the occupants, or the colour, or a sign, something, anything."

"Easy, boy. Our guy and his girl were parked Oxnard side of the Rolls. The van, or whatever the hell it was, was parked Malibu side. It made a U turn on the highway and headed back towards Malibu."

"So whatever this vehicle was, it had COME from that direction, and then went BACK there."

Flavor said: "That's how it looks. Of course, it could have been anything. A camper, kids doing night surfing, anything."

"No," McCall shook his head to emphasise his negative sureness, "Oh no. It was him. It was the perp. I'm sure of it." He turned to face the Mayor:

"We didn't have a contemporary witness, now we have a witness – "

"McCall!" Flavor's voice was like a warning shot.

" – we've placed somebody, someTHING, at the scene of a RECENT crime. And for the first time we have a MOTIVE – "

Flavor cut him off: "What motive, McCall? It isn't the blackmailer who's dead. That would be motive. What motive does the blackmailer have for killing Astaire? You're jumping to conclusions here."

McCall shook himself like a big, stupid bear or a dumb kid struggling to grasp something.

"It's the dog that doesn't bark in the night – "

"A dog that doesn't what?" The Mayor was looking at McCall as though the policeman was crazy.

"Like in Sherlock Holmes. The dog doesn't bark, and that's the unusual thing. Dogs DO bark in the night. We're seeing the right things, but drawing the wrong conclusions. Look, Astaire is the heroin addict, right?"

He plunged on without waiting for confirmation or

agreement "Astaire is being blackmailed; Astaire with-draws the money; Astaire is the old lady so scared shitless she pilots a Rolls-Royce without a licence. Right?"

Flavor stared at him.

"Right. And?"

"And she is the one who dies. So, OK, she is this frightened, blackmailed little old English lady with a great, big secret that could ruin her. Maybe she takes the gun for protection, or maybe she plans to kill her blackmailer. Only SHE ends up dead. I'm right so far, yeah?"

"The POINT, Lieutenant."

"She has VICTIM stamped in big letters all across her. And maybe that's what the killer wants, for her to appear a victim."

Flavor said, flatly: "She IS a victim, she's dead."

"Or maybe – " McCall ignored the interjection, and raised a querying finger, "maybe Victoria Astaire was head-ing out to do a little blackmailing of her own. And maybe it was the ANGEL who got even that night. Maybe she knew what he was doing, that he was the killer, or maybe she didn't. Maybe she was blackmailing him for some other reason."

Flavor asked: "And why would the killer want to appear MORE of a victim than she eventually became?"

"Because, BECAUSE, it confuses motive. Blackmailed victim tries to kill blackmailer, blackmailer gets better of victim. Motive. But I think it could be more complex than that. Suppose SHE knew something about the blackmailer, something worth him killing her for?"

Flavor said: "She drew the money, remember? She was scared enough to risk arrest driving the Rolls."

"Astaire had the gun. Whether this was a first time blackmail, or it had been going on for years, she intended to finish it that might. But suppose she was caught? She knew what could happen. So the car, the driving without a licence, drawing the money, maybe that was all a red herring. An alibi in case something went wrong."

He looked for belief in the two faces: "If the worst came to the worst, dammit, she was also a HEROIN addict. She had drawn money from the bank, driven uninsured. Who WOULDN'T believe she was being blackmailed. And the court hears how, driven to despair she . . . she . . . "

McCall looked around for the right words, ". . . she takes out her little old lady thirty-eight and kills her blackmailer. She's an aging drug addict, driven to despair by blackmail. She needs care, ladies and gentleman of the jury, not punishment. Come on, can't you see it? If she WAS caught, she knew there wasn't a court in California wouldn't have sympathy with her."

"And her heroin addiction is revealed to the world?" Flavor gave him a quizzical look, "Career finished?"

"Better than the gas chamber. Better than dying in prison. She wasn't getting any younger, remember."

The Mayor put his hands behind his head: "Do we have any evidence she WAS blackmailing anyone?"

McCall shook his head: "We'll take apart her home and private papers, but blackmailers rarely write anything down that's traceable to them."

And added:

"We find who she was blackmailing, we find her killer."

"McCall," Flavor called to him, as to a sleeping child, as though trying to gently wake him from his celebration. Her body tingled with something. A witch feeling, or was it simply the sense of discovery?

He looked up. She said: "Suppose they were both black-mailing each other?"

"Two people can't blackmail each other, it's not possible. It's a Mexican stand-off."

"They can if one doesn't know who the other is?"

"Don't get it."

"One blackmails someone she knows. In turn she is blackmailed by a stranger. Doesn't realise the stranger is the person SHE is also blackmailing."

"But when they meet, then – " Knowledge was dawning

on McCall's face.

"Then the blackmailer in the know loses the advantage on the dumb one. So there can only be one purpose for such a meeting."

The Mayor's dark head and rotund body, aided by his chair, swivelled like a tennis umpire from Flavor to McCall, and back to Flavor again.

McCall said: "So the one in the know can kill the one in the dark."

"From where I'm looking. It might not even be as strong as blackmail. The stranger blackmailer might know that the person he is blackmailing simply KNOWS something about him."

McCall asked: "Something they haven't used yet?"

"Haven't, but could."

"So he – she maybe – decides to lure Astaire to a spot, to dispose of her so – so – why?"

"Because, maybe, she feels the knowledge is too danger-ous, that she can't trust Astaire with it."

"And – I still don't get it. Why now? Why kill her now? And the rest of them? Was it the same with the rest of them? And what's the link? And this angel shit?"

His shoulders slumped and watched him where he stood, at the right of the Mayor's desk. He looked old, tired and strangely vulnerable. She resisted a temptation to feel pity.

Instead she said: "Hey, come on, this is all speculation, but it's a start. Something to chew on. It's my bet Astaire knew the Angel, when she set eyes on him at least. Only when she gets up close does she realise that the blackmailer is three things; the person she knows, the person SHE has been blackmailing herself, or who she has something pretty damn good on. And – "

"And that's he's the Angel too."

"Hell of a shock," Flavor said, "she probably knows at that moment that she's going to end up like Helm, so she pulls the gun."

"So," a big, beaming grin suddenly burst across McCall's

features, "we only have to find out who Astaire knew, what secret she had on this – person – and we find our killer."

Flavor gave him a sidelong glance: "Simplicity itself, McCall." She could not keep the sarcasm out of her voice.

He looked out of the corner of his eye at her, like an actor who has temporarily forgotten his lines: "And we start with what, exactly?"

"Aha .." Flavor nodded in the direction of the Mayor, "Well, after we have taken leave of Hizzoner, after we have cleared up our paperwork for the day, we make an appointment and prepare to descend upon the cast and crew of Pacific Coast."

The Mayor said, incredulously, and with a little peevishness too, as though suddenly, he and his amateur detective theories had been excluded from the party:

"You think the Angel could be in the cast of Pacific Coast? You're crazy."

Flavor glanced at McCall. Whatever she felt about him it was cops versus pols here. It was solidarity, it was us against them. She was black on the outside, blue on the inside, as the saying went. Whatever McCall was, he was a cop. If she was down, he'd come running, just as she would for him.

It was about all cops had.

And they were both high on exhaustion, fatigue and failure, on late nights, and – though neither knew it of the other – on the turmoil of personal crisis.

For a second their eyes met and something broke through the mutual suspicion and linked them spiritually for a moment in time, gave them strength against the hostility that lay around them like a dangerous lake. Out there in the eye of the Press and public, in here, in the cosy torture chamber of LA politics.

Flavor said to the Mayor: "Well, I don't know, Mr. Mayor. We're looking at murder, mayhem, money and sex; power, greed and revenge. All the things that Hollywood is famous for, and of course our beloved Pacific Coast, too. So I would think there is as good a place as any to look. Wouldn't you?"

91

McCall looked at her, trying not to show his sense of grudging respect for her chutzpah.

"Sir." She nodded slightly, almost a mock bow, motioned with her head towards McCall, and in seconds they were gone before the Mayor could get second wind.

Leaving Hizzoner to swivel and rock below his slimmer portrait.

Back at Task Force HQ, a young Hispanic detective holding a sheet of paper came up to McCall as he and Flavor walked through the door.

"Message for you, Lieutenant. Caller said he was a friend of yours, and to read it over exactly. He says – " the detective squinted to read his own writing – "'tell McCall if he still likes literature, the answer to the Angel killings is in the little prince.'"

"The little prince?"

"That's what he said."

"You keen on literature, McCall?" Flavor asked.

He shrugged: "Some. What does literature have to do with little princes?"

"Well, there's a famous novel called The Little Prince. Written by a French guy called Antoine de St. Exupery."

McCall's face registered blankness. "Never heard of it."

"Then this caller can't know you if he thinks you like literature."

"No. He can't know me. Hey, you going to check out this little prince book? I mean, who knows?"

"Sure, I'll check it out."

"Pacific Coast?"

"Nielsen Productions, eighteen-oh-six, Ventura. Nine: thirty."

"You got it."

When Flavor's Buick Skylark turned onto Wilshire, the van turned too, and followed her all the way from downtown, sometimes overtaking, sometimes dropping back in the heavy traffic, risking losing the car in front rather than being suspected of tailing.

It trailed her past the Beverly Wilshire Hotel, lost her briefly when it missed the lights where Wilshire Boulevard crossed Santa Monica Boulevard near the Beverly Hilton.

It caught up with her car again near the Holiday Inn, just before Westwood Village.

After that it trailed comfortably, eight or nine cars behind, past UCLA and the Veterans' Hospital.

When Flavor's car slowed, and pulled up outside a health food restaurant at the corner of Wilshire and Wellesley, the van pulled in to a parking bay.

Several minutes later someone came out of the shop and climbed into the Skylark.

Just inside the Santa Monica city limits, the Skylark slid into a parking place. Flavor got out, put coins in a meter, went into a bookshop and came out six minutes later with a bag clutched in one hand.

The van hung back at least one hundred yards, the driver noting that the Skylark's passenger remained in the car.

Where Wilshire eventually ends, at the clifftop at Ocean Avenue, the Skylark made a left at the traffic light junction next to the Sheraton Miramar, opposite the statue of Saint Monica.

The van missed the green, but from that vantage point, there was a clear view South down Ocean Avenue.

Just before the Casino Cafe, where late afternoon clients still drank capuccino and wine, chatted and read behind the shelter of the glass windbreaks, the Skylark slowed.

The brake lights of the Skylark came on, it signalled left, waited for a gap in the traffic and crossed into the maw of a private underground car park.

Above was a series of apartments, arranged, one above the other, Hanging Gardens of Babylon style, each with its own massive balcony jutting out like the prow of a ship.

When the traffic light at last turned green, the van turned

left and almost immediately pulled into a vacant metered parking space next to the grass, the trees, and the clifftop.

The apartments were diagonally opposite about fifty yards away.

A bare-chested and deeply tanned vagrant stretched out on a blue sleeping bag, and watched with idle curiosity as the van parked, but no-one got out.

Inside the cool and darkened recesses, the driver switched off the ignition, took a pair of small Pentax binoculars from the passenger seat, brought them up, scanned and waited.

Eventually the twin lenses caught Flavor, as she appeared on the balcony with her passenger. The two of them had glasses in their hands, and their mouths moved in silenced laughter.

The driver called into the interior of the van.

"Come and see your new playmates."

And the serpent voice said: "Yessss."

CHAPTER SEVEN

The bronze glass tower glistened in the afternoon sun like a crusader's shield, and the giant letters KNP glistened and sparkled like jewels in a tiara.

The elevators were draped; silent and smooth, shooting Flavor from the silver and marble lobby, up into the alpine peaks of the executive suites.

The doors sighed open and she found herself in a luxuriously carpeted lobby, fully mirrored in smoked glass of different refractions so that it was hard to place what was real and what was illusion.

Just like Hollywood, she observed. But there was a receptionist at a circular glass desk – who faced outwards, Flavor noted. The girl, no more than twenty-three, had real blonde hair, a glistening white blouse and teeth to match, above a dark skirt and stockings.

She rose from her chair, gave what appeared to be a genuine smile of welcome, and when Flavor showed her badge, said in a mid-Western accent: "Yes, of course, Mr. Nielsen is expecting you."

She sat again, a button was pressed, she breathed some words that Flavor could not hear, but obviously the recipient could, stood once more, and said: "Please do come this way."

Flavor followed, through an ante-room where two receptionist-clones sat at word processors, into a further room where a much older woman – in her late Forties – wearing very old-fashioned horn-rimmed spectacles, put out a hand and shook Flavor's.

"He's expecting you, but a second ago he was talking to London. Everyone's going home there – time difference."

Flavor smiled and nodded.

The personal assistant opened the door a fraction, said something Flavor could not hear, turned to her, and said: "He's wrapping it up. Thirty seconds."

Eventually the door was opened, and Flavor was shown into a large room with a massive picture window showing a panorama of burnt orange smog and the blurred outline of the Hollywood Hills.

Nielsen sat at one end of, rather than behind, a plain, dark wood desk, in a simple chair. It wasn't the tycoon football-field desk Flavor was expecting.

Neither was the room gross or intimidating, the movie boss office she had expected, the office that screamed its wealth and power to you.

There were some Modern Impressionist paintings – one of which appeared at first glance to be an original De Kooning – and some paintings and drawings she could not identify.

The colour scheme was muted, soft greys and dark charcoals. Only Nielsen himself was larger than life. When he stood, she could see that he was a big man, well over six feet tall, and, despite everything, her age, her position, her purpose there that day, she felt a tremor of nervousness as he reached out and took her hand in his for a firm, dry handshake.

As a kid she had seen him at the cinema, a slim, tall and

raw-boned cowboy, a handsome Army officer, a jungle explorer. And he still retained the square-jawed, clean-cut look of the matinee idol.

He was grey now, thicker around the chest and waist, but still firmly proportioned with muscle definition the well-cut clothes could not disguise — nor were meant to.

Clearly he worked out, but although his facial skin was taut, she suspected the surgeon's knife had nipped and tucked around the eyes and the chin. With such a man it seemed like tidying up, rather than vanity.

He wore a light grey suit, white shirt, and a deep maroon patterned silk tie, with a gold pin. The shoes were black, conservative and highly polished.

When he opened his mouth to greet her, his teeth were a tribute to the wonders of Californian dentistry.

The biographies said he was sixty-three, but he could have passed for ten years younger than that.

He motioned her to one end of the room that contained two deep, gray leather sofas positioned either side of a plain glass coffee table.

"Drink?" he motioned a tanned, well-manicured hand toward a row of decanters. "Chivas Regal? Remy Martin?"

"Coffee would be nice, Mr. Nielsen."

"Call me Kirk. Coffee for the Lieutenant, Marjorie, and the usual for me."

"Sir."

The PA exited silently.

"What's the usual?"

"Evian. Two litres a day. Doctor's recommendation. Do sit down, please."

"And the Chivas Regal?"

"Strictly for visitors. Despite what people think, this is not a bacchanalian business. Too many breakfast meetings and dawn shoots. Go to an industry dinner party, Lieutenant, and don't expect to stay longer than ten:thirty."

"I'm impressed." Within a minute the door opened as silently as it had closed, and Marjorie, the personal assistant, brought in a silver tray laid with a pot of coffee, a china cup, a cream bowl, a dish of brown sugar cubes, a decanter of – what was presumably – Evian, a tall, plain glass and a small dish of ice.

Clearly fresh coffee was always on hand, or it had been readied for her visit.

"May I?" Nielsen poured, indicated the cream jug, and Flavor shook her head. He handed her the black coffee.

He said: "As you can imagine, we're still reeling from the news."

"Of course. Did you know her personally? Outside of business, I mean."

"She was a great personal friend." Nielsen used a pair of silver tongs lying on the tray, selected one, two, three pieces of ice, put them into the glass, poured water from the decanter over the ice and waited as the ice tinkled and settled.

Flavor sipped the delicious coffee: "And you employed her of course?"

"Of course." He picked up the glass, and swirled the water, "Look, Lieutenant. Victoria Astaire and I had a brief affair in the late Nineteen Fifties. It's no secret. It lasted, oh, eighteen months, maybe. After that we remained friends. I married my present wife in 1968. She is fully aware of my relationship with Victoria."

"And didn't mind you employing her?"

"Victoria was a great actress. Had she been thirty or forty years younger, she'd be up there with Basinger, Pfeiffer, the whole crowd. Had she got her breaks when she WAS younger, she'd rank with Taylor, Hepburn, Vanessa Redgrave. I had no problems employing her. Half of Hollywood would be out of work if producers couldn't employ actresses with whom they'd had affairs."

He laughed, confidently, and she noticed how clear and blue his eyes were. Just like Jack's.

"Can you shed any light on her killing?"

"No." He said it flatly.

"Did you know she was a heroin addict?"

"Yes."

"We haven't released that information yet, Mr. Nielsen."

He stood up and walked to the window, then turned to her: "It is presumably why she was being blackmailed. She WAS being blackmailed, wasn't she?"

Flavor said: "How long have you known about her problem?"

He shrugged: "Since about 1964. It was something she slipped into. She told me about it, confided in me. She tried cures, cold turkey, clinics. Nothing worked."

"And you employed her – knowing that?"

"Yes," she saw a jut of chin, "yes, I did. Give me a drug addict to an alcoholic, any time. They're never late on set, they never fluff their lines, and they don't take time off sick. And unlike alcoholics they KNOW they have a problem."

"And they're fine as long as they have their supply."

"I guess so."

"And she did?"

"What are you implying – that I supplied her?" He moved across from the window, sat down on the sofa again and drank more of the ice-chilled Evian.

"You wouldn't be the first producer to do it, Mr. Nielsen."

"I didn't. She had her supplier – and before you ask I didn't know who it was, and I didn't want to know. In fact, I'm going to ask you a favour today."

"What?"

"Is it possible to keep it out of the Press – I mean, about the heroin? Apart from anything else, it doesn't reflect well on the show or on my company."

Flavor shook her head: "In this climate, in view of what's been happening? Impossible. When did you last see her?"

"When did I – ?" Nielsen laughed, "Oh come on, you don't think for a second, that I – " He laughed again, "that's quite ridiculous."

"When, Mr. Nielsen?" Flavor's nervousness had gone

now. It was just another case, another interview.

"The day before she died. She was shooting near her home – Pacific Palisades. I visited the location. Passed a few words with her, nothing more."

"She said nothing about being blackmailed?"

"No."

"She seem nervous? Acting in a strange manner, anything like that?"

"To be honest, no."

"Can you think why anyone would want to kill her?"

Nielsen shook his head: "She WAS a heroin addict, that is a strange world. But apart from that, no, not at all."

"She owe money?"

"Jesus, Lieutenant. She was making $175,000 an episode, and she did fourteen episodes last year alone. She didn't need to borrow money. Anyway, if she did, my company has its own employee loan scheme at good rates."

"Was she a lesbian?"

He laughed again, an incredulous laugh: "Victoria? Don't be absurd. As far as I know she was celibate, but she had a good run for her money in the past."

"Do you have an alibi for that night?"

"I find this incredible."

"Do you?"

"Yes, as it happens, I do. I had dinner at Ma Maison with my wife and some business associates, I can let you have their names. We went on to a charity gala for AIDS research. My wife and I got home around twelve:thirty."

"Why would anyone kill an old heroin addict, Mr. Nielsen? Chop off her head, and steal it?"

He looked up at her with his eyes, but not his face. And for a second she felt the chill of something dangerous, but it was momentary.

"You're the detective."

"I was interested in any theories you might have had."

"I have none. But it's possible that someone was black-mailing her. All the newspapers are talking about blackmail.

And of course," he spread his hands, "as I said earlier, she WAS a narcotics addict."

The intercom buzzed: "Sir, I have – "

"I said NO CALLS! No-one!" He screamed it, then said to Flavor: "Forgive me. I distinctly told them no calls."

"I'm glad you take my visit so seriously."

"Victoria was my friend, I'd like to help find her killer."

"Thank you. Did you know Art Helm?"

"Vaguely."

"You were at his funeral in Forest Lawn."

"He was a star. I'm in the business." He shrugged as if to say, you know how it is.

"So you didn't know him very well?"

"I'd met him at parties, played some celebrity golf with him, that's all."

"You employed him, Mr. Nielsen."

"Excuse me?"

"He worked for you. His last three TV films were produced by you."

Nielsen raised a bushy eyebrow: "Really? I didn't know that."

"You didn't know that Art Helm had appeared in three of your productions?"

He leaned back on the sofa and lifted his feet up onto the table, throwing his head back, closing his eyes and running both hands through the grey, but still leonine hair.

To Flavor it had the look of much-responsibility, very-tired, can't-keep-up-with-every-detail, executive cop-out. "Lieutenant, I have twelve productions on the go NOW, at this precise moment in time, not to mention Pacific Coast – and you can imagine the plot changes and re-writing involved because of Victoria's death."

"And because of that you didn't realise Helm had been on your payroll for the last five years? Also that he has appeared in a total of TWELVE Kirk Nielsen Productions ventures?"

Nielson opened his eyes, sat up, shook his head, and gave her a raised, bottom lip look of honest candour:

"To be honest, I didn't. Well, of course, I MUST have been aware of it, but when you actually asked me, I DIDN'T remember it."

He was aware of Flavor's look: "Hey, come on, there's no crime in that. Come to think of it, now, well, yup, I can recall the Vikings thing we did in Minnesota, sure, Helm was in that, and our hospital drama in Chicago. But that's about it. I think you might be better informed about my productions than I am."

He said it with obvious good humour, and then drank some more Evian.

Flavor had gone to bed the previous night at three a.m. Before that she had spent six hours combing through Jack's collection of Variety and The Hollywood Reporter, checking up on Nielsen Productions.

It was in those bound copies, as she scrutinised the fine print of the cast lists for movies in production that she found the information about Helm.

"Anyway, does this have a point, Lieutenant?"

"Well, if there is any point, it's that two people whom we now discover have a connection with your company have been brutally murdered."

Nielsen lifted his glass at her, and said: "Aha, and TWO people who – unless you can correct me – are NOT connected with my company, have also been murdered. And all by this, this, guy – what is it the Press call him?" Nielsen gave her a quiet, 'touché' smile.

"The Angel."

"Yes, the angel. The public love spooky things, don't they?"

"You didn't know Alassio then?"

"He was the . . . which one, the bank manager?"

"The hairdresser. He and Helm had been lovers, way back."

The smile was more unassuming now: "That, I believe, I can confidently say no to. No I did not know him."

"Does 'the little prince' mean anything to you?" Nielsen

paused, scratched his head, shook his head: "Can't say that it does. Is it a movie title? It sounds like something the old-style Disney people would have made. In what context?"

"It doesn't matter. May I?" She indicated the coffee: "Of course." Nielsen poured her another cup, and himself more mineral water.

"I'd like to talk to every member of the cast and crew. I understand they're all in the studio today. I can make it official if you wish, but I'd prefer your co-operation."

Nielsen spread his arms Honest John wide: "You have it." He pressed his buzzer: "Marjorie, bring in a cast folder."

Within thirty seconds Flavor had been handed a shiny white folder with the title Pacific Coast emblazoned on the cover.

Nielsen said: "In there you'll find all the cast, with colour photographs and their biographies. They know you're coming, I warned them this morning. If you get even the merest hint – " he squeezed on the word, "of difficulty from them, they'll hear from me."

He paused, "And they know it." He stood up and put out his hand: "Good luck, Lieutenant, I hope you get your man."

Flavor was hot and thirsty, and she was nowhere. There was one cast member to go, Sarah Ziegal, and Flavor flipped through her folder looking for the picture.

Ziegal was a woman in her late Forties, strong-boned face, dark hair, round compelling eyes, with a hint of amusement around the mouth.

A full-length shot showed a woman of ample bust, medium height, and still very much in trim.

Flavor asked a production assistant for directions to Ziegal's dressing room, and set off through the maze of studios and sets.

But as she rounded a corner she almost bumped into someone coming the other way, and realised with a shock that it was the woman for whom she'd been searching, Sarah Ziegal.

"Miss Ziegal, I'm Lieutenant Cartouche, Los Angeles Police Department, I – "

The woman cut her off with a dismissive wave: "Wrong babe, honey-pie, Ziegal's thataway." The woman cocked her thumb over her shoulder.

"Third down, with a zit on her face the size of a corn-cob."

Flavor was thrown: "I don't understand," she fiddled at the folder, fumbling for Ziegal's picture.

But the woman leaned forward, her face close to Flavor's: "Face mask, honey. Face mask. Hey," she stepped back and put her hands on her hips, "look again."

Flavor looked, and at first, even consulting the picture, it was still like gazing at Sarah Ziegal. But then, when Flavor peered closer, she could see a kind of heavy make-up that covered the woman's face like a bonding paint.

"Don't be shy. Look for the joins." And Flavor did, eventually tracing a line on both sides of the nose, and above the bump of the chin. It was a kind of moulding, a prosthesis nose and chin.

And the body, although the same full shape of woman on Flavor's picture, was unmistakeably younger.

She was staggered. She had the picture out now: "But you're her double. If you'd wanted to fool me, you could've. Why, what's it all for?"

"If they don't want to risk the star on certain scenes, or she's too lazy or prima-donna to shoot some stuff, and if there's no real close ups, you can shoot a face double."

"It's uncanny."

"About forty million viewers look at me and see Sarah Ziegal more times than you can imagine."

"How the hell do they do it?" For the second Flavor had forgotten her quest, and was genuinely fascinated.

"Easy. They take a moulding of Ziegal's face, then they find someone with similar face size and shape, and general body measurements. They make up a kind of mask and a wig the same colour and style as her hair."

"It doesn't look like a mask."

"Mask is the wrong word," someone called her name – Jane – and she shouted back: "I'm with you." Then to Flavor: "It's like a mask with holes. It pulls on, wig and all, over my own face. It's mainly a chin, a nose, and a bit of extra jawline. The eyes and the rest is me."

"But how do you merge it with the rest of your face?" It looked so REAL.

"Make-up. The mask edges are tight, and they're painted in to the real skin, the whole thing is merged until – unless you're way up close – you can't tell the difference."

"So when I'm watching Pacific Coast, I'm not always seeing Sarah Ziegal?"

"Not always." Again the impatient voice, and Jane replied that she was on her way. "Long shots, anything from twenty feet away and no dialogue. Getting out of cars, climbing stairs, stuff like that. Or if – like today – the star has a zit. Sometimes they'll risk shooting closer in if it's only the side of the face."

"Wow."

"Stunt people are wearing them now too. You don't pay a star eight million bucks then have her leap off buildings. In the past all the shots of stunt men had to be long shots. This way you can have an action shot and get a quarter of a second shot of the face. Within that time scale the mind can't tell the difference, even IN close-up. It actually looks like the star is doing the stunt. It makes for more realism." The stand-in laughed at the irony of what she'd said.

Flavor laughed with her: "When in fact, it's LESS real."

"This is Hollywood, honey, it's not REAL life – "

Flavor interjected, "I know, it's REEL life. I live with a screenwriter."

"Listen, I gotta go. Didn't mean to shock you. And good luck, honey, we all know why you're here."

"Thanks."

When Flavor eventually found Ziegal's dressing room a young production assistant was just coming out. She turned and rapped on the door she had just closed, and said to Flavor: "Can we have her back in 20 minutes?"

"Sure."

A voice said: "Come!"

As Flavor went in Sarah Ziegal got up to greet her, and after meeting the stand-in Jane, who was dressed the same, it was like seeing her Doppelganger.

"Lieutenant."

Flavor shook her hand: "Miss Ziegal. Actually, I've just bumped into your double."

"Ah yes, my lady Jane. A good girl, but if only she could remember that she isn't ACTUALLY me. I have a minor skin eruption, and Jane thinks – as she always does on these occasions – that it is her ticket to stardom." Ziegal's face was set.

Flavor got the message. Don't discuss stand-ins with stars. Especially in front of the help, which in this case was a young olive-skinned make-up girl who had been fussing over Ziegal even as she greeted Flavor. Presumably, thought Flavor, trying to obliterate the troublesome zit.

Sarah Ziegal was like her picture, the Irish-dark hair was still thick and lustrous, her figure was full-bosomed, and her waist was trim. It was not surprising that a woman in her – presumably – late Twenties, could stand in for this star, for Sarah Ziegal had clearly once been very beautiful.

"That'll do Selena, just leave us for a few minutes."

Without a word the make-up girl got up and left leaving the trays and brushes, the tools of her trade, on the ledge in front of the bulb-fringed mirror.

"Sit down, Lieutenant." Ziegal indicated a chair, sat in her own, and then waited for Flavor to sit and make herself comfortable. While Flavor got out her notebook, Sarah Ziegal rummaged in a large handbag, took out a hairbrush and dragged it through the luxurious locks.

It was then, as she started to ask the questions, that Flavor noticed the smell. It was faint at first, as though coming from a distance, but acrid and penetrating. It was impossible to pin it down, it was – medicinal? – with some redolence of sickness and death, a cancer ward smell.

And at the same time damp and musty. It touched her throat, her nostrils and she felt a tingle of revulsion, felt her cheeks go cold. It was the same abreaction she had once had to chèvre, French goat's cheese. Her mouth had puckered, her cheeks had gone ice-cold and then been almost physically sucked inwards by the reaction to the taste.

Flavor nervously ran her tongue around the inside of her mouth, trying to ignore the sensation, trying to get on with the task in hand.

Ziegal revealed that on the night of the murder she had worked until eight, then had driven home to her house in fashionable Brentwood, just west of Bel Air, and gone straight to bed.

Brentwood, Flavor recalled, was where the gay hairdresser Alassio lived. That didn't mean anything in itself; it was a highly-desirable area.

"So you have no alibi?"

"Alibi? You make me sound like a criminal. Only guilty people have alibis. If I'd DONE something I would no doubt have an alibi; as I haven't, I haven't, if you see what I mean."

"Do you own a closed van, or a pick-up truck?"

The actress shook her head, rummaged in the handbag, and came out with a sheaf of documents. And once more the smell, acrid, disgusting, somehow full of meaning and memory and menace, touched at Flavor's throat.

Ziegal handed over the documents. "I have a Mercedes convertible and a Mitsubushi 4-wheel drive wagon. For God's sake what on earth would I want with a van?

'Anyway, I am sure the California Department of Motor Vehicles will be able to tell you PRECISELY what I own."

Flavor examined the documents which were in order, the vehicles as Ziegal had described them.

"Yes, I am sure they will." She handed them back: "Were you friendly with Miss Astaire? On the show you were enemies I gather?"

"Arch rivals for the van Bulen TV empire. Utter garbage, isn't it? But it pays very well. Friendly? I wouldn't say that, exactly, but we got on in a professional sense. We didn't socialise."

"How long had you known her?"

Ziegal shrugged: "About, say, twenty years I suppose. She was older than me, I came into the business way after her. I think we met when we had bit parts in a couple of episodes of The Rockford Files. We did a couple of Charlie's Angels in the late Seventies, but at different times."

Ziegal closed her eyes, as if to think. At length she said: "We did a shlock-horror TV movie for HBO in, er, eighty-one I think it was – Blood of the Crypt? Yes, Vincent Price was in it – darling man."

"After that?"

"Nothing really until Pacific Coast."

"So you weren't friends?" Flavor asked again, doggedly.

Ziegal leaned in, conspiratorially, and the smell grew stronger. It wasn't HER, but it was somehow ON her. Was she taking some medication?

She said: "You'll know by now about her little, how shall I put it – problem?"

"Yes."

Ziegal leaned back, a look of smug satisfaction wreathing her features: "Then you'll understand why she was not the kind of person with whom I wished to get involved socially."

"How long had you known she had a drugs problem?"

The smug features were suddenly re-formed, alert: "Since about a year after we started Coast. Regular on-set visits from swarthy men – need I say more Lieutenant? Frequent trips to the ladies room. But I have to say, I assumed marijuana – cocaine is passé now. Heroin? I mean." She raised her eyebrows skywards.

"Sure. Well, if anything crosses your mind, I hope you'll call me." Flavor handed Ziegal a business card.

"Sure," she examined the card, then abruptly looked up, "by the way – how's Jack?"

"Jack?" Suddenly the room seemed small, and Flavor realised she was sweating. The smell seemed higher, more nauseating.

"You know, Jack? Jack Romarin, wrote The Heart Devil? I thought you two were room-mates. I've known Jack for eight years, a BRILLIANT screenwriter, got a great future – "

"Jack, of course. Forgive me, it's that I didn't realise you two knew each other. Yes, I'm sorry, yes we're room-mates, and Jack is fine, just fine, thank you."

Ziegal shrugged: "I was on the Fox lot about a month ago, and Jack was working on some piece of shit that was in turn-around from Columbia."

Flavor felt her hackles rise until she remembered that 'piece of shit' was the standard Hollywood working term for virtually any would-be movie project.

"Jack mentioned your name – " incongruously Ziegal winked, "thinks a lot of you, Lieutenant."

"Jack and I are room-mates and friends. Firm friends, but just friends."

"Sure," Ziegal said it so re-assuringly the menace in it shrieked.

"Something brewing on Jack's Apple on this angel business?"

"I wouldn't know. Jack's a screenwriter, I'm a cop, we don't mix business –"

"With pleasure? I know."

Flavor burned at the inference. She was being wrong-footed and out-flanked with the damned Jack business.

And the smell. Ziegal and the smell were indistinguishable now. It was as though she WAS the smell, something damp and old and evil, and uncannily, dangerously medicinal.

Flavor walked to the door, and turned:

"Do you detect a strange odour in here, Miss Ziegal?"

The mocking complacency was instantly washed from the woman's face.

"Odour?"

"I don't know, kinda like medicine or something."

"No, I can't say I do." The woman seemed poised now, balanced, as if for flight or fight. Flavor felt an uncanny sense of deep, deep danger.

"I must be dreaming, I've had a head cold and been inhaling decongestant, guess I can't get the stuff out of my sinuses. Thanks for your time, Miss Ziegal."

"You're most welcome." The woman stayed still, but her eyes followed Flavor.

"My love to Jack."

Flavor closed the door, and breathed deeply of the comparitively fresh air, leaning back against the stone wall, her eyes closed.

After paying her respects at Nielsen's office, she deliberately told them she was leaving and going home, but headed instead for the studio commissary. She wanted to have a word with the make-up girl, or anyone who got close to Ziegal.

Could they smell that odour too? And if so, how did they work with it? Was it just Flavor who it disturbed?

She got some coffee, saw the make-up girl at a table spooning yogurt into her mouth and walked up: "May I?"

The girl nodded and said through a mouthful of yogurt: "Join the feast."

When the girl finished her food she asked, kindly: "How'd it go?"

"So-so, OK-ish."

"Yeah," the girl ripped open the top of a milk carton, "she's a treasure. Dream to work with most of the time. Doesn't bitch like some OTHERS I could mention, but I won't, in the interest of keeping my job."

"Ever work with Astaire?"

"Once or twice," the girl crossed herself, "God rest her soul. She was a dream too. That heroin thing, it freaked me out. She was the LAST one I would've thought . . . all the over-Forties are pros, it's the kids my age . . ." she took a swig of milk, "they're the monsters."

"You're, er, Selena, right?"

"Selena Maria Perez."

"Selena, may I ask you a personal question?"

The girl put down her milk carton: "You being a police officer, just HOW personal?"

"Not police-type personal. Do you ever, well . . . do you ever SMELL anything strange when you're around Ziegal?"

The girl looked puzzled: "Like what? Booze, body odour, what?"

"No . . ." Flavor sucked air in over her teeth, trying to encapsulate that smell into words. Nothing seemed adequate. "No . . . more a kind of sicky smell . . ."

"Vomit?" the girl gave a kind of embarrassed smile, "you serious?"

"No, not that kind of sicky, more like sick person, you know when an old person is sick, and they rub stuff on them, like embrocation or stuff for their chests, and they smell all old and damp, and . . . oh shit, I don't know how to describe this properly."

Selena Maria Perez shook her head:

"Lieutenant, I've worked with actors and actresses whose breath could knock you out at twenty yards. But NOT Ziegal. She bathes, her teeth are good, she has a dietician, she doesn't cut the cheese." The make-up girl laughed: "Maybe you stepped in something out on the street."

Flavor laughed: "Maybe." But she could still feel it, smell it. It was there in her senses and her memory.

"Her handbag, maybe." That was the moment, Flavor had first been aware of the smell, when Ziegal opened her handbag.

The make-up girl put her head to one side, a slightly quizzical look on her face: "Hey, well, now you mention it. Sometimes her bag smells a little crappy. She has two handbags, you know, I mean, like a little dinky one, and then this big old-fashioned one. Normally she only brings the little one in. The big one is kinda old, and, yeah, when I'm up close it does smell kinda medicine breath type of thing. And musty, like a basement or someplace, like when you keep things down there for a while."

Flavor shivered.

"You cold?"

"No, I'm OK. What does she keep in there, the big handbag I mean?"

The make-up girl shook her head: "Don't know. These ladies get over forty, God knows. They're all taking something, pills for this, pills for that. Bet she's got a whole medicine cabinet in there, that'll account for it."

The girl drained the last of her milk and stood up: "No peace for the wicked. Good luck with the Angel."

"Thanks."

"If I smell anything I'll give you a call." They both laughed.

"Thanks Selena."

Flavor found a payphone, rang Task Force HQ and asked for McCall. The detective on the line said: "He's gone looking for you. He had his little prince caller on again today. I think McCall may have something."

"Is he coming over to Burbank? I'm at Nielsen Productions."

"He rang there, they said you'd gone home."

"Yeah, I told them that, I didn't want them to know I was snooping around the commissary talking to people not on the list."

"Well, McCall is on his way to your place. I guess he'll just have to kick his heels down there for spell."

"My place? How the hell does he know where I live, Gary?"

The detective was nonplussed: "I dunno, maybe it's on the file somewhere. He has your number, Lieutenant, what does it matter if – "

"What time did he leave?"

"Dunno. Ten, maybe fifteen minutes ago, why – ?"

But the connection was severed, and Flavor was screaming the Buick out of the KNP Productions car park, leaving rubber marks on the concrete.

And she cursed McCall for being a nosey goddamned snooping bastard. She knew she HAD to get to her home before he did.

The bronchial voice said: "Did you find the little prince, McCall?"

The detective leaned back in his chair, motioning with his right hand for quiet in the room.

"Do I know you?"

"We've met," there was a bubbly, smoker's wheeze: "You told me you loved literature." The caller gave a wheezy laugh.

"Where'd we meet?"

"Never mind. The Angel is staring you in the face, laughing at you. Did you find the little prince?"

McCall's mind was tracking like a computer: "Sure. It's a book. My colleague bought it, and read it from cover to cover. It doesn't mean anything."

"The clue is in the title."

"I think you don't know what the fuck you're talking about, and that you've never met me in your life. So do me a favour and blow it out your ass."

"Same old McCall. Try East River."

"Don't play guessing games with me."

"He's killing movie stars, remember?"

"What – "

The line went dead.

Something moved in McCall's memory, almost swam into focus, then dissolved. He let it go. It would come back when it was ready.

He consulted his notebook, then punched out the numbers for Kirk Nielsen Productions. After one ring a female voice answered.

"May I speak with Lt. Cartouche of the Los Angeles Police Department? She is conducting interviews in your building."

"One moment sir." He listened to a minute of Mozart, then the voice said: "I'm afraid she left the building thirty minutes ago. She said she was going home."

McCall fished out his address book, flipped the pages, then ran his finger along the number and punched it out. A female voice answered, and he said:

"Lt. Cartouche, please."

"I'm sorry, but she's not at home."

"When she gets in would you ask her to call me please, Lt. McCall."

"I'll try, but I can't guarantee to be here, and I'm up to my eyes in cleaning up right now, I'm going to have to go."

"Sure. Just please leave the message." McCall hung up.

He said to a detective Martinez: "Flavor has the only cleaning lady in LA who doesn't speak Spanish."

Martinez didn't look up from his work: "That's racist, I'm putting in a complaint."

"The Dodgers suck."

"I'm from San Diego, Lieutenant, remember? A Padres fan, and Viva Mexico."

McCall sipped some coffee, grimaced, and said to Martinez again: "Hey, you ever heard of a movie called East River?"

Martinez shook his head: "Nope." McCall raised his voice to take in the whole room: "Anyone heard of a movie called East River?" There was a chorus of negatives.

"Well anyone got a movie guide, you know one that lists all the movies in history, kind of thing?" There were whistles of derision and disbelief.

And he thought. Flavor will have one. Jack the screenwriter will have one. He grabbed the keys to his MGB off the desk:

"If anyone calls I'm out for an hour. I'm going to Flavor's place in Santa Monica. If she calls in, tell her to stay home."

Outside he thumbed down the roof catches, lowered the canvas top, fired the sports car into life, and eased out into the traffic.

He flipped the radio to K-Earth 101 and was rewarded with the Beach Boys: "Round, round, git around, aaayy get around, yeh, git around, round, round, I git around, Gettin' bugged drivin' up and down this same old street . . .'

The sun was hot on his face, his hands and the bare arms below his sleeves as he headed West.

Flavor's Skylark weaved through the thick flow of South-bound traffic on the San Diego Freeway as it cut through the man-carved gap in the Santa Monica mountains from the San Fernando Valley into LA, and at one point her speedo-meter needle was touching eighty.

She cursed McCall frequently and fluently. She thought they'd agreed rules. Private lives were private; no questions and no interference.

And now he was going to her HOME, dammit! Would Jack be there? It was five, maybe not. She flashed her headlights and gave a long blast on her horn as an aging, white Lincoln Continental wallowed into the outside lane.

She swung back, passed on the inside, and then cursed as the brake lights of a camper came on in front of her. Could she make it to Santa Monica before McCall did? Should she exit at Wilshire, or go on to the Santa Monica Boulevard? Which was likelier to have the heavier traffic?

Or should she push on until she reached the Santa Monica Freeway interchange, and hope the evening traffic moved quicker on the freeway?

She swerved out without checking her mirror, and squeezed between the camper and the Lincoln, then settled into the outside lane, putting her foot hard down on the accelerator.

Too late she saw in her rear view mirror the squat shape of the Highway Patrol cruiser, its red and blue lights flashing.

Flavor groaned aloud, signalled and began to ease across the freeway, out of the traffic, slowing to a halt, and the Highway Patrol cruiser was pulling in behind her.

In her mirror she saw the driver get out, put on a pair of

dark glasses and walk purposefully towards her, his citation pad in his hand. Flavor slipped out her badge. He'd probably be OK when he saw that, but it was all taking precious minutes.

She realised she was sweating.

McCall pressed the buzzer, waited thirty seconds, then pressed again. At the second buzz there was a crackle, and an impatient female voice: "Yes?"

"Is Lt. Cartouche home yet?"

"No, not yet. Who is this?"

"Lt. McCall, Special Task Force."

"Oh, I spoke to you earlier. I'm up to my eyes in it at the moment, but you can wait if you wish."

"I'd like to. Thank you."

"Please show your badge to the man at the security desk, and ask him to call me when you have. Then I'll let you in."

"Very wise," he said, drily, and was rewarded with a buzz and the sliding back of the glass entry door to the carpeted reception area.

When he reached the fourth floor, he saw the door to apartment C already ajar, and the face of a woman wearing a blue and white polka dot headscarf peering out.

"Lt. McCall? Come in."

She was in her late Forties, and when McCall stepped inside the apartment's entrance lobby, he could see she was wearing a cleaning smock, and a pair of yellow rubber gloves.

"As you can see, I have a mess on my hands, and I want to get it cleaned up before Flavor gets home. She thinks I'm SO clumsy."

She led McCall into a giant lounge along which ran full-length picture windows, a flower-lined balcony and a stunning view of the tops of palm trees, and the ocean.

There were several large, expensive looking sofas, objets d'art, some antique vases, and serried ranks of shelved video cassettes. From the reception area, McCall had seen at the end of the corridor, a half-opened door led to what appeared to be a massive kitchen.

"Nice place."

"Thanks. But look at that, God I'm so messy."

That, was the debris of a fallen plant, which had toppled, or been tipped, broken its pot, and left a debris of leaves, rich, black earth, and broken pottery across a Persian carpet.

The woman was wielding a brush and pan, ineffectually, so that she seemed to spread more than she cleaned. McCall said: "Want a hand?"

She looked up and he noticed that her eyes were ice-blue and piercing: "Would you? I confess I'm hopeless at this."

He laughed: "You're doing the wrong job." He started to scoop up earth with his hands and dump it in the pan.

"You bet. The cleaning woman doesn't come in until tomorrow, and I can't just leave it like this."

McCall looked up from the plant soil: "Cleaning woman? I thought you WERE the cleaning woman."

For a moment the woman looked puzzled, then her face wreathed with laughter, and she pointed at the smock: "Oh, this?" She peeled off a yellow rubber glove and offered her hand.

"No, I'm not the cleaning woman. For my sins I'm Jacqueline Romarin. This is my apartment."

And still McCall didn't get it. He took her hand in his, his face still puzzled: "Jacqueline?"

The ice-blue eyes twinkled: "Well, Jacqueline I was christened. But you can call me Jack. All my friends do."

He walked for a long time, all the way down the concrete cycle and jogging track, beyond Pacific Palisades, then back to the pier where he sat on the steps of the newly-constructed extension and looked out across the Pacific.

He felt cheated and tricked, like a duped and humiliated schoolkid. Flavor was gay. Jack was a woman, and not a man. His colleague was a lesbian, a dyke, and he hadn't known.

Jack. Jack! No wonder she had kept it a secret; she didn't want the world to know she crept into another woman's bed at night.

"Damn her!" He said it aloud and LOUD, and a Japanese tourist couple nearby got up and moved away. He felt foolish and humiliated and stupid, and – what else? His sexuality maligned, his manhood insulted? Possibly. He didn't know for sure, couldn't be certain, but he felt off balance, out of sync with the world.

He'd grown, well, if not to actually LIKE Flavor, during the weeks of the investigation, but at least to – what? – respect her?

That and something else he couldn't quite fathom. He'd kind of got used to her being there across the desk from him in the mornings, had begun to secretly admire her dogged persistence, her own unique way of doing things, her stubbornness in standing up for what she believed.

But to think of her as gay, suddenly knocked all that sideways. Yes, he knew, none of it mattered now, gay or straight, you weren't supposed to take sexual preference into account. Yet everyone did, for good or ill. It was part of everything, and you took it into account even if you said you didn't. Just like colour.

And it was more important than that, because it crossed some fault line that men of McCall's generation couldn't come to terms with. How could you work with a male partner, knowing that he went home and screwed – or was screwed BY – a man?

It didn't fit for McCall. He knew it was undoubtedly wrong, and he certainly didn't agree with any kind of persecution or discrimination of gays – but – he didn't know how to phrase it in his head – it CHANGED things. That was it, changed things.

To think of Flavor as gay, Jesus, he shook his head. He just couldn't come to terms with it. And then, a small, secret, self-mocking part of him asked, mischievously: And it makes her unavailable to you, right, McCall?

Get out of here. Him and Flavor, come on, man? He was an old-fashioned white boy from Detriot and she was black, new age, politically-correct.

And leaving aside the cops he'd worked with who were black on the outside but blue all the way through, his only experience of blacks was being hated by them, and locking them up.

And, of course, there was the kid he'd shot during the 1992 riots. She'd never forgive him for that – ever. There was just this wide, unbridgeable canyon between them. So it wasn't that. It couldn't be that.

Him and black women? Well, he knew all the racial sexual myths, but he'd never mixed with black women socially, so there'd been no opportunity for dating, even if he'd been available, which he wasn't, because he'd been married, and – shit – it just wasn't the thing white cops did in Detroit, anyway.

And it wasn't a sexual desire thing with him, like some cops he'd known. He had no desire for a black sexual experience just for the hell of it.

If he had, he could have had any of the black hookers on his patch. Desire Flavor? It was crazy.

He stood up, stretched, and went down to the pier rail where a Mexican family in baseball caps and T-shirts were fishing. A blue plastic pail was already crammed with their catch, and the red mouths opened and closed, hopelessly, as the fish were asphyxiated slowly from the diminishing oxygen in their death chamber.

The sun was sinking over the Malibu mountains, a golden streak of paint across the water from here to the distant hills.

And he knew suddenly, with crystal clarity, what he felt at the discovery about Flavor.

It was disappointment.

He had the gun up, rock steady, the barrel centred on the youth's chest.

"Put it down." McCall knew his voice was quavering,

"Put the gun down."

But it was as though the youth couldn't hear him. And McCall could see the gun clearly. It was a revolver, a good quality, big one, possibly a Magnum. And he could see the blued steel of the barrel, see it coming, up, up, up in the youth's hands.

There was sweat in McCall's eyes, salty, and gritty, blinding him, that and the acrid smoke that raked at his eyeballs like harsh fingernails.

"Put it down, or I fire."

Up, up, up, came the gun, and the youth had two hands on it now, and he was crouching in a police-fire stance, the mouth of the barrel pointing directly to McCall.

"Put it DOWN!"

If not now . . . McCall squeezes, once, twice, feeling the automatic buck in his hands, the pop-pop of the report in his ears like twin, painful slaps, and once, twice, two spits of red and blue flame.

And the youth is smacked backwards, flat on his back, utterly still. And it is over. A figure runs to the body, kneels over it, grabs something. McCall shouts, the figure runs, and eventually McCall walks over to the youth he has shot, and still in disbelief, stares down at the prone body, at the out-of-focus newly dead eyes, over the surprised face.

Looks for the gun, cannot find it. Knows it was there, knows now that it has been taken in an effort to brand him as the murderer of an innocent.

And above the crackle of the fires as his hearing rushes back to him like a roaring waterfall, he hears the chant of the distant, rioting, crowd: "Murderer, murderer. Pig, pig."

Then a persistent buzz, that goes on and on, relentlessly; that will not be denied.

McCall awoke in a lather of sweat, sitting bolt upright, terrifying Madonna, who had been curled up asleep on his stomach.

The cat dashed from the room, and McCall swung himself off the sofa and staggered groggily for the door.

It was Flavor. She brushed past him into the room, turned and stood, hands on her hips, eyes blazing angrily. He closed the door and faced her. Without preamble she said:

"Satisfied now, McCall?"

He gave a don't-know-what's-going-on shrug, still dazed from the nightmare.

"Don't act dumb with me. You just couldn't restrain your natural Detroit white-boy cop curiosity, could you?"

"Listen, I – "

"No, McCall, YOU listen. You had to know who was banging the piece of black ass you worked with, didn't you?"

"It wasn't like that."

"Oh no? Then why go to my home, when you KNEW I wasn't home?"

"I needed to ask you something, I was going to wait." He knew how lame it sounded. He said feebly: "I actually thought she was your cleaning lady."

Flavor laughed bitterly: "Oh really? Well, that cleaning lady is worth about three million bucks. And just wait until they invent the telephone, you're going to miss a lot of fun."

"I called you at Burbank, goddamn it. They said you'd left, I thought you'd be home when I got there."

"Oh, really?"

"It's the truth. Look, do you want to sit down? Can I get you a drink or something?"

"You're truly amazing," she shook her head, "this isn't a social call, you dumb sonofabitch."

He moved behind the soda, gripping it with both hands: "Actually, Flavor I couldn't give a goddamn who you sleep with."

She stepped forward and McCall was convinced that had there not been the de-militarised zone of the sofa preventing her reaching him, she would have struck him.

Her eyes were on fire. He had never seen such righteous anger. It frightened him.

"And just what makes you assume, McCall, that Jack and I sleep together? Huh? You an expert on these things? You fuck every guy you ever shared an apartment with?"

"It's not the same?"

"It's exactly the same."

"Jack Romarin is gay."

"You checked with your Hollywood spies, huh?"

He shook his head: "I should have known. Jack, a screenwriter. Jesus. You must have thought I was dumb. I bet everyone knew except me."

"And that offends your big macho ideal of sexuality, does it? The idea that a woman might prefer another woman, to what – " her look was one of scorn, as her eyes ran up and down him, from head to foot, taking in the sweat-stained t-shirt, the crumpled track suit pants, "to YOU? To guys LIKE you?"

From behind his defensive position he put out an accusing finger: "You don't even have the faintest idea WHO I am, or WHAT I am. So don't judge me. And I didn't say it offends my idea of sexuality. I couldn't give a shit!"

"You didn't have to say it, your face says it for you. That and your history. Well let me tell you something, Mr. Macho. Jack is gay, and she isn't ashamed of it. The only reason that I tried to keep my association with her quiet, is because of bigots like you, IN the department, and OUT of it too."

McCall said: "I'm not a bigot."

"Your history says different."

"It was him or me. That simple."

"Except they never found the gun."

"Someone took it off the body."

"You SAY. I'll let you into a female secret, McCall. You know what we women think?"

"You're gonna tell me."

"The bigger the car, the bigger the gun, the smaller the DICK."

McCall ran a hand over his forehead, wiping the sweat from his face and eyes. The whole world was coming apart in his hands.

"I think you should leave now."

"Oh, I'll leave. But let me tell you one more thing. I LOVE Jack. She is my FRIEND, and I CARE for her. I live in her apartment, and I have my own room. But, naturally, the assumption must be that because she is a gay woman, and I happen to be a woman too, then" she spread her hands, "hey presto, we must be having sex."

McCall paused before saying it, then realised he wanted to know. It could hurt, but he wanted to know.

"Well, are you? Are you having sex with her, Flavor?"

He realised there were tears in his eyes and he could hear her laboured, angry breathing, as she stared at him unblinkingly. For the first time he found it in himself to meet her gaze. He wanted to know.

"Huh? Are you? You're so fucking up-front, tell-it-like-it-is, and so goddamned righteous it hurts. So are you?"

She appeared to make a physical effort to control herself before she said:

"I'll put it this way. McCall. If I wanted to, I damn well would. Nobody tells me what to do, think, or say, not any more. And hey, if I decide that I want to, tonight, tomorrow night, I will."

She brushed past him towards the door, and once again he smelled that scent of her, that musk. He turned to her:

"You didn't answer my question. Do you sleep with her?"

"Think on it, McCall. May it torture your imaginings."

"I have enough to torture those."

"And if this is the locker room joke tomorrow, you'll pay. I promise."

"Don't worry."

She laughed, derisively: "I'm not worried, I think it's you who should be worried." Her eyes took in the sparse apartment, the threadbare sofa, the congealed food on the paper plates; the unframed thumb-tacked pictures on the wall, the higgledy-piggledly piles of weeks-old newspapers, stacked against the stained walls.

She was dissecting him and his life with her eyes, and he felt utterly sad, wretched, bleak and alone. It was as though she could see through him like an X-ray. And it astonished him that he cared so much.

He said, hopelessly: "I know you don't believe me, but I only called around for a film guide. I meant no harm. Live your life as you want to."

But she was in no mood to show mercy, and her smile was cruel: "Oh sure, I will. I don't need your permission to do that." She leaned, casually, almost triumphantly against the wall:

"It bugs you like hell though, doesn't it McCall? To think I might be having sex with a woman. That just burns you up."

He had never felt this low, this utterly degraded, not since his daughter's death.

And he said, with all the truthfulness and dignity he could muster: "Yes. To be honest, Flavor, it burns me up. As God is my witness, I don't know why it does, but it does."

She shook her head in resignation:

"There's something I never quite understood about you before, McCall."

He waited, like a bloodied and beaten boxer, for the final humiliating, oblivion punch.

"You're sad," she moved to the door and opened it. "And you just have to be the loneliest man I have EVER seen."

The sounding of its closing was like a prison cell door clanging shut for ever.

CHAPTER EIGHT

McCall poured himself a bourbon and slid the cassette into a VCR. According to Halliwell's Film Guide, East River was a movie produced in 1962, and eventually he'd found a copy in a specialised rental store called Attack of the Killer Bs on Sunset, next door to Midway Ford Rent-a-Car opposite the Hyatt Regency.

East River – starring Kirk Nielsen.

It was black and white, set in 1950s New York. Nielsen was Johnny Molano, a hoodlum with a heart of gold and a moll to match. The moll had a kid sister who tried to persuade her elder sibling to leave the mobster and join her in a flower business.

Molano was framed by gang rivals in league with a crooked cop. He broke out of prison to take revenge, killed his rivals and the crooked cops, but in the ensuing shoot-out the moll was killed, even as her kid sister raced to save her.

The last scene showed Molano – Nielsen – walking down the waterfront with his arm around the kid sister, saying:

"Don't worry, kid, from now on Johnny is going to look after you."

You didn't have to be Charles Champlin to recognise it as a turkey. McCall was about to hit the Stop button, when the credits began to roll, and from where he was sitting on the floor he eased back again into the sofa.

Johnny Molano . . . Kirk Nielsen, Jane Tenby . . . Kathleen O'Malley, Mary Tenby . . . Heather O'Malley – hey, McCall pressed the PAUSE button. Sisters played presumably by sisters.

He took the ballpoint pen and made a note of the names in a notebook by his side.

He pressed PLAY, and the list of credits rolled again. Policeman, longshoreman, taxi driver, waitress . . . Victoria Astaire! – he pressed PAUSE again.

Nielsen and Astaire in the same movie. Well, according to Flavor, he made no secret of the fact that he'd had an affair with Astaire.

Bartender, doctor, judge, prison warden, first prisoner, second prisoner, third prisoner . . . Art Helm! PAUSE. So, Helm too. It was on the file, Helm had appeared in at least three Kirk Nielsen Production enterprises, Flavor had discovered that, and while Nielsen had had trouble recalling them for some reason, he had not attempted to deny it.

It wasn't suspicious in itself. Hollywood was a relatively small community, people made friendships on the way up, and kept them. You scratched their back, they scratched yours in return. Everyone got rich and happy.

Two victims of the Angel, both in the same movie, and third victim connected to one of them by an early homosexual relationship.

There was a tie-in, only the most dedicated disbeliever in conspiracy theories could deny that. But what? And was Nielsen a part of that.

Why had the caller said East River? Why had he first said little prince. McCall tried to project the caller's thought process. He was playing games, OK, but he knew that sooner or later McCall would find out it was a movie and get to see it.

He would know that McCall would find Helm and Astaire in the cast list. So if the aim was to link the killings to Nielsen by clearly putting him in a movie with the dead twosome, then the caller would have succeeded.

But to what avail? Nielsen had no motive, and the information that he was connected with Astaire – and to Helm – had been established by Flavor with minimum effort. The caller was not telling the Task Force anything they couldn't find out themselves.

McCall re-wound the tape and made a list of EVERY member ot the cast and crew. He'd check them all out, if they were alive or dead, where they were now, for whom they worked, and if any of them had any kind of business or personal connection with the murder victims.

Later that day he went back to Attack of the Killer Bs and told them he had accidentally ruined their tape. They looked at him like he was shit and processed his $175 Mastercard deposit.

He wanted to keep the tape.

The reporter came across the art decor foyer, and put out a hand: "Hi McCall, long time no see." The detective shook the man's hand: "Well, I was persona non grata to you liberals for a while."

The reporter looked sheepish: "You know how things are."

"I sure do."

"You want something, right?"

"Clippings."

"Who?"

McCall produced a sheet of paper with around 21 names on it.

"Shit, that's a lot."

"You owe me, remember."

The reporter took the sheet: "I remember. Look, first I'll

check which ones HAVE clippings, then you can come back and check the issue in which the story appears, on microfilm, OK?"

"You couldn't just give me some xeroxes?"

"Nope, we don't work it that way. Normally it's not open to the public, anyway."

McCall laughed: "I'm not public."

The reporter gave him a quiet, quizzical look: "This about the Angel?"

"What else?"

"One of these a suspect?"

"Dunno yet."

The reporter gave the list a little wave: "But there's a connection, right?"

McCall gave a dumb smile: "We're clutching at straws."

The reporter stared through him: "Sure you are." He looked at the name at the top of the list, "We know you've seen Nielsen. He a suspect?"

"Don," McCall put an arm around the reporter and moved him to one side, "you owe ME, remember? Not the other way around."

"Well sure, but gimme a break here."

"I did, and you got a series out of it, Down and Out in Beverly Hills – the Reality. The Bag Ladies of Beverly Hills. As I recall it, Hard Copy picked up your stuff. How much did you make, five?"

"I'd like to write something; you know how big this angel thing is."

"OK," McCall put his mouth to the man's ear, "don't mention any other name on the list, except Nielsen. And you didn't get it from me. Then you call me, and I deny the fuck out of the whole thing in a way that'll sound like I don't believe a word of what I'm saying. OK?"

"And when Nielsen sues us?"

McCall spread his hands: "You're the one looking for the lead."

The reporter freed himself from McCall's embrace, and

looked the policeman straight in the eye: "But he's a suspect, right?"

McCall said: "Why not?"

"When do you want to come in?"

McCall pretended to check his watch: "Two hours."

"You're kidding me."

"Two hours, Don."

The reporter put his hands up in mock surrender: "Two hours, – you got it. I presume you don't want the contemporary stuff on Astaire, Helm, Nielsen, right?"

"Right. But ANYTHING before the angel killings."

McCall had a cappuccino and a Snickers, read a National Enquirer, walked around Little Tokyo, and returned.

The reporter took him up in an elevator, and into a hushed room with a series of microfilm machines on bare desks. Only one was being used.

He handed back the list with twelve names scored through in pencil, and said in a hushed voice: "Nothing on those people at all. Of the eight remaining, those – " he pointed to names bordered by asterisks, "feature only in movie reviews."

McCall nodded.

"Now all the others have appeared in stories OTHER than the recent stuff on the Angel, and OTHER than in movie reviews." The reporter handed McCall a separate sheet:

"Against the names are the dates of the issues in which they appeared, and it goes back to the late Fifties. You're going to be here for a LONG time. The librarian there – " he pointed to a woman behind a simple, uncluttered desk, "will give you the spools for the years in which the stories appeared. She'll show you the drill, but basically, you spool up the year and whip through to the edition you want, then go through it page by page."

"I got it."

The reporter handed over the sheets of paper: "I want the fast track on this one, McCall."

"Well, I presume you already copied this sheet," he waved the original list, "and when I've finished, you'll go through the files just like I am." McCall paused: "If you haven't already."

The reporter smiled a genuine sincere and heartfelt smile, and McCall remembered the old TV maxim expounded by Walter Cronkite. In television as in life, sincerity was everything. And if you could fake that, the rest was easy.

"As if I would."

"Don't jump to any wild conclusions."

"I'd sooner get it from the horse's mouth."

"What exactly?"

"A good tip when you're about to make an arrest. Plus the name. All the gory details about the heads and stuff. Come on, you know."

"I'll think about it."

The reporter punched his shoulder, good-naturedly: "Whatever, always a pleasure to do business with you McCall."

"And you, Don."

McCall got to work.

Flavor was hardly awake. She said, groggily, into the telephone: "Jesus, McCall, is this your idea of a bad joke? It's . . ." she squinted at the bedside clock. "it's gone three a.m."

"Get over here, soon as you can. My place." He said, with as much sarcasm as he could muster, "Unless you want me to come there."

"Why can't it wait until morning?"

But McCall had already put down the telephone, and Flavor climbed groggily out of her bed. This wasn't battered, beaten, lonely McCall, there was something in his voice, and it sounded like rebirth.

His eyes were red-rimmed, and beneath were dark rings of exhaustion, but he had showered and smelt fresh. He was wearing blue jeans and a blue cotton shirt, with moccasin

Timberlands over his bare feet.

She noticed that the apartment had been cleaned, the newspapers and stale food disposed of.

They had never spoken of her visit. Not to each other, not to anyone else. It had been said, could not be unsaid, but each – instinctively and unknown to the other – felt it could be left, to gather dust, and that somehow, with time, it would no longer matter.

"Sit." She did, and McCall handed her a thick sheaf of xeroxes.

She was still tired and muddled: "This had better be good."

"I know who called me, I know what the little prince is, and I think I know what these killings are all about." She waved the pile of papers: "And it's all in here?"

"Most of it. Want a summary?"

"Yeah."

"In nineteen sixty-six Nielsen owned a boat called The Little Prince. On Labour Day weekend he planned a cruise, Long Beach to Catalina. He had guests."

"Anyone we know? Helm? Astaire?"

"Clever girl." McCall took the file back, "Helm, Astaire, Alassio – "

"Helm's boyfriend at the time? Shit – "

"Three victims of the angel, all on the same boat at the same time."

"Other guests?"

"Sure." McCall, read from a sheet of paper, "Valerie Cruze – "

"Cruze, she was in the Chicago thing, the soap – "

"Windy City, a Kirk Nielsen Production, died of a heart attack. Then there's Joseph and Jean Angelli."

Flavor knew the couple. A former singing duo, now born-again Christians with their own nationally networked Sunday televangelical show out of Atlanta.

"But they're out of LA, now."

"Sure they're are. They have their own production

131

company, Sermon on the Mount Productions, Atlanta, Georgia." McCall was smiling.

Flavor said: "But?"

"Major shareholder Kirk Nielsen."

"Anyone else on the boat?"

"King Leonard and wife."

King Leonard was a Sixties tough-guy actor in the Jack Palance mold. He played half-breeds, Tartar warlords, and sadistic Mexican bandits.

Getting fewer and fewer roles in the early Seventies, he went into an alcohol recovery program after his wife died of leukaemia. He re-married, divorced again and was now a successful TV comedy actor.

His situation-comedy, Jack and the Beans Talk, about a new-age Beverly Hills gardener to the rich and famous, had been running for three years. The independent production company Giantkiller Productions was an off-shoot of KNP.

"So just about everyone on the boat is either, (a) dead, or (b) owes their living to Kirk Nielsen, directly or indirectly."

"Right," Flavor nodded as McCall sat down next to her on the sofa, and Madonna leapt onto his lap for a cuddle. "What's the pièce de résistance?"

"There was a Sixties movie star on that boat called Kathleen O'Malley. She was Nielsen's girlfriend of the day."

"Something happened?"

"There was a party, the newspapers hinted at heavy drinking. It looks like Kathleen got up in the night, wandered on deck, and fell over the side."

"And drowned?"

"You got it. I spent nine hours going bug-eyed looking at Times' files. This story ran for about three months. The incident, the aftermath, the body turning up, the inquest. We've been walking around with our eyes closed. This was the Hollywood scandal of 1966, this could be Nielsen's Chappaquiddick."

"What did the body show?"

"Not a great deal. It washed up at San Clemente a month

later, in a very bad condition, naturally. They identified her from jewellery, rings and stuff. Cause of death, drowning."

"What was the speculation at the time?"

"Nothing specific, but read between the lines, it was a did-she-fall-or-was-she-pushed? thing."

"By Nielsen?"

"Sure. Lots of whispers about what happened on the boat that night, like drink, narcotics, wild parties, maybe under-age girls – boys, too – nothing substantiated. You want some coffee?"

He went to the kitchen and poured them both a mug, and they sat letting the steaming fumes, and the rough, raw taste bring them awake, give them new life.

Flavor was leafing through the xeroxed clippings: "What was the inquest verdict . . ." she traced a finger, "aha, Accidental Death."

McCall put his finger on the page too, and traced to a different paragraph: "Heavily influenced by the autopsy report. No trace of drink or drugs in the bloodstream, no signs of foul play, lungs full of water. Any external damage done by sea creatures. Have a look for yourself."

She did. "So," she shrugged, "it was Offenbacher. He had a good reputation until he retired, so I am told. Before my time."

"And mine. But, look . . ." he flipped to some different sheets, "I got the clips on Offenbacher. Retired EARLY. He was forty-nine when he did the autopsy on O'Malley, and," he turned a sheet, "hey, hey he's FIFTY when he takes early retirement from the county. One year later."

"Coincidence." Flavor swallowed more hot coffee, felt it clearing her mind.

"Would've been, except," McCall pointed, "that's from Variety." Flavor read. One year and six months after the tragedy, according to the pencilled in date on the Variety clipping, Heinz Offenbacher was appointed health consultant to Cherokee Films Inc.

"And now you're going to tell me that Cherokee Films

was owned by Nielsen."

"Not owned, but he was on the board." McCall, smiled; the coup de gràce, "But until he died in an auto accident last year Offenbacher was head of medical services, Kirk Nielsen Productions."

Flavor tossed the cuttings onto the floor.

"You think Nielsen killed the girl, bribed the man who carried out the autopsy on her, then kept everyone on the boat sweet – until now?"

"It's looking that way. It's the best link we've had since this damn circus started."

Madonna stretched, then climbed off McCall and onto Flavor's lap. McCall asked: "You a dog person, or a cat person?"

She stroked the cat, listening to the reward of a rich, throaty and somewhat strangely satisfying, purr: "Dunno, I've never really thought about it before. What's her name – it is a she, isn't it, it has a she kind of a look?"

"Madonna."

"You have a cruel sense of humour if you let her out at night in this neighbourhood."

"She's had the op – right, honey?" McCall reached out and stroked his cat, and for a second his hand brushed Flavor's but they both instinctively pulled apart.

"You've been a busy bee, McCall."

"You bet."

"What now?"

"Now we see Wishaw."

"Who's Wishaw?"

"You'll see."

Flavor got up and handed Madonna back to McCall, and once again their hands touched: "Name a time and place and I'll be there, in the meantime I'm going to catch up on my sleep."

"When I said, 'now', I meant now as in this moment in time."

Flavor groaned: "This had better be good."

The man had his back to the counter, checking till receipts, and coughing, wheezily. A cigarette burned, close to his nicotine-stained fingers. McCall said: "I'm a lover of literature."

The man turned as though stung: "Mr. McCall."

"Wishaw. How's tricks?"

"Fine," he stubbed his cigarette out, nervously, and looked at Flavor, "who's your friend?"

"A police officer. You don't deserve names, Wishaw. I should have recognised your voice anywhere."

"I closed the shop in Beverly Hills."

"Correction. The Beverly Hills Police Department closed the shop in Beverly Hills. Thank God I took a forwarding address."

Wishaw took two steps back from the counter, hands out: "Hey, come on, I was trying to help."

McCall lifted the counter lid and went through, following the man who backed off until a wall prevented him going further: "Anonymous calls, riddles, guessing games. I could book you for that."

Flavor said: "Hey, McCall, ease up. He's helped."

He looked over his shoulder: "Yeah, you're right, I guess." He pointed at the bookstore owner, "You, get in back, we're all going to talk."

The man implored: "Come on, I have customers. this is a 24-hour bookstore, we never close." McCall took out his badge: "You close it, or I'll show your customers my badge and close it, that wouldn't be good for your business, would it?"

"You have no right to do this."

"You're right. But I can get a warrant and search your premises. Maybe we'll find some stuff that doesn't appear on the shelves."

"OK, OK." He pushed past McCall, around Flavor, addressing three customers who flipped through porno mags and books that adorned the shelves.

"Business, folks, have to close up for fifteen minutes.

You'll all be welcome back then." Reluctantly the late-night porn browsers filed out into the street and Wishaw locked up.

They sat in a small room that reeked of stale tobacco. McCall said, by way of introduction: "Flavor, this is Mr. Wishaw, purveyor of dirty books."

He was a bald man, mid-Fifties, Flavor estimated, and he had a nicotined, browned look about him, and yet there was something in the man's eyes, like the glowing remains of a once-proud fire, that spoke of intelligence. She nodded to him: "Mr. Wishaw."

"Wishaw and I crossed swords in Beverly Hills. He once made a very facetious remark to me as I checked his stock, right Wishaw?"

Wishaw made no acknowledgement.

"Something about me liking literature. Mr. Wishaw was attempting to be humorous. The other day when I was watching East River it all came back to me. Suddenly I remembered who our deep throat was. Hey, by the way, thanks for the tip."

"You're welcome," the man said, sullenly.

"So. What do you know about Nielsen and the Little Prince? That stuff off Catalina in Sixty-Six? That's why you called me, wasn't it?"

Wishaw palmed a cigarette like a conjuror a card, and lit it, inhaling deeply: "Sure. I wanted to give you information. But I wanted to keep my name out of it." He looked at them both, first one, then the other: "I'd still like that."

Flavor looked at McCall, it was his show. McCall said: "Yeah, you don't have to figure in this."

"OK," Wishaw waved the cigarette. "Let's get it straight. I don't like running this crummy joint. Who would? I was a writer, I AM a writer."

"What kind of writer?" McCall asked.

"Four novels, three of them published. This is the early Sixties I'm talking about here. One optioned screenplay."

"The movie get made?" Flavor asked.

"Get outta here," he waved his cigarette dismissively, "one in five hundred get made. But I did a good deal. I would've had a movie made, eventually."

"What happened, Wishaw, and how does this have anything to do with Nielsen and The Little Prince?"

"OK, I'm getting to it, man. I was doing OK, right, I had a house in Brentwood, a HOUSE, man. Like I said, four novels, an optioned screenplay. I was doing OK. I got some script-doctoring work. I was GOOD, man, GOOD." Flavor swore she could see a tear in the man's eye.

"What did you in, booze or broads?"

"Wish it had've been either, least I would have enjoyed it. Nielsen did me in, finished me, bankrupted me. They took my house, car, everything. My wife divorced me. I never worked in Hollywood again."

"How'd it happen?" McCall said it, flatly, but inside was tingling.

Wishaw laughed, a cynical, wheezing imitation of a laugh: "Oh, well, I got cocky, you know. Shot my mouth off to one or two people, then I wrote an article for one of the Hollywood mags, you know, speculating about O'Malley's death."

"Implying, what?"

Wishaw, leaned forward: "Implying what everyone else knew but didn't have the cojones to say out loud. That Nielsen wasted that girl on the boat. Don't forget she was a star too, and she could act, and she was gonna be bigger than him, and he KNEW it, couldn't stand it."

"You think he killed her?"

"Well, I can't know for sure, seeing that I wasn't on the boat. But that's what I thought, that's what I STILL think. Plus he had the hots for her sister, that was common knowledge around town. You ask me he was banging them both — probably at the same time, knowing that sonofa-bitch."

"He liked threesomes?" Flavor asked, remembering Nielsen, the cold, blue eyes, the commanding face and figure, even in his Sixties. The charming, agreeable manner. And the angry, barked rebuke to his personal assistant.

"Threesome and the younger the better." Flavor stiffened, feeling the pores rise on her arms, the film of perspiration beading her skin.

"You're saying he was a paedophile?"

"Depends on your point of view," Wishaw drew on the cigarette, leaving a hanging carbonised bough of ash, "in Medieval times girls of twelve got married, had kids. I'm not talking eight and nine here. I'm talking fourteen, fifteen maybe."

"That's paedophilia, Mr. Wishaw," Flavor said, "and it's against the law."

Wishaw said, addressing McCall: "Is she for real? This is Hollywood, honey, stars love to bang fresh meat. I could name you five stars right now that you'd cream your jeans over, and they're screwing fourteen year olds." He sat back, a kind of grim satisfaction on his face, then leaned forward, and said to Flavor, gratuitously:

"As a matter of fact one of the biggest stars of this decade just LOVES fucking twelve year old black girls, and that's the truth."

In an instant McCall had his hand over Wishaw's and there was a short, sharp scream of pain.

"Please be polite and respectful to my colleague, Wishaw, I urge you." He squeezed again, and sweat sprung out on the man's face: "OK, Christ, OK, you're breaking my fucking fingers."

McCall leaned back: "Continue."

"I was only trying to put her in the picture." Wishaw nursed his fingers. "He sued."

"What happened?"

"The magazine folded, so he turned his attentions to me. Lawyers, man, I was spending a fortune on lawyers. And he put the word out in the business; suddenly I was poison. Jesus you just don't know how much influence that man has in this town."

Wishaw drew on his cigarette, shaking his head.

"And?"

"Columbia didn't take up the option on my movie. Suddenly my publishers didn't want to know. The re-writing jobs dried up. I tried to get back into journalism – that was my major, University of Iowa."

He put his head in his hands: "No-one wanted to know. Then the cops picked me up – on a burglary charge," he looked at them, a kind of bemused astonishment on his face, "me, a burglar? Jesus, it was a fix up. Nielsen, dammit."

McCall said: "They charge you?"

"No they never charged me!" Wishaw looked at McCall as though he was crazy: "They had no evidence because it wasn't true. But each time there was a burglary in the neighbourhood the LAPD knocked on MY door. They'd, I dunno," he waved his hands in a sort of desperation, "they'd take stuff away, that your camera sir, that your stereo system, you have a bill of sale for that?"

Flavor said: "You think Nielsen was out to ruin you."

Wishaw stubbed out the cigarette: "Not OUT to, honey, DID. My wife couldn't take it. Middle of the night, the phone rings, broads saying, 'Is Ken there, please?' It drove her crazy, and none of it was true. I loved her. I wasn't fooling around."

Someone rattled the door outside, and Wishaw shouted: "We're closed, can't you read?"

Flavor said, kindly: "She left you?"

"Not until the house went. She could take the rest, I almost convinced her that it wasn't me, it was them. But there was no work, no job, I couldn't make the payments on the car, let alone the house. She went back to Des Moines in Sixty-Eight."

"But you stayed."

He looked up at them, something like defiance in the ruined face and body: "Sure I stayed. Because one day I'm going to nail Nielsen. He is responsible for blackballing me in this town, and I'm going to pay him back for that."

"And for killing the girl? You still think he killed the girl?" Flavor asked.

"Yes, ma'am, he killed the girl. He had a party on that boat, young girls, boys too, that's what I was told. And maybe his girl wouldn't play ball, so he killed her and threw her over the side."

"That's a tall statement from someone who wasn't there."

"Something happened on that boat, SOMETHING," he said doggedly, like a religious incantation. It was his faith now, he had built his whole life around it. Nothing mattered now, not the sleazy job, not the middle-age that had settled on him like decay, nothing mattered: only his crusade to get Nielsen.

McCall said: "And you think the rest of the guests on the boat knew what he did. And now he's killing them all and blaming it on some Angel of death?"

"That's what I think."

"Why all the horror movie stuff? Swords, heads?"

Wishaw shrugged: "He's in the business. It's a show, takes your attention off details."

"What's the motive?" asked Flavor.

Wishaw looked at her as though she was retarded: "Isn't it obvious? Blackmail. Someone on the boat is putting the finger on Nielsen."

"After twenty-nine years?"

"Why not? Maybe someone wanted a big pay day. Maybe someone was tired of appearing in shitty Nielsen soaps and sit-coms."

Flavor said: "You know that all the people on the boat are connected with him in some way?"

"Sure I know, everyone in the business knows. Maybe they don't know that Nielsen killed the girl, but they sure as hell know that something weird went on that night on the boat. And they know that every single, goddamn person on that boat has prospered – under Nielsen's protection."

Flavor said doggedly: "Then why kill the goose that lays

the golden egg?"

"The big pay-off. Or maybe Nielsen was laying off the help, figuring he'd done enough. That it was all too long ago to harm him."

She looked at him, and she knew that Wishaw believed all the rest of the things he'd said, but he didn't believe that. It was the missing bit of the jigsaw for him as well.

She said: "It was all a long, long time ago. People said things, then, memories fade. How come you still believe it all now?"

He looked at McCall, and indicated a drawer: "May I?" McCall gave a curt nod of permission, and Wishaw opened the drawer and took out a bulging manilla folder.

"You don't seriously believe I just THOUGHT about this all these years?" He waved the folder like a battlefield standard, the rallying point of his cause. "I've collected every bit of evidence about him and that goddamn boat I could."

McCall put out a hand, and Wishaw handed him the folder: "Take the autopsy. There was ONE pathologist at that autopsy, Heinz Offenbacher – "

"We know about him," McCall said.

Wishaw waved a dismissive hand: "Oh sure, that he quit working for the county and went to work for Nielsen. Yeah? But did you know that Offenbacher bought a house for one hundred thousand dollars in La Jolla – in 1966? Do you know what kind of place that bought you, then?"

"In La Jolla?"

"Yeh, where no-one knew him, or the story, or could have cared less if they did. And under a different name. I only found out because I watched the bastard like a hawk. He bought it under his son's name."

Flavor took out the Marlboro, offered Wishaw one, and lit both: "You're saying he faked the autopsy?"

Wishaw waved a hand to indicate equivocation: "He didn't need quite to fake, if you know what I'm saying. I'm saying, he didn't LOOK too hard." He bit on his lip, and jabbed a finger. McCall thought, He's obsessed.

"O'Malley's cadaver was a month in the water, eaten by the fish, decomposed, right? So you can forget looking for obvious signs."

McCall said: "Maybe, but bullet entry and exit wounds, limbs fractured by gunshot, organ punctures indicating attack with a knife, are different from animal or shark tears. Spinal dislocations or torn neck ligaments from strangulation, there's a million – "

"Yeah, a million things, if you're LOOKING!"

"The report of the autopsy said no narcotics or alcohol in the bloodstream."

"If it was HER blood. Offenbacher took the sample, no-one else. The samples come back negative, he finds nothing, death by drowning. Big Hollywood tragedy, end of fucking story. But not for me, McCall."

McCall exhaled with a whistle through his teeth: "Look, I'm sorry about the hand, back there."

"Forget it, I'm a scumbag. That's what this town has turned me into. I deserved it. Ma'am, I apologise, I meant no disrespect."

Flavor had been thinking, and had not paid close attention to the last remarks: "What? Oh, forget it. Was the girl buried or cremated?"

"Buried. Hey, it was a big funeral at the time, Kathleen O'Malley wasn't Liz Taylor, but she was big in Sixty-Six."

"Where?" Flavor asked.

"Forest Lawn, Hollywood Hills."

"That's where they put Helm."

"History repeating itself," Wishaw said, with a hint of triumph.

McCall said: "Like you said, you weren't there. So what makes you think he killed the girl and threw her overboard?"

"Because I learned a little something about our Mr. Nielsen."

"Give."

"He's done it before."

CHAPTER NINE

The dark scuttling ceased, but the figure kept itself in the darkness at the edge of the dim light. What did the onlooker feel; hatred, pity, contempt, revulsion – even fear?

Yes, all of these, but stronger than all those sensations, a curious satisfaction at what could only be termed its creation.

"Play," the voice from the darkness said, piteously, "let me play."

"Take the food," the onlooker replied, and the plate was pulled, with feral speed, into the darkness.

"Soon. Soon you will have a new friend with whom you can play."

"Friend." The invisible voice said, with a kind of wonder. Then each retreated to its own world.

Flavor sat in the shaded, screened-off area of the Casino Café below her apartment, sipped espresso and studied the bulging file with its crumbling, yellowing clippings that lay beneath the clear plastic cover.

Prize Exhibit A from Wishaw's personal file on Kirk Nielsen was dated August 14, 1950. A clipping from the Manchester New Leader, Manchester, New Hampshire.

A boating accident. One Kurt Knudsen, 20, and his girlfriend Eileen Watkins, 17, had taken a row boat out from Weirs Beach onto Lake Winnipesaukee. An unexpected storm had blown up, with high winds and driving rain. The first hint of tragedy was when Knudsen, a summer lifeguard and strong swimmer, had struggled ashore exhausted, and raised the alarm.

His girlfriend was missing. A search was launched, but nothing was discovered until the next day when pieces of the boat began to come ashore. The girl's virtually naked body was found on a beach near Wolfeboro 24 hours after that.

Beneath that clipping, others, including the one on the inquest. Death by drowning. Verdict, accidental death. A faded, dotted newspaper picture of Kurt Knudsen. Even then you could see the resemblance. Knudsen was Nielsen.

That day, as Flavor and McCall had sat with Wishaw in a West Hollywood coffee shop, he had given them HIS interpretation of events.

"I did some detective work on Nielsen. He gives his birthplace as Manchester, New Hampshire. It isn't, it's Laconia, which is maybe an hour away."

Wishaw had fingered his clippings like an evangelist his Bible.

"One lie. He gives his school as Manchester High, well only for the last year before graduation, before that it was a school in Laconia."

"So what, Wishaw?"

"Patience, McCall. His parents moved after the business with the girl. Public pressure, I guess. No matter what the police thought, the people there knew better. They KNEW Knudsen."

"When did he change his name?"

"Mid-Fifties, after his Army service, and when he got to Hollywood." Wishaw drew a xerox from his file. It was a police charge sheet.

"This is why the locals didn't believe Nielsen." He handed it over, like a mother her month old baby. The Laconia Police Dept had charged Kurt Knudsen, later to be Kirk Nielsen, with two counts of statutory rape, sex with a minor who was deemed incapable under the law, of giving her consent to sexual intercourse.

The date of the charges was June 5, about three months before the boating tragedy.

"What did he get, reform school, what? And how did he get out in three months?" Flavor had asked.

Wishaw took back the sheet, triumphantly: "The case was not proceeded with. The girl and her parents pulled out at the last minute, refused to press charges."

"How'd you know all this, Wishaw," McCall asked, suspiciously, "how'd you get hold of that thing?"

"Moved there man, got a job tending bar. People drink, they talk. All the old guys remembered that sonofabitch Nielsen."

"Why did they refuse to press charges?" Flavor had asked.

Wishaw shrugged: "Ain't that big a town. Juvenile court, no names, but it would have got out anyway. Maybe Knudsen's people put pressure on, who knows?"

"Who was the girl?"

Wishaw gave them both, but especially McCall, his smug-told-you-so-smile: "Eileen Watkins."

"And you think he killed her."

Wishaw thrust the file forward like his battle standard: "Look at the evidence. She could have sent him to prison, reform school, ruined his life. Only she fails to testify, right?"

"So he's clear," McCall shrugged, still puzzled.

"Yeah, but now she has a hold on him. And I think he was still banging her. You know, discreetly, like OUT ON A FUCKING ROWBOAT, for example."

Flavor nodded: "Then?"

"She gets scared, cocky, whatever. This time she's going to tell. Knudsen-Nielsen is going to jail. So," Wishaw shrugged, "he goes over the side with her, holds her under maybe, he was six feet tall plus, a lifeguard, she wouldn't have been hard to kill."

"There WAS a storm," Flavor said, doggedly.

"His good luck. Storm or no storm, she would have drowned, believe me."

"All neat, pat and convenient."

"You got it."

"I'm not talking about the maybe-murder, I'm talking about your story," McCall said.

"Yeah, sure, it's an accident, McCall, and then he has another girlfriend, and she just happens to have an under-age sister, and, oh my oh my, there's a boat – on the ocean this time – and his girlfriend goes and drowns. Doesn't it strike you as too much of a coincidence?"

Flavor said: "Are her parents still alive, the girl who drowned in New Hampshire?"

Wishaw shook his head. "No, they were mid-Forties even then. But she has a sister, and she's alive."

He produced a sheet of paper with an address on it.

"Have you spoken to her?"

"Tried, ten years ago, wouldn't have anything to do with me. You ask me Nielsen has got to her too. But," he spread his hands, "you two are cops, how could she refuse you?"

When Wishaw had gone, Flavor had looked at McCall and said: "Well, what?"

McCall looked puzzled: "It reads well, it reads TOO damn well. And he's obsessed with it, the files, the note-books, the clippings, it's his whole life. This man travels damn near three thousand miles to be a bartender so he can play detective."

Flavor said: "Yeah, he comes across like that. But just because you're paranoid doesn't mean someone isn't out to get you."

McCall had stirred his cold coffee, as though the answer might lie in there: "Well, Knudsen is Nielsen, we know that."

"And he was charged with two counts of statutory rape – "

"Dropped."

"OK, dropped, but there IS a dead girl, and then ANOTHER dead girl, both drowned. And then, nearly thirty years later, and in the space of a couple of months everyone on the second boat starts getting knocked off like the ten little – "

"Indians," McCall wagged an admonishing finger, "ten little Indians."

"Would I use the N-word?" She laughed. It felt marginally better between them. Neither had ever mentioned her visit to his apartment, nor the issue that provoked it. They had let the hours, the days, the weeks, act like a healing process, scar tissue to cover the wound of their confrontation.

And in an odd way it was as though her outburst, as vicious and wounding as it had felt to McCall, had somehow punctured a poisoned sac of tension, unspoken bitterness, and resentment that had lain between them.

She couldn't figure out why, but the issue of Jack, now that it was out in the open – now there was a third party – had clarified for her. Now she could focus on what she was, and what she wanted.

"We could pull Nielsen in, really put him on the rack, get a search warrant, ransack his place."

"You think you're going to find heads in his refrigerator, Flavor, really I mean?"

The waitress freshened their coffee, and Flavor waited until the woman had departed: "Nothing would surprise me on this."

"And if we pull him in and he walks? Then our ass is grass and Nielsen's lawyer and the Press are lawnmowers."

McCall's mobile phone squawked itself alive on the table.

He activated it and put it to his ear: "McCall." He pulled out his notebook, took a ballpoint from his inside pocket and began to write. After about two minutes he terminated the call.

"We-e-e-ll. We got our last missing victim in place. Smith from the Valley."

"Yeah?" Flavor leaned forward, this was the one that had always puzzled her, infuriated her, with its lack of place.

McCall consulted his notes:

"Our all-American boy Richard Smith was born Leon Filipe Andrade in Vera Cruz, Mexico. His father, now deceased, was José Andrade, ship's master. He emigrated to the United States on December 14th, 1961." McCall paused: "He was the captain of The Little Prince, Nielsen's boat."

Flavor leaned back and gave a long, low whistle.

"Andrade died of cirrhosis of the liver in 1969."

"The kid was on the boat," Flavor said it through clenched teeth, "he was a kid on the boat with his Daddy, and now he's been killed for it. He couldn't have been more than what, seven, eight?"

She remembered now the cheap, tin Mexican flag lapel badge that had glistened, and caught her eye when they'd interviewed Smith's widow at the neat, almost obsessively clean, one-storey house in the San Fernando Valley.

"Remember the little Mex flag, McCall? She just couldn't bear to put it away. It was all that was left of her husband's heritage."

The proud, racist widow with her stiff, Southern back. She'd married a greaser, a Mexican boy, and she had spent her life remaking him in the image she wished.

When the two detectives had asked whether her husband had any alcohol problems, Mrs. Smith saying, proudly: "We are a Temperance family. His father died of drink, so we know the misery alcohol causes."

They just did too, Flavor thought. A Mexican kid with a drunk for a father who must have lost his job when drink took a hold. And he'd met this Southern belle. How she must have hated her attraction for him, and how he must have spent his miserable life denying who he was.

And then he paid with that life because he had gone with his father for a day on the ocean. What had he seen? Had he seen anything? What could a seven or eight-year-old boy have seen or heard that made someone come back, when the boy was a man, and sever his head from his body.

She thought of youth, childhood and innocence. Her own, Smith's, how time's fingers somehow grew sharp nails and reached out to claw the innocence from you like a ripped and violated garment.

McCall drained his new coffee: "Whoever this is – if this IS Nielsen, he won't stop until everyone on the boat is dead. Go to new Hampshire. Flave, do it now, tomorrow, as soon as you can get there."

"You think the dead girl's sister will talk?"

"She might. If she thinks Nielsen DID kill her sister, and if she has been intimidated all this time, maybe she'll come out into the open now."

"And we do what with it?"

McCall thumped the table, making the cups rattle: "We'll get Nielsen in, search his house, his cars, his boats if he has any, we'll shake him down so hard his fixed teeth crack. We'll confront him with what the girl says, with the stuff from New Hampshire, then The Little Prince. Maybe he'll crack. We'll grill that sonofabitch like a hamburger."

They parted outside the Thrifty drugstore at the corner of Sunset and Fairfax. The Crown Books store burned out in the riots incredibly still lay open and charred, like a blackened, gaping tooth. Singed volumes still stood on charcoaled shelves, brown-edged pages flapping in the breeze of passing traffic.

McCall said: "We're getting somewhere. I feel it."

She nodded, then fell silent. McCall put on his sunglasses:

"When do you get your car out of the shop? You wanna ride anyplace?"

She looked at her watch: "Six. But come on, you're three blocks from here, crazy to go all the way to Santa Monica now. I'll call a cab."

"I don't mind."

"No, I'll get a cab." She paused, looking into the traffic, as if for a cab, then she turned, abruptly: "About that time, at your apartment, you know, when –"

He put up both hands, palms facing her: "Forget it. It's over. I was out of line, totally. My fault, I deserved it."

"Hell, McCall," she looked away from him, unwilling to face the dark squares that were his eyes, gazing instead up Fairfax, up to the hazy hills and canyons that rose beyond Sunset, at the houses that perched precariously on every habitable slope and ledge. Like nesting birds, she thought, like nesting birds.

She turned back. "No, it was me that was out of line – "

"Your life, I – "

"Shut the fuck up, McCall, please! It was an accident, I know that now. Jack told me. I mean, the look on your face, she said you looked like a kid caught playing with himself."

"I felt a jerk."

"Yeah, but I should have been open about it – living with Jack, I mean. I should have just said, hey, you know, like my room-mate is – " she faltered, stopped. "If it wasn't for pigment, McCall, you'd realise I was blushing."

He fingered his sunglasses: "Got these from Stevie Wonder, can't see a damn thing. Like I said, it's over. Forget it."

"No," she shook her head, "it's not over, and I won't forget it. What I said to you, those things, you know . . . were vicious, hurtful, rude and WRONG. And I apologise."

He shrugged nonchalantly from behind his emotion-protectors: "You were more accurate than you realised – with the personal stuff, anyway."

"Well I'm sorry more than you realise."

"Well, thanks, and I'm sorry for the other stuff, you know."

"Could you lean down a little please."

"Pardon me?"

"Just lean down towards me. You're a big man, McCall."

He leaned forward, awkward, curious, and she kissed

him on the cheek. The brush of her lips felt like fire on his face, and he could feel his heart begin to race, and the blood pound in his head.

"I'll call you from New Hampshire."

"Do that. Meantime I'll try to talk to every surviving guest on that boat."

"Keep safe."

"You too."

He walked past her and turned right, into the drugstore parking lot, when he heard her call: "Hey McCall!" He turned.

"The answer to your question is no."

For a second he didn't know what she meant. Then he knew.

She called again:

"I'm not."

Flavor drained the last of her espresso and put the file back into her shoulder bag. She was booked out of LAX on an 8 a.m. United flight to Boston, and from there she would take a rental car and drive to New Hampshire.

Jack was doing some emergency re-writing on The Heart Devil's location in the Mojave, so Flavor intended to take in the 7.15 performance of Bob Roberts that was re-showing at the Criterion on the Santa Monica Broadway. Then she'd eat dinner at the Broadway Bar & Grill, go home, book a cab for the airport, pack and sleep.

She was aware that if it had not been for McCall and the bungled Deep Throat calls from Wishaw, not to mention Wishaw's personal crusade against Nielsen, they'd still be floating in the shadows and the shallows.

At the beginning, when McCall had the edge over her, that had burned her. Now? She didn't for the life of her know why, but it seemed not to matter anymore.

She knew though, that the moment in his apartment had been a seminal one. She had seen him as big-gun, little-dick, macho Detroit white-boy, and also as someone who was maybe sexually interested in her in the worst way, simply because she was black.

Then she'd seen him in the pathetic apartment and she'd said those terrible things to him, about him; those wounding, awful things, and had seen the words pierce him like arrows.

And at that precise moment, she had seen him as he was; as perhaps the saddest and loneliest person to whom she had ever been close. And at the height of her self-righteous anger, she had used that as a further instrument to hurt him.

But when her temper had cooled, she saw those things from a different perspective. She saw someone who was already deeply wounded. She could not know why, and suspected she never would.

And the hurt and the fear, she suspected drove him somehow. She had said, with poetic viciousness, when he asked her if she was sleeping with Jacqueline Romarin: "May it torture your imaginings."

His reply had branded itself on her conscience: "I have enough to torture those," and his words had haunted her on the slow, reflective drive back to Santa Monica.

What tortured McCall? Shooting the black kid in Rodeo Drive during the riots? And dammit all, Flavor, she had admonished herself, the enquiry DID clear him. Other witnesses said they saw the kid pull a gun and draw a bead on McCall.

That? Or something else, something that had happened in Detroit. Her visit had stung him into some action too, she realised that when she returned to the apartment, roused from sleep in the early hours to share his information.

She had seen the changes then, the paint, the clearing up, the – what? – new pride?

What tortured his imaginings? She knew what tortured hers. What had he left behind him in Detroit that he still carried with him?

She joined the short ticket line outside the Criterion.

She thought of Mississippi, the troubled childhood, then the growing into young womanhood, of her mother and father who she had barely known, when their pickup ran off the road into a tree killing them both.

Flavor thought of her grandmother, the woman who had brought her up, who had given her the love and nurturing without which it is impossible for a human to grow and love too.

"Where you at, Flavor, where you at girl?" Wizened old grandma, who, when Flavor was at police academy, one night just lay down in the big brass bed, comfortable in the clean white sheets, closed her eyes, went to sleep and never woke up.

We leave what we know, Flavor thought, and we go on a journey, a necessary journey. Like the line in The Song of Hiawatha that her grandma had quoted her in act of what Flavor now knew was incredible courage and unselfishness.

'Leave thy father, leave thy mother, leave the black tents of thy tribe apart.'

When at last she regained a normal childhood, she turned to books and to learning as a hungry man to food. When she reached high school she was the brightest kid in class. At graduation her Grandma's smile was so big, she told Flavor: 'I could've spanned the Mississippi river with it."

She was lucky — she knew that now — she got a scholarship from a black students' fellowship to study psychology 2,000 miles away at the University of California at Los Angeles, the famous UCLA.

She was 18 years old and terrified. She had been away from home just once, on a high school quiz team trip to New York city. She had never lived alone, or with anyone other than her grandma, and she had no brothers or sisters.

But, 'Leave thy father, leave thy mother, leave the black tents of thy tribe apart.' Her grandma had said it to her, that night before she left, when she didn't want to go, didn't want to leave home, leave Mississippi. When Flavor just wanted suddenly to maybe get in a local college, and come back in three years as a schoolteacher. To settle here, near the river, to have status, a black girl who made good, who the small town could be proud of. The world was large and frightening.

Her grandmother had understood her fears, and understood too that the fears must be overcome: "You gotta go girl. You'll never forgive yourself if you don't. Has to be a time for goodbyes. Remember Hiawatha."

"I never knew you could recite poetry, grandma."

And her grandmother had smiled that gold-toothed smile, and replied with some mystery and some satisfaction: "Lot of things I know that you don't know I know, girl."

So she got the bus to Memphis and the plane to Los Angeles, big, bewildering, brown-smoggy LA. But she loved UCLA, the people, the course, the sheer BIG-ness of mind and thoughts and horizons after Mississippi. It was, literally to her, another world. And what the scholarship fee didn't cover, she earned by working long evenings in a hamburger joint up on Sunset.

The students called them 'Mcjobs' with some disdain. And when she got home to her shared apartment a long bus ride away in Inglewood, late at night, with the taint of food on her, she'd look in the mirror and remind herself.

"You're doing a mcjob now, Flave, so that you won't spend the rest of your LIFE doing a mcjob."

Then as graduation approached, she realised with the feeling of someone standing on the edge of a precipice that she had not the faintest idea what she wanted to do as a career.

Until one day she saw a newspaper recruitment campaign for the Los Angeles Police Department that laid special emphasis on highly-qualified ethnic minority entrants, offering fast-track promotion for the right people.

And it hit her like a bolt from the blue. Police officer! Why not? Cops in Mississippi had always been the ENEMY, red-faced white boys, with just a sprinkling of what her people always called 'tame niggers'.

But here in LA, she knew it was different. This was a multi-ethnic city, black, white, chicano, asian, it was like the melting pot America always fondly imagined it wanted to be.

To go home to Mississippi a police officer, a *Los Angeles* police officer. And if she could make a difference, actually make a difference to what went on out there, if she could stop things happening to people that had happened to her.

Her decision was reached on perhaps that factor above all the others. So she applied, was interviewed, was accepted, went to police academy and qualified.

She worked as a patrol officer in East LA for two years, made sergeant in three, and exactly five months after her 28th birthday, she made Lieutenant. She knew a lot of the other cops in the department resented that, felt that it was an ethnically-biased promotion, and maybe it had been.

But she knew she was GOOD at what she did, good enough to qualify on MERIT, not on race, whether the people who promoted her had understood that or not.

And she didn't just LIKE the job, she LOVED the job. In five years she had become the job and the job had become her. She was Flavor Cartouche, police officer, it was her identity, the soul of her. She could not imagine being anything else.

She knew her people had to see black cops, see GOOD, HONEST black cops in senior positions, see cops acting without fear or favour to all races, it was the only way.

And Flavor believed in law and order, believed in it passionately. It was a noble cause in an age when noble and cause were both dirty words.

She had not been back to Mississippi for two years, but when she had returned she'd seen the look in people's eyes in her home town when they saw her. She was not just the black girl who had the college degree, she was the black girl who went to Los Angeles, to UCLA, the Lootenant in the Los Angeles police force, who had been interviewed on CNN when during her time as a detective she had helped nail Hans Tooter, Mr. Chocolate Chip.

And their faces said: We're proud of you.

"Ma'am?"

155

She came out of her reverie with a start: "I'm sorry, one ticket for the 7.15 performance of Bob Roberts, please."

She bought a tub of popcorn and melted butter, and a Pepsi, and settled in her seat. When the lights dimmed, she realised she wanted this right now. To sit, cocooned in the comforting womb-like darkness of the cinema, and be transported into another, more colourful world, a world away from corpses, boats, drowned girls and severed heads.

And anyway, she wanted to OGLE, there was no other word for it, Tim Robbins. There were precious few white guys she found attractive, but Tim Robbins was one. The movie started. If McCall was 15 years younger, she thought, and if he lost 20 lbs, and if – hell, no, NO-ONE could look as delicious as Tim Robbins.

Flavor did not see who tailed her, who observed her lost in thought, then buying the ticket. Who followed her into the cinema, and settled, just three rows behind her.

She did not see who watched her, and not the movie.

McCall opened a tin of Purina and fed Madonna, then he showered, changed and went back downtown. There he put a call through to Sermon on the Mount Productions in Atlanta, Georgia, identified himself, and asked to speak to Joseph Angelli.

He was connected to a woman with a deep Southern drawl, who insisted on calling him back to verify his identity. When she was satisfied she said: "Sir, Mr. and Mrs. Angelli are in London, England, for talks with British television." I'll just BET, McCall thought. They are scared, and they are running.

"Do you have the number there please, ma'am?"

"Yes I do, but I am only releasing it you because you are a police officer, you must give me your word you will not give out the Angellis' location or this number to any other party."

"You have my word."

"You realise they are eight hours ahead, it is one a.m. in London right now."

"Yes ma'am, I do. May I have the number, please."

He got it, then severed the connection, accessed the international code, and tapped out 44 71 836 1533.

There was an electronic pause, then a strange, repeated brr-brr, ringing tone. A correct male British voice said: "Good morning, Savoy Hotel. May I help you?"

"This is the Beverly Hills Police Department in California, please connect me to Mr. Angelli's room please." He put the receiver under his chin and waited. After several rings a sleepy yet suspicious voice answered: "Yes?"

"Mr. Angelli, I am sorry if I've woken you. My name is Lieutenant Rory McCall, of the Task Force dealing with the angel killings."

"You say."

"Mr. Angelli, you are at liberty to call me back to check my identity – "

"Hold on." There were muffled voices, a plastic slither sound as someone put a hand over the telephone, a male voice, a female reply, and at last Angelli came back on the line: "What's your partner's name?"

"Lt. Cartouche."

"Are you big or small?"

"Big."

"Yeah, you sound like him, but we have nothing to tell you, so leave us alone. And we won't be here to tomorrow, so don't even try to contact us."

"Mr. Angelli, listen to me for a moment. You and your wife were guests in 1966 on a boat called The Little Prince, owned by Kirk Nielsen . . ." he heard the harsh, amplified intake of shocked breath.

"We have reason to believe – Mr. Angelli?" The line had gone dead. He called again, and when the Savoy Hotel answered the Angellis had beaten him to it. The man said the occupants of that room had left instructions not to be disturbed.

McCall wondered: Could he ask the London police to send a man down to see the Angellis? To ask what? To find out, what? It wouldn't work, not unless he or Flavor went to London, and by that time the Angellis would be long gone.

McCall and his wife had planned to visit Europe the year after they married. London – Paris maybe, Venice, Rome; and they would have if she hadn't got pregnant in the Spring. And when Helen was born they vowed they'd make the trip when their daughter was old enough to appreciate it. Somehow other things came up, they put the trip off, and now it was too late.

He consulted his notebook and punched out another number. Three minutes later he replaced the receiver. King Leonard of Jack and the Beans Talk would be happy to see Lt. McCall that evening.

McCall put his feet up on the desk and scratched his head. King Leonard had been on The Little Prince the night Kathleen O'Malley had died. He must have been aware, like the rest of Los Angeles, and increasingly the rest of America, what this murderer they called the Angel was doing.

He must have known before anyone the connection between the killings and guests on The Little Prince – of whom he was one.

So why was he so confident, so unafraid? Of course, McCall reasoned, he wouldn't need to be frightened at all if it was HIM doing the killing.

It had gone dark by the time Flavor emerged on the pedestrian precinct, which was now thronged with families and strolling couples.

People were eating and talking noisily at tables in the fenced off outside areas of the restaurants that lined the open-air mall.

Some shops were still open, and musicians played for coins and dollar bills, each player a sufficient distance from the other so that somehow the noise of a blues saxophonist, a guitarist with a twelve-string, and a violin trio near the Broadway Bar and Grill, seemed to complement and not clash.

She and Jack were regulars at the Grill, so the maître'd greeted her warmly and found her a table for two outside, up against the rough-brick walls.

Despite the earlier popcorn she was hungry, so quickly ordered Louisiana Blue Crab cakes with cracked mustard remoulade, Colorado Lamb with fresh mango chutney and grilled new potatoes, plus a glass of Burgess '89 Chardonnay.

The watcher saw Flavor take her seat and settle back with the wine.

The watcher waited.

King Leonard's house was Spanish Colonial with four corner turrets, and gardens overflowing with palms and bougainvillea. Concealed lighting suffused the shrubbery with a soft, orange glow, and arcs starkly highlighted the white walls, and the russet-tiled towers and roof.

There was the usual alarm system, but McCall could see no sign of any human agency guarding Leonard. The wrought-iron gates opened as soon as McCall announced himself over the inter-com, and he drove the MGB up the tiled drive.

Leonard was waiting to greet him, standing outside an open, nail-studded thick timber door. It looked genuine. McCall had the feeling the door had been looted from a turn of the century Spanish monastery and exported to LA to feed someone's Iberian fantasy.

He was a big man, McCall's size, but raw-boned, with not an ounce of spare flesh. Off to one side McCall could see the darkened tennis courts. He guessed Leonard must play every day to keep in that kind of shape.

In the gigantic living room was a massive, open, stone fireplace that stretched some twenty-five feet, and there was a minstrel's gallery off to one end.

McCall was offered, and accepted, a bourbon. Leonard opened a concealed refrigerator, took out a condensation-weeping can of Dr. Pepper and popped the tab.

"Cheers."

"Cheers. You must know why I'm here." McCall looked around. "And no lawyer? I thought you guys never moved without some highly-paid mouthpiece to protect you?"

"I don't need a lawyer. I have nothing to hide. I'm only surprised it took you so long to get the connection."

"You could have called, Mr. Leonard."

"You're the detective, I'm the television star."

"They say you're gonna be bigger than Cosby."

King Leonard laughed, revealed perfect teeth: "I couldn't live so long. Cosby is General Motors."

"And you're Chrysler?"

"I do OK."

"So why aren't you worried?" McCall sipped his excellent bourbon, "I mean, we both know what's going down here. Alassio was on the boat, Helm, Astaire. Even Smith, the guy the angel killed in the Valley."

Leonard gave a puzzled look: "Never got that one."

"Remember the captain, the Mexican guy? Smith was his kid. Changed his name later on."

"Aha!" Leonard tapped his nose with a finger, "that was the one that had me puzzled. I remember the kid, skinny, black hair, Christ he couldn't have been more than six, seven maybe."

"Yeh, seven or eight. Why aren't you scared Mr. Leonard?"

Leonard shrugged: "Why should I be?"

"If you were the killer you wouldn't be."

He shook his head: "It's not me. I think you know that. I have alibis for all the killings. Coincidental as it happens, but I still have them. If you wish I'll fax every detail to you tomorrow; venues, witnesses."

"That won't be necessary. Did you know that the Angellis have taken off to Europe?"

Leonard laughed: "There you go, could be them. I never did trust that new religious fundamentalism of theirs, and then there's the name. Angelli." He had the decency to smile.

"They were in Atlanta. Live television, remember?

Anyway, whoever it is, he'll want to kill you too." Leonard acknowledged the fact with a slow, deliberate nod of his head.

"Lieutenant, I'm sixty-nine years old. The handouts say sixty-four, but I was there when I was born and I had a long friendship with my mother, so I KNOW. Something will get me, soon. Cancer, a heart attack, stroke – Alzheimer's." He shrugged: "So."

"This guy chops your head off."

"Not if I can help it." Leonard put a hand under the cushion of the chair in which he was sitting, and pulled out a nickel-plated automatic. "I can use this. There's one in my bedroom drawer, another in the kitchen. And they're all loaded." He put the gun back under the cushion.

"Mind the help doesn't shoot itself."

"If he wants me, this Angel," he spat the word contemptuously, "he can try."

"Is it Nielsen?"

Leonard shrugged: "Could be, who knows?"

"You work for him."

"In a manner of speaking."

"Does he owe you favours?"

"No."

"May I?" McCall stood up and refilled his glass from the crystal decanter.

"Did Nielsen kill Kathleen O'Malley that night?"

Leonard took a long swig of Dr. Pepper: "Now YOU, have been talking to Wishaw."

Despite himself, McCall was knocked off balance, and it showed in his face.

"Come on Lieutenant, it's obvious. The guy is cracked, a screwball. He's obsessed with Nielsen, has been for twenty-odd years, everyone in Hollywood knows that. Except you, it seems."

McCall sipped his drink: "Seems he has reason."

"At the time, maybe. Nielsen didn't take too kindly to those accusations. I know he was a bit of an oddball where girls were concerned, but he LOVED Kathleen O'Malley, he was distraught when she died. I saw him at the funeral, I'm telling you."

"Wishaw says Nielsen ruined him."

Leonard swigged some more Dr. Pepper and gave a little sigh of satisfaction as though it was Chateau Lafite: "Think about it. Nielsen is a big star, suddenly this nut is accusing him of murder. He had to sue, he had to put Wishaw out of business, otherwise he would have been the laughing stock of Hollywood."

King Leonard squeezed the can and there was the metallic crack sound as it dented.

"And he was genuinely outraged that he should be accused of murdering the girl he loved. This town is about power. He had to show who was boss."

"He played rough."

"It's a rough town. But listen to everything Wishaw says and you'll end up writing in the margins of the LA Times and sleeping in Echo Park." He gave a good-natured laugh.

"Something happened on the boat, before O'Malley drowned, maybe? A party, under-age girls, boys? What happened out there?"

"Get outta here. My WIFE was on the boat. God rest her. Under-age kids?" He shook his head.

"Nielsen has a reputation."

"Sure he does – well, DID. A lot of stars banged young girls then, it was the fashion. Autre temps, autre mores."

"But he wasn't banging young girls that night, that what you're saying?"

Leonard got up, went over to the fireplace, leaned on the mantel, thought for a while, turned to face McCall.

"This between you and me? One on one. You don't tell the Press, and no scandal?"

McCall inclined the glass in his direction: "Sure."

Leonard walked back, took a deep breath: "It was a party, right? A private party. A party outside the city limits, on a boat. The captain and the kid had their own cabin, totally private, they didn't see a thing that went on."

"What went on?"

"Nielsen, me, Angelli, we had our wives or our girlfriends with us, OK, Helm was with some guy, but we all knew what he was, it was accepted. Cruze and Astaire were sharing a cabin."

"A lesbian thing?"

"More like a SMACK thing. Anyway, after dinner, we all partied. This is between you and me, right?"

"Absolutely."

Leonard put down the Dr. Pepper: "OK. We did a lot of drugs out there, that night. I mean, EVERYTHING, dope, uppers and downers, smack, mescaline. It was a pharmacist's vacation out there."

"Flying, huh?"

"Stratosphere, and now look," he held up the soft drink can like a white flag of surrender, "the wages of sin. I quit the booze shortly after my wife died."

"And no kids out there, no under-age girls, or boys?"

"Helm's chico could have been technically under age, but I mean nothing orgy, you know what I'm saying? The captain and his kid stayed out of the way, just like I said. After that, a private party, just the eleven of us."

A rocket fired in McCall's brain, illuminating his sky.

"You mean ten?"

Leonard faltered: "Yeah, that's what I said, ten."

"You said eleven."

"Slip of the tongue."

"With the exception of the captain and his kid you were ten. Nielsen and the O'Malley girl, two, Helm and Alassio, four, Cruze and Astaire, six, the Angellis, eight, you and your wife, that's ten, not eleven."

"Sure, ten." McCall could feel the chill in the room.

"You said eleven, Mr. Leonard."

A facial muscle twitched like a semaphore in Leonard's taut, tanned face.

"I MEANT ten!" The familiar face was tensed and

twitching with anger.

McCall got up and slammed the bourbon onto a polished side table so that the contents slopped onto the expensive surface.

"But somehow you said eleven, Mr. Leonard. And it's what, nearly thirty years ago, and just like that you can summon up the number." McCall clicked his fingers: "Just like that. That night must be emblazoned on your memory. And you said, eleven."

The sitcom star made a wild gesture with his hand, and the Dr. Pepper spilled through the drink hole onto the polished stone floor.

"Listen, McCall. I won't say this again." He enunciated each word, "It-was-a-slip-of-the-tongue. OK? Jesus, ten people, TEN. Maybe if Cruze or Astaire had a guy that night it would have been eleven, but it wasn't, it was ten. TEN!"

McCall thought he saw Leonard's hand moving slowly towards the cushion beneath which lay the gun. No-one knew McCall was there. He had told no-one, and he had been greeted by no servants, if Leonard was desperate enough . . .

"Touch it and I'll break your arm."

Leonard's hand stopped, and now, all composure gone, he was confused and blustering.

"The interview is over, Lieutenant. I tried to help you, I tried to be frank and co-operative, and look where it got me. You threw it back in my face."

"Why did you say eleven?"

"If you wish to talk to me again contact my lawyers."

But McCall was closing in; near enough to see the faint cosmetic surgery scars like cycle tracks around the jawline; to see the lines of re-planted and weaved hair that strode off across the scalp like the serried ranks of a vineyard.

Near enough to see the devil twins of fear and lie in the man's eyes.

"There was someone else on the boat that night, wasn't there Leonard?"

"You're crazy."

"Who was it?"

And, aware of what he was doing, the RISK, he took Leonard's jaw in both hands and squeezed:

"WHO ELSE WAS ON THAT FUCKING BOAT?"

CHAPTER TEN

On a hot, steamy summer day as she plays in the oozing river mud, the once-little girl, who is older now, tells her best friend her most secret secret.

Tells her the secret she has sworn she will never, ever tell. About the cellar, about the man who promised to banish the demons, but who simply brought others, about how she had believed him, and how she showed her gratitude, sitting there on the dusty, ex-Army cot, as the flashes blinded her.

And to her horror her best friend tells her that what happened was wrong, tells her the dirty, awful reality, tells it to her in shocked and awed whispers.

The girl cries for days, cannot tell her grandmother the reason, for the man is still there in the village. He looks at her each morning as he walks down to the river, looks at her like the Devil himself.

And one day, months afterwards as the sad girl sits, as she normally does when there is no school, in the circle of women as they gossip, laugh, smoke, chew and spit, she hears a tale so horrible, so wondrous, she feels the hair on her scalp prickle.

The next day, and in the hot languid summer days that follow each other sluggishly like footsteps in the glutinous Mississippi mud, she starts to make her doll.

She fashions it with care, sewing the scraps of material so they represent as closely as possible the coveralls the man wears, and the threadbare red-checked shirt beneath.

With broken off pieces of straw she plaits with nimble girl fingers an imitation of the straw hat with which the man covers his head from the noonday sun. Then she adds a wisp of red thread for the scarlet bandanna he wears around his throat.

She steals the needles with the care and patience of a graduate of the academy of deceit, one every two days, so that her grandmother will not notice, steals them until she has six, the prescribed number.

The moon is full this night, and she is ready as she sits alone on her rough bed in the tiny room, listening to the cacophony of crickets.

She inserts each needle, one, two, three, carefully into the man-doll, as she remembers from the story of the women; then four, five and six.

She takes the doll and lowers it, face forward into the enamel wash basin full with limpid water. Watches it float, doll arms out, circling slowly.

And that night she sleeps fitfully, fearing, dreading, that what she has done will work. At the same time, with a child's contradiction, praying for the success of what she has done. But the next morning as she sits on the step, the man passes and looks at her as before.

The eyes say: Do not tell.

For a whole week he passes her, and she knows she has failed, that the old women knew nothing, and in her bed she weeps with shame and humiliation.

But the next day the man is not there, and at noon a cry

*goes up, there is shouting, men and women rushing past her,
down to the river.*

*She follows, one hand nervously to her mouth, the other
clutching at the hem of her cotton dress. And she sees the
corpse, sodden, torn and bloody.*

*The girl looks in fear and awe at what she has surely
done. That night she waits to see if the demons are banished
by her killing of the man.*

That night the demons still come.

Flavor was startled.

"Finished ma'am?"

She looked up, quickly at the waiter: "Yes, I have. I'm
sorry, I was thinking. I didn't hear you."

"Dessert, coffee?"

"No, no thank you, I'll take my bill please."

She was slightly frightened, as she always was at these
momentary trance-like interludes, seconds of what she could
only put into words as 'otherness'. And now there was a slow
crawl up her spine, like an insect tracing gossamer feet, and a
sensation in her brain like – what was the phrase? – like
someone just walked over her grave.

She looked up, around her, a feeling, indefinable but very
real, that watching eyes were on her. But she saw nothing,
just throngs of people walking in the warm night air,
listening to music, people laughing and chatting, eating and
drinking.

Witch? She laughed inwardly and derisively. If you're a
witch Flavor how come you can't find the Angel? She paid
with her Visa card and set out for home.

The watcher was ahead of her now.

The elevator stopped and Flavor crossed the hall to her
apartment door, keys ready.

The lights went out. Total blackness.

She stood stock still, her skin instantly clammy with fear.
Slowly, carefully, she transferred the key to her left hand,

and with her right now free, she slid the Smith and Wesson from its shoulder holster.

There had never been a power failure in the halls or elevators of this building as long as she had lived there. It could, of course, be mechanical failure, but she was taking no chances.

She turned, slowly, carefully, putting her back against the apartment door. She could see NOTHING. She had never realised how totally enclosed this landing was, there was absolutely no light source.

Flavor heard the hum of the elevator descending, and knew that it was not a power failure in the whole of the building.

The sound diminished and there was total silence around her. From somewhere outside she heard the distant wail of a police siren.

It's an accident Flave, a power failure, a fuse or something. She traced an arc in front of her, tracking the barrel of the Smith and Wesson back and forth.

There was a sound off to her right like something dropped.

She spoke the words more confidently than she felt: "If there's someone there you'd better show yourself buddy, because I'm about to start using this gun."

Only silence.

Had she imagined it? This was like being blind, she had never realised before what being blind must be like. She had seen this hallway and landing so often she imagined she must know it back to front.

But now she could not remember how close the elevator was, or where the buttons were. She knew she had her back to her door, but at what level was the lock? Slowly she brought up her left hand behind her back, searching for the lock.

Then a torch beam stabbed from the darkness like a laser, blinding her, dazzling her, and a voice said: "Are you OK? We got a blown fuse."

And after the shock had rippled through came the wave of relief. The janitor. The beam shone like a lifeline to safety and she moved towards it, her free hand groping into the light, the gun held out at her side and pointing to the floor.

A mistake.

A warm, animal, human thing, flesh, a hand, closed around her mouth, and a blow like iron jarred her wrist, sending the gun spinning from her grip.

And with a stab of terror that turned her bowels to water, she felt the sharp point pierce the skin of her neck, and the warm, almost incontinent feel of the tiny rivulet of blood that flowed from the instant wound.

A voice said: "Say hello to the Angel."

McCall drummed his fingers on the desk and waited impatiently for the bleeps, then left his message: "Me. Call me before you leave. It's urgent. There was someone else on the boat, someone we didn't know about. Don't go to New Hampshire 'till you've spoken to me." A pause, "It's ten now. CALL ME!"

He replaced the receiver.

Flavor said: "What do you want?"

"You."

It was just a shape and a man's voice in the darkness of her apartment. She could see the light that filtered into the room from the street below reflect dully off the steel of the blade he held.

"I don't understand."

"You do. I want you cop bitch. I want your pussy. You're trying to find me. I saw you on the TV." There was a short, manic giggle. "I found you instead." And the short giggle, like a punctuation mark.

"You're famous. Aren't you Flavor?"

"I don't think so."

She had no gun, he had the sword, cutlass, whatever it was. And it was razor sharp, she could still feel a tiny trickle of blood where he had pressed the point of the blade into her skin.

A blade like that could cut off –

She stopped. She tried to still her emotions, to suppress the trembling hands and the tremors that shook her spasmodically. Fear was an enemy, fear was his ally.

"It's so easy. You wait for the elevator, fuse the lights, place the torch opposite from you on a timer. I've done it before."

"Are you Nielsen?"

"What?" There was a note of peevish anger in the voice.

"Who are you?"

"I'm the Angel."

"You said you wanted me, I don't understand."

The shape moved closer in the gloom and she could hear the sexual rasp of his breathing. He was exposed and erect.

"Like it?"

"My God."

"Why shouldn't I? Women like you, coloured women, niggers, harlots, Jezebels . . ." She could almost hear tears of rage and frustration.

She tried to act to save her life.

"You want me."

"You deserve me. Are you a dyke? All fucking black women are dykes. I'll fuck some sense into you."

"Sure you will."

There was a dangerous swish and thwack in the darkness and she felt the movement of air close to her face and realised the man had wielded the sword. If it hit anything, tissue, muscle, bone, tendons. She shuddered.

"Can I call you the Angel?"

Silence.

"When we do it, can I call you the Angel?" God help me, help me.

"Do you like – " she hesitated a long, deliberate, second "movies?"

"Filth, all of them," the man lisped, she heard it as an

effeminate and soft squishy sound.

"Yes, they should be – eradicated."

"Eradicated."

"The police confiscate movies. I confiscate them. They are filth and trash and perversion and I confiscate them so people will not be corrupted. I keep them, to protect people."

She felt she was going insane, there in the darkness, trading words with a psychotic sex killer. She could imagine the blade cutting into –

"You keep them? Here?"

"Yes, I keep them, sometimes I look at them when I'm alone to see what filth they are. Depraved."

Silence. She waited, listening to the rattle of his tortured breathing.

"Some of the things, men with girls, young girls, men with two girls, black, white, men who – "

"They're here, in this room?" His breathing was quicker, harsher, he made small grunting noises. Was he doing something to himself in the darkness?

"On the shelf – hundreds of them. Shine your torch." The man shifted in the darkness, there was a click and the torch beam painted light across shelf upon shelf of video cassettes.

"I'm going to kill you – afterwards, do you know that? I'm going to make you kneel and chop your fucking bitch head off your body."

She shivered in mortal terror. Her voice, not her, just her voice said: "It's your right to kill a bitch."

The grunts intensified. She said, quickly: "Have you ever seen them? The bad ones?"

The torch beam went back and forward, lingering like a voyeur over the racks.

"So many," the voice said, in a kind of awe.

"Would you like to see one – before – "

"Filth!" the voice cried, "filth!"

"Yes," her voice was almost a plea, "that's why I keep them, because no-one must see them. Only the special ones, the ones who are pure, the ones who cannot be corrupted."

"The Angel is pure."

"Yes, then you shall see one, before – ?"

The torch beam snapped off like a broken spear.

"Before."

Flavor moved tentatively: "May I take one down? I need the light to see the titles."

One second, two, three. Just silence. Five, six, she realised she was holding her breath.

"Take one."

The torch beam snapped on and Flavor moved hesitantly into the light. Praying now, praying fervently, Hail Mary, Mother of God, Blessed Art Thou Amongst Women.

Please Jack let it be there. Please, God, please Jack, please Clint, please Harry, please God. PLEASE. She stopped. The title on the spine said: Dirty Harry.

"Wait." She froze. The beam moved like a finger, up and down the box.

"That is a movie about a cop. A bastard faggot cop with a big gun."

She turned into the light that blinded her, turned into the glare, into her destiny, and lied with all her face, body and heart.

"The title is for the uninitiated. It is for those who might otherwise stumble upon it and be corrupted. Beneath this, only the pure can see."

She couldn't see, she was blinded, tears streaming from her eyes as the long seconds went by.

"Take it."

She pulled down the box, flicked open the plastic VCR container. Please God, I love You, PLEASE!

Her hand reached inside, pulled out the thirty-eight Special, turned and fired twice into the light. The blast was deafening, drowning out all but the highest pitch of the animal howl of pain.

And then she began to scream and scream until she found the light, and saw at last the broken, bloodied pathetic thing that had held her captive.

McCall held her hand, gently: "He's not our man. He's not the Angel."

She looked up at him, fearfully: "The sword, the things he said . . ."

"He's a psycho with a history of sex offences, done time in Soledad, and been living in a half-way house at West Covina for the last year. He'd seen you on the TV and developed a kind of fixation."

"How'd he know where I lived?"

"Dunno, but he has a history of tracking females, getting into their apartments. You're lucky."

She nodded. "I'm lucky all right."

"Who put the gun there?"

"Jack. It's her little joke. You know, Dirty Harry, come on, punk, make my day."

Madonna came up and nuzzled at Flavor's hands, licking her with a rough tongue. Flavor picked her up and held her — close.

"Is he alive?"

"Yup. One shot missed him — you have a BIG hole in the sofa, your second smashed his scapula, that's probably why he shouted so loud."

"The sword?"

"One of those short-bladed Samurai things, he bought it out of a catalogue."

"It was sharp." She rubbed the Band-Aid on her neck.

"I'll bet. Want to stay here tonight?"

She looked up at him: "Would you mind? I'm not sure I could spend the night in that place, not after this. Jack comes home tomorrow, but I'll be in New Hampshire."

"You're crazy, after this? Anyway, there's statements, and we've got the Press and TV on our backs."

"A good reason to go to New Hampshire."

"Whatever. Drink the rest of your brandy and crash. You can have the bed, I'll take the sofa. Don't worry Flavor, clean sheets!"

"I'll feel kind of safer, knowing you're here."

"Pleasure."

"Night. Hey, you were going to tell me something."

"It'll keep."

He bedded down on the sofa. Maybe it was crazy, but HE felt safer – no, not safer, what? More secure, more comfortable, more like a FAMILY? – knowing SHE was there.

McCall was asleep in an instant, and did not dream. The next morning when he tiptoed in gingerly with coffee, she was sleeping like a child with the covers pulled up to her chin.

So was Madonna.

CHAPTER ELEVEN

"My sister was in love with Kurt Knudsen, and from everything I saw he was in love with her."

Outside in the small schoolyard, the cries of the children were like excited seagulls, and in the warm, cosy classroom, dust motes danced in the stream of sunlight playing on the Stars and Stripes.

"It was a long time ago, Miss Watkins."

"Yes, I admit that," the schoolteacher said, taking a long, errant strand of greying hair and pushing it back into place, "but those kind of things you don't ever forget."

Flavor twiddled her pen over the blank page of her notebook: "The locals believe he killed her and made it look like an accident caused by the storm."

She gave a contemptuous snort: "Kurt was MY sister's boyfriend, I knew him. These people around here, the type who gossip. Nothing but ignorant, superstitious fools. They'd burn witches if they could."

"But why would they say such things?"

"Because he was better-looking than they were, smarter than they were, he was going places and they were going nowhere. It was jealousy, plain and simple."

Flavor wondered if Miss Watkins had been in love with her sister's boyfriend. Maybe still was?

"Your sister was a strong swimmer. How come she drowned and he didn't?"

"He was a lifeguard, for God's sake. He swam in all weathers. Eileen was good in the water, strong, but it's one thing swimming in a pool or in calm weather, another when the waves are as big as a boat, and it's hailing and raining. And that water is cold out there."

"You don't think he could have saved her?"

She shook her head: "If he could, he would have. I saw that boy afterwards. He was distraught. He'd swum with her holding on, he'd pulled her along. He'd done everything humanly possible to save my sister. He was exhausted too, remember, she slipped away, went under, he tried to find her, but he couldn't."

"And you believe that?"

"Yes I do. I remember that day like it was yesterday. It was late afternoon, and I knew they were out in the rowboat, and I knew they'd go far, it was the only damn place they could be alone, without Dad or some other busybody trying to find them . . ." she paused, and looked at Flavor. "You know about that?"

"Sure, we'll come to it."

"I saw the clouds, they were like ink, and low, right over the lake. It was spooky. You could see the rain coming down like a curtain, then hail, the water was churning up."

There was a higher than normal cry from one of the kids, and Flavor saw her head come up, like a bird that has sensed danger to its young. Then the cry subsided, and she relaxed.

Flavor said: "It wasn't forecasted?"

The schoolteacher shook her head: "No. There was no warning. He couldn't have planned it, if that's what you were driving at."

Flavor remained impassive. The woman continued: "I don't suppose that funny little man from Los Angeles – oh, come on, Lieutenant, don't think I didn't know who sent you here, everyone knows about that snoop – I don't suppose he told you the GOOD things about Kurt Knudsen?"

Flavor stretched awkwardly on the tiny desk seat: "Why don't you call him Kirk Nielsen? He's been that for a long time now."

She pulled a little face: "I guess to me he'll always be Kurt Knudsen. Even when I see him on the TV or the movies, I don't think Kirk Nielsen, I think Kurt Knudsen."

"What good things?"

"Like the lives he saved out there," her mottled, age-spotted hand waved towards the window and beyond to the sheet blue expanse of the lake."

"How many?"

"Four people in ONE Summer, and one of the kids was just five. Each owe their lives to the man you think is a murderer."

"I didn't say that."

"You didn't have to. I watch the TV. You're coast to coast, Lieutenant Cartouche." The teacher pushed her spectacles up momentarily from the bridge of her nose and massaged each side of her nose, and under the eyes. She coughed nervously. She HAD been in love with Nielsen, Flavor was sure.

"He had sex with your sister when she was under-age. Statutory rape. He was charged, but someone persuaded her to drop the charges."

Miss Watkins pointed to her bosom: "Me. I persuaded her, and she only made the police statement in the beginning because Dad MADE her. There was no other complainant. Even the Laconia Police Department was embarrassed by the whole thing. Kurt was the most popular kid around."

"She was under age." Flavor said it doggedly.

"How old are you, Lieutenant?"

"I'm thirty."

"Then you're lucky. You don't know what it was like then. All good girls were virgins, and if you slept with someone you were a slut. Sure Eileen was under age, in New Hampshire! If she'd lived in Georgia or Virginia or somewhere she could have married Kurt and had a couple of kids."

"You're saying she was a willing party to what went on?"

"Very willing. She consulted me. She loved Kurt, he loved her. He respected her. He didn't try to force her into anything, it was a decision they reached. They didn't flaunt it and they took precautions."

"Who found out?"

She looked out of the window, out to the lake and to her youth: "Dad. He found a rubber contraceptive in her handbag and went wild. He went through his own daughter's handbag, can you imagine that?"

"He went to the cops?"

She nodded: "He insisted she made a statement, virtually forced her to. He used to use a hickory stick on us when we were kids, you know. Anyway, I talked to her. She knew Kurt could go to jail. It would have finished him."

"Was that the only pressure she got – what about Nielsen?"

"Kurt? Dammit it all he couldn't come within a mile of the house. Police instructions, and if he HAD, Dad would have shot him."

"So no pressure."

"Just good sense."

"What about the rowboat?"

"It was a while later, and things had calmed down, the charges had been dropped. After all it was the only place they could get some peace and quiet."

"Do you think they had sex out there?"

"Well they were crazy if they didn't."

"She could have threatened him, held it over him, said she would tell unless . . ."

The teacher's look was triumphal: "Unless what? She

LOVED him, he loved her. The day she came of age they were going to get married. Believe me, there was no mystery out there that day. I don't know how any of this fits in, but Kurt Knudsen was a fine boy, and he's a fine man."

A hand-held school bell began to clang, and outside a woman's voice called the children back to class.

Miss Watkins said: "Look, I'm sorry, but I have a lesson right now. I'm not sure what else I can tell you."

"You've been kind."

"Talk to the male morons in this town and you'd think Hollywood was Babylon."

"Hey, I live there and I think that."

The older and younger women laughed together.

"Will you see him soon – Kurt, I mean?"

"Yes, I suspect I shall."

At that moment a little schoolgirl head poked around the door and called: "Miss?"

The schoolteacher called kindly: "Hi, Maureen, just form a line outside the class and you can enter shortly." The little head disappeared.

"Is he a suspect?"

"W-e-e-ll," Flavor tipped the flat of her hand, back and forth, "he IS connected to all the deceased."

"He didn't do it. He wouldn't do that. He's not capable of it."

"Sure?"

"Absolutely. He couldn't hurt a living thing. Beneath all that macho tough-guy, he's soft as ice-cream."

"I hope so."

"Will you give him my love? Tell him we could do with a visit from our favourite son."

"Of course." Flavor eased her legs from beneath the desktop.

"Thanks for everything."

"You're welcome." They shook hands. As Flavor reached the door, Miss Watkins said: "You know Kurt has a big sister, right here in town."

She turned: "I didn't know that."

"She's in her Seventies now, a little frail. If you speak to her I should be circumspect. She doesn't follow the news."

"Yes, I'll do that. Where does she live?"

"Somewhere on Jefferson, up in the 1200s ..." the teacher thought for a moment, "try 1220, if it's not that, someone will know her, she's lived there most of her married life. She's widowed now."

"Thanks."

"She'll tell you just what I told you. And maybe it's not what you want to hear."

Lottie Hansen nee Knudsen told Flavor just what Miss Watkins had told Flavor, and Miss Watkins was right, it wasn't what Flavor wanted to hear.

She realised that what she wanted to hear was that Kirk Nielsen was a psychotic maniac who had deliberately murdered Eileen Watkins, then gone to Hollywood and murdered Kathleen O'Malley in much the same way, and was now murdering everyone he thought might be aware of that fact.

Flavor realised she wanted the simplest of solutions, and Nielsen was the simplest of them all. A double murderer who killed to silence either witnesses, blackmailers or both.

Instead she was being told what a nice guy he had been in his previous life as Kurt Knudsen. She was tired from the long trip from LA, stiff from sitting for almost six hours – in Coach – she just wanted a long, hot bath, a Marlboro, maybe a Scotch, and instead she was sipping execrable tea served to her by a 72 year old widow.

And as it went dark outside, the woman showed her the mantelshelf collection of framed pictures of her brother. Nielsen in a late Sixties studio black and white publicity still; Nielsen in Army uniform and forage cap; Nielsen in high-school football rig, leather helmet pushed back on his head, smiling broadly; Nielsen in bathing drawers perched on a lifeguard's high chair.

Lottie had not seen her brother for ten years. He rarely came East and she was too frail to make the trip to the West coast.

Flavor felt tired, drained, above all, disappointed. She looked at her watch, cleared her throat and coughed politely.

"Well, Mrs. Hansen. Thank you for the hospitality. I guess I must be going."

"You're quite welcome. You know, I have to say I think it's just perfectly fine that the police force has coloured women officers now. It's not before time."

Flavor thought, Wow! She said:

"Thank you. But actually black people refer to themselves as African-Americans now."

"Do they really? African-Americans. Yes, I suppose that IS logical, since your forefathers came from Africa. You know in my day I have to say that the coloureds were not treated well at all."

"No, ma'am. Well the world has changed." She put her cup down, "I guess I'll be heading back to the motel now."

"Oh no you won't, young lady," Mrs. Hansen poured more tea, defiantly, into Flavor's cup: "It's not every day I get chance to talk to a coloured – I'm sorry, what was that – ?"

"African-American," Flavor said, gloomily.

"Yes . . . police lieutenant from Los Angeles, and besides, you haven't seen all the pictures of Kurt."

She started to rummage in a small black box on a table next to her, and even in the gathering gloom Flavor could see what looked to be a whole pile of family photographs.

It was look-at-the-happy-snaps time, and there was no way out of this one.

"There he is at age eight months." One by one the old woman handed over the curled, age-faded snapshots, and the darkness grew deeper.

And one by one Flavor glanced politely, murmured something inconsequential, and wondered to herself why it was that old people seemed to live in permanent darkness.

Nielsen at two. On his tricycle. In the bath. Held by his mother, a sour faced woman with a hatchet jaw. On his father's shoulders, hands on the man's head.

"This was at a fancy-dress party, I think he was about ten." Flavor took it, looked politely, looked again, squinted in the near-darkness, held the picture even closer.

"Mrs. Hansen, could you put a light on, please?"

"Of course. You want to see better." She fumbled with a lamp next to her, there was a click, and suddenly Flavor could see the snapshot.

It was black and white, faded so it was almost sepia. It was the young Kirk Nielsen, real name Kurt Knudsen, in costume.

He was dressed as an angel.

He had wings, and a little halo that seemed to be held up by some wire that sprouted from behind his neck. And in his right hand, what chilled Flavor to the bone, he was carrying what looked to be a real sword, or bayonet.

She looked up at the old woman, who was pleased to see her visitor taking such an interest: "How old did you say he was when this was taken?"

"Oh gosh, I just said so, didn't I? Ten, I think."

"What kind of fancy dress party was it?"

"Heavens, I have no idea."

"Why was he dressed as an angel?"

"I don't for the life of me know. Some kids like to be pirates, cowboys, Kurt liked to be an angel, I guess?"

"An angel?"

The woman put her hands to her forehead as old people are wont to do when trying to remember.

"It's more than fifty years ago, I don't . . . well, yes, he had a craze. Like all kids, he had a craze. We had some religious books, with illustrations, angels, heaven, that kind of thing. I think he was rather taken with angels."

Flavor looked again at the picture: "Who made the costume?"

"Mother and me. The wings were a wire frame, I think,

and we put material over it, then we put kind of straps so he could put the wings on." The woman gave a little childish clap of hands: "Oh, we spent such a long time making that costume."

"Why is he holding a sword?"

"Sword?" Flavor handed the picture over for the old woman to see, and she put on her spectacles from the side table: "Oh, the sword. Well, actually it's Dad's bayonet. He brought it home from the Great War. He was in France you know, oh yes, Argonne Wood. He was a hero."

Flavor said slowly: "Why does Kurt have it? Angels don't carry swords."

"Dad let him play with it when he played angels."

"How the hell – excuse me – how do you play angels?"

The woman said: "Don't worry about me, I'm very broadminded. But you're not drinking your tea."

"I'm sorry," Flavor picked up the cup and took an impatient sip: "How do you play angels, Mrs. Hansen?"

"Well, I think it was like pirates, you know. And in one of those books – they had big illustrations – and in one of them, the angel must have had a sword. Maybe it wasn't an angel, but Kurt was just a kid, maybe he got mixed up. Heavens, I don't really know."

There was a tight feeling around Flavor's throat. She said: "Do you still have the book?"

"Goodness, I wouldn't know. I shouldn't suspect so. When Mom finally died we divided all the stuff up, and I think Kurt took the books. Yes, I think you'll find Kurt has all the books."

"Thank you."

"There was a set, and they were bound. In leather. They'll be worth a lot of money now. A collector's item."

"He liked playing with the sword?"

"Bayonet," the old woman corrected her, "from the town of Bayonne in France, where it was first invented."

"Forgive me. He liked playing with the bayonet?"

"Until Daddy took it off him, that was a shame, I'm sure

he never intended – " the woman stopped, gave a little smile, "still it's all a long time ago. Water under the bridge."

Flavor leaned forward, into the musty, slightly-damp, old-person smell: "Something happened? What didn't he intend?"

"He never meant it, I'm sure. He wouldn't harm a soul."

"What-didn't-he-mean, Mrs. Hansen?" Flavor said it almost as one word, through gritted teeth.

"Killing Napoleon."

"What!?"

"That was his name, Napoleon."

"Your brother killed a boy named Napoleon with your father's bayonet?!"

The old woman gently smacked Flavor's hand, like a mother admonishing a daughter: "Don't be silly. Not a boy. Napoleon was a rabbit, Kurt's pet rabbit."

Flavor released a long-held-in stream of breath.

"Kurt killed his pet rabbit – accidentally?"

"Yes."

"How?"

"It was an accident?"

"HOW, MRS. HANSEN?"

"I'm afraid he chopped poor Napoleon's head off."

McCall pinned Wishaw to the supermarket car park wall by the frayed lapels of the man's sports jacket.

"Your source for all this shit on Nielsen was José Andrade, right?"

Wishaw nodded, affecting nonchalance: "Sure he was my source. How did you know?"

"Because you were at his funeral." He freed a hand, took out a crumpled clipping, and read from it. "Long Beach News, July 16, 1969, funeral report of José Andrade. Mourners include a K. Wishaw."

"Poor old José, I knew the booze would get him eventually. I first met him when a friend of mine chartered a boat, and José was the captain. I liked to pop a few cold ones in those days. Then after the death of Kathleen O'Malley I saw his name in the news reports. I remembered him, and I had my suspicions about that night. So on a hunch I went down to Long Beach. I knew he hung out down there, and I figured if anyone knew what went on that night, it would be him."

"And why should he tell you and not the police?"

"Because the police meant trouble with Nielsen, like I said. And I knew José was a lush. He wasn't exactly discreet the first time I met him. The cops should've got him loaded, at a certain point drunks just talk and talk. They can't help it. Anyway, he wasn't hard to find, he used a bar called the Tahiti in Long Beach. McCall, can you put me down please?"

McCall released him, and made a pretence of brushing down Wilshaw's crumpled lapels: "And he gave you the dirt on Nielsen."

"He'd heard a scream in the night. It woke him, he stayed awake a while, then he heard feet on the deck, whispering." Wishaw paused. "Then a splash."

"That's all?"

"Isn't it enough?"

"No. Why didn't he tell the police this?"

"Like I say, he knew how powerful Nielsen was."

"But he told YOU?"

"In vino veritas, McCall, it means – "

"I know what it means. Why didn't you tell me Andrade was your source on this?"

"Because Andrade's dead, he's out of harm's reach. But he had a kid, he'll be a man now, I didn't want to put him at risk in case Nielsen found out."

"Too late, Wishaw, he did – or someone did. The guy in the Valley, Richard Smith, was Andrade's son."

"Shit!"

"You got it. What exactly did Andrade think went on that night?"

Wishaw shook his head, fumbled in his pockets for a pack of cigarettes, lit one and inhaled deeply: "Wasn't sure," he exhaled a stream of smoke, "except that he had an instinct that something strange was going down out there. After dinner he's packed off to his cabin, him and his kid. During the night he hears a scream, and then, the next morning a major movie star is drowned. He didn't need a picture."

"Does Nielson know how much you know, or THINK you know?"

"He knows I KNOW. And I DO, McCall, I KNOW it's that motherfucker behind all this."

"Then you'd better watch your step." McCall put his arm around Wishaw, and it wasn't a friendly gesture. "In the meantime, come for a ride with me." He motioned to the MGB: "You ever been in an English sports car?"

"I start work in 30 minutes, I haven't got time for a pleasure ride."

"It's not a pleasure ride." McCall motioned to a payphone at the end of the supermarket wall, "Call in." He produced a quarter from his pocket: "It's on me."

McCall held up a glossy black and white photograph of a group of mourners seated to one side of a casket. On the back of the photograph was a red stamp that said, Los Angeles Times.

He jabbed a finger at the mourning group: "Her, the one in the headscarf and dark glasses, who is she?"

Wishaw took the picture: "Heather O'Malley, Katherine's kid sister. The funeral was on the TV news at the time. She was a kid, an actress too. She wept through the whole thing. She shared an apartment with Kathleen."

"How old is she here?"

"Fifteen or sixteen, slightly older maybe. Can't quite remember, but she was a kid, I remember that. Kathleen looked after her, like a mother to her. So I'd read."

"You said she was an actress?"

"Yeah, I think it was her sister got her work, nothing major. I think maybe she did a couple of pictures with Kathleen."

"Like East River."

Wishaw gave McCall a long, strange look: "Yeah, like East River. What is this?"

"She was on the boat that night, did you know that?"

"No, I swear." Wishaw was shaking his head vigorously, stepping backwards, as though being accused of some crime.

McCall waved the picture at him and the light caught the gloss: "If you're lying to me I'll fuck you over from here to Thanksgiving."

"I swear." Wishaw looked as though he was telling the truth, "she was on the boat? Jesus. NO-ONE knew that. You mean Nielsen kept that quiet from the cops? There has to be a reason for that."

McCall gave him a withering look.

"Thank you. You said Nielsen had the hots for Heather too, and that he liked them young. Well, this was the perfect perv's dream. Two sisters, one under age. I truly believe he was screwing them both." McCall paused: "Probably at the same time."

A look of real pain, like a dark cloud, passed over Wishaw's face, but he quickly recovered:

"Who says she was on the boat?"

"Someone who was there."

"And he tells you now, why?"

"I persuaded him. What happened to the girl, where did she go?"

"It's a long time ago."

He saw the dangerous gleam in McCall's eyes. "I swear to God, I don't think anyone saw her again after that. She went back East, or to the Mid-West or someplace."

"And that was it, right, you never heard of her again?"

Wishaw hesitated.

"This is your thing, Wishaw, you know every spit and cough. You never heard of her again?"

"Look, it may be nothing."

"Try me."

"Variety, early Seventies. Just one of those things, I was

browsing through. There was a cast list for a movie being made on location in Missouri. I can't remember what it was called. But one of the cast was called Heather O'Malley. It struck me, naturally. But O'Malley is an Irish name, I'll bet there's thousands of them."

"If she's still alive, I'll find her."

"How?"

"I'll ask the gardener. I've a hunch he knows."

Wishaw looked justifiably puzzled.

Jack's voice echoed over the 3,000 miles: "You owe me a new sofa."

"With pleasure."

Her voice became serious: "You were lucky. Are you sure you're OK?"

"The trip did me good. And there's movement on the case, I think it took my mind off what happened."

"Thank God for the gun, I mean, I'm a card carrying liberal, but if we hadn't, if I hadn't put . . ." her voice quavered, and Flavor could almost hear the tears.

"Hey, Jack, come on, I was the one it happened to, no point in YOU getting upset."

"My home, the thought of someone coming in to my home, saying those things, God."

"So let's drink to Dirty Harry. That was inspired."

Jack seemed to perk up: "It's re-loaded and in a new place."

"Magnum Force?"

"Don't even try to guess. Tell you when you get back."

Flavor heard her flight called: "Gotta go."

"Shall I wait up?"

"Forget it, I have to see McCall."

"Maybe you should move in with him."

"Jesus, that was uncalled for."

"That's all I hear from you these days, McCall, McCall, McCall."

"I WORK with him, Jack."

"Yeah, so I see."

There was a pause and just the electronic amplification of their breathing down the line. Flavor broke the silence:

"How's The Heart Devil coming along?"

"I had to write a new final scene, in 24 fucking hours, damn near had a nervous breakdown. But they shot a lot of stuff, and they're happy with the script – at last. I didn't mean to snap at you, honey, I'm sorry. Can we have dinner tomorrow night? Just you and me, a cosy night in?"

"It's a date." Flavor put down the receiver and headed for the departure gate. In the Santa Monica apartment the telephone rang within seconds of Jack replacing the receiver, and she lifted it thinking maybe Flavor was calling again.

It wasn't, but she knew the caller, and agreed to a meeting.

McCall sat across the table from Beverly Hills' most famous and celebrated TV horticulturist. But this wasn't the slow-talking, full-of-wisdom gardener the public knew and loved.

This was not the Jack who talked to the beans and to whom the beans talked back, who knew the folly of material-ism and the essential emptiness of the Me generation.

This was mega-star King Leonard with his lawyer and a tape-recorder and a look so formal he must have worn it last for a funeral. The tape was running.

McCall said: "Mr. Feldman, I should like to thank you for making your client available for interview so soon after my request."

"Noted," Feldman said.

"I have some questions."

King Leonard's eyes flickered to his lawyer. Feldman said: "For the record my client has instructed me to issue a $5 million dollar law suit against you, the Beverly Hills Police Department, and the Los Angeles Police Department, for violation of his civil rights under the constitution of the United States, for assault, injury, harassment, and emotional strain, following your unprovoked attack on him at his home, and for which he is, as of this moment in time, receiving counselling."

McCall said: "Bullshit."

"I beg your pardon?"

"Your client is attempting to obstruct a murder investigation. He's lucky he's not in jail. He's also very lucky he has not yet become a victim of a serial killer."

Feldman ignored him: "I am, as of this moment in time, seeking your suspension from both the Beverly Hills Police Department, and this murder investigation. I wouldn't be surprised if there is a criminal prosecution." He leaned forward and pressed the pause button on the tape: "You're history McCall."

He let the tape run on.

"And let the record show that my client is ONLY here today as a public-spirited citizen anxious to uphold the law."

McCall took out his handkerchief, blew noisily, pretended to examine the non-existent contents, and put the handkerchief away.

"You told me that Heather O'Malley, sister of the deceased Kathleen O'Malley was on a boat, the Little Prince, that night Kathleen O'Malley died. You told me that Heather, an under-age person, took narcotics. I wish to know where Heather O'Malley is now. Mr. Leonard?"

Feldman said: "My client has no knowledge of the whereabouts of the named individual. Furthermore, my client denies that he gave any such information of the type you describe, even uncautioned and despite the considerable duress under which you placed him. He was the victim of an unprovoked assault by you while in his own home. Your question is therefore irrelevant and insulting."

"Look at me Leonard." The star did, and McCall could see he was frightened. "I think Heather O'Malley could be a significant witness in the Angel murders. I think she was present on a boat belonging to Kirk Nielsen off Catalina Island in 1966 when her sister, Kathleen O'Malley, drowned.

I have reason to believe that the events on the boat that night have a material bearing on the killings currently taking place. So I ask you again, do you know where Heather O'Malley is now?"

Leonard put his hands together, and slowly, rhythmically gave derisive applause.

"Quite a speech Lt. McCall."

"I need to know."

Leonard looked at Feldman who nodded imperceptibly.

"For the record I have no idea of the location of the named person, nor whether that person is living or deceased. Neither have I ever said, nor do I believe, that she was on the boat that night. That is an elaborate fabrication, a figment of your fevered – and possibly insane – imagination."

Leonard sat back in his chair with a smug grin of satisfaction that the tape could not record.

McCall moved away to the window and looked down eighty feet to the flower beds and neatly-clipped lawns. An automatic sprinkler had laid a mini-rainbow across the grass.

He knew it was the end. There was no other way. He had to find Heather O'Malley. McCall turned around, walked over to the door of the interview room and locked it, putting the key in his pants pocket.

"What are you doing?" It was Feldman.

"Shut up, Feldman, you two-bit shyster lawyer. You've been corrupt for as long as I can remember, taking fat fees to let people walk the streets who should be behind bars. You should die soon."

Feldman grinned with genuine pleasure: "The tape is running, Lt. I believe the last might just constitute a threat to my person."

McCall took the recorder, walked to the window, opened it, and dropped the small machine to the lawn below. It burst in a little explosion of black plastic and brown spools of tape.

"You're finished, McCall. Like I said, history. You're Stone Age, a dinosaur. Cops like you are over."

McCall took out his handcuffs from his back pocket, grabbed one of Feldman's wrists and snapped a cuff on it. Feldman squealed and McCall cuffed him across the face with the back of his hand.

"Shut up." The lawyer was dry with fright. McCall then snapped the other cuff on an exposed pipe that ran down one corner of the room.

Leonard said: "Jesus, he's crazy."

He walked backwards, badly scared, back to the window. McCall followed, picked him up around the waist and began to feed him head first out of the open window.

He screamed.

McCall said: "Tell me where she is."

Leonard croaked: "You're crazy. You won't do it."

McCall said: "Yes, I am; and I will," and then he fed more of the TV star out of the window until his head, torso and thighs were hanging into the abyss.

"Please!"

"Tell me!"

"I don't . . ."

McCall released his iron grip a fraction, and more of Leonard slid into space.

"Please God, I – "

"Where IS SHE?"

Leonard was making hysterical, terrified, squealing noises.

Feldman began to holler in a dry, parched call, and McCall heard someone rattling the lock of the interview room.

"Five seconds."

"I can't, she'll – "

"Four, three . . ."

"If I – "

"Two . . ."

Leonard was held just by his ankles now, and someone was putting their shoulder to the door.

"One . . . TELL ME!"

Leonard told him.

CHAPTER TWELVE

Flavor turned her Skylark into Havenhurst and as she approached McCall's apartment, realised there was a gaggle of bodies gathered on the sidewalk outside his apartment block.

She pulled over, found a parking place, and it was then she saw the TV cameras, the microphones, and the expensive professional Nikons.

She got out of the car, locked it, and they saw her, recognised her, turning as one body, moving like some wriggling creature of assembled parts across the road towards her, blocking traffic, shouting questions. Car horns started honking.

Flavor said briskly: "First thing. Back on the sidewalk, let the cars through." Like naughty kids, somehow individuals again, they sheepishly obeyed. She said: "Now, what is it?"

A female reporter from KTLA asked: "Lt. Cartouche. Do you have any comment to make?"

And Flavor said, genuinely puzzled: "On what? I've been out of town."

"On Lt. McCall's suspension."

Flavor said inside: Oh, Jesus, what has he done? But recovered enough on the outside to say: "I have no comment at this time, until I have spoken with Lt. McCall." Then she pushed through the questioning mass, aware that the TV lights were switched on now, the video cameras running, the flash guns banging away, and what the TV reporters would say in their front-of-camera pieces: "Despite his suspension, Beverly Hills Police Department's Lt. McCall was visited at his West Hollywood apartment late last night, by his former colleague and joint Task Force co-ordinator, Lt. Flavor Cartouche of the LAPD. On her arrival, Lt. Cartouche refused all comment. She spent . . ."

Flavor rang the bell, and heard McCall's slurred voice over the intercom: "Go away, no comment." Luckily the mikes didn't get it, and she breathed: "It's Flavor, open the goddamn door."

When she got into the building his apartment door was on the catch, and when she let herself in, found him in the kitchen with a full glass of bourbon in his hand.

Without preamble she said: "What the FUCK is going on? The ratpack tell me you've been suspended. Is this some kind of a joke?"

He waved his drink, and some spilled onto the linoleum. He gave a mock bow, and she thought: He is LOADED.

"Regretfully not, Flavor, regretfully not. Badge, gun and future are all now in the possession of the Beverly Hills P.D."

"And you're off the case?"

"Could be I am OFF to jail."

She sat down:

"Tell me."

"W-e-ell, remember King Leonard?" She nodded: "He gave you some stuff you were going to tell me about."

"Yup. Well, I got that bit by threatening to squeeze his immaculate chops into porcelain fragments. Breach of all regulations, of course. But even THAT couldn't persuade him to tell me what I REALLY wanted to know. So I told him unless he came downtown with his lawyer I'd arrest him then and there, call the Press, and let them photograph him being thrown in jail for the night.

'He couldn't bear that and having his famous Hollywood ass messed with by the animals in the tank, so he turned up with his overpaid Gucci-shod little shyster legal eagle in tow. And suddenly, my oh my, not only was he struck dumb, Flavor, but I was facing a telephone number lawsuit and the threat of them going for a suspension."

"So you threatened him?"

"I figured if I was going to be suspended, and then lose every cent I had to a bunch of shark lawyers I might as well get good value for money."

"Jesus, you didn't hit him? They must make them dumb in Detroit."

"Yes, quite so, Flavor of the month," McCall took a gulp of his drink, made as if to gargle it mouthwash-style, then swallowed it noisily, "Dumb I think is what they make them. But actually, hitting was mild by comparison."

"Oh my God, what?"

"Oh my God it is. But I NEEDED that information, NEEDED it. It was vital, and I tell you it is going to break this case – for you, of course, since as of about noon today I am history, to quote Mr. Feldman."

"What DID you do?"

"To persuade Jack the Giant Killer, or Jack Frost or whatever he calls himself, to talk I . . . well; basically I held him out of the window by his ankles and threatened to drop him unless he told me what I wished to know."

"Tell me you're kidding."

"Read the Times tomorrow."

"You're beyond belief. Where was his lawyer while this was going on?"

"Feldman? Oh, he was handcuffed to the hot water pipe."

197

"You are absolutely beyond belief."

"How long does it take to pay off $15 million dollars if you're paying monthly, OUT of a job and IN jail?"

She couldn't help it, she laughed: "Oh well, let's say I'd start founding a dynasty fast."

"Do they have a Western Union office in San Quentin?"

"You're very drunk McCall."

"Utterly correct."

She went up, took the drink out of his hand, and there was no resistance as his fingers opened for her. She poured it into the sink, came back, took both his hands in hers, and looked into his eyes, expecting to see some beaten-dog look, some hopeless dispiritedness.

Instead there was a fiery reflection of a kind of dogged victory, and that puzzled her.

"That stuff isn't the answer."

"Maybe not."

"You dumb, DUMB, shit. What did he have that was worth going to jail for; losing your job and your career for?"

"Kathleen O'Malley's sister, Heather, was on the boat that night. She was the wild card. They had a narcos' party out there, every kind of drug imaginable. I think Nielsen was screwing both the girls, probably at the same time. And I think all the victims in this case knew that Heather O'Malley was on the boat, too. Maybe they were involved, some orgy thing, God knows. And who knows what else they knew, something they probably got killed for, even after all this time."

She held his hands out in front of her, like a mother with her child's hands, gently raising and lowering them as she spoke:

"And you think if we can find Heather, and she sheds some light on how her sister died, it'll finger Nielsen, and then put all the angel killings into perspective?"

"I do, I do. Sweet Molly Malone, I do."

"Oh, McCall. Was it REALLY worth doing what you did?"

Her hands felt good. Comforting, like a mother's hands. He felt a bizarre kind of peace. And he thought about what she'd asked. Had it been worth it? Had it, really? He looked up at her, noticing the texture of her skin, the milky white of her eyes around the brown pupils.

For a long second he wished that the case would never go away, that the angel would go on, that they'd always be one step behind him, and that way, he and this woman would somehow always be around one another. He just liked her being there. He liked her stroking his cat. He had liked seeing her chin over the top of his sheet as he brought her coffee the morning after she had stayed over.

He liked her touch – what was it that a woman like her brought to a place, to a person? That transformed it, made it, and him, more than the sum of their parts?

And he hated himself for enjoying her touch, her company, the civilising essence of her presence. For he knew he had forfeited the right to have such feelings.

And was it all worth it? The end of a career just to make a reluctant witness tell what he knew, something that MIGHT make the case come good?

He thought of the suave evasions of Leonard, of his silence and lies even as people who had been his friends were dying; of the smug certainties of Feldman and his kind, the warped new centurions, protecting the guilty, shielding their clients behind the intricate woven parapet of legal technicalities, delaying tactics and downright lies, and of all that had brought criminal justice in the United States into such disrepute.

He said: "Yes, Flavor, it was worth it. It was the only way."

"Your career is effectively over, you realise that? After the kid in the riots, now this – there's no way out of this one. Even if you don't go to jail you'll never be a cop anywhere in LA after this, perhaps nowhere."

He sighed, like a very old or very sad man: "I realise that. Well, it had to end some time. Police officers have a shelf life, and I am, way, WAY past my sell-by date."

"I think you're probably the best cop I've ever met."

He flopped heavily on a battered kitchen chair, as though suddenly weary: "Thank you for those few kind words."

"Do we know where she is now?"

"Now this is what was worth them taking my gun and badge. Heather O'Malley is right here in this little ol' town."

"She lives in LA?"

"Been right under our noses."

Flavor let go of his hands, and he felt an almost physical sense of loss. She said:

"I'm tired, McCall, it was a long flight, and I have information of my own. You're loaded, I'm sober, and that makes it worse, so please, just tell me where she is."

"Tell ME what you found out in New Hampshire."

Flavor straightened up and went to the fridge, pulled out a Tres Coronas, flipped the top, took a long pull of the ice-cold beer and said:

"TELL ME!"

"Available to millions through the miracle of the cathode ray tube, a star of the small screen, a character beloved of the American public."

And suddenly the drunkenness vanished like a mask from McCall's features and the knowledge was like sobriety on his face.

"Heather O'Malley, under age partaker of narcotics on Kirk Nielsen's boat, witness no doubt to her sister's death, is now none other than – Sarah Ziegal of Pacific Coast."

"This is serious?"

"It cost me my job, it'd better be. Faced with falling eighty feet face first to the ground, King Leonard, volunteered – " McCall laughed, "that O'Malley changed her name in the mid-Seventies. He further vouchsafed that she and Nielsen have been thick as the proverbial thieves since then, and no doubt way, way before."

Flavor said: "Shit!", with genuine admiration.

McCall said later over the coffee: "The TV will call it crisis talks."

"They can call it what they like." She took a long gulp of the scalding, refreshing coffee. "How are we going to work this now?"

"Work what?"

"The case."

"I'm suspended, damn it."

"Not by me. We're in this together."

"I can't be seen to be doing anything official. Can't question, no access to files, and if they think you're co-operating with me they'll burn your butt too."

She shook her head: "Uh-uh. Suspend BOTH cops in charge of the Angel case? Then they WOULD look bad. And I'm black, McCall, politically correct, above suspicion."

He looked at her, searching for irony, cynicism, candour?

"So – what do we do?"

"I'll think on it? Anyway, I'm pretty sure now that it IS Nielsen. All we have to do is prove it. Maybe he didn't drown that girl in New Hampshire, maybe it was coincidence. But a kid who dresses up as an angel, who is obsessed with angels in a book, who decapitates his pet rabbit with a bayonet. That is TOO much of a coincidence."

She poured them both more coffee. The kitchen clock said 3.10. Outside it was pitch black and quiet. Even the media mafia, who had lurked like hired assassins, had now gone home.

He drank some of the coffee and grimaced as it sloughed the bourbon off his tongue:

"Yeah, it HAS to be. He has the kid sister on the boat and no-one is told, not the police doing the original investigation, not the coroner, no-one. It's the best kept secret of the whole affair. Then little grieving Heather goes to ground, and turns up years later as Sarah Ziegal. No way he can claim he wasn't aware of that. She just HAS to have something on him?"

"Which makes her, King Leonard, and our friend Mr. Wishaw, the next ones on the list, right?"

"Right, should we pull Nielsen in now – correction, will

YOU pull him in? You could get a search warrant for his home on probable cause."

She thought, chewing her lower lip: "OK, he lied about Heather O'Malley, but that was 1966, and this is now. I'm not sure anyone would or could take action against him now. King Leonard has withdrawn what he said about drugs being on the boat, and as you're on suspension for allegedly threatening to kill King Leonard, no-one is going to listen to YOU. If we – I – pull him in, all he has to do is sit tight behind his lawyer, and we're nowhere."

"So we – I can't stop saying that – go to Ziegal."

"Yeah, I'll buy a nose-peg."

"Don't get it."

"You will if you ever meet her. That lady has an odour they could bottle to ward off skunks."

"A big TV star smells?"

"To the Heavens," Flavor finished her second cup of coffee, draining it: "I gotta go. Actually, it's a weird smell, I've never smelled anything like it before. McCall, can a smell be creepy, you know, kind of make you feel scared?"

He shrugged: "Dunno. People say you can smell fear, but this is not the same thing."

"I'll call you. In the meantime get a good lawyer. I hear Feldman is available." They laughed.

"Seriously, could you get gaol time for this?"

Again he shrugged: "It's possible. It's assault, threats to kill, forcible detention – that's Feldman – yeah, if they wanted to throw the book."

"But you think you can work a plea bargain to avoid going to gaol?"

"I'm hoping it won't even get to court. You know, I suddenly feel a pressing need to retire on the grounds of ill-health. I'll agree to take counselling, do some community work, you know the way it goes. I won't be the first cop to take that road. And I didn't actually DROP him. I'm a sick cop, under strain, still crazed by grief – "

"What?"

"You know, strain of overwork, stuff – "

"You said grief, what grief? Is there something I don't know, McCall?"

He smiled, easily, amazed himself at how easily deceit came: "Angel victims, you know, seeing them up close, decapitated bodies. Yeah, I think I might stay out of gaol, but it'll be close."

"Would you have? If he hadn't told you? Dropped him I mean?"

"To be absolutely honest, Flavor, I don't know."

"Then, McCall," her look was unflinching, "maybe counselling wouldn't be a bad idea."

The strains of Vivaldi's Four Seasons greeted Flavor as she closed the door of the Santa Monica apartment. She looked at her watch. It was 4.20, and she was utterly, utterly exhausted.

She realised that on the East coast, where she had spent the last three days, it was 7.20, and her brain and stomach were on Eastern Standard Time, not Pacific Time. She had risen yesterday at six, so now she had been up and awake for over 25 hours.

In addition she had spent almost six hours sitting in a cramped coach class seat, flying between Boston's Logan and LAX.

The living room was lit by two shaded lamps, and a small, fragrant candle still burned in an ornate Nepalese silver holder.

Jack often burned the candle when she meditated or did her Yoga.

The violin of Nigel Kennedy was dramatically, rhythmically well into the second movement of Winter, as Flavor called softly: "Jack, are you up?"

Only the deep sweeps of the violin. Flavor moved across to the sound system and shut off the music. She ejected the CD tray and checked the multi-disc container. It was full. Jack often put on five continuous hours of suitable music, usually classical, then relaxed and left it, even after she had retired to bed and fallen asleep.

Flavor, in turn, had become used to the distant lulling sound of Bach or Mozart as she herself fell asleep. It had always been strangely comforting, and now she instinctively re-started the music.

She called again: "Jack, are you asleep?"

The beauty of the music, the violin that seemed to sweep its bow across her very heart, the high-like buzz of exhaustion, suddenly made her feel like crying. Not from sadness or despair, or happiness or elation, just for the sheer act of it, like relief or relaxation, and she felt a moist tear form in the corner of her eye.

The smaller, occasional dining table against the balcony window appeared to be set, and a wine bottle stood near a plate. Flavor walked over. There was a glass with some red wine still in it. It was Banda Azul Rioja. On the table was a serving dish with the remains of what appeared to be a vegetable dish, and a plate, its knife and fork neatly arranged close together, side by side in the center of the plate, pointing away from the eater.

There was a coffee cup and saucer, virtually empty. A coffee jug, Flavor lifted it, there was still some coffee in it. She touched the jug with the back of her hand. It was cold.

Opposite was another place-mat, but no glass or plate or cutlery. But Flavor saw the tiny remains of a piece of food on the edge of the mat. And the chair opposite the eater was pushed back.

She went out and into the corridor, and into the kitchen, switching on the light. The double sink was empty. She knelt down and saw that the red light on the dishwasher was on, but that the machine had completed its cycle.

Flavor opened it. Her skin began to crawl. Inside was one matching dinner plate, one coffee cup and saucer, a coffee spoon, a knife and fork, and one wine glass.

Why had Jack had dinner with someone, and put THEIR dishes and cutlery, but not her own, nor the coffee pot, into the dishwasher?

Winter, the nadir of the year, the season when things died. Now, the violin strings seemed to vibrate on her skin, like chalk scratched down a blackboard.

She went out, up to Jack's door, and rapped with her knuckles, hard. "Jack!"

There was no reply.

She knocked again, then tried the handle. The door opened.

"Jack, are you asleep right now?"

The room was in darkness, but the blinds were partly open and civilisation's orange street glow illuminated the room.

Flavor's eyes adjusted, gradually, and she stepped into the large room. Jack's bed was near the window, and she called again: "Hey, Jack!"

And she stopped. It was bizarre. Jack was praying. She was on her knees next to the bed, her hands clasped in front of her. She was praying, but Flavor could hear no words.

"Jack," she called softly, "Jack, are you OK?"

But the silent, kneeling devotion continued uninterrupted, and Flavor stepped further into the room. As Jack's figure came closer, Flavor saw that her friend was praying, but with her head out of sight under the duvet.

One step more, and Flavor stopped. Rooted. Riveted. Unable to move, hardly to breathe, certainly not to speak. The fear, and the sheer horror of what she was witnessing, gripped her like a vice, and her heart felt like it was being squashed.

Jacqueline Romarin, Jack the screenwriter, gay Jack, who loved her, and whose love Flavor had just begun to learn she could never return in the way the woman wanted, was dead.

She had been decapitated.

And Vivaldi stopped. Winter ended, the Four Seasons died, and silence crept over the house like a black shroud.

Slowly, fearfully, hating herself, Flavor began to back out of the room, back to sanity and light. She wanted help, she wanted McCall and strong policemen in uniform. For this was the cellar, this was darkness and fear and madness and terror, this was the thing that she knew she had to confront, and could not, not now, perhaps not ever, and thus was in its thrall, a slave to its power.

But not now, not NOW, tomorrow I will confront it, but not NOW, please!

She realised when she got to the bathroom, that her teeth were chattering, and her hands were shaking like someone with a palsy. She sluiced water over her face, half-spat, half-vomited some dark bile into the sink, turned on the faucet and rinsed it away.

Flavor looked into the mirror. Coward, she said, cowardly nigger, chicken-shit jigaboo coward. Just like they always said in police academy. Can't trust the niggers, man, no spine, no guts, frightened of the dark.

Those rolling eyed caricatures of her mother's youth, Step 'n' Fetchit, and – coward: "Coward," she said it aloud, "shameful coward."

She went to the living room telephone, picked up the receiver, dialled 911, asked for the police, and then she saw it, standing next to the telephone, so close she had not immediately noticed it.

An angel. A carved wooden angel, just like the rest – except ... She picked it up, ignoring the female police dispatcher's voice that now filled her ear.

The angel was either painted, or heavily varnished, its surface covered in a shiny dark sheen. She held it up, into the light from one of the lamps. It was almost – almost black.

A black angel. It was meant for her. Tonight was meant for her.

Flavor wept.

CHAPTER THIRTEEN

The van stopped beneath the statue, and the occupants looked out through the smoked glass that muted the harsh day's glare.

"Tell her about your new playmate."

And the voice came, like a slither: "Yes. Yessss . . ."

McCall said: "There are no words I can say."

Flavor stood facing the sink, her body ice, numb, like some hanging carcass. Everything in her, every sense, every feeling, seemed to have frozen.

She said over her shoulder: "No, nothing anyone can say. Except, if I hadn't gone straight from the airport to your place, perhaps if I'd come here first, or . . ." her shoulders sagged hopelessly.

"Then you'd be dead. And in case you think it was either-or, you're wrong, she'd be dead too."

"Or I could have stopped it."

"Jack knew the killer, that's obvious. She didn't suspect.

She had dinner with him. What makes you think you would have known different?"

Flavor nodded, woodenly.

McCall said: "Did they check for prints, the plates, glasses – ?"

"Clean," she replied, dully, "only my prints, Jack's or our cleaning woman on anything. Whoever did it had the – " she hesitated, she wanted to say, had the OBSCENENESS, but instead said "– the sense to put their dishes in the dishwasher. And that, after you've just – " she couldn't bring herself to say it, "that is cold-blooded. This maniac has ice-water in his veins."

McCall put a hand out tentatively and touched her shoulder, and slowly she turned around.

"Did you check her diary, the answering machine, her friends, colleagues, did she tell anyone she was expecting – "

"No." Flavor's voice was hard, but brittle like dead wood. "She wrote nothing down, there's nothing on the machine, Jesus I only spoke to her that morning as I was leaving Boston."

"The telephone company – "

"We've checked all the outgoing calls for that day. Business stuff, her agent – and before you say it, anyone she called has an alibi for the evening."

"Does she know Nielsen?"

"Jesus, McCall, get a life, EVERYONE in this town knows Nielsen. Everyone who is in the business, anyway. Jack was a screenwriter."

"Did you check his alibi?"

Flavor's nostrils flared in irritation: "I cannot just go back to him each time – " she hesitated, "each time . . . this . . . happens, and ask him where he was. And damn it all, don't you think if it IS him he WILL have an alibi, given what he must know from King Leonard about what we know and suspect?"

McCall threw up his hands in a kind of defeat.

"If I was just back on the case."

"Well you're not." She brushed past him, went in the refrigerator and took out some Evian.

He stayed still, looking straight ahead, then felt her hand on his shoulder, and turned.

"Hey, I'm sorry, McCall. It's, I dunno, I can't think. It's like someone has stuck a knife in my side, and all I can think all the time is Jack, poor Jack, if only . . ."

He took the Evian from her, lifted a glass down from a shelf and poured her some water: "It's not your fault."

She took the glass and drained it. "It is, it IS my fault. You saw the wooden angel – black, goddamnit – this maniac wanted ME, not Jack."

She put the cool glass up to her forehead and rolled it back and forth between her hands, her eyes closed.

"He wanted ME. Poor Jack." She started to cry, silently, tears coursing down her face, and she angrily brushed them away with her hand.

"You need some rest."

"And you need to get the hell out of here." McCall turned. The voice belonged to one of the Task Force team, a cheerful Hispanic.

"Come on Carlo, I'm visiting with a friend."

"They'll burn you downtown if they learn you're here. You're suspended, don't forget. Then there's the Press."

"Give me a minute. No-one will see me leave."

"A minute." The detective left McCall and Flavor alone once more in the kitchen.

He stepped forward, and she put a hand up palm flat out, like a stop signal from a traffic cop: "Don't! I don't need comforting."

"We'll find him."

"Oh yeah?" her look was undiluted cynicism, "and then?"

"Then, what?"

"You know what'll happen."

"Sure. He'll go to the gas chamber."

"And that'll bring Jack back, bring Helm back, Alassio, any of them?"

"You're a police officer, you know the way it is."

"But he won't even go to the gas chamber, will he? I mean, no court is going to accept this guy is sane. It's a defence lawyer's dream isn't it? A guy who maybe dresses up as an angel, who keeps the heads of his victims? The trial will be a carnival of shrinks, each one outdoing the other for an explanation of why this guy is a poor, sick, misunderstood weirdo. He'll sit out the rest of his life in some hospital while Jack and the others . . ." She shook her head in a kind of bitter resignation.

McCall replied:

"It's never satisfactory. Hell, Flavor, I hate the system most of the time, but it's all we have."

"Says the man who somewhat breached the rules of interrogation."

"My cops are a different generation. You're the ones now, for God's sake don't start talking and thinking like me. As for Jack, well, all I can say is that time – "

"Oh come on, don't say time is a great healer. I expect that from a priest or the guy at the funeral home, not from you."

"I was going to say time is all you have. It might not work, but it's all you have."

She poured herself some more water, drank it, and laughed a bitter, hurting laugh. She looked up into McCall's eyes: "You're really not a bad guy, you know that."

He said grimly: "I've been here."

"Yeah, I think you have. Want to tell me about it?"

"Nope."

Flavor shook her head, side to side, side to side: "God, I actually just cannot believe she isn't going to be here. I mean, I saw her, saw her like – and I still cannot believe she's gone."

"You loved her, didn't you." It was a statement, not a question.

Flavor nodded, ruefully: "Yep, I loved her. Didn't realise how much until now. Didn't want to go to bed with her, she was gay, I wasn't, but I loved her. And, you know, she was a GOOD person. Sounds trite, but it was true. She never pressured, you know, the gay thing, not really."

"I wish I'd met her more than the once."

"Oh yeah?" Flavor raised an eyebrow, "she didn't like just about anything of you. I think she saw you as a rival."

McCall laughed: "I'll bet."

"Believe it. When a gay person is attracted to someone and they think that person is hanging round too much with someone of the OPPOSITE sex, then that is the worst rival of all."

"I can remember when it was boy–girl, girl–boy. The rest has passed me by."

Flavor gritted her teeth, trying not to cry: "Yeah, well, it's all water under that goddamn proverbial bridge now."

"McCall?" It was Carlo. "Better run, man, I heard on the squawk that the chief was on his way. If he finds you here and calls Bev Hills they might just have you arrested."

"OK." McCall said to Flavor: "You going to stay here?"

She gave a wild, lost look: "I don't know. I honestly don't know."

He leaned forward and squeezed her arm: "Whatever you do, call me."

"Yeah," she looked off through a curtain of tears, seeing nothing but the sea mist of her own misery, "I'll call."

For now the Mayor stayed still in his swivel chair as Flavor sat in front of his desk.

But he fiddled nervously with a sheaf of documents, shuffling and reshuffling them.

"Lieutenant, I can arrange for you to be taken off the case immediately. The chief and I are both in agreement on this. Just say the word, and you're off. This was a traumatising event for you, and you might feel you need some therapy or counselling. It is also clear that you have become a target for this maniac. We can organise protection."

Flavor was numb. It was as though her skin, her veins,

her very fibre was sclerotic. She sat with her hands folded into her lap, looking at the Mayor, but seeing through him, into the wall, and out into the strangeness of the future.

The voice that was hers, but that seemed to come from someone else, some automaton within her, said: "Sir, I would very much like to continue to lead this investigation, despite what happened – no, especially because of what has happened."

The Mayor said, kindly, but with what seemed like a reluctance that would become apparent shortly: "Well, of course, in view of what you have been through, and the work you have put in on this case, we will go along with whatever you wish."

"Thank you."

The Mayor coughed behind his hand, cleared his throat. He was embarrassed. Whatever he was about to say, was going to be difficult.

"Lt., under the circumstances, this is a little, you know, difficult."

"Sir, please say what you have to say."

"Well," he got up, clasped his hands behind his back, and walked from behind his desk, "I don't have to tell you what a field day the media has been having this week. Miss Romarin's, er . . . status, your friendship."

"We were room-mates, sir, that is all."

"Yes, of course, I'm less concerned, that is we are, the Chief, the City Council, less concerned with that, than with the lack of progress in this case. First there was the unfortunate business with Lt. McCall, now this. We were wondering if perhaps, fresh faces, a new – "

"No!" She was on her feet, and the ferocity of her reaction made the Mayor step back in alarm, "no." She deliberately softened her voice, "No sir. Please. Please do not have me taken off this case, not now of all times."

"I understand how you must feel. But we have not even had ONE arrest. This is a city living in fear now, and that is not a tabloid cliché."

"I'm aware of that."

"Will you ever find this angel?"

"I'm certain of it. Before he was suspended Lt. McCall came upon some new information. With that, and what I learned during my visit to New Hampshire, I believe we are on the verge of breaking this."

"Am I going to be privy to this information?"

"Sir, out of context it may not make a lot of sense. I hope you will continue to put your trust in me and allow me to reassure you that it is a significant step forward."

The Mayor sat down again behind his desk, fingering a long silver letter opener, absent-mindedly cleaning beneath his immaculate nails. "I seem to have heard something very similar from you and Lt. McCall before. The news that Victoria Astaire was a drug addict, theories of blackmail and counter-blackmail." He raised an eyebrow.

"We'll get him," Flavor said, doggedly, "and it would help if I still had Lt. McCall."

"Uh-uh," the Mayor shook his head from side to side, "this city has witnessed enough destruction as a result of police brutality to let another rogue cop stay on the streets. We'll be drafting another senior officer to work with you as soon as we can find someone suitable."

"Sir, I've never asked before. But is there something in Lt. McCall's background I'm not aware of, something that may have made him do what he did?"

The Mayor's face was grim: "I certainly wouldn't divulge any personal information on a serving police officer, even one under suspension. Anyway, he's not an employee of the City of Los Angeles, or its Police Department. It was an arrangement, remember that. I suggest you speak to Beverly Hills."

"Sir."

The Mayor coughed again, and swivelled in his chair to face his dieted portrait. "There's something else."

"Yes?"

He swivelled back to face her: "We naturally thought,

after – after what happened, that you'd want to come off the case."

"And?"

"You have to understand that the Chief and I are under tremendous pressure. This is news all over the world now."

"And?"

"You have thirty days, Lieutenant. No arrest, no charges within thirty days, you're off the case."

McCall didn't answer his buzzer and she saw him come jogging down from Sunset Boulevard, went in with him, and waited while he showered and changed into jeans and t-shirt. She brewed coffee.

He said: "Bastards. After what happened to Jack, how could they?"

She gave a look of resignation: "They were expecting me to fall apart with grief, and want to come off the case. I think they believe that crap in the Globe and the Enquirer, that Jack and I were fucking up some lesbian storm down in Santa Monica."

"Thirty days, huh? Well, we can do it in thirty days."

"It's we again now, is it?"

"Unofficially it always was. I want to show you something." He went to a kitchen drawer, brought out a brown paper parcel, unwrapped it and placed a .45 Colt Gold Cup automatic in the palm of his hand.

"They took my own gun, and I needed some firepower just in case the angel came calling."

"It'll be on Current Affair. Steve Dunleavy says suspended rogue cop in Angel case buys big gun. You're crazy."

"Nope. The guy I bought it from won't tell. It's legal, and I'm a resident of the State of California, but if he picks up a telephone and calls the TV, I'll pick up a phone and call the Feds, and he knows it."

"Blackmailer." She said it with as much light-heartedness as she could muster.

"It's a dirty old world, Flavor."

"Ain't that the truth."

They ate dinner on the terrace at the Silver Spoon. McCall demolished a steak, but Flavor just picked at a salad, and ate so little the waiter asked if everything was OK.

"Are you still at the apartment?"

Flavor shook her head: "Can't bring myself to. I've got a deal on a motel up on Wilshire. It's got a kitchenette, it's all I need for the moment."

"Yeah."

They drank coffee in his apartment, and Madonna sat on Flavor's lap while she and McCall discussed the case. Sarah Ziegal was at her home in Palm Springs, and the next day Flavor planned to drive there to interview her.

McCall said: "She'll know that you know. Leonard will have told her."

"Maybe. But this is a murder investigation. If she refuses to co-operate I can give her all kinds of trouble, not to mention telling the Press what happened. Neither she nor Nielsen will want that kind of trouble."

"Pity I can't come with you."

"Yeah."

They sat in silence for a moment, then Flavor got up, stretched, and said: "Guess I should be going."

"Sure. I'll walk you to your car."

"Bye Madonna." She stroked the cat under its chin and heard its gravelly purr.

On the sidewalk, she stopped, so suddenly that McCall almost collided with her. "You OK?" She said nothing: "Flavor?"

She turned: "I don't want to be on my own tonight McCall. I don't know why, tonight I mean. Well, I do know. I'm scared. Not of the angel, not of being killed, just scared. Of the dark, of being alone."

She stood stock still. Like a statue. McCall said: "Hey, no problem, you can stay. Glad of the company. Madonna'll love it. Come on." They went back into the apartment, he changed the sheets, made himself a bed on the sofa, they said goodnight and he settled down.

He must have fallen asleep, because he awoke with a start, her hand on his.

"I'm sorry, I didn't mean to wake you."

"It's OK? What's the problem?"

He could see her shape in the half-darkness. She was wearing one of the shirts he had handed her, and below its flap her legs were bare. He could smell her musk. And he thought, I can't allow myself the luxury of this. I can't allow myself to want, or to care.

There was a moment's silence in the gloom. Then he felt her hand close on his.

"I have to trust you, McCall. Please say I can trust you."

"I don't understand."

"I can't be alone tonight. I have to have someone near me, I CAN'T be alone. Just lie with me, on the bed, and hold me, hold my hand, but not . . . I can't – can you just hold me tonight? PLEASE?"

He closed his other hand around his and hers, and squeezed: "Sure, I can just hold you tonight, Flavor. It would be my greatest pleasure and privilege to just hold you."

And they slept like that, her back curved into him, his arm across her shoulder, holding her hand. Madonna lay curled in a furry ball at her waist.

In the night he woke, just once, and her bare neck was inches from his lips, and he remembered his promise, but he could not resist it, and he gently brushed his lips against her skin, and heard her murmur, groan, and move softly in her sleep.

And he said to himself. It is just one night. Even the wretched of the earth are not denied all happiness. And then he slept once more, and woke to the light. And as he did, as if on instinct she squeezed his hand and smiled.

McCall smiled too.

She came off Interstate 10 just before Thousand Palms and turned South-West, taking the six miles long narrow two-lane blacktop into Palm Desert. On the outskirts of the town she pulled in at a gas station, bought a local map, and located Redwood Drive.

It was on the edge of town, where civilisation met the desert, where swimming pools and sprinklers and lawns lay in uneasy proximity to sand and sidewinders and scorpions. 1419 stood in far larger grounds than its neighbours and the rear garden touched up against the lower slopes of a cluster of low hills, bare except for meagre scrub and cactus.

The driveway was a semi-circle, and there was a large multi-vehicle garage to one side of the house. Flavor parked, got out, and before walking to the porched doorway she stood on tiptoe and tried to peer into the garage through two windows in the wall that jutted out beyond the confines of the house.

But the glass was filthy, almost opaque with grease and dirt, and she could see nothing. She tried to clear a spyhole with a wet finger, and looked again. It was then she realised that there was black paper up against the glass. No-one was meant to look in.

She pressed the bell, and heard it ring dully, somewhere inside the cavernous interior. She waited, rang again, and after a few seconds saw the spyhole darken as someone peered out, then heard the rattling of locks.

Flavor had somehow expected a maid or servant to answer the door. But it was Sarah Ziegal herself. She was dressed in a towelling jogging suit and sneakers. Her hair was up in a bun, and she wore no make-up. Her face was lined and dried from the desert sun, and from encroaching middle age.

Flavor showed her badge: "Lt. Cartouche, Los Angeles Police Department. We met in Burbank."

Ziegal nodded: "Yes, I remember you." She stepped back: "You'd better come in. I will not say your visit is a surprise."

She walked in front of Flavor down a long, carpeted corridor, to a door, which she opened. Inside was a study, or den, with book-lined shelves, a fake antique desk, several armchairs, a small TV and a telephone.

Ziegal pointed to an armchair: "Please sit down." The window was covered by blinds, but through the slats Flavor glimpsed a swimming pool. The water looked an unhealthy green, and the paving around was overgrown. She saw weeds that had poked persistent fingers out from cracks in the surround.

"Well?" Sarah Ziegal put her hands behind her head and sat behind the desk in a stiff, upright chair.

Flavor got out her notebook, a tape, and then read Sarah Ziegal her rights. She replied: "I have nothing to hide, go ahead."

"Your real name is Heather O'Malley. You are the sister of Kathleen O'Malley who drowned off Santa Catalina in 1966. I'm correct in that?"

"I don't accept your definition of real. I was christened Heather O'Malley, but I changed it to Sarah Ziegal in 1972, which is everyone's right. I did not want to trade on the memory of my dead sister, nor be held back by it for that matter. Yes, of course, Kathleen O'Malley was my sister."

"I understand that you were on board the boat the night your sister died, but that you did not tell the police that at the time, neither did Kirk Nielsen nor anyone else present."

She paused: "Your erstwhile colleague forced that confession out of Mr. Leonard. It couldn't possibly EVER be used in evidence in a court of law."

"I'm not planning to use it in a court of law. You were on the boat, weren't you?"

"Yes."

"Then why did no-one say so at the time? You would have been a material witness."

The smell was there. Flavor had noticed it from the moment she had walked behind Ziegal to the study. It was less an odour, more an atmosphere.

The first time it had made Flavor want to gag, now it simply frightened her, made her almost physically draw herself in, tightly, her arms, stomach, knees, as though she was about to be attacked.

"Oh, be serious. WHY? Because I was under-age, because there were drugs on the boat, and drinking, a gay couple. Can you imagine what a field day the Press would have made of that? I'd probably have been carted off to some home."

"Were you part of it? The drugs . . ." Flavor paused, "the sex? Any of it?"

Ziegal threw her head back and laughed uproariously: "Don't be absurd. With Kathleen there? She was my big sister, she kept an eye on me. I just wouldn't go anywhere without her, and I wouldn't let her leave me behind. To be frank I think she would have been happy to. Kirk was her boyfriend. I think they would have liked some peace and quiet."

"How did Kathleen die? You were there, what happened?"

Ziegal tried to speak, choked on it, turned away, put her hand over her face, the fingers splayed, recovered, turned back.

"Yes I was there, and it happened just like everyone told the police. There was no mystery about it. OK, they didn't tell the captain I was there, and afterwards they didn't tell the police. I've told you why. I had a bunk in Kirk and Kathleen's cabin, it was the only place they could keep me secret. I must have been a bit of a gooseberry. I went to bed before them, I don't think I even recall them coming in – there'd been a party in the dining area – they were doing drugs, you know that."

"You approve of that?"

"I should care less. And Hell, it's so long ago who would care now? These days half Hollywood blows its nostrils out on a regular basis."

"Tell me what DID happen."

Ziegal ran a hand across her taut and puckered eyelids: "Who knows? Kirk woke me, about five o'clock, I think it was. He said Kathleen was missing. He'd searched the boat, couldn't find her."

"Did you look again?"

"Yes, bow to stern, woke up the rest of them, then the captain. She was gone. We launched a boat, it was foggy I recall. We called for her, everything."

"Did anyone radio the coastguard?"

"Yes, the captain put out a Mayday or something, you know, man overboard, or whatever it is they do."

"You're sure she and Nielsen were not fighting?"

"No, he loved her. REALLY loved her. If you're suggesting he did anything to harm her, you're wrong. As God is my witness he would never have harmed Kathleen. She was the ONLY woman he ever really loved. He loves her to this day."

"He remarried a long time ago."

"Maybe. That doesn't alter what he still feels for Kathleen, I'm sure of that."

Flavor took a chance.

"Are you aware that Kirk Nielsen is a suspect in the Angel slayings? We now know that every single victim was on that boat the night your sister died. And I think you know something you're not telling me."

"I'm afraid you're deluded. What reason would Kirk have for doing such terrible things?"

"Revenge."

"For what?"

"I don't know – yet. Perhaps someone was blackmailing him and he didn't quite know who, so he decided to kill everyone on the boat."

"Except there's nothing to blackmail him for, certainly nothing that went on that night. And I'm still alive, so is Mr. Leonard. So are the Angellis, as I understand."

"Narcotics? An under-age girl? That's reason for blackmail."

Ziegal waved a dismissive hand: "Come on, THEN maybe, but not 29 years later. I am sure there must be a statute of limitations on these things."

"You could become the next victim of this killer, don't you realise that?"

"I'll take my chances. I have no plans to answer my door to anyone carrying a sword who I don't know." She laughed carelessly and the facial lines stretched and strained like a safety net.

"But of course, if it was YOU, you wouldn't have to worry at all, would you?"

She pretended to seriously consider the question, and replied: "No, I don't suppose I would, but as I haven't killed anybody I don't think that applies. You haven't by any chance arrived with some secret evidence tucked up your sleeve that you propose to whip out like Hercule Poirot, have you, Lt?"

Flavor ignored the sarcasm: "When I questioned you at Burbank you lied about knowing Victoria Astaire. And she was on the boat too."

"Yes, I lied. It didn't seem like it. I hardly remember her from the boat, and the next time I met her was when I'd said, an episode of the Rockford Files, I seem to recall."

"You also told me you knew Jacqueline Romarin, my room-mate. Was that another lie?"

"Of course not. I knew her professionally, and only a little. The last time I saw her was down at Fox where she was doing some work on a script in turnaround. In fact it was shortly before Victoria Astaire died."

Flavor swallowed hard: "You will be aware Jacqueline Romarin was murdered?"

"Yes. I'm so terribly sorry. You and she were very close." Ziegal smeared innuendo like poison over the final word.

"And, of course, you will have an – "

"I was dining with Kirk Nielsen and his wife."

"If I thought it was you who killed Jack, I'd kill you personally, you know that?" The words slipped out like flatulence, gone in a moment's reckless, grief-stricken burst of temper.

Ziegal leaned back in the chair, head tilted backwards, arms and hands straight in front of her. It was almost like watching a wild cat stretch, or a cobra about to strike.

Then a near-beatific smile crossed her features:

"I will choose to overlook that, because I wouldn't wish you to end up in the wilderness like your erstwhile colleague."

"I've nothing more to say."

"Then," Sarah Ziegal spread her hands, "if you have no further business with me, I shall say goodbye."

She stood up. Flavor said abruptly: "Except – did you have sex with Kirk Nielsen when you were under age?" She paused: "And – or – since?"

Ziegal looked at her like she was a biological specimen. "Why, what a cess-pit world you must inhabit, Lieutenant. I think perhaps I'll take a leaf out of King Leonard's book, and have my lawyer present at any further interview."

"That's your right."

"But then, who knows, you might handcuff him to a pipe and threaten to throw me out of a high building in a bid to extract some confession from me."

Touché, Flavor thought.

She turned her car onto Maple, tasting the dead dregs taste of disappointment. As she passed the corner of Sycamore Drive, a church sat on a corner lot. A white clapboard structure with a spire of black wood spars, it seemed more appropriate for a New England village than a town in the low desert of California. A small scrolled board on the open lawn said: Church of the Holy Saviour. Pastor Emmett D. Lightower.

Flavor drove on, went downtown, saw a Denny's, parked, went to the counter and ordered coffee. This case was like a soufflé. It was risen and all puffed up and virtually-ready-to-eat, then someone opened a goddamn oven door and you had nothing.

She lit a Marlboro, and a stern looking waitress said: "I'm afraid you can't smoke here, ma'am." She pointed to a no-smoking sign.

"I thought at the counter . . .?"

"Whole restaurant now. As of yesterday." Flavor stubbed her cigarette out in her saucer and cursed. The Republic of California was turning into George Orwell's Big Brother state dressed in a nanny's apron.

She sipped her coffee, thinking about McCall, thinking about Jack, everything all mingled and mixed up like a kid's messed up meal. Last night had been good. For the first time since – what, EVER? – she had felt secure. It had been strange to feel the touch of a man, even a hand on a hand, after all this time.

Sometime in the night she had felt, in her sleep, what she thought was the touch of his lips. Perhaps she had been dreaming, but whatever the sensation was, real or imaginary, it had not been repulsive to her, as she had once thought it might, when the time came again. And then all she could see in her mind was Jack, dead, mutilated dear Jack, her remains in a morgue awaiting burial.

She had been so real, so substantial. Jack, with her million dollar spec screenplay deals, her committed gay propaganda, but her Platonic love too, her wisdom and her patience. Her woman's instinctual understanding, and the friendship she had hoped might become sexual love, and that was never to be.

And McCall, of whom Jack had been so jealous, and of whom Flavor knew she was so fond. Something was wrong there, something deep, something she couldn't get at. Trust him to get into trouble. That was his reputation, from even before she'd had to work with him. Quick Draw McCall, rubbing everyone the wrong way from deputies in Palm Desert to – . She stopped, put down her coffee, a strange tingle in her stomach.

What? That deputy here in Palm Desert, something he'd said when they'd interviewed him, something about the victim. What? Absent-mindedly she lit another cigarette, and just as quickly stubbed it out when she remembered.

How the widow of the dead man hadn't wanted scandal. How only she had known he was decapitated. And why?

Why? Well, what woman wouldn't want to keep it all quiet if her husband had been with another woman in a compromising situation, when he was killed? And. And, he was . . . a PASTOR! A pastor with the Church of the Holy Saviour in Sycamore Drive. And that was one block from Sarah Ziegal's home.

Flavor threw a dollar bill and some change down on the counter and left. The Church of the Holy Saviour was closed, but a passer-by directed her to a nearby house, the home of the present pastor.

Pastor Lightower had been at the church just two years, but he gave her the address of a church worker who had been a volunteer for over thirty.

The woman was a healthy, rotund widow in her early Sixties. Flavor gave her identity, and said she was making enquiries about the murdered pastor.

The church worker remembered it vividly, what a shock it had been for everyone, what a good Christian the pastor had been.

She went away and made them tea, and produced a plate of cookies to go with it. And gradually Flavor turned the conversation around to general things, life in Palm Desert, the summer heat, bugs, famous residents, Flavor not even sure quite what she was aiming at, at what she could discover.

"I hear that Sarah Ziegal from Pacific Coast has a home around here someplace."

"Sure does," the woman pointed towards her lace curtains, "a block from here on Redwood."

"How long has she had a place in this neighbourhood?"

"Gosh, twenty-five years, more maybe. Comes here a lot, she can't stand Los Angeles, that's what I heard."

"She ever visit the church?"

"Not now, used to. But not any more." The woman shook her head: "Sad business."

"The pastor, yes."

"Well, sure, the pastor, but her son dying like that, too.

He LOVED that church."

"Sarah Ziegal had a SON?"

"Sure did. Sweet kid, crippled, you know. Not quite all there. But he loved the Lord. He used to come to church in his wheelchair, his Mom pushing him, and his little face used to light up when we sang the hymns, though I don't suppose he could understand a word of them. I just hope the good Lord is looking after him right now."

"When did he die Mrs. Schumacher?"

The woman puckered her face, thinking: "Sometime in the Seventies, I can't rightly remember when. He was a sickly child, not long for this world."

"Can you remember how old he was when he died?"

Mrs. Schumacher shook her head: "Goodness me no, it was hard to tell HOW old he was, poor thing, all twisted up and crippled like that. Him all covered up, cold all the time, even here. Don't think I ever saw much more than his face and hands."

Flavor took her leave and drove back to Ziegal's home. Sarah Ziegal opened the door once more.

Flavor said, without preamble: "You didn't tell me you had a child, Miss Ziegal." The actress stepped back into the hall: "Come in." Flavor went into the hall, and once again the smell, the ATMOSPHERE, hung like an invisible mist in the room.

The woman closed the door, and turned to Flavor: "And should I have? Was my late son part of your enquiry?"

"I think just about everything is part of this enquiry now. Please tell me about him." They went back to the study. Sarah Ziegal rummaged in a drawer, took out a file, flipped it open and finger-walked through the sheafs of paper until she found what she wanted, extracting two documents.

She handed them to Flavor: "That's all you need to know about my son. His birth and his death. That is his birth certificate. He was born on August 24, 1962 in Ladue, Missouri." Flavor held up the document and scanned it. The name of the father was listed as: Not known.

"Who was the father, Miss Ziegal?"

"A rich man, a married man, now sadly a very, very dead man. Do you know Ladue?" Flavor shook her head.

Ziegal said: "It is a rather nice and expensive suburb about 11 miles west of downtown St. Louis. Kathleen and I were born in East St. Louis, which you may or may not know is actually in Illinois, across the Mississippi."

"What kind of upbringing did you have?"

"Well you could say that metaphorically speaking East St. Louis is also on the opposite side of the tracks – watery as they are – from Ladue. Kathleen got out first through marriage, then acting."

Flavor interrupted: "I didn't know Kathleen O'Malley had been married."

Ziegal frowned: "It was a brief thing, she did it to get out of East St. Louis, it didn't last."

"I'll say, she was just a kid."

"They got a quickie divorce after eight months, it wasn't working out anyway. You were asking me about MY child."

"Yes, I'm sorry, the father was from Ladue?"

"Yes."

"How'd you meet him, you were just a schoolgirl?"

"He was the son of one of my father's few surviving friends. He'd made good. Anyway, he was thirty and very, very respectable. But then isn't that the way? I told him that unless he paid for a proper birth, I would go to Ladue and shout the news to the rooftops. He nearly had a heart attack, poor man. Actually I think he would have done the right thing, anyway. He picked up the tab for the hospital, post natal care, everything, and as a family friend, of course."

"How old were you on August 24, 1962?"

"I was fourteen years old."

"Statutory rape. Your 'poor man' committed a criminal offence."

"With my agreement and encouragement."

"The law deems you legally unfit to give such encouragement."

"The law, as someone once said, Lt., is an ass. I was fully aware of what I was doing. And anyway, it's rather too late for you to find him, if you could."

"What did your parents say about this?"

"My mother was dead, my father virtually senile. Kathleen brought me up, not my father."

"She was in Hollywood at this time?"

"Kirk Nielsen met her in St. Louis when he was on location, and they fell in love."

"She was very young."

"Four and a half years older than me."

Sarah Ziegal looked at her watch irritably. "Is there much more of this?"

Flavor looked down at her notes, and without looking back up, said: "Yes, some. Did the police ask you to name the father?"

"Of course. I told them to go to hell."

"Didn't anyone try to make a court order for you and the child?"

Sarah Ziegal ran a hand through her hair: "You know, I RESENT having to answer these questions. It is nearly thirty-three years ago, and my child has been dead for twenty."

"This is a major murder investigation, Miss Ziegal. And you should have revealed to the police originally, the fact that you were on board the Little Prince the night your sister died. You were a material witness."

"It is all so long ago now, what can it possibly matter?" she replied, with a kind of refined boredom.

She had aged badly, Flavor thought, exposure to the sun clearly hadn't helped, and she had that almost Katherine Hepburn style of affected superiority about her manner. Flavor wondered how much was real, and how much an act.

She said:

"I have a right and a duty to ask these questions. I could arrest you if you'd prefer."

Ziegal smiled and it was as though a cloud had passed

over the sun: "And after the arrest, what, a charge? Come on Lt., you've already become a laughing stock, you and that redneck goon colleague of yours. You can't afford any more mistakes. As it is you're running out of time, I hear. And I'm intrigued; how on earth does a person like – well, you know – get on with a bigot like that?"

Flavor bit the inside of her check until she tasted blood.

"You have a choice. Answer here, or I'll make life as inconvenient for you as possible. It's over a 100 miles to LA and that's where the hell you're going unless you talk now."

"Ask away, dear Lt., ask away."

"Did they try to take your illegitimate son from you?"

"Why not say, bastard, Lt? You'd like to, wouldn't you?"

Flavor ignored the taunt:

"Well, did anyone try to get a court order for you and the child?"

"Yes. On the grounds of my moral delinquency, I believe it was called. We got over that."

"How, did you 'get over that'?" Flavor put emphasis on the words to indicate how brusquely she felt Sarah Ziegl had tried to get round it.

"This is America, money can solve a lot of problems. My sister was being escorted by a major movie star. Need I say more?"

"Did Kathleen come back from Hollywood, to help you with the pregnancy?"

"Yes, whenever she could."

"East River. Did you do that AFTER your pregnancy, during, or before?"

"Before. I went to Hollywood for a week. I was a kid, I didn't know what the hell I was doing. Both Kirk and Kathleen were kind. If you've seen the movie you'll know it was virtually all indoor sets. They shot my stuff in a week flat."

"After the birth; they wouldn't have let you bring up a child, not at fourteen, even if there wasn't a court order. I understand he was handicapped."

Sarah Ziegal made the rather tense hair-moving gesture again, and said: "Yes, he was. Kathleen arranged for him to be cared for initially in a special home for handicapped babies and toddlers here, in California."

"Why here?"

"Because part of the deal was that I would come to live with Kathleen, and I wanted to be near him. When I was deemed grown up enough my son came to live with me. With some of what Kathleen left me, I bought this place, employed a nurse and a housekeeper, and I came back here when I could. By the early Seventies I was making a career for myself in the business. My son lived here until he died."

Flavor said: "I was told you went back to St. Louis after Kathleen died. Certainly you seemed to disappear."

Ziegal shifted slightly in her seat: "For a spell, then I came here."

"What was the name of the special home where he was originally nursed?"

"I'm not telling you. It's not relevant, and you will not be able to get your hands on confidential medical records, so forget that."

Despite herself, Flavor was taken aback. Ziegal seemed both conciliatory, in that she readily admitted to the information Flavor had, and yet was also confident and belligerent.

She picked up the other document: "This is the death certificate?" Sarah Ziegal nodded. Flavor read: January 13, 1975. Cause of death bronchial pneumonia. It was a City of East St. Louis death certificate, signed by Dr. Ivan B. Tanowitz.

"You were back home when your son died?"

"Yes, visiting friends. I was foolish, it is very cold in Missouri and Illinois in winter. One of the great things about California, especially the desert here, is the dry heat. He felt the cold terribly."

"Where is he buried?"

"He was cremated."

229

Jesus, Flavor thought, it's like playing tennis with a pro, you whack 'em over and she whacks 'em back without breaking sweat.

"Why keep the house after he died? You have a place in L.A. Doesn't the heat get you down, especially now, in the Summer?"

Ziegal shook her head: "In LA I'm a star. Here I'm just the poor woman who used to have the handicapped kid, I bought cheap, it's comfortable, and only a couple of hours from LA. When I'm here I can relax."

"Do you have any staff now, you answered the door yourself, both times?"

She shook her head: "No, I live alone. I have enough people around me in LA."

"What was your son's name?"

"Gregory."

"What was the problem with him?"

"It was congenital. He was born with spina bifida, and encephalitis, more commonly known as water on the brain. For the first week or so the doctors did not think he would live. His legs did not develop properly in the womb, and never grew properly in childhood. He was, I suppose you would say, deformed. He could barely walk, and then only occasionally with the aid of callipers. He spent most of his time in a wheel-chair. There was also some brain damage, probably caused during the actual delivery."

"Poor kid."

"People die of the strangest, smallest things, yet Gregory survived. It was almost as though he was meant to live."

"But he did die young, twelve?"

"Twelve and a half. The miracle was that he lived so long."

"But don't you think it ironic that it was NOT his condition that killed him, it was pneumonia?"

"Such children are vulnerable to conditions like that. It is PART of their condition. Today, no doubt, I would have known about some of these pre-birth conditions, and been offered an abortion."

"Do you WISH he'd not been born?"

The question seemed to jolt Ziegal like electricity, and her face came up, alert. She waited a few seconds and said: "Yes, to be frank, I do. For his sake, not mine. I loved him."

"I'm sorry."

"Feel sorry for Gregory, not me, he's the one who needs your prayers."

"Are YOU religious, Miss Ziegal?"

"No, my remark was hypocrisy. No world with a God would produce the likes of Gregory."

"You've never married?"

Ziegal shook her head, briskly, from side to side: "No. What man do you think would take on a woman with a monster child?"

She added: "Oh, I can see it in your face, Lt. 'Not even a star with millions of dollars?' Well, I only really started to earn AFTER Gregory died."

"But you still never married?"

"It was my choice."

"You called Gregory a monster? That seems a cruel epithet for your own child."

Ziegal looked a long time at Flavor; an embarrassingly long time, not answering the question, just looking. And Flavor felt unease, fear almost. She had a witch moment, a moment of almost uncanny vision. The moment told her. She is EVIL. Then Ziegal broke the silence as though it had never existed:

"Those who love are entitled to criticise. I may call him what I wish. We are too prissy today, too politically correct. We dare not say what is in our hearts. He WAS a monster. A more humane society would take such children and drown them before the mother was even aware to what she had given birth."

Flavor tried to meet the cruel stare: "You astonish me. I have met many parents of handicapped children who get great joy from them."

Ziegal waved a dismissive hand: "Save me the sentimentality. Yes, yes, of course, we know all that. Finding the gem in the field of stones that is your crippled child. I too had such moments. But I still believe he was better off dead than alive. You can have no idea how such children suffer."

A tangible wave of hostility, almost like static electricity, jolted Flavor, and the smell surrounding Sarah Ziegal seemed higher, distilled into a putrefying, nauseating essence.

Flavor realised she was holding herself rigid, and looked down hurriedly again at her notebook:

"Didn't Gregory have any kind of life here? Couldn't he go to school or church? Didn't he have any friends? I mean, handicapped people can do the most amazing things, have fun, learn to – ?"

Ziegal said curtly: "No, he had no friends, the other kids just made fun of him."

She reached over and took back her certificates: "He couldn't be accommodated in a classroom, he was in a wheelchair, remember. Eventually I paid for a special tutor. He could talk after a fashion. Reading was beyond him. He liked to look at pictures, to watch TV, he got some joy from that."

Flavor pushed on, knowing what Mrs. Schumacher had told her about the boy's wheelchair church visits, almost inviting Ziegal to agree, to tell Flavor about the church trips.

"But couldn't you have taken him to church, couldn't he have joined the Boy Scouts, or anything? They have sections for handicapped kids now."

"I regret that those things were not possible."

"What on earth did he do all day?"

"Look at pictures, watch television. Wait to die. He was born to die. He seemed to accept that."

"That seems very harsh."

"Until you have been in that position you cannot know. So don't JUDGE me. Will that be all?"

Flavor shifted in her seat:

"Do you ever read the supermarket tabloids, you know,

the National Enquirer, the Globe?"

Ziegal gave her a look of almost undisguised contempt and said one word: "*Please.*" It meant, please don't insult me by even SUGGESTING I would sully my mind with such publications.

Flavor couldn't resist it, she wanted to get a dig in, a little knife thrust, to wipe that smug, superior look off Ziegal's face.

She said: "Oh, they're not so bad Miss Ziegal. And I would have thought, you know, 'TV star's crippled love child' would have been the kind of thing they'd have liked."

Ziegal tensed, and the barely concealed lines on her face broke out like a rash. The tightened flesh on her jaw strained against the bone. Flavor thought: A little cosmetic help from medical friends there, Ziegal.

"Yes?"

Ziegal ran her hand back through her hair in what was rapidly becoming a nervous tic: "Well, you clearly know them better than I did. A year before Gregory died I saw someone photographing us from across the street. Then I was telephoned for comment by an English reporter with a very low class British accent. I had no comment to make, but one such magazine carried the story anyway."

"What about the newspapers?"

"Ignored it. Thank God the Press proper still has some standards." Ziegal pushed her chair back, and stood up: "I think if you want more, it will have to be in the presence of my lawyers. And I hope you will agree I have been VERY co-operative."

Flavor nodded. She wanted to leave this room, leave this house, leave the – presence – that was it, PRESENCE, of this woman, for it disturbed and frightened her.

"Yes, thank you. You've been very co-operative." Sarah Ziegal saw Flavor to the door, and said, as a parting shot, "Don't call again. Call my lawyers." She closed the door.

Flavor drove to the Sheriff's office, and she was in luck, the same deputy she and McCall had spoken to, was on duty.

Flavor had a copy of the 1974 "angel" killing file back in Los Angeles, but she wanted to see it again NOW. The deputy who'd had the run-in with McCall remembered her – and worse, remembered McCall.

He agreed to her request to go over the file of the murdered pastor again, but as he handed it to her, he said with a triumphant grin: "See your good old boy got himself into one hell of a lot of trouble up there in Los Angeles, didn't he?"

Flavor forced herself to smile. "He sure did."

She began to flip through the file.

"He'll get us peace officers the wrong kind of name."

"Sure will."

She got the file on the dead man, Pastor John Donnell. November 18, 1974, was the night Anne-Marie Fullerton made her terrified telephone call, the night she claimed to have been with Donnell when he was murdered by someone dressed as an angel.

Killed on November 18, and less than eight weeks later, the crippled boy Gregory, who sat in his wheelchair in Pastor Donnell's church, wheeled there by the mother who now denied it, was also dead, from bronchial pneumonia, way away in cold, wintry, Illinois.

Jesus, what was it? Flavor whacked herself on the forehead with the file. What WAS going on? Somehow she knew in her gut that all the deaths were linked, but how, HOW?

"Problem, Lieutenant?"

Flavor ignored him. Ziegal was Heather O'Malley, who was the murdered woman's sister, who was Nielsen's lover, drowned in possibly mysterious circumstances, and now everyone – virtually everyone – who had been guests on the boat were DEAD.

Now the killer wanted her, Flavor, and presumably McCall too. Had killed Jack. Flavor closed her eyes. Had killed poor, poor Jack.

Was Ziegal involved, AND Nielsen, a conspiracy, and if so, why? Had she killed her own son and then faked the cause of his death? Why would she do that? Had the poor, crippled, brain-damaged kid seen or heard something?

She had called him a monster, said he was born to die, said she regretted he had ever been born, yet also claimed to have loved him. Surely anyone who had murdered their own child would not freely tell a police officer that she regarded that child as a monster?

Yet whoever was behind the killings had not bothered to take the risk that the little captain's son on the boat had seen or heard nothing.

But this wasn't a handicapped kid with few faculties, Andrade's son was a normal boy, who, if he saw or heard something, might have made something of it when he grew up.

Gregory, even according to an independent eyewitness, was a cripple in a wheelchair. And he had NOT been on the boat, what possibly could he have known, seen or heard that would make his own mother kill him?

Was it the death of the pastor? Had somehow he been privy to information about THAT death? How could anyone fear a handicapped, brain-damaged child?

And what could the pastor have known or done to have made Nielsen, if it WAS him, or Ziegal or BOTH, want to kill him? And why was Ziegal lying about never having taken her son Gregory to church?

Flavor hit herself once more on the forehead with the file, and said, aloud: "Fuck, fuck! None of it makes sense."

"You're really having problems with this one, hey Lieutenant, that's what the TV says? Word is you're off the case by the end of the month too, 'less you can come up with some answers."

She looked at the vacuous grin over the double-chins, at the sagging belly that strained at his gun belt, and she searched for a crushing retort, the devastating put-down, but there was nothing there, the tank just rang hollow and empty.

She went back outside into the searing desert Summer heat, ready for the long drive home.

CHAPTER FOURTEEN

Los Angeles sweltered in an August heatwave – 103° at the Civic Center – and the case stuck like a rabbit in melting tar.

The revelation that Sarah Zeigal was the long, lost sister of dead Kathleen O'Malley, and that all the victims had been on board the Little Prince that night the star died, was a seven-day wonder.

Nielsen called a Press conference to deny any involvement in the murders and to quote his alibis. The LAPD chief – without informing Flavor – held his own Press conference, to confirm that the LAPD would NOT be re-opening the enquiries into Kathleen O'Malley's death.

And there had been no more deaths – not Angel deaths, anyway. The rest of LA was killing in a frenzy. Blood-boiled husbands blew away their wives, frayed housewives plunged kitchen knives into couch potato husbands, jammed and sweat-soaked freeway motorists pulled guns on drivers who sneaked by them on the shoulder.

In East and South Central LA the gangs were tetchy, itching, hot and murderous, and drive-by shootings multiplied. Each night the sheet-covered victims littered the news broadcasts.

And Angelenos seemed to have developed a strange feeling of Robin Hoodism about this Angel killer. OK, he was whacko, but hell, he wasn't blowing away liquor store clerks, he wasn't kidnapping and raping co-eds, or luring schoolkids and doing unspeakable things to them.

Hey, real people were dying out there, not just fag hairdressers, AIDS-infected stars and million dollar screenwriters.

So, let's wait for the arrest, the trial, the book, the movie, and in the meantime, when will this heat ever END? This was California, not Florida, it was like a sauna out there.

And LA was change, flux, it was about the new, the HAPPENING, and suddenly the Angel was old, it was yesterday. The mass psyche of the city wanted new, NEW, and above all an end to the stifling heat that lay like a soaking blanket over the city.

As if by magic the climate of fear in the movie community began to dissipate. Flavor and McCall watched in wonder. It was as though they accepted, by process of osmosis, and without any continuation to its logical end, the conclusion that all the killed had been on the boat, the Little Prince.

So the only people who needed worry were those who had been on that boat or connected with it. And that left, well, WHO, they asked at Ma Maison, and Spago, and in the studio commissaries?

It left the Angellis, roaming Europe someplace, it left King Leonard, Sarah Zeigal, nee Heather O'Malley, and it left Kirk Nielsen himself.

Maybe one of them was the murderer, maybe all of them – conspiracy theories were popular – but as far as victims went, so the buzz went in Beverly Hills, and Holmby Hills, at the top of Mulholland, in Bel Air and Malibu, we're clear.

Stars returned from Europe, security companies started

laying off the help, surplus Germanic guard dogs were whimpering to the SPCA.

It was . . . . . OVER.

Pity the heat wasn't.

Flavor and McCall sat at the small, plastic table in the dog-eared garden at the rear of his apartment, sipping wine cooler. Madonna sat motionless beside the wine and soda bottles, like an object in a still life.

It was midnight, still 84 degrees, and the heat rose from the ground in waves, hanging like weights on the three stunted trees that framed the garden.

Flavor wiped a hand across her forehead and sweat flew off in a spray. She looked tired and dispirited, as though the heat, humidity and the lack of movement on the case had drained the spirit from her.

"I can't believe this. Mississippi yes, but California? Don't let anyone ever tell me again they don't need air-con here."

She took the wine bottle and rolled it against her face, but it was already warm. "You got a cold one of these?"

McCall got wearily to his feet. He felt wiped out, sluggish, as though something primeval and swamp-like oozed through his veins rather than blood.

When he returned, she took the ice-cold bottle unopened, and ran it over her fevered skin. "Wow."

Madonna turned her head, watched Flavor, then resumed the silent sentinel pose.

"What now?" McCall asked.

Flavor gave a resigned shrug of her shoulders.

"I'm damned if I know – properly anyhow. Nielsen is all alibi-ed from here to Labour Day – "

"Yeah, and that means nothing. I could walk three blocks and find you two guys who'd give you an alibi for a hundred bucks."

"He was seen in public at least ONE time."

McCall swigged at his wine and soda and it tasted warm

and bitter, like the bile of defeat in his throat.

"So he got someone else to do one – all of 'em maybe – it doesn't mean anything. You know he's involved, I know he's involved, the sonofabitch himself knows it."

"And we can't prove it, McCall, there's no forensic, no witnesses, no real motive. The LAPD couldn't give a damn about 1966, half the population of the city wasn't born, then, so, you know – "

She plucked the wilting straw from her glass, tossed the soggy reed aside, then quaffed half the glass's contents: "Jesus but that is vile when it warms up. Get a wine merchant, McCall."

"Sure. Give me the fresh." She handed him the bottle and he uncorked it.

She emptied the remaining contents of her glass into the parched shrubbery, and filled the glass to the brim with fresh, cold wine.

Flavor took a big, long sip:

"I gave the guys a pep talk today, like, it ain't over 'till it's over, we can do it guys, win this one for the Gipper. They weren't buying it. It's five minutes to go in the last quarter of the Superbowl and we need three touchdowns."

"Well, it ISN'T over till it's over."

She laughed a bitter laugh: "Sure, but you try telling them that – or ME, for that matter. They saw you canned, they know I'm on notice, they're not stupid. No-one wants to be around failure, it smells."

Even the traffic noise, the ever-present LA muzak, the Angelenos' lullaby, seemed muted, as though the heat was like a muffler on the burble of the cars on Santa Monica and Wilshire boulevards above and below them.

"Who'll take over?"

"Don't know. Haven't been informed. It doesn't matter, it's cosmetic. This is going to be shunted off into a siding and left to rust. When no-one is looking in six months or nine, the chief will sidle up and put the thing out of its misery."

"And tomorrow?"

She drank some more wine, and grimaced, it was warming already: "I thought maybe you could talk to Wishaw, unofficially, you know, and maybe I'll take a look at O'Malley's gravesite. We never did check it out, maybe the angel lays flowers there or something, Jesus, I don't know, anything."

"You have some feeling about Wishaw?"

"A kind of hunch thing, nothing more. You know, it's like he's so obsessed with this, with Nielsen. Why? OK, he got screwed, it happens, he was in the business, it's Hollywood. But it's dossiers, and detective work, and the whole thing freaks me out when I think about it seriously. When he mentions Kathleen O'Malley I swear there's a gleam in his eye. Just like the teacher in New Hampshire, the sister of the girl who drowned in the lake – "

"The one who deep sixed our Nielsen murderer theory?"

"Her; but, it was when she talked about him I was sure she was in love with him. Same with Wishaw, I think he somehow had the hots for O'Malley."

"She's been dead awhile for that."

"Still, you could go over it with him again, why, how, who, shake the whole bag up and see if it falls in a different order."

He raised his glass: "Your wish, my command."

"Is that thing in your bedroom they call an air-conditioner actually working?"

"Well, you can be hot and deafened, or hot and quiet."

"That bad, huh?"

"The guarantee ran out when Eisenhower was President."

"I might just sleep in the shower – with the water on."

"I'll take the bath."

Since the night she had asked to stay, and had slept beside him on his bed, Flavor had never returned to either Jack's apartment at Santa Monica, or the motel facility she had rented on Wilshire.

She had brought a suitcase over, and neither she nor

McCall had spoken of it. She was staying, and McCall had not questioned, queried or tried to discuss it with her. It was as though speaking of it might break some spell.

He did not wish her to leave, and he was content to lie there, he, Flavor and Madonna, a chaste threesome, each night. He knew he desired her, but that was an animal thing. She was a woman, and he had been without a woman for a long, long time.

And yet, when he lay beside her at night, and she was willing for him to hold her, her body against his, it was not that he did not feel desire, he did, but it did not dominate.

She was there, and the presence of her was so comforting, so PLEASING – there was no other word – that he marvelled at the sensation of it.

And when he slept, it was more soundly than he had done in ten years.

She was being led down the cellar steps, the rough, once-trusted hand in hers, but now she knew what the man was, for she knew she was grown, she was an adult, she was a police officer, and this was all a dream.

Yet still she walked down the steps in the place that housed the demons, and now the cellar was a graveyard, a place of raised, dank, moss-covered tombs, of towering statuary and gravestones.

And over the graves slithered rattlesnakes, scores of them, curled around the inscribed memorials to the dead, sliding over crosses, forked tongues flickering.

The man looked down at her, and she knew now that HE was dead, too, because his face and hands were those of a cadaver, and she saw, coming out of the darkness, Sarah Ziegal, bringing the awful, putrefying smell with her.

If she was grown, if it was a dream, she knew she could waken. But when she tried, she could not, and the corpse's hand was tight and unyielding on hers, pulling her further down towards Ziegal, towards the snakes, towards death.

Ziegal leaned upon one statue that towered over a grave,

and beckoned to Flavor, who realised that the statue was that of an angel, its hands clasped together in prayer, wings flowing down its back.

The angel had a face, the face of a negro child, and the child was alive. It looked up at Flavor and smiled.

Flavor realised the face was hers.

She tried to scream, and it was as though her throat was stuffed with cotton wool. No sound emerged, only a dry rasp, and her mouth was a silent O as she was led, step by step towards Ziegal and towards Flavor's own childhood face.

She came awake sobbing, shaking with tears, and the convulsive movement of her body woke McCall.

"Are you OK? Were you dreaming?"

She couldn't answer, instead she thrust her face into his chest, and her hands clutched at him, and she kept her head buried close into him for long minutes, as he stroked and soothed her, like a father would a child.

At length he felt she must have fallen asleep, so when she spoke she startled him.

"McCall, do you believe in voodoo?"

"I don't know, why?"

She fell silent for a few moments:

"Do you think you know me?"

"No, I don't know you Flavor."

"If I told you I was a murderer, that I'd killed somebody, what would you say?"

A shaft of silver moonlight cut through the curtains and across the bed like a lance, and McCall had uncanny feelings. That things were abroad that could and may change this night. People talked of sea changes and of watersheds. It was said that sometimes in time and life, something shifted, and lives changed because of it.

He sensed it like an animal. It was as though he was primeval, and that senses long dormant were now awakening.

He said: "I'd like to hear the story."

She told him.

Her parents had died in a car crash when she was five, and she was brought up by her widowed grandmother. Home was a small, rural and very poor Mississippi community that sat hard by a river from which most people made their living by fishing. The river and the swamps around could be dangerous; there were alligators and water moccasins, but generally human, animal and reptile stayed clear of the other species.

There were cotton fields to be picked on the edge of town, and the women made money this way.

The village had a man who was, by the benighted standards of the place, rich. He lived on the slightly higher ground at the edge of town, on land that did not flood, and that stood above the mists that sometimes swirled, waist-high into the village, so that it seemed as if dismembered torsos floated across a grey sea.

His home had foundations, it was linked to sanitation by means of an overground pipe, and it had a basement. The man called it his cellar, and the gossip of the village was that he kept the bodies of his relatives buried down there.

The village gossips and busybodies spoke of strange events, of lights at night, of terrible things that went on in the big three-storey house that perched over the village like an evil guardian.

One day, when Flavor was nine, she sat on the river bank, her bare feet in the cool mud, when suddenly the man was next to her. She looked up at him fearfully, but at first he said nothing, then sat down beside her, and she was too scared to move.

The man asked her if she was afraid of demons, and Flavor said with childish naïvety and outright honesty, that she was. Did they ever come in the night, the man asked? Did she ever hear them rustling in the roof or murmuring in the dark corners of her room? Did she hear their evil whispers beneath her bed?

Flavor's face said that she did.

Then mark my words carefully, the man whispered, for they will come again tonight. I will send them.

And that night they came. She heard them in the roof, fancied she saw their shapes in the corners of her room, and lay in terror as they whispered beneath the bed.

Once, in the night, she woke in horror to what she was certain with a child's certainty, was the cobweb-light touch of corpse fingers on her face.

She lost her appetite, lost weight, only exhaustion could plunge her into sleep. She could not concentrate, and her schoolwork suffered.

Weeks later the man found her again, down by the levee; found a thin, frightened child, deaf to the pleas of her grandmother who begged to be told what was wrong.

The man asked if Flavor now wished to banish the demons. She nodded dumbly. Then you must come to my house, at a time that I will tell you, when we can be alone, and you must tell no-one before or afterwards, the man insisted.

For the demons live in my cellar, he said, safe in the darkness during the day, and at night they roam the village, entering the houses and the bedrooms at will.

But I have the power to banish them – for those I wish.

So she went, when her grandmother was at the market, and the man's wife was away from the village. And the man led her by the trembling hand down into the cellar, where the demons lived, and with a flick of the switch the light flooded the cellar. There, he exclaimed triumphantly, the demons are banished.

And if you do as I say, and tell no-one, and be my friend for ever, the demons will never again come to your room.

The gratitude flushed her skin like fever, and so when he showed her the old Army cot, told her she must sit there, and must first remove her clothes, she did so.

Just a photograph, he said, and you must arrange your hands, like this, so.

As she spoke those words, Flavor felt McCall tense on the

bed next to her, heard him say something inaudible under his breath, heard him say it over and over, like an oath.

"Are you OK?"

He grunted something like agreement, and she continued.

After she had done with her hands what the man wished, after touching herself, then the flash of the camera blinded her.

McCall said: "My God." And there was a strange choke in his voice. She reached for his hand, and found it was balled into a clenching, unclenching, clenching fist.

And the worst part, if it was possible for something to be worse than that, Flavor told McCall, was that the man had lied. Because that night the demons still came. And they had never really been away.

McCall was swearing, over and over, the same foul, offensive word, over and over, as though somehow oblivious to the presence next to him of the woman – the child – who had told him the story.

At length he seemed to recover and asked: "Did you tell someone, the police?"

Flavor had not told the police, or her grandmother, but months later, distressed and disturbed, scared beyond reason, she finally confided in her best friend, Sheree, telling her what the man had done. Sheree told her it was wrong and dirty.

McCall said with a desperate intensity: "Why didn't you tell your grandma or the police, someone in authority?"

She shook her head: "I was too scared. To be honest, I thought the demons would kill me. I thought he controlled them."

"Poor kid, you must have been frightened out of your wits."

"I can't tell you. I'd heard my grandma and the old ladies talk about voodoo dolls, about making people die. They said it happened in Africa, if a witch doctor did it."

She stroked her fingers over the tightened, angry fists, traced upwards and squeezed his arms: "Jesus, McCall, I know this sounds old hat, pins in dolls, silly superstitious crap, but this was backwoods, even for Mississippi, and some of that stuff has been handed down by word of mouth for generations."

"I'm not laughing, believe me."

She hugged him: "Thanks, it was real to me. I made this doll, I dressed it, I stole the pins from my grandma, I stuck them in the doll, and floated it in the water. That way the guy was supposed to drown."

"And he did, right, and so you think you're a murderer?"

"Less than a week later. I killed him, I KNOW it."

"You don't know it. You were a nine year old kid and you stuck pins in a doll. Maybe there was an autopsy, maybe he had a weak heart, or maybe he couldn't swim, you don't KNOW."

"Suppose I DID, suppose it was me?"

"And suppose when I was nine I threw the morning newspaper onto somebody's front porch and they tripped over it and died? That was then, this is now. Spells, voodoo dolls, come on?"

She would not be comforted.

"I think I killed him. I believe it to this day, that I murdered someone, I took a life – "

His voice cut across her savagely: "Well, good. GOOD. He was a child molester, he was scaring you half to death, so what the hell if he drowns? He's lucky he just drowned. Maybe if someone had got their hands on him . . . someone . . . if . . ."

He was trembling, vibrating with some kind of passion she had hardly recognised in him before.

And he was thinking, Yes, yes, he's lucky. And maybe it WAS voodoo, and if it was, then McCall was FOR it. He was for the power of the victim, the weak, to fight back with weapons that the strong, the cruel and the vicious could not combat.

If the fate of the man, and the reason for it, was as Flavor had said it was, then it was beyond what McCall had known as justice, and he had sworn to uphold justice. Could there be, he wondered, a justice that transcended the laws Man had created?

He came from the daylight world of the normal and the rational. He had built his life around rules, and procedure and the remorseless grind of a not perfect but ultimately righteous system that pursued the guilty.

He realised with a start, that Flavor was speaking to him:

"You know, back there, when I was crying, I'd just had a bad dream. I was back in the cellar, and Sarah Ziegal was there, snakes all over, it was a graveyard, and I was an angel."

He ran a hand over the lustrous sheen of her hair that seemed almost luminous now in the moonlight.

"Flavor, you're grown now. It's over. They're dreams, and when you awake they finish."

"Yeah, sure." She nestled closer into him, and he cuddled her, whispering reassuring noises. They were silent for a long time. Eventually she whispered:

"You awake?"

McCall said: "Yes, it's good like this, like an oasis."

"Can I talk some more? I need to."

"Talk."

"Do you know what a coward I am?"

"No," McCall said, evenly, "tell me, what a coward are you?"

"When I found Jack, when I saw her – like she was – I ran, McCall. I ran like a rabbit out of that room. I am a police officer and I've seen a thousand corpses, mangled, hacked, shot, and I still ran."

"She was your friend."

"Which makes it worse. I was frightened. Frightened of the dark, of the Angel, of that body without its head. I wanted you there, the man I'd wronged so much."

"Come on."

"No .. uh-uh," she shook her head, and he felt her hair against his arm, "I was so right, and you were so wrong. Not for anything you'd done, just because, oh, you were wrong; wrong colour, wrong generation, wrong attitude."

He said nothing. She wanted to talk. It was a path and it was leading somewhere, and she had to take the steps. And he wanted the peace of another's thoughts, another's pain, to sap the pain from him.

"Oh, but I wanted you then all right, you and your big gun and big body, and all those old-fashioned cops, white, black, I didn't care, in their uniforms, strong and male, because I was back in the cellar, shaking and terrified, and I was a scared nigger – "

"Why do you use that word?"

"I can say it, I'm allowed to say it. I was a scared jigaboo bug-eyed spook chicken-shit nigger. You know what they used to say in police academy? Not to our faces, even they couldn't do that today, but so we could hear, or so it would get back to us? They used to say when it comes to it, the niggers can't cut the mustard. The coons will cut and run, the spooks have no guts. And when I was running – and I WAS running – from that room. When I couldn't stay with my dead, lovely friend, I could see those redneck faces McCall, I could see them in my head, and they were laughing, oh boy were they ever laughing. The coon lady cop with the fancy name and she's running just like any old shack darkie from the Georgia woods with a posse of KKK on her tail."

"Can I say something?"

She moved in the darkness, and her skin seemed like deeply beaten and darkened copper in the strange light: "Sure."

"I have no PC track record, but some of the best and bravest cops I ever worked with were black. The other stuff is redneck crap, I KNOW, I grew up with those guys. If they think it works, they'll use it."

"Yeah, but it's about US, it's about what WE feel, whether deep down, inside, you think: Is it true, when it comes to the OK Corral are we just Step N'Fetchit?"

"What proof do you need for yourself, Flavor? You come

out of the Mississippi backwoods, you get an education, you get through police academy, you make Lieutenant, at twenty-eight years old. I was forty."

"You make a good case for me."

"You've earned it."

"It's the cellar, McCall," he heard with unease the frightened gasp of her breath, "one day I've got to go into the cellar, and I'm terrified. I'm not brave. I want to be brave and I'm not brave."

He brought her head up to face him:

"You want to know from brave, I'll tell you. Brave guys do it, the ones the fools can call cowards don't, and the irony is there's no such thing as cowards because nobody says you have to do it, no-one can make you, and no-one KNOWS how bad it is. Because whatever it is, only YOU are there when it happens.

'So I don't give horseshit for bravery or cowardice. But if you want to be brave, do it. Instead of walking away, stay, instead of stopping, walk down the cellar stairs, even if your ass is Arctic with fear, and your fucking hands shake, and you can't breathe, and you want to die. Just walk on down and shake hands with fear and say, Fuck you baby, 'cause here I am, now what you gonna do?"

He realised HE was shaking.

"That's bravery. That's all, it's doing it, rather than not doing it. And you know what the worse thing can happen to you, you can DIE. So if you're prepared for that, what's to fear?"

She said into his ear: "You been there?"

"Yeah, I've been there, and it's not worth shit, not worth giving a damn over. The silly, technical truth is that I've been brave, and I've been a coward, and the difference between the two is like I said. One time I did it, another time I didn't. So what does that make me, a hero or a coward?"

She lay quiet, and suddenly McCall noticed that the tone of the silence had changed. It now gave off a deep hum like the key of some orchestral bass instrument, and at the same time it was as though it had taken shape, and someone had hung it like a curtain across the room.

And it waited, this orchestral, tangible thing, to sound an overture and draw back on the first act of some great play.

Dark, resonant silence that hid a million players, a host of voices, who, when the cue was given, would chorus some momentous happening.

He sensed it, he smelled it.

There WAS something abroad this night, some agent of change. Tonight the world would move, would shift a fraction on its axis, and he and this woman would be changed, irrevocably.

He had no expectation, no hope and no fear. He was calm with an almost religious acceptance. What would be would be, he knew that, understood it, welcomed it.

There was a movement at the foot of the bed, and Madonna leapt in that tiny, effortless aerial leap of cats, and stood there, motionless, eyeing them.

McCall felt Flavor turn slightly to look down to the foot of the bed, and saw Madonna shift a fraction. Then the cat's head twitched, just once, she gave a great yawning miaow, and scuttled from the room.

McCall thought: Madonna knows too. She knows, just as I know. She can sense it like a storm. This is my witch moment. Lying here, next to this woman, with touch but no carnality, by being with her, talking with her, spending time with her, it is as though I have drawn some of what she is, some of that uncanniness she possesses, into me.

In return is she drawing my pain, as I selfishly hoped tonight, or can she draw also my strength? Will she draw my fear and my shame?

The silence hung, immeasurable, until at last he felt her stir, and she brought her face level with his, both their features bathed naked by the moonlight.

Her eyes were open, her face set, not solemn, almost enquiring, and she looked into him, into his eyes, through the windows of his soul, into the core of him.

And he thought, without fear. This is me, this is McCall, Flavor, can you see me, can you see the secret, and the shame, can you see in through the pitiful facade that fronts this wasted interior?

This is me, all of me, look into me and weep. For I cannot be loved, can I?

She gazed at him for a full minute, looking at him almost as Madonna sometimes did, with a kind of quizzical benevolence. He wanted to say out loud, like a bitter delinquent: Well, Flavor Cartouche, there you have it. There it is.

This was what it must be like to be discovered, to have your soul turned inside out like a thief's pockets.

And then she kissed him. Flavor Cartouche, black woman, frightened child, high achiever, kissed Rory McCall, white boy product of Detroit, who held a secret shame to his heart like a concealed crown of thorns.

It was like no other kiss that had passed between them, it did not give thanks, or gratitude, or timid, blushing affection, it sent a message that electrified him with the possibility of the impossible.

At first it was just a schoolkid's lips-against-lips kiss, but he knew it was the herald trumpet of a dawn he had never believed could break.

Her hands came up and she pulled his face closer into her, then drew back. He could taste the moisture of her lips, a bead of it hung like dew on his, and his tongue tasted it.

She said: "I love you, McCall. I didn't before, couldn't before, didn't even think of it as a possibility before; and then it came, like the sun. Please, please tell me that you love me also."

He looked at her like men must have looked at hitherto undiscovered valleys or mountain peaks. He was, in truth, seeing her properly for the first time.

He said: "Yes, of course. I love you so very much."

She kissed him quickly: "When? When did you know?"

He shook his head, smiling: "I don't know, just when I did. When I did."

He leaned forward and kissed her, felt her lips part for him, entered her cave, felt the delicious taste of her. He moaned slightly.

She said: "Others wanted, others pressed. You waited. You repaid my trust. Why?"

"Because, because," he stopped, and kissed her eyes, and it was the most exquisite moment, "because it was all pre-ordained." And, McCall, thought: It was voodoo, Flavor, it was the dark, harsh, sometimes-just God of that world to which you introduced me.

She said: "Will you please love me and live with me for ever until the moment we die, together, at the same second? Will you do that for me, McCall?"

He ran his face over hers, his nose across hers, felt the bone of his strike the bone of hers, felt her cheeks on his, the rough contours of his chin on the soft skin of hers. There had never been such a Paradise.

"Yes, for ever and ever, until we both shall die."

"Until we both shall die. So shall we live for ever and ever and ever?"

"Yes, for ever and ever. And then we wish, we'll die together, at the same second." He laughed at the marvellous, absurd, possible magic of it all: "The world is ours."

She said, looking at him intently, and still quizzically, as though she could still not quite believe what words were being said:

"I LOVE you, isn't that so marvellous and strange?"

"If I wished, I could fly right now, I could carry you across the hills."

She laughed: "On a broomstick? A WITCH! A male witch. And a poet, a romantic."

He kissed her again: "Of course, the poet was locked inside me like St. Valentine, and you turned the key in the cell door."

"I should have known. A big, redneck cop who could quote the lyrics of Dory Previn."

He said: "'Come marry me, and we shall all the pleasures

make'. I cannot remember the poet's name."

"How about McCall?"

She kissed him wildly, passionately, and they clawed at each other like animals. She pulled at his T-shirt, and he fumbled with the buttons of the shirt she had borrowed from him. He failed, clumsily, and ripped at them, uncaring.

The shirt swung open, and he gasped as his hands found her breasts. They felt like over-ripe pears beneath his large hands, he thrust his head forward and his mouth found her huge, erect nipples.

"God." He took them in his mouth, first one, then the other, marvelling at the size and taste. He ran his tongue along the valley divide between her breasts and tasted the salt sweat of her.

He brought himself level with her face until they were facing each other diametrically, eyes, noses, mouths aligned.

His words rang like crystal: "You are so very beautiful and dear to me, Flavor."

She beamed with pleasure: "Am I beautiful, McCall? No, I am, I know, I know you're speaking the truth. Imagine me, beautiful." She hung her hands around his neck.

Now he knew what it meant for words to mean exactly, mathematically what they were supposed to mean, with no colouring or shade, nothing chipped to fit, just sheer, precision-made, exact words.

And now he knew also about love, what love meant. And he said, to the ghosts and the memories, and to the one he had so grievously wronged. Forgive me, for I cannot resist the strength of this love, mine or hers. I am weak, and I cannot stand out against this. Forgive me.

He was free-falling in space, tumbling from the sobriety of loneliness and grief into the intoxication of love with this woman.

She said, suddenly:

"Be inside me, McCall, come into me. Join with me. Nothing else for now, we have a lifetime for that, just please enter me."

He pulled the shirt off her shoulders, saw them bare in the moonlight, marvelled at them, and he realised – as if conscious of the conjuring trick – that his T-shirt and pants were gone.

She moved sightly, and he felt a sensation of shock and delight, like a diver hitting water, as she lowered herself, and he moved upwards and they met, in harmony, in synchronisation, he entering her, enveloped by the welcoming moist wetness of her, she impaling herself on the hardness of him.

And as they moved together, he realised with an awareness that had eluded him all his life. I am making love. This is what making love means. MAKING, love. We, together, she and I, are creating love. It was so simple and so wonderful.

Their bodies glistened in the heat of the night, she threw her head back and moaned, fell forward, kissed him, sucked at his face, bit him gently, rotated on him, and he marvelled at the majesty of it.

And eventually, he climaxed, unable to stop it, unwilling to, receiving no verbal or physical hint from her that he should not, and it went on and on, like a crashing wave of pleasure, body linked with mind in a mystical union at which he could only wonder.

Yet he was still hard, and she threw herself back and forward on him, her pubis grinding against the bone of his pelvis, and she was giving small cries, almost of fear, and something else, bass and deep down, like a volcano restrained, and then she bared her teeth, like an animal, threw back her head and moaned, not loud, just a long, unbroken moan that went in an arching parabola to its zenith, then tumbled slowly down into silence.

She placed her hands flat onto his chest, then the fingertips came up, tracing his neck and chin, feeling his lips like a Braille mouth, until her fingers caressed the line of his nose with a child's tenderness.

She said: "My love. My only true love."

And then they slept. Together.

Glued by love and the perspiration of their bodies, they slept. And when the silver hue of moonlight began to fade like old paint, and it was dawn's first dull primer that swept the sky, McCall awoke, opening one eye.

She was already awake, propped up on one elbow, looking at him.

"You're beautiful. Did anyone ever tell you that you are beautiful, McCall?"

He shook his head: "No. No-one ever told me that. And maybe you should call me Rory now."

"No, don't you see, you're not Rory, you're McCall? Believe me, I know."

She slid down next to him, and he felt the moist suck of her lips, like the tide, as she kissed him.

He said: "You know, at first I was afraid to sleep in case I'd discover it was a dream, that none of it was real. Then . . ." he shrugged.

"Then you did, and it wasn't, and it is." She kissed him again.

"Until we both shall die?"

"Until we both shall die."

"Will the magic ever fade?"

"No, McCall. Nothing born this way can ever die."

"The rest of the world will seem alien."

"It is; we'll have our world."

She fell in to him, moulding herself to him like plastic, and he felt her outline along the length of him like a Siamese twin. He said: "How long did I sleep?"

She cast a glance over at the clock radio: "An hour, maybe. I only woke up about five minutes ago. I programmed my mind, I wanted to watch you asleep."

"An hour, wow," he ran his splayed fingers along the knobbled ridges of her spine, "I feel like I've slept for a day. I could run a marathon."

"Oh, yeah?" Her look was wicked.

They heard the soft pad of paws, the gossamer brush of fur on wood, looked, and saw Madonna at the door, half in, half out of the room. She was looking at them intently.

Flavor said: "Honey, could you come back in, say, an hour? We have important business to attend to. If you're restless, go out the cat-flap and walk around a little."

The cat gave a little twitch of its head, made a clicking noise that sounded strangely like a disapproving 'tut-tut', turned on its paws, and disappeared with a last arrogant flick of its tail.

McCall lowered an eyelid: "You and that cat have something weird going. I swear it understands everything you say."

"Cats and witches. Do I have to paint a picture?"

"Clearly not. What's the important business?"

He was hard against her, and now there was time, now there was the space given by the prospect of a future that stretched out before them like a promised land.

"I'll put it in one word. Nike."

"NIKE?"

"Just do it."

He did.

CHAPTER FIFTEEN

The porn store looked even more bleak in the morning, the clientele even more furtive and hunted, the wares like night-time whores in the unforgiving glare of daylight.

McCall rapped on the counter and a pale, thin man appeared: "Yes?"

"Mr. Wishaw here?"

"He's the night manager."

"I know that. But it's only seven:thirty, I thought he may still be here."

The thin man eyed McCall suspiciously, then said: "He didn't show last night. I'm his relief. Who are you?"

McCall was about to give his identity, his hand was in his pocket for his badge. And then he realised that he was no longer Lt. McCall, he was a civilian.

And it didn't matter, because now he was the McCall who had love, and had a future. And not being a police officer anymore did not matter.

"I'm a friend."

"Wishaw has no friends."

"Where does he live?"

Recognition began to dawn on the man's face: "You're the guy from the TV, the cop they say's going to gaol."

He leaned back, smugly: "You've got no right to go hassling Wishaw. They took your badge, I seen it on the TV."

McCall smiled, shook his head, ruefully: "Can't fool a guy like you."

"No sir."

"Wishaw is a friend, and he could be in danger. I need to see him."

A smug smile: "Nope. That's confidential information."

McCall said: "Do you have a light?"

"A light?"

"A light, man, for a cigarette, you know."

The man eyed McCall suspiciously, then rummaged under the counter and brought out a cheap, transparent cigarette lighter.

McCall flicked it, saw the bright yellow flame, then adjusted the nozzle so that the flame was high and strong.

"So where's your cigarettes?"

McCall shook his head: "Gave it up. Bad for you." The flame flickered in a small draught. With his left hand, McCall reached out and took a porno mag. Two muscled males in leather jackets and little else embraced their way across the cover.

McCall took the flame and placed it against one corner of the magazine. The glossy magazine took light slowly, but when it did, and the flame caught, it flared into a torch.

"What the fuck are you doing?"

"What I'm going to do is walk this along every rack out there, unless you give me Wishaw's address."

The man slipped on his smug smile like a mask, but it was a bad paint job, because he wasn't sure. He said: "No you won't. You don't want to go to gaol. A cop? Go ahead, DO it."

McCall looked at the man, carefully, the magazine now disintegrating, blue smoke in the air, charred fragments splitting off, spiralling upwards. Customers were looking over in amazement. One headed quickly to the door, and McCall noticed that the exiting customer had pocketed a magazine.

McCall said: "It's over. The old days are over. Give me the address or I torch your stock."

The man shook his head: "You won't do it."

"When are you people going to learn." McCall threw the burning mass onto the nearest rack, and the paper caught.

"Jesus!"

The man was fast, but McCall quicker, snatching the fire extinguisher from the wall rack.

"Fuck man, the whole store is going to go, the whole street."

The rack was ablaze, the photographed petrified sin consumed by fire as if in some Biblical judgement.

"Tell me!"

"You're crazy, you'll kill us." The air was choking with black smoke. McCall heard an alarm go off in the back of the store . .

"TELL ME!"

"Olympic Boulevard . . I . ."

"Number!"

"3660, I think . . ."

"Apartment?"

"Eighteen, Eighteen A . . . use it, USE IT!!"

McCall snapped the clip on the extinguisher and sprayed the foam, expertly, dousing the rack, playing the nozzle on the hot, charred wall, then turning his attention to black but glowing chunks that drifted throughout the store.

When he'd finished the air was thick with smoke and the smell of charred paper, and gobs of foam littered the store. Above the clamorous clatter of the store's fire alarm, they both heard the distant wail of a fire siren.

McCall turned to the man: "3660 Olympic, Apartment

Eighteen A, right?"

The man nodded, gulping.

"What happened here was an accident." The man couldn't speak. "It was an accident. If you say otherwise, and if I get a visit from the LAFD, I promise you I'll come back and finish the job."

The man had a look of sheer terror on his face.

"And now," McCall waved a hand at the hot debris, "you know I'll do it." The man nodded, and McCall was gone.

The apartment block was in the shadow of the junction of the Santa Ana & Long Beach freeways at Commerce. McCall had to step over two youths who sat in the corridor stairwell, and who eyed him, unblinking and menacing.

He heard the buzzer ring inside the apartment, but no-one opened the door. He rapped heavily on the door with his knuckles: "Wishaw, it's me, McCall."

Nothing. He found the supervisor, a Korean man who spoke very little English, but understood the word 'Police', and seemed so impressed by the simple authority of it he did not ask for identity, before letting McCall into the apartment.

The dead, trapped heat hit McCall in the face as though someone had opened an oven door, and he felt sweat break out in his armpits and crotch, across his forehead.

He fumbled for a switch, flipped it, and a sickly yellow light from a weak bulb cast a jaundiced mantle over the tiny room.

When his eyes adjusted, McCall said "Jesus Christ."

The room had been turned into a shrine. Every inch of wall space was plastered with photographs, posters, and newspaper clippings. In one corner was a narrow, single un-made bed, in another a small stove and sink.

The floor was littered with box files and scrapbooks. Next to the bed was a heavy, unfashionable iron desk of the type favoured by offices in the Fifties.

McCall went over to one wall. On it was a full-length portrait of Kathleen O'Malley, blown up commercially from a newspaper photograph; it was blurred and indistinct.

There was a poster from East River, snapshots and publicity stills, all thumb-tacked into the walls, and surrounding them like shabby relations, newspaper clippings. He looked at one from the Los Angeles Times, and noted the date in the top right hand corner. 14th May, 1963.

The clipping looked yellow in the light, but when McCall pulled back the curtains, blinking at the sudden daylight, astonished by the heaviness and opaqueness of the fabric, he looked again and noted that actually it was in remarkably good condition, slightly yellow, but not what one would expect for a piece of newsprint over thirty years old.

He looked back at the curtains, remembering their weight, and how completely they kept out the light.

And it registered. WISHAW NEVER DRAWS HIS CURTAINS. He lives in this dim hell so his portraits and clippings will not fade. It was a mausoleum.

McCall knelt at the cardboard files and began to rummage through them. It was all Nielsen, the drowning, obituaries, tributes, and the growing career of the man Wishaw believed had drowned Kathleen O'Malley.

It was like Flavor had said, he was OBSESSED with her, loved her, was in love with her, in that way of the weird sicko world in which he lived. The world where anonymous losers convinced themselves that if only they could get close enough to a star, that star would realise the extent of the powerful, enormous love the inadequate carried in their hearts.

But SHE WAS DEAD, for God's sake, she'd been dead since 1966, why, how, could he carry this obsession over nearly thirty years?

McCall turned his attention to the desk, tipping out old chequebooks, circulars, fliers. He emptied the drawers onto the floor, looking urgently now, for something – he did not know quite what – something that would put a spotlight on the yellow, psychotic world of Wishaw.

He found a red metal file that was secured with a padlock, wrenched it, stamped it, and pulled at it, until at last the metal snapped with a brittle twang.

Publishing contracts, a screenplay option, a letter from an agent dated 1963. A birth certificate. He ran his finger over it. Wishaw was born in St. Louis, Missouri. McCall's heart began to beat a little faster. He rifled through the letters and certificates, glancing at them, speed-searching.

It was at the very end of the file. A marriage certificate, 31st March, 1962, City of St. Louis, Missouri. Ken Wishaw, bachelor, occupation journalist, married Kathleen O'Malley, spinster, occupation actress.

McCall got to his feet clutching the certificate, biting hard at the inside of his mouth. Wishaw was MARRIED to Kathleen O'Malley. He had MARRIED her. And she had left him, maybe within months, left him to pursue stardom, to sleep with Kirk Nielsen.

And then she'd drowned. Wishaw had married again, but it was a front for his later obsession. He still loved Kathleen. He could never get over her death, could never forgive Nielsen for what he believed the man had done.

Flavor had been right. Wishaw WAS in love with Kathleen O'Malley, so in love, he'd married her.

It wouldn't be just Nielsen, he wouldn't be able to forgive any of them, anyone who'd been on the boat that night.

McCall said aloud: "Oh my God."

He went into the tiny, grimy bathroom with its shelf rack of basic toiletries that presented themselves in a parade-like loneliness. Apart from two threadbare towels the room was bare.

McCall returned to the living area, and found the small clothes closet. Jackets and pants hung on wire hangers. He fiddled for a light switch, but could find none, so dropped on his haunches and began to feel in the gloom.

Several boxes met his fingers, and he pulled them out, tested them, felt them empty and discarded them. Then his fingers felt something metallic and cold. He closed his hand on it, and ran the hand upwards. The thing was long and vaguely tubular. He pulled it out, and held it up.

It was a scabbard, and in it was a Samurai sword. McCall went in his pocket, took out a hankerchief and wrapped it around the sword's haft, then eased the blade out of the scabbard.

The blade was spotless and it gleamed like hope even in the poverty of light that fell upon it. McCall put his thumb tentatively and gingerly against the one of the sharp double edges, felt the sting, and saw the tiny, surprised pop of blood.

It was like a razor.

McCall wiped it clean, and carefully eased it back into the scabbard and replaced it in the cupboard. He could not find this. Flavor had to find it, she would have to get a search warrant, citing probable cause, so that any trial against Wishaw would not be prejudiced by the matter of illegal entry.

Would the Korean supervisor remember, and tell the police that a policeman – a big one, so high – had already been in the apartment?

McCall cursed. He cursed his stupidity, Flavor's, everyone's for not seeing it. Wishaw wanted revenge for what he felt was the murder of the former wife he still loved. Somehow he had inveigled himself into the homes of Alassio, Helm, and Smith, and had somehow lured Victoria Astaire to Point Dume.

All along they'd been looking for the wood, and seeing only the trees, as obsessed with Nielsen as they had believed – for the wrong reasons – Wishaw was.

And now it was so obvious, Nielsen wasn't the Angel, Wishaw was.

But Wishaw had gone, perhaps for ever. McCall cursed.

Flavor showed her badge, and was greeted by a dark-suited friendly man, who disappeared into an office and emerged several minutes later to give her directions to the gravesite of the late Kathleen O'Malley.

Flavor went in through the gates, drove her Skylark up Memorial Drive, took the first right into Evergreen, and came round, as she had been told, in a loop past the statue of Moses, back on herself, then turned right into Celestial Drive.

The drive was a half circle, and there Flavor saw it. She was not shocked, or surprised, it was almost an embellishment on the evidence they had.

A towering angel, wings upswept, head downcast, its hands clasped together in prayer, towering over a black marble plinth. Flavor stopped the car and got out.

She stood at the base of the statue, looking up at the angel with its blinded, opaque stone eyes. She read the words: "Kathleen O'Malley, 1944–1966. God took her in His arms and sat her alongside His angels."

She looked, one last time, then drove back to the entrance of the Hollywood Hills Forest Lawn cemetery, and found the dark-suited man.

She asked him if others had enquired about the location of the grave, if flowers were left there, if the grave received visitors. She waited while he checked, received mostly negative answers, but a positive promise to call her if anything of the kind was resolved.

Flavor headed for her new home in West Hollywood. She felt calm now. She knew that she did not have the answer, and that the deadline was two days away, but she felt no panic.

What had happened last night had changed her. She was different now, it was not a romantic fairy-tale cliché, it was the simple truth.

Even after what had happened to her as a child, McCall was not the first man with whom she'd had sex. Flavor had deliberately plunged, anxious to get it over with, like a timid swimmer and a cold pool, into an affair when she was at UCLA.

It had lasted three months, been unsatisfactory, and she had ended it with the minimum of pain. In her first year as a police officer she met an actor, and he had romanced her. She was flattered, and eventually went to bed with him more out of gratitude than anything else.

Sometimes the sex act had been not unpleasant, but no more than that. When she was close, and intimate with the two men who had been her only lovers, she had felt – squeamish – it was the only word she could use to describe it.

It was like a geographical feeling of place and time; that she should not be HERE, with them, she should be THERE with . . . who? She had been attracted to Jack, to her personality, her warmth, and if she was honest, with a kind of coquettish pleasure that Jack wanted her.

It was only really after she met McCall, after she had been around McCall, that she realised – not, at that stage that she wanted HIM – but that she did not want sex with Jack, or with any other woman.

Last night had not been inevitable – she didn't know what McCall felt about that, or truly believed – but suddenly she had known it was right.

And at that moment, when they declared their love, when they were intimate, she knew that she was in the right place and time, that she had found her place, and found HIM.

So now she WAS different.

He called the carphone and got a recorded voice telling him it was switched off. So he dialled his own answering machine, listened to his voice, and left a message.

She was opening the door when she heard McCall's voice on the machine, but by the time she reached it he had finished the message and hung up.

She replayed it, and had to sit down. Wishaw! Wishaw! They'd been looking in the wrong direction. All the time, their informant, their confidant, him!

Flavor dialled her office and spoke to a colleague. A probable cause search warrant to go into Wishaw's apartment. Without giving too much away she hinted that there might be a sword or something in the closet, and that it might be sharp.

McCall would be back soon anyway, Olympic Boulevard was only about 30 minutes away. She took a long, hot shower, her mind buzzing with it. Wishaw! She herself had said he seemed to be in love with Kathleen O'Malley, and both Flavor and McCall had agreed the man was obsessed.

How had he gained entry into Jack's apartment? How had he persuaded a star like Victoria Astaire to keep an appointment with a failed writer turned porno manager? And Alassio, and Helm, and the bank clerk Smith in the Valley?

She towelled herself dry, wrapped the towel around herself and went into the bedroom to get a T-shirt and jeans. She looked around it, at the crumpled heaps of male shirts and strewn pants, and thought. This was where my life changed.

Flavor opened the closet and felt on the top shelf for the clothes she had laid out there. McCall had obviously moved them. As she began to fumble around under piles of his clothes, she disturbed a brown manilla envelope that slid off the shelf, caught her on the shoulder and spilt its contents on the floor.

Cursing, she knelt down to put the stuff back in the envelope. She froze. They were pictures, about half a dozen Polaroid color pictures, and a larger color one.

The pictures were of a girl aged about eleven. She was naked, her hands were tied in front of her, and she was staring directly into the camera.

The girl was clearly terrified. The camera had caught her fear and dragged it into the posterity of the lens.

Beneath the Polaroids the larger picture was a portrait and had obviously been taken by a professional. It was the same girl, but a little younger, and she was smiling and confident.

The girl had freckles, and braces on her teeth. Flavor looked back, her teeth gritted, back to the obscene Polaroids. It was definitely the same girl.

Flavor heard the door open, and McCall's voice: "Flavor, you home?"

She came out into the living room, the Polaroids in her left hand, splayed out like a hand of cards, the portrait in her right hand.

He saw them in her hand and said: "I'm sorry. You shouldn't have found them. I should have put them somewhere you wouldn't find them."

The previous night seemed like another age now. She held the pictures out before her like a challenge, a rebuke.

"McCall, why?"

He shook his head: "Please don't ask me. Please."

"I can't believe it; not this, not something like this, not you."

He looked up to his left, to the ceiling, to nothing.

Her face hardened: "You have exactly thirty seconds to tell me what this is all about, who this girl is, before I arrest you McCall. I swear I mean it."

She could hardly get her breath. She was choking, her lungs rose and fell, the whole room felt it was closing in on her. The silence screamed at her.

"OK, I warn – "

"She's my daughter, Flavor. The girl is my daughter."

He had turned to look at her, and there was a fierce sorrow in his face, and she saw the silent tears coursing one after another down his face, dripping onto his jacket and shirt, speckling them with the dark drops.

"I don't understand, McCall. I don't understand anything. Your daughter?"

He moved over to the sofa, sat down heavily and put his head in his hands. She sat down next to him, and reached out her hand. He took it, like a child, not daring to look at her as he did so.

She said gently:

"Tell me."

He looked up, and his face was hard again, but guilt ran across it like a sabre scar.

"It's like I say, she's my daughter. She WAS my daughter. She died on October 23rd, 1980, well that was the pathologist's estimate, anyway."

"The pictures?"

He took one, looked down at it: "The picture was taken by the man who kidnapped her." He paused: "Raped her. The man who killed her."

"McCall, I am so, so sorry. I never knew."

"And why should you know? It didn't make any headlines outside of Michigan, just an every day run-of-the-mill pervert kidnapping girls from the mall, taking their pictures, doing —" he stopped, choked, and cleared his throat noisily.

"How old was she?"

"Her name was Helen and she was ten years old, born on October 25th, 1969. She would have been eleven two days after she died. We'd planned a party, with a cake, and candles, and we'd bought her gift. We bought her a horse. She had always wanted a horse."

"Honey," he looked up, and as he did, Flavor kissed his forehead and his eyes, "you shouldn't keep these. It isn't healthy. She's at peace now, and you need peace too."

He shook his head wretchedly: "I'm NOT healthy, I can't forget or forgive."

"Why should you forgive, he did a dreadf – "

"Not him, ME, it was MY fault."

"How could it be your fault?"

He got up and paced the room.

"This guy, Badakian, that's his name. He'd killed three girls, and we were hunting him. His MO was to go into mall car parks, wait for some young kid left unattended, then grab her. So, you know, we put out appeals, posters, telling people not to leave their kids alone in car parks, not for a second."

"OK."

"And we staked out places, concealed in vans with spyholes, binoculars, cameras. We had decoy kids, young officers passed off as kids. But he never showed."

Flavor stayed quiet, and McCall looked away a long time

before turning to her: "Helen wanted to go ice-skating, and it was my day off, the first in two weeks. So I said I'd drive her there. And on the way she asked if we could get some ice-cream from Baskin-Robbins. At the mall."

"Oh, honey . . ."

McCall shrugged: "It was like, a minute, two maybe. I just said I'd nip in and get a quart. Pistachio, she loved pistachio. And I told her to hang on for me, I even left the keys in the car, and engine running, I offered it to him on a platter, I . . ."

His breath came in harsh gasps.

"When I came out, the car was gone . . ." he shook his head, his eyes looking into the past, looking into the empty space where his car and his daughter should have been, "it was – gone." His face still registered disbelief; "He took the car and Helen."

She came next to him, slid her arms through his, and held him tight.

"I ran, I ran from the lot, up the road, I had my gun out, and I was running, and everyone thought I was crazy. A black and white pulled up, they probably would have shot me, but I'd worked a beat with one of the guys."

He shook his head again: "A Pontiac Le Mans, 1974, cream with a red vinyl top, two door. And they couldn't find it. There was an APB out in five minutes, and no-one saw it Flavor, no-one saw a damn thing."

"What happened?"

"Three days later we got a call from a hunter who saw the car in some woods way up North. It wasn't our jurisdiction but we went up there. The sheriff's office had found this cabin, and the guy had opened fire on them, so it was, you know, a siege."

"He was the guy?"

McCall nodded: "Eventually he came out with his hands up. Told us where the bodies were: trussed up, out back in some woodshed. She'd been dead for two days."

"You found her?"

He nodded, dumbly, like an exhausted man: "Yes, I found her."

"What happened to the guy?"

"Badakian? Insane. Locked up in a high-security hospital facility. Last I heard he was learning Spanish. Can you get that? Spanish? Wouldn't being insane preclude against learning Spanish, Flavor, wouldn't it? Not sane enough to die, but damned sane enough to learn Spanish."

"Honey, HONEY." She crushed her face into him.

"But, like I say, he couldn't have done it without me. Couldn't have done it without the big, dumb cop with the useless gun, who broke all his own rules, who left his ten year old daughter alone in an unlocked car, with the engine running, and a maniac on the loose. I gave him a gift of my daughter. I said, 'Here, take her.' "

She looked up, and saw the self-disgust all over his face.

"We found the pictures in his cabin. He used to take them, and after the kids were dead, he'd jerk off to this stuff."

"Why KEEP them? It's insane, you should burn them. Keep the GOOD memories of her."

She felt him grope for a handkerchief and blow his nose noisily.

"I have my reasons. After the funeral I just worked. Mary, that was my wife, well, we got divorced. She couldn't take it. I mean, maybe if it had been, just, you know – but the way it happened. She blamed me, and she was right."

"But why keep the pictures?"

"Ever had a tooth, and maybe you lose a filling, or some enamel, and you can't get to see a dentist for a couple of days, and your tongue just won't leave that tooth alone? That was me. The pictures were the tooth, and I LIKED seeing them. Because they reminded me that it was MY fault. And I reckon Helen deserves that, that each day of my miserable, goddamn life, I look at those, and I say 'I'm sorry, and I'll do better today.' And I don't care what happens to those scumbags out there, who know all the tricks and the loopholes, and the smart lawyers, because they're bad guys, and by God if I have anything to do with it they're going away."

She took out her own pure white handkerchief and wiped his eyes with it.

"You make more sense now, McCall. Now I know what tortures your imaginings – do you remember me saying that to you?"

"Yes, yes I do. And you know, sometimes, when I used to feel I couldn't go out there again, when I was scared, and sick of crawling into a sewer every day, I'd take down those pictures, and I'd look into that terrified face . . ." Flavor felt tears drop onto hers, "look into it and it would say to me: 'Coward! You can't go back? Well, how can you NOT go back?' "

"Do they know in Bev Hills?"

"Yes," he wiped his nose. "the chief knows. I applied to the LAPD originally. After Helen died I had two good results with serial killers. But they wouldn't take me. I'd taken counselling, but they thought I might go rogue."

She laughed a little: "You did."

"Well, I think I earned that right after all this time. I'm only sorry – for her, for Helen – that I blew it with Leonard."

Flavor detached herself from McCall, went to the sofa and picked up the portrait of McCall's daughter.

"Put the other ones back in the envelope. Frame this one and put it on the wall. She's your daughter, and I'm sure she loved you."

He threw his head to the sky, his face red and tear-stained, and it was almost as though he was about to howl from pure misery.

"What did she think, Flavor, what did she think, at the moment she died? About me? I was her FATHER, and I abandoned her. A father should protect, I would have died for her, he could have killed me, but I let him take her. I let him take her."

She closed with him again: "Do you believe in God,

in Heaven?"

He shook his head, wretchedly: "Don't know. I did, we went to church, but afterwards . . . No, not now. I believe in justice, and revenge."

"She's dead McCall, she is dead. And wherever she is, she bears you no hatred. You were her father, and whatever life she had, however short, she could not have had without you. She was part of you, your creation. It is a tragedy that she died, but now she is at peace. That's what death is for, so that in the end, there is always peace."

"I hope so much she is at peace."

"And I think she would want YOU to be at peace too." Flavor leaned over and propped the portrait against a mug of pencils on the desk. The freckle-faced ten-year-old smiled out at them.

"Don't keep her in the cupboard. Let her be part of what you and I can be now."

Then she walked him, slowly, as though he were a cripple, or injured, her arms around him, laid him down on the bed, and lay down next to him.

McCall cried for a long, long time, before he slept.

CHAPTER SIXTEEN

Wishaw drove with the fixed intensity of the possessed. He knew, absolutely, that his murderous rage was righteous. Kill, and be killed. It was said in the Old Testament. An eye for an eye. They murdered, he could murder.

There was no law that could ever reach them. Wishaw had known that for nearly thirty years. There was no law, no justice, no reason and no peace.

There could be no peace for him, EVER, until she was fully revenged, until the life they had so wilfully taken – HER life, the life of the only woman he had ever really loved; and the life they had ruined – HIS – were fully paid for in kind and in blood.

On the back seat of his rented car, hidden beneath a frayed and threadbare blanket in its scabbard, was the twin blade of the one that remained in his closet, in the shrine-like apartment he had called home for so long.

He had not made the Angel, the Angel had been created by Ziegal and Nielsen. It was the sickly, deadly child of their hate. And when THEY were ended, then the Angel too, would end. Wishaw knew that with his vicious new certitude.

Simple telephone calls had established that Ziegal was at her second home in Palm Desert, so much easier to reach than when she was in Los Angeles.

And Nielsen would join her at some point, for were they not co-conspirators still stained from the bloodied dagger of that night of murder aboard The Little Prince?

Wishaw knew what he would do. He would gain entry to Ziegal's home, and kill her in the same manner in which the others had died; that would be fitting.

Then he would find Nielsen, and kill him the same way. Then Wishaw would call the police, wait for them, and tell them about the Angel, tell them the truth at last.

Perhaps they would put him in the gas chamber. Wishaw didn't care. He would write his book before he died. He would write about the injustice aboard The Little Prince, about the Hollywood stars who got away with the murder of the woman he loved.

And then Wishaw would write about the Kiss of the Angel, and MILLIONS would read him. The movie companies who had so cruelly rejected him, thanks to the influence of Nielsen, would now flock to buy the rights.

He would get the fame and critical acclaim of which he had been cheated for so long.

Flavor and McCall came out of the apartment.

She said: "Wow! That is some place."

Two uniformed policemen in a patrol car looked meaningfully over at the two of them, and one of them, a man Flavor knew, covered his mouth with his hand and said something to his colleague. There was a sniggering smile on his face.

When they were out of earshot, McCall said: "Everybody's gonna know I went in there with you. You're asking for trouble."

The patrolmen were staring and Flavor returned the stares: "I don't give a damn. You went in with me because you are a material witness."

"What you mean is, I made an illegal entry into those premises the FIRST time, and I had no business being there the SECOND. What if they learn that?"

"You came by some information that Wishaw may have one of the murder weapons in his apartment, and as a good citizen you informed your local police. Later I went to the scene with you, that is perfectly proper."

"If they question the Korean, they're going to know I went there posing as a cop."

"You ARE a cop, McCall, one of the best damn cops I've ever known."

"The law says different, and the whole world knows you're living at my place now. This isn't going to help your career."

She shrugged: "Get in the car, doomsayer. When we get Wishaw and he confesses, or we link him somehow with forensic, they're going to love me."

McCall said, but only to himself, I doubt it. And somehow? What? A smell, a feel, a sense of unease.

"There's been an APB out for 24 hours, and you've known since this morning that he rented a car from Alamo down at LAX. How come he isn't in custody?"

She got in the car without answering, conscious of the patrolmen's gaze. He got in next to her, and she gave him a delayed answer: "Could be he's dumped the car and crossed the Mexican border."

"But logically he must be heading for Ziegal or Nielsen, or both."

She nodded: "They're warned, and both have declined protection. They've both promised to sit tight."

"Where?"

"Ziegal's in Palm Desert, Nielsen's here. The LAPD have a watch on Nielsen and the police at Palm Desert have a car outside Ziegal's place."

"For how long?"

"Long as necessary."

"Something not right about this."

"Like what?" She started to fiddle in the glove compartment, then cursed silently.

"You out of cigarettes? Come to think of it I haven't seen you smoke since – hey, since you first stayed at my place."

She laughed: "I've given up, but for a moment there I forgot, force of habit. Maybe we can patent you, McCall, and stick you on arms like a patch. You worked with me. And speaking of addictions, there's a lack of Snicker wrappers up at Havenhurst."

He looked away sheepishly: "'Thought I'd better keep in some kind of shape now I'm not alone."

She leaned across and kissed him. Saw that the patrolmen saw it, didn't care.

They looked at each other for a long time, and she said, carefully: "You OK? About, you know?"

He nodded: "Yeah, actually I'm OK."

Something had been lifted from his shoulders. The pain and regret and the shame would always remain a part of him, like a scar. But he felt now it was a scar he could look at with peace; a scar whose livid intensity would fade in time; she had waved some wand and helped him to understand it as part of his past, not his present.

He had dumped the bitter agony like a burden, by the roadside. He had carried it long enough. Something Flavor said had worked like a combination to a safe containing the secret of escape.

She had said: 'That's what death is for. So we can have peace.' And he had thought about that. If there could not be peace after death, then what WAS death for?

His daughter was at peace now, and the past could be seen for what it was, another time, another life. If his daughter could be at peace, then he, McCall, could allow himself some peace also.

When he had awoken from his tear-drugged sleep he had

taken the brutal Polaroids, the evil souvenirs of pain and shame that he carried like the tattooed number of a former death camp prisoner, and he had burned them in the sink.

The flames were cleansing, and the blackened ashes washed away like the greasepaint of a mask he had been forced to wear.

His daughter, whom he loved, and missed beyond speaking of it, and for whom he would still weep when the pain was too much, was now the girl in the portrait, frozen in youth and innocence.

Flavor said: "You were saying something wasn't right about this?"

"Heck, I don't know."

"It's like you said, it's a shrine in there, he was MARRIED to Kathleen O'Malley, he has MOTIVE, he has OPPORTUNITY – "

"But how did he get in to see Helm, Alassio – to see Jack: And how did he lure Victoria Astaire to Point Dume? I mean?"

"That's a twin-blade set in there, McCall," she thumbed across to the scruffy apartment on the run-down street, "Mail order, the torn-out page from the catalogue is still there. Twin Samurai swords. And there's only one in there. So he has the other one. That blade is sharp enough, and tough enough to sever a head from a body, right?"

"Sure, oh sure. But I've known Wishaw a few years. Always thought he was a scum-sucking sleazebag, but I never thought him capable of this."

"Honey, the QUIET ones. It's always the way. They lead secret lives, and when they go, they go for blow."

"Maybe. Did he know Jack?"

"Not that I'm aware of. But he WAS a screenwriter."

"Was he a member of the Guild?"

"He must have wished. To be a member of the Guild you have to have something produced, movie, TV, something."

"So – shit, she had DINNER with him, Flavor."

"Or them, maybe it isn't just Wishaw."

"And why Jack, I can understand the others, but why should he have such a grudge against you he'd want to kill you, or your room-mate?"

Flavor pulled a face: "Dunno, but he may have thought if he got me or Jack you'd ease up or something, maybe he . . ." her voice fell lamely away.

"And there was no wood in the apartment, no chippings, nothing he could have made the angels with, it's . . . shit," McCall rammed his fist against the dash, "it's bugging me."

"You were the one found the blade, found the certificate. You seemed sure enough at the time."

"Yeah," he bit his lip, "seemed so logical at the time."

Flavor stuck out her hand and pulled on a finger: "One; at the moment he's the best we've got. He's linked to The Little Prince because his ex-wife got wasted on that boat, and we've always believed that was the key." Flavor pulled on her second finger, "Two, he's on the run, with a sword. I mean, why would a guy like Wishaw buy a sword, TWO swords, then disappear carrying one of them? What other reason except that he is the Angel and is determined to either get away or finish the job?"

"Yeah, you're right."

Flavor pointed to one of the policemen: "See him? His name is Henry, Michael Henry. He once asked me out on a date."

"Did you go?"

"No."

"Why not."

"Because he isn't my type, and anyway he has horse-breath."

McCall laughed, choked, giggled. And Flavor said: "Yeah, Henry, you never made first base, and you're all burned up with jealousy, right?"

But the patrolman knew he was being talked about, laughed at, and he looked away.

McCall said: "Why'd you do that, Flavor?"

"Because they're sitting there all smug and comfortable

counting the days to their pensions, and they're laughing at your discomfort, and you're smarter than both of them."

"So, what the hell."

"You're my man, McCall, you are my man, and I don't like people attacking my man." She gave him a wide-eyed innocent grin.

He said: "You're incorrigible. Let's go home."

"Let's go home. Yes, sir, I like that, let's go home. OUR home."

"Our home, isn't that WEIRD?"

She started the engine: "It's just about the best thing I've ever heard."

Wishaw came in from the desert on foot. He had practised this many times before, rehearsing it like some special operations soldier who knows that one day he will need the nerve and the courage to cross the dangerous border.

A small dune protected him from view as he surveyed the garden that touched green up to a chain mesh fence and then abruptly surrendered to the sand.

He lay there until the sun sank and the purple of dusk spread its cloak over the desert. He lay and watched.

He lay and was watched.

The Chief was formal, courteous, but insistent. With the finality of a judge's sentence, he said: "It is over, Lieutenant. You gave it your best shot, and it wasn't enough. You need not reproach yourself. You're formally relieved."

Flavor was on the carpet, literally, in front of the big, mahogany desk, and as she heard the words she felt her world retreat, shrink miscroscopically like some object viewed through the wrong end of a telescope.

She had already made her protests, rationalised her rationales, pleaded her pleas for more time, and they had bounced off the chief's armoured resolution like arrows off a tank.

There had been a deadline, she knew that, but with

Wishaw's disappearance, his becoming the object of a man-hunt, she had assumed . . .

She said finally, desperately, almost bitterly: "Sir, with respect, I should like to know if my relationship with Lt. McCall of the Beverly Hills Police Department has any bearing on this decision?"

Fuck 'em. If she was off the case, she was off, but she wouldn't go quietly in some conspiracy of silence. Let them be confronted with what they hated most, plain speaking.

But the Chief just tut-tutted, poo-poohed, no bearing at all, private matter, not taken into consideration, she could rest assured, private life, public duty, no conflict whatsoever, wholly matter of operational efficiency.

Flavor knew. It was bad enough Black Murder Cop's Lesbo Room-mate Beheaded. Now they had Black Murder Hunt Cop in Love-Fest with Rogue White Cop After Lesbo Pal Slaying.

And there was nothing she could really, EVER say to counter that. Love was a language people like this had never learned. The Chief added: "You've played an important role in this. When the suspect is caught and tried, I am sure you will receive an appropriate commendation."

But the face said: You're an embarrassment, you made waves, you stood out. OK if you'd succeeded, but you failed.

My career just effectively ended, she thought with a rush of shock.

I dug my own grave. First Jack, then the Angel, now McCall. I got all the way here, walked the hardest road, from Mississippi to respectability, a life and a career, and now it has all been in vain.

She was given a curt nod of dismissal and turned to leave the room. At the door she paused and turned, to see looks of weary exasperation like hosts with a tiresome guest who lingers too long.

"Yes?"

"Sir. Me and Lt. McCall – "

"I've assured you – "

"It's real, sir. I mean, we actually love one another. It happens even to people like us."

The Chief couldn't resist it.

"I believe you." He paused for effect: "Your funerals."

She had been awake a long time, McCall's head cradled into her shoulder, his big arm across her stomach, the blonde hairs on his fore-arm highlighted as the sun began to finally filter into the room.

Flavor had hardly slept. She was beyond anger, beyond bitterness or remorse, she felt only a strange kind of calm and logic.

The man beside her was a factor in everything that had happened. What she had discovered with him was worth a career, was worth the glittering and ultimately tarnished prizes she had once coveted.

She now knew what mothers felt, and she had never before understood. That the child was worth more than everything. Was THE reason, THE answer. She felt that with McCall, and maybe one day they would have children too.

It was over with the LAPD, that was clear. Wishaw would be caught, presumably; convicted, presumably; and she knew with vicious clarity that she and McCall would be out of the final scene, discarded in pieces of celluloid on the cutting room floor like the cut scenes of out-of-favour actors.

But there could be life after the police, and there were other Americas than Los Angeles.

Flavor knew it would be uncharted waters, mined and shark-filled, given their different colours, but there was a life for them; they would MAKE a life for themselves.

Yet there was a harsh truth she had to face, perhaps ultimately they would BOTH have to face, whatever they felt about each other. They had FAILED. Individually, and as a team. They had failed as detectives, as police officers.

The Angel had killed with impunity, and was still at large. Why hadn't they seen the Wishaw possibility until it was too late?

Had she been so unconsciously bound up in McCall, first in hostility, then in comradeship, and latterly in love, and he in her, that they had missed seeing wood for trees?

The telephone rang and she grabbed at it, feeling McCall murmur and moan in his sleep.

The voice said: "It's Carlo. I thought you'd want to know this. They found Wishaw's rental car in San Bernardino."

"Yeah?" She was bolt upright in the bed.

"And there's a sighting of someone fitting his description boarding a bus for Phoenix."

"When?"

"Thirty-six hours ago."

"Hell. Where does the bus stop?"

"Indio, then Desert Center, Blythe, a run through to Buckeye, then into Phoenix."

"Any sightings of him getting off?"

"The CHP are checking all the bus stations up to Blythe, and the Arizona Highway Patrol are doing Buckeye and Phoenix, but listen, there's more. Last night the police in Palm Desert got a 911 about a prowler back of Redwood Drive – "

"Ziegal's place!"

"She'd asked for the surveillance on her house to be ended, but it was a neighbour made the call. He says he saw a guy with a small backpack in the desert at the back of the houses, so the local guys went round to check it out."

"They find anything?"

"Kind of. They checked the street, went to Ziegal's place, she let them in, they checked the place top to bottom, nothing." Flavor heard the flicking of a notebook page, "They, ah, went out back, shone their flash lights and saw what they thought was a kid."

"A kid?"

"Yeah, too small to be an adult, ran off into the desert. So they hung around in the car, lights off, watching for a couple of hours. Zero. Sounds like some kid goofing off."

"You say it was Ziegal herself who let them in."

"That's what they said."

Flavor bit her thumbnail and thought.

"That's about it."

She came out of her tiny reverie: "Hey, yeah, thanks Carlo. I shouldn't know any of this. You have a new boss as of yesterday noon."

"Really?" the voice said, with mock astonishment, "Then I insist you totally disregard this information."

She laughed: "I owe you."

"Make it a cold one. Not sure what this amounts to, but there it is."

"Thanks."

"We think you got a rough deal. Good luck to you and your guy."

"We'll make it – thanks again, Carlo."

Flavor slipped quietly out of the bed, pulled on jeans and a sweat shirt, and laced on a pair of scuffed Reeboks. She took the polished leather shoulder holster with the .357 Smith and Wesson, off the chair-back, and buckled on the harness.

She went to the bathroom and quickly cleaned her teeth. Facing the mirror, her mouth full of dentifrice foam, she asked herself. What is it? What is it you intend to do?

And at that moment, she didn't know. But she knew her skin tingled and there was a strange topsy-turvy sensation in her stomach. She felt that things were shifting in her subconscious like some game where panels have to be moved and slotted until a pattern is complete.

She rinsed, gargled, and dried her mouth with a towel, then moved into the living room, picked up the telephone, and dialled, from memory, the number of Kirk Nielsen's Beverly Hills home.

A housekeeper answered and when she asked for Mr. Nielsen, was told he was out of town. Mrs. Nielsen was there, but was still sleeping, and the housekeeper said she was not prepared to disturb the lady of the house.

Flavor severed the connection, got a new tone, and

dialled Sarah Ziegal's home in Palm Desert. As the number rang Flavor looked at her watch. It was 6.50 a.m. If Ziegal answered she'd be angry, and Flavor did not even know what she would say if a woman DID pick up the phone.

But the long rings went on, no machine kicked in, and Flavor thought of that empty house, the corridor, the study where she had sat opposite the actress, and Ziegal, poised and arched, like a cobra ready to strike.

And that overpowering essence of evil.

She replaced the receiver.

If the prowler last night WAS Wishaw, despite what the cops thought they saw, then he must be long gone, because Ziegal was OK, the cops had confirmed that, and the intruder had not got into the house, because they'd gone through the place.

Flavor looked at the portrait of McCall's murdered daughter, then closed her eyes. Sometimes, doing this job was like swimming in a sea of evil.

Flavor opened her eyes and said aloud: "Do it."

For a moment she considered waking McCall, then dismissed it. It was a wild idea to go there anyway, even she was off the case now. But McCall was under suspension and might face charges; she couldn't risk the local cops stopping the two of them.

She found a pad and pen, scribbled a note, and left it outside the bedroom door. She got her bag, her car keys, pulled on a leather jacket, and went out, closing the door quietly behind her.

CHAPTER SEVENTEEN

McCall awoke slowly, stretched, realised Flavor was missing, and felt an inexplicable start of alarm at her loss. He called her name.

The apartment was silent. He swung out of the bed, pulled on his shorts, and as he opened the bedroom door his feet caught on the note Flavor had left.

He picked up the ripped out notebook sheet and read: 'McCall. Gone to Ziegal's in Palm Desert. Suspect Wishaw is hanging around there. Maybe in hiding. If I don't call by noon, send the cavalry to 1419 Redwood Drive. Love you. F.'

McCall cursed, rushed back into the bedroom and dressed hurriedly. He opened the closet and took the Colt Gold Cup automatic from its newspaper wrapping, and stuffed it into the waistband of his pants, the butt under his T-shirt, then he put on his sports jacket.

He checked his watch. It was 8.20. What the hell time

had she left? He went to his parking space, unlocked the MGB, climbed in and turned the key.

Nothing. Not a whirr, not a turn, not even a clunk. The battery was stone dead, or the solenoid had gone. He cursed, got out, lifted the hood, checked the battery terminal leads, then turned the ignition key once more. Nothing.

He looked around, gripped by a sudden sense of panic. Call the AAA? Goddamn it, he remembered he wasn't even a member of the triple A.

The foreign car specialists on Fairfax? They came in at eight. But even if they sent someone out straight away – and he wasn't even sure if they did call-outs, it'd be, what? – a half hour at best.

There was a garage at the bottom of Havenhurst on Santa Monica Boulevard, maybe they'd come out. He banged his fist on the canvas hood. Damn it. In the next bay was Mrs. Annameyer's Chevy Impala, and for a wild moment he considered hot-wiring it, then instantly rejected it. His catalogue of law-breaking could do without Grand Theft, Auto.

Apartment 14. He rushed back to the block, went up to the second floor, found 14 and pressed the buzzer. He waited, nervously, then pressed again.

He didn't know why, but he had a terrible sense of danger. Had Flavor heard something? He dimly remembered the telephone going earlier. And why would she go to Ziegal's place now? And alone?

The door opened and a very sleep-crumpled middle-aged woman in housecoat and hair-curlers, said: "Lt. McCall? Actually, I've been meaning to speak to you about your cat, she's – "

"Mrs. Annameyer, may we discuss that another time. This is an emergency. May I please borrow your car?"

"Borrow my CAR?"

"Rent! RENT your car." He had his wallet out, flipping out the notes. When he'd last checked there was about 130 dollars.

"Well, I don't know. I was going to my daughter's this morning."

"A hundred and thirty dollars, Mrs. Annameyer." He peeled them off one by one into her moist palm, two fifties, a twenty, three fives, three one dollar bills.

"A hundred and thirty EIGHT dollars. Please! I'll look after it. You have my word." Her eyes were still unsure, but the patina of greed was slowly glossing over her anxiety.

"Police business."

"No chases, like on the TV?"

"No chases – cross my heart and hope to die."

"We-e-ll . . ." she turned, waddled off and came back with a bunch of keys. The plastic ring said: Hug a Mom today.

"Gas?" he said, anxiously.

"Filled up yesterday. You'll replace it?"

"Absolutely."

"Be sure and – "

But he was gone, and seconds later she winced as she heard her engine roar, and her tyres scream as he reversed out of the space, and burned rubber as he shot up the ramp into Havenhurst.

Only the currency, warm and moistening now in her closed fist, made everything seem better.

Outside Palm Desert Flavor pulled into a gas station and called Ziegal's home from a payphone, but heard just the long, ominous repeated ringing tone.

She drove on, past the Church of the Holy Saviour, turned into Redwood Drive, and pulled over outside Sarah Ziegal's house. There were no cars parked on the curved driveway, and the blinds were drawn on the windows.

Flavor sat and watched. And it was as though the house stared back malevolently. It was now nearly eleven, and the sun was high and hot, yet the house seemed to live in its own shadow. Flavor shivered.

She remembered that other house of her childhood, the

289

one on the slightly higher ground on the edge of her home town. At length she got out of the car and walked slowly up the drive.

The house watched, the blind-drawn windows like sun-shaded eyes. Flavor checked the garage windows, scratching at the darkened glass, until she remembered that they were covered on the inside to prevent anyone seeing in. And once again, she thought: Why?

Who had secrets in their garage? She approached the big black front door, and rang the bell, watching the spyhole from the corner of her eye to see if it darkened slightly, a sure sign that someone was peering out, checking the visitor.

There was nothing. Flavor rang again, listening to the empty tone echoing inside the closed house. She hammered with her fist on the door, calling out: "Miss Ziegal? Lt. Cartouche, LAPD."

After a minute without reaction, Flavor walked to one side of the house, and along a paved path until she reached a wooden fence about six feet high. There was an inset wooden door that Flavor tried to open. It was locked.

Looking around she could see that the street was quiet, torpid in the blazing sun that now began to burn her face. Quickly she reached up, grabbed the top of the wall, hooked her feet on the door latch, clambered one leg onto the top of the wall, and hauled herself up and over.

She landed on the balls of her feet, crouched, tensed and stayed like that, looking around her. In front of her was the swimming pool she had previously glimpsed through the half-drawn blinds of Sarah Ziegal's study.

This was not the Hollywood fantasy pool, the heart-shaped extravagance or the mock-Grecian indulgence. The poolside paving stones were cracked and scarred, and weeds poked out from the gaps between.

The pool was long, and looked uncannily like a European coffin, bulging outwards two thirds of the way along its length, then tapering back in.

It was full of water, but not the kind anyone would wish

to swim in. It was dark, virtually opaque and covered in algae. Some aged and dirt-covered pool furniture lay next to a derelict barbecue set. It was as though the occupants who had once enjoyed this outdoor area had long ago fled.

Flavor unholstered her gun, unchambered it and checked that all six rounds were in place. She pushed the chamber back in, then kept the gun out at her side, barrel pointing downwards, her finger across the trigger guard.

This was guard-dog territory, and if Ziegal had one it would surely have put in an appearance by now. But if some 60 lb Rottweiler did come hurtling at her, she wanted to be ready for it.

Or anything else.

The cop in her said: This is unlawful entry, Flavor. And she didn't care. It was beyond all rules, and codes and rights. It was the new world she was in now.

If Wishaw was here, this was not the academic forensic cut and thrust of a courtroom. It was life and death. His, or hers. She moved around the back of the house, looking for some method of getting into the house, an unlocked door or a window carelessly unlatched.

Despite a careful inspection she found nothing. She made a decision; pausing in front of a door that led to a massive, open and empty kitchen she hesitated for a second, then reversed her gun, and smashed the glass with the butt.

She put her hand gingerly through the gap, found the key, carefully unlocked the door, removed her hand just as carefully, and let herself in.

Flavor stood, feet initially crunching on the broken glass, ears attuned for the slightest sound. And waited.

McCall drummed his fingers against the steering wheel as the rush-hour traffic moved at a crawl where the Hollywood Freeway intersected the Pasadena at Downtown.

Eventually the sluggish vein of vehicles cleared, he put his foot down to the floor and the aging Impala picked up speed. He swooped in and out of lanes, the speedometer needle hovering around seventy, praying no traffic cop would pull him over.

And damn it all he didn't even know how much further ahead she was. He passed West Covina and the sign for the Forest Lawn Memorial Park at Covina Hills.

He flashed back in his mind to that other Forest Lawn ceremony; Helm's funeral at Hollywood Hills. That seemed as though it had happened in another world, to another man.

Except the reason for his presence was the same as today. The Angel. McCall gunned the Impala for all it was worth. He had asked Mrs. Annameyer about the gas, he hadn't asked about the oil.

Nothing moved in the house. Flavor could hear her own breathing.

She realised she was almost hyperventilating, and deliberately tried to slow her intake of air, taking in measured lungfuls, and feeling her whole body calm.

She shouted: "Ziegal? You OK?"

Flavor felt frightened, but also slightly foolish. Perhaps Ziegal was shopping, or visiting with friends. Flavor had gained illegal entry into a house where the owner might be asleep, sedated, or out.

As the sound of her voice diminished, silence flooded back like the decreasing rings of water closing over an intruding stone. It was then she noticed the smell, the smell she thought of in the way humans pigeonhole things as the Ziegal-smell. Sinisterly medicinal, a smell of illness and damp and darkness.

She walked through the kitchen, still holding the gun outwards, her grip relaxed, finger still outside the trigger guard. She had no wish to shoot herself – or anyone else – accidentally.

The kitchen was spotless, there were no recently-cooked food smells, nor the aroma of coffee. She went through into a dining room, the table bare.

Gun in hand she checked out every room downstairs,

including the study where she had once questioned Sarah Ziegal. In that study, on the desk was a closed business diary. Flavor flipped it with her left hand, flicking through the days immediately prior to that day.

There were seemingly innocuous notations, a dinner here, a lunch there; a Los Angeles 213 number, a name, Jane Carson. A small flame of recognition flashed briefly in Flavor's brain, then went out as abruptly like a dead star.

She flicked through the pages. A manicurist appointment, an interview with a TV magazine. August 24th, the written entry, 'G's birthday.' The G would mean Gregory. Today was her dead son's birthday.

Out of curiosity Flavor flicked back to February, then January, the month the boy had died. She went through each day, but found no reference to the anniversary of his death.

Suddenly Flavor stiffened, and the tiny hairs on the nape of her neck stood out on end. Somewhere in the house, beyond it or beneath it, there was the almost imperceptible muffled sound of metal on metal, like some iron door clanging shut.

Cautiously she stepped out of the study and into the corridor, and stood, head cocked, almost like a wild animal, listening intently.

The sound was not repeated.

Slowly, deliberately, measuring her step quietly, she moved to the foot of the long, curving stairs and started the climb. At the top she paused on the landing, and moved to the nearest door.

She listened, took a deep breath, kicked in the door, and pushed her back up against the wall, her gun in both hands. When there was no response she went slowly in.

The bedroom was empty. She repeated the process with each bedroom in turn – seven in all, nerves strung taut and tight. Each room was empty. Five bathrooms in all, each neat, ordered and empty of any human life.

One bathroom off the main bedroom was clearly used by Ziegal, animated with her collections of expensive designer toiletries, treatments and perfumes. The smell was fainter here, almost overpowered by the scents and the residue aroma of baths and showers taken, but she could still detect it.

The rest of the bathrooms were hotel or hospital-like, arranged as if for guests or patients who have so far failed to arrive.

Flavor went back downstairs and moved along the bisecting corridor in the opposite direction. She found two further large rooms, one graced by a Steinway grand piano. In the other the floor was stripped and polished pine board, and the room contained a Stepmaster, an exercise bike, a powered treadmill walker with computer graphics and arm-rails, and a full set of stainless-steel weightlifting and bench-press equipment.

It wasn't unusual. Stars were keen on physical fitness, and today even middle-aged women went for the burn with weight-training.

At the corridor's end Flavor found another door. Opening it she discovered a utility room with a giant Maytag washing machine and tumble drier, and beyond she could see through a half-glassed door the gloomy outline of the interior of the multiple garage.

Imagining a footfall behind her, Flavor swivelled, gun outstretched, finger inside the guard, on the curved trigger. Her heart was pounding.

But there was nothing, only the phantom of imagination, and slowly she turned back to her task, moving through the utility room, instinctively feeling the surfaces of the washer and drier with her left hand, and getting only a cold response to her touch. It was like an abandoned home.

She peered through the glass panels of the door into the musty, warm darkness of the garage, and could see at least three vehicles, two cars of different shape and outline, and a third bulkier, higher-sided vehicle.

She opened the door, cautiously ran her hand up the wall, and found a switch, tripped it, and three strip lights stuttered into life with a spasmodic jerk.

Flavor crouched back into the cover of the utility room, and waited; but nothing moved in the illuminated garage. The car nearest to her was a large Mercedes saloon with a personalised California licence plate that boasted: 'Nielsen.'

Flavor could feel the blood pound in her temples. She felt the hood of the Mercedes, and found it very hot. Nielsen had driven here and recently. Why had he got away from the guard protecting him from Wishaw? And where was he now? In the house somewhere?

She could hear her own harsh breathing in the silent garage as she moved to the next car. It was the latest Mercedes sports convertible. Ziegal had said she owned such a car, so presumably that was hers. It had a normal California licence plate containing letters and figures, unlike Nielsen's personalised plate. Flavor checked the convertible's hood. Compared to Nielsen's the car was cold. It hadn't been driven for hours, that was obvious.

Flavor moved on to the next vehicle. It was a grey, Ford Econoline van. She knelt to look at the license plates, and tensed as she recognised the dried-blood red of a Missouri registration.

She had once asked Sarah Ziegal if she owned a van. That was after the witness had spotted a van near the scene of Victoria Astaire's murder at Point Dume.

The actress had laughed at the idea, and said it was checkable. And Flavor had checked, and Sarah Ziegal had no such van registered to her, the DMV in Sacramento, the state capital, had confirmed that.

But someone visiting this house, or living in it, owned such a van registered in the State of Missouri. And Flavor silently cursed herself, for by Ziegal's later disclosures the woman was born just across the state line from St. Louis, Missouri. Flavor should then have asked the Missouri and Illinois DMV's to run checks on Ziegal.

Flavor tried the handle of the rear door only to find it locked, but as she did so she winced in pain as her leg caught painfully on a metal protuberance. She knelt and examined it. It was a metal runnel, grooved and oiled with raised sides. On looking she found a similar one on the other side of the rear of the van.

The runnels went perpendicularly into specially milled entrances in the bottom of the van's rear doors.

She racked her brains as to where she had seen the like before, then remembered UPS and Federal Express parcel trucks that sometimes had small hydraulic lifts installed to deal with heavy packages.

The rear doors opened and a platform was lowered mechanically down the runnels. Some organisations and charities installed them so they could lower disabled people in wheelchairs from van to ground. She checked the hood of the van; normal temperature.

She froze. The sound again; possibly amplified by the concrete floor of the garage. It seemed to come from below, a dull, muffled boom with that sense of metallic collision. Flavor closed her eyes, trying to locate it.

Was it directly beneath her, or was that a trick of accoustics, and it was in fact somewhere way off, in an attic perhaps, or even outside of the house?

The heat in the garage was stifling, and she was sweating, realising too with a faint sense of self-revulsion that she had not showered that morning.

She checked the windows and found black paper encrusted against each glass panel. She looked around the garage, taking in the normal paraphernalia of suburban America. An orange garden hose on a large green spool looking like a snoozing snake; a lawn mower, a lawn trimmer, several grimy pool parasols, some stacked plastic chairs, a heavy, gas-powered barbecue, several spades and forks, some packing cases, several cartons bearing brand names of kitchenware and hi-fi equipment. A pile of old Sunday supplement magazines. Some fertiliser and old plant pots.

Flavor turned to go, then stopped. A garden hose, a lawn

mower, a lawn trimmer, a gas-powered barbecue, spades and forks. A gas-powered barbecue?

Outside was a perfectly good, but left-to-decay barbecue. And it was clear that Sarah Ziegal didn't hold cosy neighbourhood cook-outs judging from the state of the pool and its surrounds.

So why another barbecue? This was America, Ziegal was Hollywood, such people just bought because they had money even if they had no need. But a second barbecue? She went over to the matt-black equipment, touching it almost suspiciously as if it were some ferocious but temporarily dormant animal.

It was heavy, and hardly moved at her touch. She pushed again, putting her bodyweight against it. Two things happened. The barbecue moved on its rubber wheels and she saw the plastic-encased chain that was tied to one strut, and disappeared into a drilled hole in the garage floor.

She pushed it more until it was clear of its original parking space, and saw a big curved metal ring set into a recessed steel flap. On the flap was the triangular nuclear sign in black and yellow.

The barbecue set was to conceal the flap. Anyone coming out simply had to pull on the chain from inside to clear the flap. Peering closer she saw a small, shiny metal plate riveted into the large steel flap. Printed on it was: "Nuclear fallout shelter, manufactured by Belleville Construction, 1232, Mark Twain Avenue, Fairlawn Industrial Park, Farmington, Mo."

Beneath her was a nuclear bunker.

She stood up, trying to calm herself, to slow her heart that pumped and thumped like a steam hammer beneath her ribs. She shook her head, and said aloud:

"No. Jesus, I can't."

McCall's voice that night when both their worlds changed. 'If you want to be brave, do it. Instead of walking away, stay; instead of stopping, walk down the cellar stairs, even if your ass is Arctic with fear and your fucking hands shake and you can't breathe and you want to die. Just walk down and shake hands with fear and say, fuck you baby, 'cause here I am, now what you gonna do.'

But Jesus, McCall, that was in a warm bed, the conversation a prelude to love, and you also said, didn't you, that there's no such thing as cowards because nobody says you have to do it, no-one can make you, and no-one knows how bad it is? Because there is only YOU there when it happens, you said that too, McCall.

And it was all metaphorical, the cellar was just a metaphor; and now. She prayed; help me, McCall. And the inner mocking voice said; yeah, you're just a chicken-shit jigaboo who wants to run like a frightened shack darkie from the Georgia woods. A nigger wanting help from The Man.

That big redneck instructor at police academy, with his stage whisper. A nigger will always cut and run.

All the dreams and the terrors and the memories. She closed her eyes, and the witch voice challenged her. Make them go away, Flavor, make them go away. This is the only way.

She opened her eyes, knelt down, and pulled on the recessed handle, swinging up the metalled section of the floor with a flatulent sigh of hydraulics.

The Ziegal-smell belched out, and hit her like the foul breath of a subterranean monster. A warm, medicinal dampness, something vile and ill, a smell redolent of decay and neglect.

She gagged slightly, then steadied herself.

Beneath her she saw the first metallic steps of a staircase-ladder that led down into an eerie glow from subdued red lighting. She peered in and listened, trying to banish the smell from her mind.

It was silent down there, with the exception of a low hum of electricity.

She told herself. I don't have to go down there. Despite everything McCall said, despite the witch-voice, I don't HAVE to go down there.

And then, as if it was happening automatically, involuntarily, she watched as first one leg moved, then the other, and one foot was on the first step, and the second foot followed.

Slowly, Flavor Cartouche descended into the literal depths of her childhood nightmares.

McCall had the air-conditioning on full but the Impala was still like an oven. He rolled down the window and it was as though someone had opened a furnace door.

He cursed: "Shit, it must be 120 out there."

He'd passed Banning five minutes previously, and was almost at the first of the exits for Palm Springs. The temperature gauge needle was edging dangerously up into the red, and the oil warning light had been on for the last fifteen minutes.

He dared not stop, and the car, labouring against the heat, the years, and this cruel and unusual punishment, battled on.

This is what it must be like, McCall thought, as the fear gripped him, to be a twin; to feel someone else's pain or danger as though it was happening to you. She was in danger, he was sure of it.

The car engine missed – it was just a hiccup, almost possible to believe it had not happened – then the straining, overheating engine struggled valiantly on.

McCall gritted his teeth. It had to last until Palm Desert. It had to. He could argue the toss with Mrs. Annameyer later.

Her feet echoed eerily on the metal steps as she climbed slowly down, left hand on the rail, right hand and gun outstretched.

When she reached the bottom she found herself in a passage lit by red lights protected by bars, the type found in military establishments.

Slowly, willing herself every step of the way, she moved on until she reached a steel door. She paused and listened, and hearing nothing, pushed with the palm of her hand. The door swung open and once again she heard the breathy swish of hydraulics. Everything was power assisted, as though for someone without strength.

She flattened herself against the wall and waited, then stepped in through the opened space. It was a room, lying in an oblong crossways across the route indicated by yet another doorway directly opposite.

The smell dominated the room. If the smell WAS Ziegal, ORIGINATED from Ziegal then this is where she spent most of her time, not in the house, because here the smell permeated the very molecules of the place.

The room was similarly lit, and in one corner a single, metal-framed bed was covered with a dark, rough blanket. To her left was a single metal table, two spartan looking chairs, and on the table, a plate, and mug that looked, in that light, to be made of garish plastic.

But it was the walls that thrilled and chilled her. Two portraits, each occupying the full height of each wall. One showed a female angel – essentially a woman with wings sprouting from her shoulder blades – holding a sword in one hand, and a severed head by the hair in the other.

The remaining portrait was, on closer look, actually a blown-up and thus slightly blurred photograph. Flavor recognised the statue above Kathleen O'Malley's tomb.

She moved forward, stiff and knotted with tension, the sweat pouring from her in streams, forward to the next door. She pushed gently, and once again the hydraulics took over and the door sighed open. The sound unnerved Flavor, it was uncannily like the aspirations of a sleeping child.

She waited, then moved cautiously into the next room. This was bigger, and at each side Flavor saw bolted, metal-frame storage racks containing industrial-size cans of food, so identified by simple white labels; and clear plastic containers of what was labelled as purified water.

It was as though someone was genuinely waiting to sit out a nuclear holocaust down here. In the Sixties, at the height of the cold war paranoia, yes, but now, in the Nineties with the Soviet Union collapsed, the thought of a global, super-power mega-nuclear exchange virtually unthinkable?

A clicking noise froze her. It was like a door opening, until she remembered that these were not normal doors, and then, seconds later, another click, and a whirring noise that jolted her heart with adrenaline until she recognised the sound as an electrical motor kickstarted into action some-where deeper in the bunker.

She tried to think rationally. Air must be pumped in, filtered, and the pump must be controlled by some air-purity gauge or thermostat.

Behind a rack of storage shelves was a kitchenette with bottled butane gas cylinders, and hard-block miniature cooking stoves normally used for instant cooking by troops.

Another door, and once more the soft child-sigh of the door opening. Another sound, not distant, here in this new room, a rapid machine-gun rate of clicks, that was somehow known, and yet anachronistic. She tried to place it, trying to put a picture to the sound.

She stepped further into the room, and stopped as her eyes took in the movement of light, the spear-like flashes of black and white stabbing into the red gloom.

Another storage shelf blocked her full view, and when she stepped around it, gun outstretched in a two-handed grip, she was more astonished than frightened.

She was in a room furnished like any living room might be. A couch, two easy chairs, table lamps, a television and VCR, a carpet, some ornaments.

And there, in the centre of the room, the cause of the partly-remembered clicking noise, a 35 mm movie projector, focusing its strange blue-white light in a square against one blank wall of this bizarre underground room.

She glanced up at the crackling, scratched black and white images, men and women naked and ludicrous, writhing in a melange of flesh.

She looked away from the harsh light, refocused, and

peered into an as yet unexamined and darkened corner of the room.

Flavor gasped, stepped back, her chest tightening, and thumbed the hammer back on her Smith and Wesson in two audible clicks.

For in the corner was a stiff-backed armchair, and there was a clear silhouette of someone sitting in it.

CHAPTER EIGHTEEN

McCall was driving through a vapour trail of his car's own steam and blue-black smoke, the Impala groaning, grinding, grunting and protesting like a tortured galley slave.

He was three miles from Palm Desert, he could see the town shimmering in the distance below the low hills like some mirage, when the car finally juddered, gave an almost human death rattle, and rolled silently to a halt, smoke pouring from the hood like lifeblood.

He got out, tried to flag down a Toyota that sped past without stopping, then began to run, the mid-day sun like a giant branding-iron that scorched him across his head and face.

McCall felt the Colt like a spear digging into his side, regretted the extra years, the extra pounds, regretted the slide into middle-age.

He stopped quickly, and looked back, breathing in the air that rose from the pavement in almost tangible waves. Not a car in sight, and three miles to the town. In this heat it would probably kill him.

McCall started to jog.

The sound of Flavor's voice echoed in her ears.

"Whoever it is, step out into the light so I can see you, arms away from your body, then lie face first on the floor, arms and legs outstretched."

The silhouette failed to answer. She repeated her order and received the same mute response. The barrel of the Smith and Wesson was aimed at the dark torso, and she felt her finger touch gently on the trigger, easing into the pressure that would snap the hammer forward onto the shell.

You can't do it, Flavor, not like this. Could be deaf, could be asleep, unconscious. Could be dead, even. She fumbled for the torch she had seen on the couch, never taking her eyes off the silhouette.

She held the torch out with her left hand, pointed it and brought her thumb down on the pressure button. The beam shot out and painted the silhouette with light.

It was Sarah Ziegal, and she was not asleep, because her eyes were wide open in frozen terror. Flavor took a step forward: "Ziegal?"

Sarah Ziegal was quite dead.

That became obvious in the most horrific way, because as Flavor got closer, perhaps it was the vibration of her footsteps, or simply some involuntary settling of the corpse, but Sarah Ziegal's severed head detached itself from its resting place, and rolled at Flavor's feet.

Flavor screamed.

The gas station was a shimmering image in the distance as McCall put one foot before the other in a parody of running, his feet like divers' boots, anchoring him to the ground, a tight vest of scorching heat searing his lungs.

His tongue was shrivelled leather in his sand-blasted mouth, and he felt that his blood was boiling. The sun was directly overhead, and it seemed like a blow torch turned on his skull. Inside it was as though his brains were being fried, like in the anti-drugs TV advertisement.

He couldn't see, the glare was blinding, the salt in his eyes was like gravel, his heart pumped, lurched, missing beats like the engine of the abandoned car.

But he staggered on.

Flavor sat now, knees bunched up against her chin, in a corner of the room away from the body and the head, the gun still held in two hands in front of her, like some crucifix to ward off evil spirits.

She stayed that way for a long time, scared, paralysed with fear, hardly daring to take her eyes off the grim, dead relic of Sarah Ziegal.

All the things Flavor had felt came back to haunt her. That smell and that sense of evil, all wrong, WRONG. It WAS Wishaw, after all. The van, the Missouri plates, all red herrings, coincidences.

She should have INSISTED that the woman have proper protection after Wishaw went missing, INSISTED on it. Ziegal's death was Flavor's responsibility.

The projector clicked on, a macabre, almost surreal back-drop to the harsh reality of the room. Two naked age sepia-ed women were performing some sexual act on a writhing male whose face was obscured by their bodies.

Flavor looked away. This was Marat-Sade's Charenton asylum come to life. A headless corpse, portraits of angels, an aging 35mm blue movie.

She knew she had to act, had to move, get up, push on, find Wishaw, find Nielsen, if that was possible before Wishaw killed him, arrest Wishaw, go back to the sun, to light and sanity.

But she felt so weary and so scared, and as long as she stayed in the corner with the gun, Wishaw couldn't hurt her, Ziegal couldn't hurt her, none of the ghosts and the demons and memories down here could hurt her.

Without warning the movie came to an abrupt stop, the end of the reel broke free and whipped and flapped around in a rotating frenzy. It broke some spell in Flavor. She got to her feet, found the off switch, and stilled the projector.

Using the momentum, she pushed on, skirting the Ziegal remains, went through a door-less gap in the wall and found a small bathroom, illuminated by the same sickly red glow.

Flavor went in, and it was like stepping into something half-way between normality and a doll's house, like some contorted fun house view of a bathroom. Everything was smaller, and at a lower level, including the basin, the lavatory, and the bath. The smell pervaded the room.

She checked the cabinet. Shaving foam, razor blades, female deodorant, a box of sanitary towels.

Who in God's name lived down here?

She left the bathroom and went back into the corridor. The doors were gone now, each room was connected to the other by a uniform gap in the wall.

In the next room she found a steel cabinet, like one might find used as a cupboard in an office, opened it and saw that it was a makeshift wardrobe. There were racks of clothes on thin, wire hangers, women's blouses, men's shirts and what appeared to be a pair of child's jeans.

In one corner of the same room Flavor saw a large, white chest about four feet deep, and two and half feet across, and six feet long. From it she could hear a faint electrical hum.

It looked like the kind of deep freeze one might keep in a utility room. The courage drained out of her like water from a sick man's bowels. She instinctively knew what it was, and what she would find there.

The rest was mystery. Somehow this had become Wishaw's lair. Somehow he had a connection with his dead wife's sister, and now he had murdered her. There was no need to look in the freezer, she knew with utter certainty what was inside.

She shook her head, slowly from side to side at the horror of her thoughts: "Oh, Jesus Christ."

Flavor knew she had to get out of that bomb shelter NOW, she had to retrace her steps, go up the stairladders, run out into the sane world, call the Sheriff and let them come with men and guns and lights, let them descend into this hell and confirm what she already knew.

But still the voice, the haunting, redneck mocking and challenging voice said: The nigger will always run.

Flavor said aloud to herself, to the childhood ghosts, to the taunters and the doubters, and above all to her own negative self-image:

"Fuck you. Fuck you ALL."

She took the several steps to the freezer. There was a lid, with handles, and she felt the slight resistance of the rubber seal grips as she pulled upwards.

The horror was no less because she knew what she would find. No less at all. From the coating of ice that covered them. The frozen heads of Smith, Alassio, Helm, Astaire, and of Jacqueline Romarin stared up in the final rictus of death.

Another head lay face downwards under the layer of ice. Flavor knew whose head it was. She had been so utterly wrong about him from the beginning, as she had been wrong about Sarah Ziegal.

And because of that, he had met his death here in this evil cellar. Kirk Nielsen had not been the Angel any more than Ziegal had. Now he had become a victim of the Angel.

Steeling herself, she reached down with the barrel of the Smith and Wesson, disturbing the web of ice crystals, trying to turn the head over. Kirk Nielsen, lifeguard, lover, movie star turned mogul, rescuer of drowning children, with his patrician grey hair –

And yet this head did not have –

She turned the head.

It was not Nielsen, it was Wishaw.

And at that precise moment every light in the bunker died, including the deathly white light from the makeshift morgue over which she leant.

Total, utter blackness.

And the voice said:

"What a stupid bitch you are."

McCall knew he could go no further. He ran to a staggering stop, and stood, swaying in the road. There was nothing left. Nothing. He tried to shield his face against the merciless cudgel of the sun, but he no longer had the strength to lift his arm, and it swung down under gravity and its own weight, crashing against his side.

His stomach convulsed, and he vomited a thin bile, too exhausted to wipe if from his mouth and chin. Something was crashing about in his skull, side to side, like the clapper of a bell.

The tar of the pavement swam in and out of focus. He tried to fix his eyes on something that might keep him conscious, but failed.

He vomited more bile, feeling the stinging, acrid taste in his mouth and nose, and then some unseen giant picked up the whole of the planet, desert road and all, and smacked McCall solidly in the face with it.

"You just never got it. From the beginning, you could never understand it, could you? You and your white trash friend both."

"Who are you?"

The blackness was Stygian, total. But she knew, the voice was unmistakeable. It was Nielsen. And he was right, she didn't understand anything. Wishaw. Ziegal. Nielsen. This bunker and its bizarre accoutrements, the porn movie, she understood nothing.

"Nielsen?"

The red lights came up slowly, and he was standing about six feet from her, his face suffused with the red glow of the lamps, a gun in his hand.

"Why did you come today? There was absolutely no reason for you to come today. You'll die because of it."

The gun was still in her hand, pointing out and downwards,

and his gun was pointing directly at her. If she moved, he would shoot her directly.

As if reading her thoughts, he said: "The gun, lower it to the ground, don't drop it, and I'll watch you every inch of the way." She bent her knees and placed the gun on the floor.

"Now stand and kick it gently to one side." She obeyed him.

And once again, somewhere off in the bunker she heard a sound, a metallic sound, and she stiffened.

Nielsen said, mysteriously: "Don't scream, that will only bring him."

"I don't understand."

"You don't need to. Why did you come today? If you had not come this all would have been finished, all of it."

She realised she was no longer scared. The fear, the imagination, was now incarnate. And although the flesh had a gun, it was somehow less terrifying now there was some human rationale in this bizarre place.

"Because I had a hunch Wishaw was here. I thought he was the Angel, that he had come here to kill Sarah Ziegal. To kill you. You're right, I was a fool."

Nielsen laughed:

"Wishaw was a fool, and a man with an obsession. Oh, he'd come to kill us all right, because he thought Sarah and I killed his precious ex-wife. The maniac has pursued me half my life, so he thought he'd become the Angel for a night."

Flavor edged her foot gently outwards, trying to re-locate her gun.

"But he couldn't be the Angel, because YOU are."

Nielsen shook his head, the red light bathing his face like blood: "You still don't see, do you? I'm not the Angel."

"I see the remains of Helm – the rest of them . . ." momentarily she choked up with emotion, "I see the remains of Jacqueline."

Something clanged in the distant recesses of the bunker, and her heart leapt, this time with hope, not fear. Could this be rescue? Was it past noon now? Had McCall alerted the local police or sheriff, and were they even at this moment coming down into the bunker?

It was as though Nielsen could read her thoughts. He said: "It's not your gallant rescuers, Flavor. There are no rescuers. You can't know who it is, but I urge you for the moment, for your own sake to keep silent. Do not scream, or make a loud noise. Do not hasten the moment. Now he eats, and when he is sated he will return."

"Who is HE?"

"In time," Nielsen moved around at a slight angle, and as Flavor turned with him, her toe touched the discarded weapon. How long would it take to reach down if his attention was distracted? How long to reach down, pick up the gun and fire?

She said: "Why did you kill Sarah Ziegal – the rest of them, why?"

"I didn't kill her. I came here after she telephoned. I parked the car and found a note in the kitchen telling me to meet her down here." He stammered: "I called her name, she didn't answer. I heard the projector running, so I came through. She was sitting in the chair. At first I thought . . . then I could see . . ."

He paused.

"I was scared then, I knew he'd done it. He'd turned on her. I loved her in my way. Have you ever lost someone you love, Flavor?" He did not wait for her response.

He was looking through her, a murderer horrified by death.

"Seeing her dead, like that, in the darkness. It was like it was, a stranger, someone else. You've seen bodies . . ."

Flavor nodded assent.

"Is it always like that? You know it is the person, but the face is not theirs. Someone you have loved, without life, it's . . ."

She saw his eyes wander, thought she might have a split second to reach down – but then the chance was over, as his eyes snapped back, alert once more.

"I couldn't bear to look at her, to touch her, couldn't hold her. Should I have held her Flavor, just once more, in my arms, tell me that?"

She shook her head slowly: "I don't know Nielsen."

"I just couldn't . . ." he shivered as his mind contemplated the idea.

"Aren't you used to death by now?"

"No," he shook his head slowly from side to side, "you never get used to it."

"Just to enjoy it."

His face changed and the mask of tragedy was replaced with stunning speed by the facade of whimsy.

"Not the act, the results."

"You're going to kill me."

"Of course," he said it petulantly.

"Tell me why? Why you did it all."

He laughed: "And you hope, like in one of the bad movies that as I carefully explain to you, you will snatch my gun, or one of your colleagues will step conveniently from behind a curtain."

"Why the statues, why the beheading, why – everything, I must know?"

There was a pause, and she thought she saw Nielsen cock his head slightly to one side, as though listening.

Then it was as though he had ignored her question. He said: "Against my judgements on other matters I find you sexually attractive, Flavor. Simply carnal, nothing spiritual."

"All you boys are the same, Nielsen, you despise it but you want it."

"Tell me, when you were a young girl, did men make passes at you, older men; did they try to have some kind of sex with you?"

A shiver wracked her body.

"Yes."

"Of course. We men are animals, it's the way we are. The honest ones admit that they like young girls, sometimes the younger the better."

He paused.

"When I came to Hollywood I went to a party given in my honour. I was taken to a room, and there was a girl in it. And I mean, a GIRL. She was twelve years old, Flavor, can you imagine?"

The cellar. Flavor could imagine. This was horror within a horror. She had delved fearlessly into a nightmare to be confronted by a bigger one.

"I had sex with this girl; actually, it was expected of me. Unfortunately," he waved the gun in a kind of shrug, "after that, I had a penchant for similar activities. Nothing too sick, nothing below twelve."

Flavor felt a wave of cold nausea pass over her and quelled it.

"You're wondering where all this is leading. Believe me, it leads to the destination you seek."

Again, the distant scraping sound. What time was it? She dare not look at her watch. Help me McCall.

"But such activities are dangerous, punishable by imprisonment. I have no feelings on it, I simply knew that I had to have the thing I wished. Like a drug. I was addicted, and I loved my addiction. And the risk made it . . ." he paused, and his voice seemed to take on an extra, sexual tension, "BETTER."

"You could have sought help."

"Shut up!" his voice was like a guillotine, "I don't need your new age prattle. I liked to fuck young girls, and it wasn't hard to get such a girl, not in Hollywood. But I KNEW I needed one I could trust, a regular companion, someone who could be seen with me, could visit my home, without suspicion."

"And you found her."

"Oh yes, Flavor, I found her."

"Her name was Heather O'Malley, aka Sarah Ziegal."

He nodded: "Yes, Heather O'Malley, but your statement is only partly correct, as you will see."

"Your own girlfriend's sister."

"Spare me the bourgeois disgust."

"How could you, didn't Kathleen object?"

Nielsen moved forward a pace, and for the first time she could see the hooded eyes, reddened by the light, and she thought, he's insane.

"Object? Kathleen ARRANGED it." Flavor remembered the final scene of East River, Kirk Nielsen walking away with the fourteen year old real and fictional sister of the dead heroine, saying: "I'll take care of you from now on, kid."

And Nielsen had been 'taking care' of her, in his own perverted way. At some point Kathleen must have objected. So he had taken Kathleen out on his boat and arranged a drowning.

His under-age sexual conquest had then gone into a chrysalis, and emerged as Sarah Ziegal.

Flavor's foot was still touching her gun, still waiting for any opportunity, still hoping that the noise might be McCall searching for her, or the police he had alerted as she had asked him in the note. She said:

"And when Kathleen became jealous, perhaps threatened to go to the police, you drowned her, just like your other girlfriend back in New Hampshire."

He shook his head; long, long turns of the head.

"I didn't kill Kathleen O'Malley, Flavor. No, no, no."

"Then who did – Heather O'Malley nee Sarah Ziegal maybe? Sibling rivalry?" she said it bitterly.

Nielsen said:

"No-one killed Kathleen O'Malley in 1966 because up until a short while ago, Kathleen O'Malley was still very much alive."

Kirk Nielsen lay in the large, circular bed that occupied the majority of the forward cabin, a naked sister cradled in each arm.

He was still erectile. He nudged Kathleen, and she opened her eyes, wearily. She was very drunk, very tired.

He said: "Do it. Do it with your mouth."

A voice said: "Let me, Kirk."

Kathleen faced the hard, cruel eyes of her under-age sister, and the whiplash tongue greeted her:

"What's your problem, lush?"

They faced each other like cats, fangs drawn, ready to fight. Nielsen liked that. He liked the rivalry, the corruption of the elder sister who had procured the younger, then the usurping of the sexual hierarchy by the younger sister.

Before, back in New Hampshire, he had seen the jealousy of the two sisters who had fought for his favours. He had reproduced it now. He enjoyed seeing that closeness severed, the sibling intimacy wrecked by competition.

He liked to destroy illusions, and the biggest illusion was friendship and loyalty. Here were two sisters, almost twins, almost Doppelgangers, closer than anyone could ever hope to be.

And he had come between them like a wedge, so that now they competed and jousted, and snarled and fought over him.

That night, out in the back cabin, the captain and his son safely in their quarters, they had made a movie; low budget, with just a handful of actors.

It would never be seen by other than they, and none of them would dare speak of it to others, because they were all implicated, Helm and his boyfriend Alassio, Victoria Astaire and Cruze, the Angellis, King Leonard and his wife.

They'd all joined in, various permutations and combinations of human body and sexual gender, fuelled by booze, narcotics and perverted desire.

Heather was the wild child, the pièce de résistance at that table of debauchery. Officially she was not there. The captain and his kid hadn't seen Heather O'Malley, and only the selected guests knew of her presence.

And they were all bound in this conspiracy of sin. All the heterosexual males had had sex with the under-age girl, and the wives had watched. The single women had enjoyed their own playful tangible curiosity, and the homosexual males had achieved far more response from their allegedly straight counterparts than they could have wished for.

It had all been, for Nielsen, both an exercise in eroticism and an immensely interesting insight into human sexual behaviour.

"See what you can both do," he taunted the two sisters who competed to offer him sexual favours.

Suddenly Kathleen leaped across the recumbent Nielsen's body and tore into her sister, scratching, and pummelling. Nielsen was galvanised, tugging them both apart, angry now.

"For Christ's sake, what is it with you two, you want to wake up the whole boat?" He jerked a thumb at Heather. "She's not even supposed to be here, for God's sake. If the captain finds out and anyone discovers what went on here tonight, we'll all get thrown in gaol."

He pulled the sisters into his body, stroking their hair: "Come on, we've got a nice scene going here, don't spoil it." He could not see Kathleen's eyes, and if he had he might have been forewarned, for they burned with hate.

Nielsen got up, climbed over the younger sister, cut another line of heroin, snorted it through a rolled-up bank-note then came back to the bunk, where Heather and Kathleen still stared sullenly at each other.

He realised with regret that sooner or later it would have to end. It was becoming trouble. And that was a pity, because he was – perversely – in love with Kathleen, and Heather was wild and YOUNG, Kathleen was a great lay, and together, when they competed, they were DYNAMITE.

The heroin hit him with a rush, and within a minute he passed out.

Flavor said: "You're evil."

"I'm human and I have the courage to indulge my fantasies. What are your fantasies, Flavor? Fucking white men, is that your fantasy? Are you fucking the officer McCall?"

She put her foot gently on the gun and began to draw it

towards her with microscopic slowness.

She said: "Tell me the rest."

Nielsen awoke, realising there was nobody left at his side. He opened his eyes and saw Kathleen sitting in the small galley that ran off from the forward master cabin. She was smoking a joint.

He sat up, brushing against Heather's body. "You OK Kathleen?"

She looked up at him, didn't speak, just drew heavily on the reefer. He felt a stirring of unease. "Kathleen?" She turned away.

Nielsen looked down at Heather, who seemed to be immobile and sleeping heavily. He pulled back the sheet that covered her, and noticed there was absolutely no movement of the naked body.

Panicked, he tugged at her shoulder, rolled her over, and felt the heavy, unresisting body, saw the closed eyelids and the purple thread of exploded veins on her cheeks.

He turned to Kathleen in the galley: "Jesus Christ, what have you done to her?"

He put his ear over Heather's heart, heard nothing, felt the pulse. Nothing. She was cooling by the second. He got up slipped into his shorts, and went over to where Kathleen sat pulling on the big joint.

The scent of marijuana was pungent in the small space.

"You killed her?" He gripped Kathleen by the shoulders and shook her: "You fucking KILLED her."

"Yes." She nodded gravely through the smoke, "I killed her. She was asleep. I got a pillow and put it over her face. She didn't make a sound, well, she struggled a bit, but nothing really. It was so easy."

"Gimme that," he took the reefer from her, and took a long pull, drawing the smoke down into his lungs. He handed the cigarette back and put his face in his hands, speaking through splayed fingers.

"We'll both go to the gas chamber. They'll gas us."

316

She shrugged, nonchalantly, as though everything was far away: "Not you. Me. You didn't do anything."

"Didn't DO anything! She's on my boat, I've been screwing her, an under-age girl, now she's dead, in MY bed. Are you crazy? Kathleen, she's your sister!"

"I hated her," she looked up at Nielsen who had removed his face from his hands, a look of utter despair on his face, "did you know that?"

"Hated her? You're like twins, you look alike, dress alike, live together, Jesus, don't tell me you hated her."

"She was my best friend, my kid sister. And then – " she paused, "when she – when we . . ."

Nielsen poked an accusing finger: "You agreed to it, don't say you didn't. You joined in, she was enthusiastic, there was no coercion, dammit."

"Sure." She stroked his face with appalling tenderness.

"Because I knew it was what you wanted. I didn't want to lose you. I didn't want you going with some stranger, maybe being arrested, sent to prison. And I joined in, enjoyed it, I admit it. But when I learned she was carrying your kid, I HATED her. It was like she'd taken some part of you."

Nielsen eased her back to the bed.

"It was an accident, dammit, you know that. And you can't have kids, otherwise we would've. Anyway, it was an accident. And it's a fucking freak, how could you be jealous of that?"

Kathleen shook her head: "I loved it more than she did. Because it came from you."

"It'll die soon, the doctors said so."

"No," she shook her head, "I won't let it die."

"KATHLEEN!" He took her by the shoulders and shook her vigorously: "Forget the kid, FORGET it. Your sister is dead, you murdered her, and unless we think of something quick we're both going to San Quentin."

Kathleen said: "I'll tell them I killed her. I'll tell them she consented, that she liked it; I'll tell them . . . tell them she seduced you – "

He hit her once, a hard, stinging slap across her face, and it stopped her.

He spoke slowly, in a low, determined voice: "Listen carefully to me you stupid, STUPID bitch. She is not old enough to give her consent. It's statutory rape. Even if they don't gas me for complicity in her death I'll go to gaol. I'll be finished. Anyway, they'll think I killed her because she threatened to tell. That's what they'll think."

"I'll tell them. She was a liar and a whore, even though she was my sister – "

He slapped her again, then grabbed her by the lapels of her dressing gown, her face inches from his: "They'll make you say anything they want. We're not Joe and Doris Plotnik from Smalltown, USA, I'm Kirk Nielsen, you're Kathleen O'Malley, don't you understand? They'll CRUCIFY us."

Nielsen let her go, and she sagged, all fight gone.

He looked around the cabin, as though somewhere there was a means of escape from this deadly entanglement. He turned back to her: "They'll find out about the kid. A fourteen year old girl had my child. A monster."

Nielsen made a low moaning sound of pure anguish. "Even if they don't gas us, even if we get out of prison eventually, we'll be ruined. I'll lose everything I've worked for. This was just the BEGINNING, Kathleen, don't you understand that? There's more, more of everything. This was just the START. Now we'll lose it all."

He put his face into his hands. She came up and put her arm around him: "I'm sorry Kirk. I wish it was me, not her. I just couldn't take it any longer."

Yes, he thought viciously, I wish it was you as well. Heather was evil, but Heather was the best lay he had ever had. Tight, horny and gave head like a pro. He'd screwed her at thirteen and she wasn't a virgin then.

He looked up into Kathleen's bloodshot eyes, thinking: Yes, I wish it was you, bitch. And then, like the sound of a faint, bugle call to a beleaguered garrison, came the thought. Louder and louder, real, not an apparition; an escape, a way out.

It was like a pure crystal in his mind. It was possible. And it was his only chance, THEIR only chance.

He said: "It CAN be you, if you want."

She said dumbly: "Kill me, I don't care."

He took hold of her hand: "Not kill you, Kathleen. Swap you. Take your gown off, your slip too."

"Kirk?"

"Do it, or would you prefer them to do it at San Quentin when they strap you into that chair and choke you to death on cyanide pellets?"

She took off her clothes, and stood naked.

"Help me." He went to the bed, stripped the covers, and turned Heather O'Malley's dead naked body over, and began struggling to put on Kathleen's discarded slip and dressing gown.

"I said, HELP me." She did, clumsily, still drugged and inebriated, and they got the slip on, then the silk dressing gown. Through gritted teeth, panting from the exertion of lifting a dead weight, Nielsen said: "They fit."

"We're the same size, but what are you doing?"

Nielsen said: "Listen to me carefully. Tonight, Kathleen O'Malley – YOU – is going to go on deck, full of booze and drugs, stumble, and fall overboard into the cold Pacific Ocean. And drown."

"What?"

"Tomorrow morning, early, I will discover she is no longer in my bed. I will raise a hue and cry, then call the coastguard. I doubt if anyone will find the body for a while, not with these currents."

"I don't get it. You pretend that I have drowned?"

"You will hide down here, maybe in the head, until we get back to LA. When it's safe you put on HER clothes, get off the boat, and you go back to your apartment. Then I'll come and break the news about your sister."

"Jesus, Kirk, what – "

"You'd better follow this, because it's the only thing that can save you and maybe me too, from the gas chamber. She shares an apartment with you, goddamnit, she LOOKS like you. You know her better than anyone else. The only friends she had were me and you. She dropped out of school, no-one knows her, except you and me."

"They know ME, I'm five years older, Kirk I'm famous."

"Sure, sure . . ." he bit his nails, "We can do this, we can pull it off. The world thinks Kathleen O'Malley is dead. Her younger sister is in seclusion. When she comes out for the funeral, if there ever is one, she's in dark glasses, a headscarf."

Kathleen sat, naked, confused.

"Our doctor, dentist?"

"Shit!" He bit down beyond the nail, onto his thumb. "She have any operations, appendix removed, anything like that?"

Kathleen shook her head.

"You?"

"No."

"Cavities?"

"Neither of us."

"Right." He was thinking desperately.

"Same colour eyes . . . marks, small scars, anything like that?"

"No, I don't think so."

"Let's check it." He went over the body, looking for a birthmark, a childhood scar. There was a small cicatrix on her kneecap, but it was tiny. And if she was in the water for weeks surely it would disappear . . .

"But how can I become her?"

He stepped forward and grabbed her wrists: "You're an actress, goddammit, so ACT. Act the best part of your life, because your life depends on it."

"Kirk, I have a career," she almost wailed.

"Unless you do this you have NOTHING, can't I make you understand that? You disappear once the dust settles, you're overcome with grief. Then maybe after five years or so, when everyone has forgotten, you can change your name and come back, restart your career under another name. I'll look after you."

"Can we still get married, like you promised?"

The weight of the burden was crushing him. He took her hand: "There is going to be a media fest over this. Theories, speculation, and someone, somewhere is bound to hint that I killed her. They're not even going to smell at the REAL truth. But if I then marry her kid sister — and that's who you are from now on, Heather O'Malley — they are going to come down on me like a ton of bricks. Marriage is out."

"Kirk," She leaned into him, her tears on his cheek.

"Money won't be a problem. When it's time, I'll get you work. Go back to St. Louis for a while. After that we can carry on, like we are."

He realised, as though she was an asp crawling from a fruit basket he held to his bosom, that from now on she was a deadly danger to him, and for a wild, insane second he contemplated killing her too.

It wasn't possible. Here in this chamber of death he was being wed to her in a ceremony of murder, tied to her now more securely than by any vows.

He realised she was speaking to him: "Will they find her?"

"Eventually. I hope to God by then she's so eaten by the fishes no-one can recognise her."

"Fingerprints!"

A shock wave went through Nielsen. If her fingertips survived immersion, decomposition, fish damage, they would know it was Heather and not Kathleen. Various studios had taken fingerprints of Kathleen for security reasons. They wouldn't match. He thought of the strange metal sphere at San Quentin, the door locking, the pellets hitting the bath of cyanide, of the fumes, of being strapped in the steel chair, choking . . .

For fingerprints you needed the tips of your fingers.

"Help me." Together they dragged the naked body into the small galley. "Light the stove." She did so, fumbling with the matches, dropping one, putting the second out in her nervousness, succeeding with the third.

"What are you going to do?"

"You'll see. Help me raise her." They struggled with the cadaver, and Nielsen took one of the dead girl's hands, and held each finger in turn over the flame.

There was a stench of burning flesh, and he heard Kathleen gag. He repeated the process with the second hand, then sweating and exhausted, he trailed the corpse back to the bunk.

He looked at the body with its scorched fingertips, desperately trying to think. When they identified a decomposed body, what? What did they look for?

Clothing? That would mostly rot in the sea; jewellery, rings?

"Rings. Kathleen, give me your rings." She wore a signet ring on her right hand, and a big white diamond on a gold band on her third finger left hand. It had been their symbol that they were betrothed, though no public announcement had been made.

She pulled off the signet ring with difficulty, and Nielsen slipped it onto the rapidly stiffening finger of the corpse's right hand.

"The other one," he said, urgently.

"Kirk, it was your gift. It's my engagement ring."

"Goddamn it, give it to me," he grabbed her hand and wrenched at the ring. She gave a piercing shriek of pain, and he hit her again with the back of his hand. "Do you want to wake the whole boat? You want everyone on deck for when we dump her?"

She sobbed with the humiliation, and slowly eased off her treasured ring. Nielsen put it on the body's third finger, left hand.

Dental records. No two sets of teeth were totally alike, even if neither of the girls had cavities. If they chose to identify the corpse by its teeth, then some other course of action would have to be taken.

It all depended on if – or where – the corpse was washed up. Money could buy a lot of things, perhaps it could buy some selective blindness. After all if a badly decomposed corpse was washed up, and if Kathleen O'Malley was missing, if everyone on the boat thought so, if her sister identified the rings as those of her missing sister, why need it go further?

He would cross that bridge when it came to it.

"Now listen. When you get back to the apartment, you cut your hair to the same length as hers. It's the same colour, same style, so that's not a problem. Then you lie low. You speak only to the police, no Press, and no neighbours. You put on a lot of make-up, like you'd been crying, you wear dark glasses, and a scarf all the time."

She was crying, deep heavy sobs that wracked her body: "They'll know, Kirk, they'll see my face, they'll KNOW. How can they not know?"

"They'll not know because you are DEAD, and this is your sister. Who'd think different? And Heather – you're Heather now – is not even on the boat, remember? They'll ask Andrade the captain for an inventory of passengers and you – Heather O'Malley – will not be on it."

"What about – tonight, the party, the movie . . .?"

Neilsen gave a bitter laugh:

"They won't suspect either, they'll just think you – forgive me, KATHLEEN – got wasted and walked over-board. As for Heather, they'll know we'll want to keep her presence a secret, and believe me they'll want that just as much as we do. Don't forget, I have the documentary proof of what went on here tonight."

She saw the reel in its cardboard carton in the corner of the cabin.

Nielsen smiled: "Sure. That can send any one of them to prison for twenty years, Astaire, Druze, the Angellis, the Leonards, not to mention our two faggot friends."

"But they'll know! They'll know it's Heather, not me."

He grabbed Kathleen's jaw, viciously: "They won't

know, because they won't see Heather again, ever. They won't know unless you tell them. Kathleen O'Malley is dead, Heather is alive. And you will be Heather O'Malley. From now on you ARE. Kathleen is dead, and you are HEATHER! You're HER."

"The cops?"

"You weren't here – Heather, were you? You were at home, in your apartment. Why should they think differently? No-one here is going to tell them. And anyway, Hollywood is going to be in mourning for Kathleen O'Malley."

"We're perverted, sick. I'm a murderer."

Nielsen found a Bourbon bottle in a cupboard of the galley, and poured them a large shot each. She took hers in large draughts, gulping it down.

He put his arm around her, and said gently: "It's the only game in town now. No option, honey, no other option."

She looked up at him, and he saw through the tears, through the mock sorrow and self-scourging.

"If they do find Heather – "

"Kathleen, they'll find Kathleen. You're Heather now."

"If they find – her – will there be a funeral? She should have a resting place, something suitable."

"Oh sure, Forest Lawn. And we'll put a statue up, a big one . . ." he thought back to his childhood, "We'll put up an angel to watch over her."

"Will I go to . . ." her voice trailed off.

"Sure. You'll attend your own funeral."

"What about the kid, what about Gregory, I have to bring him up. He's her child, hers and yours."

The friendly arm tightened on her menacingly:

"Don't call that monster mine. Gregory will die soon, the doctors said so."

McCall thought he was dead and in his shroud. Something wet and cold covered his face, and he was icy cold. For long seconds he did not know what had happened, then he remembered collapsing.

He groaned, and felt the wet flannel pulled off his face.

A woman's voice said: "Well, he's alive anyhow."

He opened his eyes, and shut them again as the light blinded him. A man's voice, an old voice said: "They're sending an ambulance, they'll take care of him."

McCall opened his eyes a slit, and the light was like cactus needles. His head throbbed with pain, and he felt as though he had been kicked all over.

He sat up, groggily. He was on a couch in someone's home. He saw an old woman in dungarees and a red baseball cap. She eyed him and said, to someone McCall couldn't see: "He's coming round, Jake."

A man in coveralls and three-day whiskers swam into McCall's vision: "How ya doin'?"

McCall swung his feet off the couch, and it was as though some spirit level bubble sped up, down, and up again in his head. The whole room began to spin.

"Oh, oh," he put out both arms and steadied himself.

The old man knelt creakily and looked at him: "You got heatstroke, boy. We've sent for a doctor."

And then he remembered, everything. Flavor, why he was here. He said, anxiously: "Where is this?"

The man said: "Palm Desert's about a mile up the road."

He wiped his eyes, and said, groggily: "Do you have a vehicle?"

The man laughed: "Sure. Got the pick-up, found you flat out in the road back there. Hadn't of found you the sun might of killed you."

McCall got groggily to his feet, his legs felt like jelly.

He said it formally, absurdly, he had no purchase on their services, he was no longer an acting police officer, he didn't even have any money, he had given every cent he possessed to Mrs. Annameyer.

"May I please ask you a favour?"

"Ask away, boy."

"Could you run me to Redwood Drive, and I'll pay you later. I have . . ." he almost laughed at the phrase ". . . I have an urgent appointment."

The woman said: "What about the ambulance?"

"When it comes, send it to Redwood Drive. I think we might need it."

CHAPTER NINETEEN

They dragged the body of Heather O'Malley to the steps of the forward cabin and out onto the bow deck, as the boat rolled gently in the hint of breeze.

Nielsen looked aft, looked amidships, heard and saw nothing. They'd all be in a drugged, alcoholic sleep now, surely? They'd collectively consumed enough booze and dope to anaesthetise an elephant.

Heather, like Kathleen, was slim and light, but now in death she dragged like an anchor as they sweated and cursed, pulling her along the narrow bow, her arms and legs constantly snagging in ropes and protrusions.

Once he thought he heard a sound, and looked up quickly, then resumed his task. They reached the bowsprit and paused. The moon came out from behind the clouds, and Nielsen saw the look on the real Kathleen's face as the horror of what she had done, and what she was about to do, began to dawn.

327

He hissed at her; "It's the only way."

She nodded, teeth gritted.

Nielsen said: "Let her go." They heaved together, and winced at the fat slap as the body hit the water. Back in the cabin they smoked another joint and drank some more Bourbon until Kathleen – the new Heather – fell into a troubled sleep.

But Nielsen stayed awake until dawn crept stealthily in through the heavy curtains like a returning late night reveller. Soon Nielsen would raise a hue and cry, and get the boat's captain and passengers on the phantom and futile search for Kathleen O'Malley.

Only one of the guests bothered him. Nielsen had seen a glimpse of the head before it dodged down out of sight. It was bad luck, damned bad luck. But somehow he didn't think the man would say anything.

For the voyeur had his own secrets he would not wish the world to know. In addition Nielsen would make it his business to look after him, look after all of them. Words could be said, favours offered, their careers would prosper along with his.

And if there was ever the hint of blackmail, then Nielsen would not hesitate to kill. They could only gas you once. He made the tiniest of chinks in the drawn cabin curtains, looking out at the heavy dawn mist that hung like widows' weeds over the grey Pacific, blotting out the coast of Catalina Island.

It was all a gamble from now on.

The gun was under Flavor's right foot now.

She said: "You fooled them all for twenty-nine years."

"We," he corrected her, "Sarah and I – oh I think of her as Sarah now, not Heather or Kathleen. She was reborn as Sarah."

"Didn't she object when you married?"

"Ah, well," Nielsen affected to look rueful, but under the red glow the expression was simply macabre, like a circus clown's mock sadness.

"She had to be persuaded that it was necessary. As I said, I could not marry the sister of my dead lover, people might have gossiped."

"You bribed the coroner."

"I HELPED him persuade the police that our identification, that of myself and Kathleen's SISTER, was sufficient. I begged him to avoid for us the extra strain and grief further identification procedures would cause."

Nielsen smiled the false clown's smile.

Flavor said: "And he knew, of course, that to be nice to Hollywood's Mr. Nielsen could do him no harm in the future." She paused: "As it so proved. You did give him a job, eventually."

Her sarcasm hung like vapour in the air.

"I put on absolutely no pressure. Although the body was badly decomposed, the rings were intact. She was the right sex, the right body size, everything pointed to it being Kathleen. There was no mystery. So, of course, no dental records were required."

There was a sound, nearer this time. Flavor stiffened and saw Nielsen's head come up, suddenly alert.

"He's coming back."

"Who? Who is coming back? Who lives down here?"

"You'll soon know."

She said, hurriedly:

"Why did you start killing? Was one of them blackmailing you?"

Nielsen said it bitterly:

"It's all Wishaw's fault, all of it. He wasn't blackmailing us, it was worse than that. You can buy off a blackmailer, you can't make a deal with an obsessive. He'd been married briefly to Kathleen. I took her away from him. Then he thought I'd killed her. Stupid man, if only he'd known the truth, that she was still alive, that he could see her on his TV set.

"The man was obsessed with what he thought was her

death. He wouldn't leave me alone. I sued him, I made his name stink in Hollywood, I RUINED the man, but he was like a limpet."

"What did he do?"

"He was planning to write a book about Kathleen's death, after all this time! He approached everyone for interviews. Alassio saw him, so did Helm. I know, they told me. I think they enjoyed tantalising me.

'Wishaw even had the damn cheek to approach me! We began to wonder, Sarah and I, if others had seen or heard something. If maybe they even suspected what we'd really done. Maybe the child had seen something. Kids can hide, they're small. Suppose he had seen something, remembered it, and suppose he told Wishaw? Then if Wishaw did his book and the police re-opened the investigation . . ." the whole plot of future possibilities and dire consequences ran away with Nielsen's tongue like a tangled conspiracy.

"Then why not just kill Wishaw? Wouldn't that have been preferable to this . . ." she half choked, "this slaughter?"

Nielsen shook his head:

"I would have killed him like that," he snapped his fingers, "but I couldn't. His vendetta against me was Hollywood history, I would have been suspect. I couldn't afford any raking over of the ashes."

The murderous coldness of the man, the sheer perverted logic. Dangerous to kill one person, less dangerous to kill three, four – everyone else on the boat that night.

"So you started to kill everyone who had been on the boat that night?"

"Oh no, I didn't kill ANYONE. I didn't kill a soul."

As he spoke she tried to feel whether the tip of her foot was resting on the butt or the barrel of the pistol. She wanted the butt nearest to her. But the gun slipped under her probing foot, and the metal scraped harshly on the concrete floor. A mistake.

Nielsen looked down.

"Oh, Flavor, you've seen all the wrong movies. You keep the bad guy in black talking while you try to retrieve your gun. This time kick it towards me. Do it!"

She hesitated.

"Or die right now."

She kicked the gun towards him.

"Are the pieces falling into place now? Has your diminutive backwoods brain found the full picture yet?"

He was looking at her with scarcely concealed contempt. She said as calmly as she could:

"If YOU didn't kill them, who did?"

"Just as you read in the newspaper, Flavor, The Angel! That terrifying creature who leaves wooden angels on the headless bodies of his victims."

She said, as calmly as she could: "And did the Angel kill Sarah Ziegal?"

"Oh, yes, the Angel killed her too. And soon he will kill you. After that, I," he waved the gun like a magic wand, "shall kill the Angel. The story will end, here. I shall destroy the bunker. There will be mystery for a little while, then the world will forget. It always forgets, I can assure you, the world always forgets."

She looked into the red-haloed eyes. He was truly mad.

"And the Angel killed Smith, Alassio, Helm all of them?"

"Yes."

"And he would have killed everyone on the boat until there was not a witness left alive?"

"Eventually. Now I think the point is made, so the Angel can be put to rest."

She took a deep breath: "Would you say the Angel is insane, Nielsen? Would you say he needs help?"

He laughed a laugh of genuine amusement:

"It is my belief that only the genuinely creative genius can become mad. I assure you the Angel has never had the wherewithal to become truly mad. He is, perhaps one would say, CRAZED, by birth, by circumstances, but not mad, Flavor, not in the criminal sense I believe you have in mind."

That long-ago, rough hand, holding hers, leading Flavor the child down into the cellar, leading her to a tyranny of possession and nightmares. Free yourself, the witch voice had said. Bravery is doing it, McCall had said. The worst that can happen is that you can DIE.

She would not be held by tyranny, held in a cellar by a new madness. Flavor looked Nielsen straight in the eye, holding his gaze.

"Only the criminally insane would speak of themselves and their crimes in the third person, Nielsen; speak of them as though they were committed by someone else. You ARE the Angel, aren't you? No doubt some force greater than you, some inner voice, a voice from God perhaps . . ." she could not keep the sarcasm from her voice, it filled her throat like phlegm, "TOLD you to do it. Why not acknowledge that and say 'I, killed'? Why not refer to yourself as you are, a demented, sick – terribly sick – man?"

He looked at her as though it was SHE who was mad, and not he.

"Me? The Angel? Oh, Flavor. You think I am some Dr. Jekyll who becomes Mr. Hyde? That I am so mentally sick I am not even aware that it is my alter ego who commits the crime? Do you?"

"Yes," she said, flatly, "I believe that."

"Well, let me try to enlighten you. I am not the Angel. I refer not to me, but to a person you have not, as yet, met."

She tried to still the anger, the tears, the frustration and incomprehension. And also the held-down terror that bubbled, and threatened, like nausea.

It was like some Armageddon of spiritual will. She struck down a demon, defeated a fear, and the awful twins rose again like unslayable zombies. There was some terrible secret here, and she was not privy to it.

"Then if you're not the Angel, who is? Because it's not Kathleen – Sarah Ziegal, because she is dead. Who does that leave Mr. Nielsen?"

His eyes burned as if in fever, and he moved closer.

"Why IT, the thing, the creature."

"What?"

"Don't you understand Flavor, can't you comprehend this, this MADNESS that exists around you?"

"No." And she couldn't, didn't; didn't understand at all. The face came closer and closer, and the words hit her like blows.

"Gregory! GREGORY is the Angel!"

Someone, something was moving in the bunker. Flavor could hear the noise clearly now. And the smell; the smell was getting stronger. All thoughts of rescue had fled like cowards. Whatever it was to which Nielsen referred was in the bunker with them. And it bore the dreadful smell, the foul fragrance Ziegal had carried with her. Had it been her proximity to whatever lived down here, or something in her handbag, some possession or item of apparel?

Nielsen also knew something was moving in the bunker. She saw him cock his head and listen, as though measuring how near the person – thing – was. Yet he made no move to go. Clearly he was waiting.

Whatever unholy alliance this was, Flavor knew with utter certainty that when the as yet unseen presence arrived, she would die.

She said, slowly: "When I interviewed Sarah Ziegal she told me that Gregory was dead. She also told me it was SHE who had given birth to him when she was under age. That he was crippled and sick."

He gave a dismissive snort:

"The facts are as I outlined them in my description of that night. Gregory was born to Heather when SHE was under-age. All the certificates you saw were fakes."

"Why fake his death?"

Nielsen paused, without speaking for a long time, as though looking back into the past. At last he spoke:

"Have you ever been in a farmyard and seen those aberrations of birth that nature produces? Two-headed kittens, calves with five legs, have you ever seen those things Flavor?"

She nodded. She had seen such things as a child. Once the unhealthy curiosity of the onlookers had been satisfied the unfortunate creature had usually been drowned. Freaks frightened people. They were unconsciously regarded as an affront to nature and couldn't be allowed to live.

"Then you will understand Gregory. The child was – IS – one of God's cruel tricks. He was hermaphroditic – truly. I believe there are only a handful of true hermaphrodites in the world, humans born with the physical sexual characteristics of both genders.

'He – we called him he," Nielsen giggled, almost hysterically, "one had to call Gregory something. He has male genitalia, a penis and testes. He also has a vaginal orifice, a womb and ovaries. He is a rare freak, Flavor, a medical phenomenon."

Flavor felt a warm rash of fear and revulsion sweep over her body, and the heat in the bunker felt like a poison ivy that prickled her skin.

She said, haltingly: "He lives here? This is his home?"

"Home? Such a touching word for such a dark reality."

The smell was GREGORY.

"You imprisoned him here?"

"After the funeral the real Kathleen went back to St. Louis. Gregory was in a special home there. As if God had not punished him enough, the – thing – was also a cripple. He was born with a congenital malformation of his lower spine, his legs were barely developed. He also had – the common term is water on the brain – he was not expected to live."

"But he did."

"You have to believe that we did everything for him." Nielsen said it almost plaintively, with a wheedling whine in his voice: "I hired the best doctors. I spent hundred and thousands of dollars. When we deemed it ready, Kathleen became Sarah Ziegal and moved here."

"No-one noticed that she was what they assumed was Kathleen O'Malley's sister?"

Nielsen smiled his red-tinged clown's smile: "Surgical alterations, Flavor, a nip here, a tuck there, some very expensive rhinoplasty and orthodonty."

He waved his free hand: "And a new star is born. A change of name in Missouri, perfectly legal, and the trail goes cold. I start her slowly, a bit part here, a bit part there, then a support role. It was not as if she did not have the talent. After that – " he let the obviousness of the rest hang unspoken.

"And Gregory?"

"The desert dryness and the warmth was supposed to be more comfortable for him. He was susceptible to lung infections in damp or cold climates."

"Sarah said he died twenty-one years ago."

"Twenty-one years ago he was brought down here, into this bunker. Apart from – " Nielsen laughed a dry, almost regretful laugh, " – excursions, he has spent all that time down here."

Flavor tried to take in the enormity of it. Twenty-one years in this man-made subterranean prison. It was beyond comprehension.

"Why?"

"Ah, why, why, why? Let me start by saying that Gregory used to like angels, Flavor, he used to like angels. There was little in his brain; he couldn't read, couldn't write, couldn't comprehend much above the most basic of communications, but he liked angels. When I was a child I became obsessed with angels. Perhaps . . ." he stopped.

"When he first came to live in this house as a child, he found an old illustrated volume I had left on a shelf here. He stared at the pictures for hours on end. He had this remarkable talent for drawing and painting things – for copying – did you see his handiwork out there?"

The painting she had first seen. The avenging angel with the sword, clutching the severed head.

"Yes, I saw the painting."

Nielsen stopped speaking, stopped moving.

Was he listening? Had he heard something she had missed? Was this Gregory returning?

Abruptly he continued: "Sarah used to take him to the local church. Of course, no-one knew of his peculiar condition. He was just a crippled kid in a wheelchair. He liked the ceremony, the prayers and the hymns. He had no knowledge of what they meant, they were an entertainment, like the television, or the pictures of angels.

'The pastor was kind to him, he seemed to be the only person with whom Gregory could really communicate. One Halloween the church held a costume party for the children. I do not think they really approved of Halloween, and it was their way of controlling it.

'Sarah and I made Gregory an angel costume with a halo and wings. When I was a child I had such a costume. We even put luminous paint on his costume so that he would glow when the lights were lowered. I have never seen the wretched child so happy."

Flavor said flatly: "Gregory killed the pastor." It was a statement, not a question.

There was a slight catch in Nielsen's voice as he went on.

"Gregory was about twelve. We had seen him crawl, but we didn't know he could walk sometimes. He was getting out of the house at night. We began to find things in the house, dead things, without heads, or cut in half. A rat once, a snake, a desert fox. I had two Samurai swords that I'd brought back from the Army, and a bayonet belonging to my late father.

'Sarah kept them here on the wall. I thought of Sarah as my real wife, and this as my real home."

"And Gregory as your son?"

He went on as though Flavor had not spoken, almost as though he had not heard her: "A sword went missing. Gregory must have taken it. To reach it he must have been able to stand, to climb onto something. I ransacked the house but the sword was nowhere to be found. He must have had a hiding place for it in the desert."

"The pastor," Flavor said gently, "how did it happen?"

"One night Sarah called me in a panic. I drove down. She took me into Gregory's room . . ." his voice tailed off.

"Tell me, Nielsen, tell me what you saw."

"It was like a nightmare. Gregory was in his room, sitting on the bed. He had found his angel costume, added to it, reconstructed the papier maché wings. We never knew he could . . . He had even daubed himself in the luminous paint. And in his hand . . ." Tears were in Nielsen's eyes now.

"He must have come across the pastor with his mistress in the desert. That the pastor was seeing someone was the worst-kept secret in Palm Desert, though no-one ever found out who the woman was. I think everyone knew except the pastor's wife.

'Perhaps Gregory saw them kissing, or maybe even having sex. He couldn't have understood what was happening. But he loved the pastor and his wife. God knows what went on in that monster's mind when he saw the pastor with this woman. One of them must have fired a pistol at Gregory, because he had a deep furrow in the flesh at the top of his shoulder."

"Why didn't you simply tell the police?"

"Oh what a tangled web we weave, when first we practise to deceive. We did not wish the origins of Gregory's birth to be unduly checked. And imagine the scandal? They would have discovered that Ziegal, was – or so they thought – Heather O'Malley. My visits would have been noticed. Romantic trysts with the sister of my drowned lover? Suspicion, Flavor. And think on it: one of the biggest names in Hollywood linked to an idiot hermaphroditic child murderer? A monster I had kept secret, a monster who had decapitated a man of God? No . . ." he shook his head from side to side.

"So you locked him away, down here, away from the light, away from the world. How could you do that?"

"First she took him back to the mid-West, and his death

was announced."

"More bribes?"

"Simple forgeries. No funeral. No-one in East St. Louis knew Gregory. When she returned to Palm Desert with Gregory hidden in the van, she simply announced that he had died and been cremated during her absence. She had the certificate to prove it. Who would check? Everyone knew Gregory was doomed to die. Then, if he needed treatment she simply flew in some struck-off doctor from the East and paid him handsomely. She would put Gregory back in his old room for the duration of the visit. No questions were ever asked."

And while she was away arranging the scenario for the faked death, she arranged for a Missouri company to build a nuclear fallout shelter for her, Flavor thought.

Hundreds of thousands of dollars to build a prison for a dim-witted, half-crippled freak of nature; a purpose-built prison ready for his return and incarceration.

What tortures that clouded, limited mind must have endured.

"It was her idea," Nielsen said, almost as though in mitigation, "It had to be secure and hidden. It could not be seen, and she and I were away for days on end after she joined the cast of Pacific Coast."

It seemed to Flavor now that there was no nightmare dark enough that one could not plunge deeper. A half-witted, half-crippled, murderous hermaphrodite, buried alive here in the darkness and the soft red lights. With just a TV, books and his own angel fantasies for company.

She asked with disbelief: "Why didn't you just put him out of his misery?"

He waved the gun like a souvenir of his previous resolution on that score: "I SUGGESTED it. She couldn't, don't you see? This was her DUTY. She had killed her own sister, imagine the lifelong horror of that. From that day she vowed she would protect her sister's child until the end."

"Even if that meant locking him up in the darkness for

the rest of his life?"

"Yes."

Flavor shivered. There in the humid, sickly warmth, she shivered. Some things were worse than death. Madness. 'Let me be not mad,' King Lear had pleaded with the Heavens. And was there ever a more heart-rending plea. She pleaded too, to the darkness. Let ME be not mad.

She was at the core of insanity, deep in the dark heart of madness. There was nothing lower in the world now, no deeper bowels of Hell on earth.

They had taken this wretched, botched creation, this thing that had murdered not knowing what murder was, and had turned him into their weapon of destruction.

The outer being of her, the bodily shell around this interior of revulsion, the Flavor Cartouche who had walked down the steps into the bunker, spoke again:

"But when you thought Wishaw was on your trail you both decided to act – using Gregory?"

"I wanted nothing to do with it, it was HER idea. She even threatened that if I didn't go along with it SHE'D tell everyone the truth about that night. I HAD to go along with her."

Flavor heard what she thought was the soft brush of fabric, or a footfall. It came not from far off, but from somewhere chillingly close behind her, in one of the rooms through which she had passed.

Somehow he had bypassed them. Were there other passageways? She felt her skin crawl and her body hair stand up on end. Flavor felt the wash of icy fear.

They had turned Gregory into this thing who killed, who beheaded. This was the Angel of their creation, and he was down here with the one remaining culprit – and with Flavor.

Had Nielsen heard that most recent sound?

"Who arranged the meetings with the victims, Sarah?"

"Yes. I was never involved at that level. She had the perfect entrée, being who she was, and of course, she was still on intimate terms with most of the victims. She told them it was a personal matter, swore them to secrecy about whom they were meeting, hinted at consequences if they told a soul. It seemed to work. None left a note or message indicating who they were seeing. You saw the van in the garage?"

Flavor said: "Yes, I saw it."

"It is adapted to take a wheelchair. Occasionally she would take Gregory to see his real mother's grave at Forest Lawn. He loved the angel statue."

The wooden angels, carved in the image of the statue above the supposed grave of Kathleen O'Malley – in reality the last resting place of the younger sister Heather.

"It was easy enough for Sarah to see the victims, then make an excuse, go out to the van, and let Gregory in. His very appearance terrified them. Sarah had given him a sword, and, of course, he already knew how to use it."

"How did – ?"

"She made them kneel – she had a gun, of course. Then Gregory . . ."

"And you were her alibi?"

"I had no choice. My wife went along with it. She didn't know what we were doing, but she didn't want trouble."

"Did Gregory carve the angels?"

Nielsen nodded: "He made them in the image of the statue above his mother's grave. The first was a mistake, he dropped it at the scene. After that it was Sarah's idea to incorporate it. She wanted everyone to think it was a serial killer, a maniac, and that the angels were his trademark."

"The black angel?"

Nielsen shook his head:

"It was supposed to be you that night. She developed this hatred of you, at first I could never understand why."

Flavor spat it: "The nigger with the badge who had the audacity to try to catch her?"

Nielsen gave a long, drawn-out sigh.

"It wasn't racial. She hated you because – I do not have to lie now, so you can believe me – she hated you because you were beautiful. She had grown to hate beauty. She hated

Jane, the girl who was her face double, she hated her make-up girl, she hated her younger co-stars on Pacific Coast, anyone who was young and attractive. I think anyone younger and more attractive reminded her of Heather. It was as though she wanted to destroy beauty itself."

The word beauty dropped into the darkness of that soulless night like a precious stone into a bottomless well, vanishing, swallowed, no sound of its fall. If she lived through this, Flavor doubted if she could ever hear that word in the same way again.

She realised that she was weeping silently. Beauty. The rational, self-justifying beast spoke of beauty, and it tripped a held-back dam of emotion that threatened to swamp her.

"You didn't even leave them with any dignity. Not even a full body to bury. Couldn't you have spared them that? Instead, you let him bring those things here to . . ." she faltered, choking on the futile words and the tears.

Nielsen seemed to notice the tears now.

"I do not expect you to understand. But the heads were his toys, they were his . . . friends."

Flavor shook her head from side to side in distress.

"Christ help us."

"There is no help, Flavor. Ask Gregory. If only he could understand he would tell you. There was no help for him. He never really had any friends, except the pastor. Then he killed his only friend."

The tears were in Flavor's mouth, running over her lips onto her tongue, she could taste the bitter salt of them.

"Then for twenty-one years he saw no-one except me and Sarah, or the occasional doctor. Living down here, he didn't understand, he was lonely. The heads became his toys, his friends. He spoke with them, played with them."

Flavor groaned in real agony.

"And as long as he was promised a new friend, he was happy."

Nielsen paused:

"Then he would do anything Sarah asked him."

"Heads," She breathed the word like an obscenity.

"We couldn't take them away from him, so there had to be somewhere for him to keep them, in case they deteriorated."

Flavor felt as though she was in a vortex, somehow out of control, spinning away into the blackness of some crazed infinity. She remembered the crackling and scratchy black and white home movie. The movie they shot on the boat?

"Nielsen, the movie that was showing down here, was that the movie you made on the boat?"

"Of course. Sarah used to show it to him, and tell him that the people on it – with the exception of me, of course – had hurt his mother. So when she went to visit the victims, she knew he would not hesitate."

Flavor said slowly:

"Did she make the appointment with Jack so that she could get me?"

"I told her she was being foolish and emotional, that it was not necessary to kill you. She thought you would be there that night, she didn't know you'd gone away. Sarah knew Jacqueline Romarin, because they were both in the business, and it seemed an easy way to get at you."

"They had DINNER together." Flavor screamed it. "DINNER!"

He pointed the gun at her in what looked remarkably like a gesture of weakness: "I had no part of it. I only know how she did it. Jack gave her permission to park in the service area at the rear of the apartments. Gregory stayed in the van. She had dinner with Jacqueline, then left, jamming the service entrance open on the way out. Then she took Gregory in via the service entrance and elevator. When she rang the apartment door bell Jacqueline presumably thought Sarah had forgotten something."

Silence.

Nielsen said: "But she let Sarah back into the apartment. Maybe she should have asked herself how Sarah had got back into the apartment without using the security buzzer."

Flavor wiped tears and mucus from her eyes and nose with the back of her hand.

"But if she had dinner with Jack, Jack must have told her I was away in New Hampshire. Sarah KNEW I wasn't there. She knew she couldn't kill me that night."

Nielsen said nothing.

"She knew, and yet still she went back with Gregory. And they left the black angel. She had Jack killed to SPITE me!"

"I had no part – "

Flavor clenched her fists, moving dangerously forward, and Nielsen raised the gun in panic. "I'll kill you, believe me, I'll kill you."

She bit her lip in fury, bit it until it bled, and she could feel the warm, salt taste of the blood mix in a stinging cocktail with the tears on her tongue.

"I wish she was alive. I wish Sarah was alive so I could kill her, so I could kill you BOTH!"

Whatever composure Nielsen had lost, he seemed to regain. He said calmly: "Step back." She didn't move. "Step back!"

He pointed the gun at her upper leg.

"Step back or I'll fire one shot into your thigh. You will hurt, Flavor, and bleed. He likes blood, you know that now."

She hesitated, then retreated a pace.

"One more."

She took a pace backwards.

"You have to believe me. I came here today to finish it. I had planned to kill Gregory, it was the only way to stop Sarah. It was all out of control, and I suspected Wishaw was coming here. Gregory is cunning, he has made tunnels out of here, I believe that is how he found Wishaw prowling around, and killed him. Whether you believe me or not is now irrelevant. I meant to finish it."

"If Gregory can leave the bunker at will, why doesn't he escape?"

"Escape where? This is his home, as you say. There is

shelter here, and food, and clothing. You haven't seen him dress, have you Flavor. He can be a woman, he can be a man, he can be a CHILD. Here is his theatre, why should he not return?"

She gagged, and spat a ball of blood and mucus on the floor. In the world of the normal she would have felt self-disgust, here she felt nothing.

She said, thickly, her bitten lip swelling rapidly: "Why did Gregory kill her?"

"I don't know. When I came down here I found her like this. I came down here minutes before you. Gregory had gone. Now all we can do is wait for his return."

Once again the noise. A touch of material on metal, Nielsen didn't hear it, but Flavor did, and realised the source had moved. Now it was off to the right, somewhere in a pool of darkness.

She dared not look for fear of alerting Nielsen, but she had the sensation a deer must feel. A deer could smell a lion like she could smell the thing that stalked them.

For the two of them, she and Nielsen, were being stalked. Something – presumably Gregory – was watching them like a predator in the darkness.

McCall said tetchily: "Doesn't this damn thing go any faster?"

The man gave him a withering look: "S'going a damn sight faster than you was when we found you."

McCall took the Colt out of his waistband, saw the man's face, and said quickly: "Don't worry, I'm a police officer – kind of."

He checked the magazine, slid it back inside the butt of the automatic, then pulled the slide back to make the gun ready.

"As soon as you've dropped me, find the nearest 'phone and dial 911." McCall looked at his watch and his eyes felt like they were operating independently in two different heads.

344

It was 12:05. She'd said if she hadn't called by noon, send in the cavalry. Well it was noon plus, and she hadn't called. Of course, he wasn't there to take the call, but it didn't matter. He KNEW she hadn't called.

He knew damn well she was in trouble. If he was wrong . . . hell, he WASN'T wrong. McCall said to the driver: "Tell them you have two police officers on a murder enquiry, and you suspect one officer is down. Remember – officer down, say it like that."

The man nodded, and spat laconically out of the aging pick-up's window: "Sure. I'll say it just like that."

Officer down. Shit, McCall thought, I hope it isn't so. And even the unspoken words, the mere act of thinking, sent echoes through his throbbing head like shouts down a high-sided valley.

Flavor said: "And when he returns?"

"Do you know what the date is, Flavor?"

"The date?" Yesterday had been . . . "It's the 24th of August, why?"

"Think. That date has a significance here."

Flavor remembered just minutes before, but what seemed like a lifetime ago, checking Ziegal's diary. The 24th of August was . . .

"My God, Gregory's birthday."

"Indeed. Today, Gregory is thirty-three."

"You're insane too."

He ignored her: "On a birthday you receive a gift. I intend to give Gregory a gift. I shall give him a new toy for his birthday – a new friend with whom he can play."

Her legs suddenly felt enormously heavy, her stomach light. Where was her courage, where were the guts that had brought her into this place, now she faced this dreadful truth?

"Yes, Flavor. I shall give him the gift of your head. Remember the Nazi killer, Adolf Eichmann, the one the Israelis kidnapped and hanged? He once said: 'I shall leap into my grave laughing, knowing I have the deaths of six million people on my conscience.' I can understand that. After one the rest are irrelevant, and although I did not personally kill anyone, my complicity is obvious. So Eichmann's position is mine – in miniature. I am too far in to stop now, and I feel almost nothing. Because there is no God and no Heaven, no punishment and no Hell. There is only the here and now, the carnal sensations."

"You're wrong, Nielsen. They're all waiting for you. Smith, Alassio, Helm, Astaire – Jack. All of them."

He laughed a smug, confident little laugh.

"I doubt it. And when Gregory has taken his gift, I shall finish the job. His birthday shall also be the day of his death. I shall use your revolver. Then there will be a fire, a big fire."

She felt incredibly calm, although her legs still felt like lead. Something moved, off in the darkness, behind and to the right of Nielsen, something murky white, like a ghost.

"Don't be ridiculous, Nielsen. Fire doesn't destroy teeth, bones. They'll know what went on here. All the money in Hollywood won't buy you out of this one."

He paused as if to consider it:

"No, you are quite correct, fire does not destroy teeth, or bones. I do not wish it to. Sarah Ziegal is mad. Sarah Ziegal has a secret bunker in which she keeps – something, some strange burned creature that was the Angel. She telephoned you, perhaps, you came here, you found Sarah beheaded, you found the heads of the victims, and you shot Gregory – it is your gun I shall use, as I said."

The ghostly shape moved.

"You are the heroine who has killed the Angel – but sadly, he managed to kill you before he died. A conflagration ensued. After all, the bodies will be, with the exception of Gregory, both beheaded. Then, of course, there will be the rest of the severed heads. The police will quickly establish what happened."

"And what if they check your alibis for Sarah?"

"I was only ever asked for one. And I shall stand by it. It

will not matter. There is no killer, no culprit, no evidence, NOTHING."

"You are here – now."

"No, I am at home – "

"Your housekeeper told me – "

"My housekeeper will say what I wish her to say. She's from Chiapas, Mexico, her Green Card depends on me." He looked almost nonchalant.

"No-one saw me arrive, no-one will see me depart. The fire will not start until very late tonight. I am . . ." he bit into the words, "NOT CONNECTED. The Angel killings will stop. Ergo, Sarah Ziegal was behind the killings. There is nothing, I repeat to you Flavor, NOTHING to connect me with those killings."

He gave a shrug:

"Anyway, just as in 1966, I have no choice. I cannot let you live, I cannot let Gregory live. It is a matter of practicality. I regret your death, I do not regret his. He is a monster. Soon you will see just how MUCH of a monster."

"No," she said it calmly, "he's not the monster. You are. You and she were the monsters. You're worse than anything he could ever be."

"I am obliged to destroy him."

"Destroy him? Nielsen, whatever he has done he is not an animal, he is human. He's your child, you bred him, don't you feel anything? For God's sake you are his FATHER!"

It was as though she had struck him or turned on a deafening noise. He thrust his gun hand and free hand up to his ears, as if to block out the sound, and cried out:

"Shut up! SHUT-UP! Don't say it."

She looked at him in amazement, suddenly seeing the chink in the armour, the soft underbelly of vulnerability.

"My God. Now I see why you want to kill him. You hate him most of all because he reminds you of yourself. And you know you gave him life. He is your sins made flesh. He's all the evil in you, reproduced, isn't he Nielsen?"

He raised the gun: "I'll kill you. I won't wait for

Gregory."

"When you look in the mirror, do you see Gregory? Do you, Nielsen?" She thrust the spear in, remorselessly:

"You're Dr. Frankenstein, and he's your monster. You had sex with a CHILD, and you bred your monster. He's yours Nielsen, he's your son, your daughter, both in one. There is a God, and he punished you with Gregory. Your BALLS spawned him."

Nielsen's look was pure pain:

"He should have DIED! We should have killed him in the womb."

Flavor laughed in his face; laughed at the cellar, and the memories and the demons, and at the dark, evil place that life had become. She would die, but she had beaten it.

"Does he even KNOW that you are his father? Did you ever tell him, Nielsen?"

"SHUT-UP, I said."

"Does he?"

"No, and he'll never know," Nielsen had the gun centred on her body. She could see the extra tension on his face, he was about to squeeze the trigger.

"He'll die not knowing I'm his father."

She heard no warning sound, no movement in the darkness, her whole life was focused now on the barrel of this gun. Her only thought was: I showed no fear, McCall, try to understand that I showed no fear.

The slithering whisper slid like a snake from the jungle of darkness. A sibilant wet hiss of sound that froze Flavor's spine, and rooted her to the spot.

She saw Nielsen go rigid, eyes widening.

The serpent voice said:

"YOU-ARE-MY-FATHER?" And louder: "YOU-ARE-MY-FATHER!"

CHAPTER TWENTY

The man-woman that was Gregory stepped from the darkness.

Nothing could possibly have prepared Flavor for this apparition.

The ghostly whiteness she had glimpsed in the darkness behind Nielsen was not a garment, it was the naked flesh of a creature too long denied the light, and now the smell was overwhelming.

It was the distilled essence of his condition, his medicine, and his confinement. It was the stench of something buried alive, long ago.

She was transfixed, beyond horror, riveted by a compelling and voyeuristic fascination. She realised it was to malign the colour to describe Gregory as white.

He had no colour. It was as though he was bloodless, drained of the very stuff of life itself. The effect was of a nothingness, a lack. In shape he was squat and small, no more than five feet in height, and utterly devoid of hair on any part of his anatomy.

Gregory was as Nielsen had cruelly described him – like one of the tragic farmyard freaks of Nature. Suspended from his flattened, muscled chest were – it was too much of a perversion of the word to describe them as breasts, with that connotation of beauty and succour – appendages that resembled the withered dugs of a dried-up crone.

Gregory's eyes were red-rimmed and almost albino like in that strange lighting.

The face was the blueprint for some nightmare future race bred for life underground. A round, hairless skull with mice eyes, a flattened nose and little below the mouth except a tiny jut of chin.

But it was the mouth itself that sickened.

Wetly-red lips, the shape of them and the mouth they made, not circular, but somehow irregularly broken like a sea-anemone moved by water.

And as she watched, transfixed, the lips pulled back as a plant opening to catch a fly or plankton, shrinking back to reveal toothless red gums.

And then from the obscene mouth, this creature she had been told was a monster, incapable of communication, a deeply retarded thing, a body brought by circumstance to murder, and then taught again to murder; from this mouth came the incredulous words:

"You! YOU are my father!"

It was as though each word somehow began and ended with a multiple ssss sound, a sucking wetness that touched a deep disgust in the ear of the listener.

Flavor noted, almost as an afterthought, that Gregory held a Samurai sword in what were bizarre, over-sized hands.

It was as though Nielsen had become paralysed, shocked into statue-like immobility. Gregory moved, slowly, in a strange, crab movement, his stunted legs bowed and bent like some Thirties' rickets victim.

The white bullet-head cocked to one side, and looked at Nielsen as a dog may gaze quizzically on its master.

The voice sucked on another word: "Father?"

Gregory moved nearer to Nielsen in the trundling, crab gait. He loosed one hand from the sword, and placed it palm up, like some human baseball mitt, so out of proportion was it to the rest of his body.

The hand stretched towards Nielsen.

"My father."

Nielsen was motionless, unblinking.

Gregory said: "Play with me, father. Be my friend."

It leant on the sword now, like a cripple, the arm and pleading hand just an inch from Nielsen's face. It was almost Biblical; a blind beggar pleading for alms, pleading for love, pleading for some human touch in a world devoid of pity.

It was also a child pleading for recognition from its parent.

For a second the three of them were frozen like that, a tableau of players in that hideous drama. Perhaps it could have been different if Nielsen had made some gesture of kindness, had said even a word of love, responsibility or kinship.

If he had uttered something that might have penetrated the brain of this tortured thing he had fathered.

Nielsen said nothing, instead he came alive.

He stepped back and raised the gun, his hands palsied with fear.

Flavor screamed: "Nielsen – no!"

Gregory had two hands on the sword now, the mouth open in a sea-cave grimace of fear.

Nielsen fired.

There was an ear-piercing, deafening boom, a whine of metal hitting stone, the screech of a ricochet, and the stench of cordite. Gregory moved, not backwards, but forwards, bringing the sword up, the blade raised high above his head.

Nielsen fired again.

A piece of Gregory's neck exploded in a six-inch high, black-red gout of blood and flesh, and he gave a high, agonised scream.

He swung the blade.

It picked up a swishing blur of red light, and then there was a sickening abattoir sound as razor-edged steel met flesh, sinew, bone and artery.

Nielsen made no sound as the arterial blood sprayed in a curving fountain, then crashed lifeless in a great slap and thud of heavy flesh.

The monster to whom he had given life – and who had taken his, turned, his torso sashed with his father's blood, looked at Flavor, raised its head and gave a hideous animal cry of agony to the barred Heavens.

She ran – for her life.

Flavor had a few seconds start, and she was in the next room before she heard the cry of anger and the sound of pursuit. She ran doggedly, everything now just an avenue of her escape.

She reached the stair-ladder and began to climb. Within seconds she felt the extra movement and weight on the ladder and cast a fearful glance down.

The white, now-murderous face looked up into hers, as the giant hands clasped the rail.

A chunk of flesh the size of an apple was missing from his neck, she could see raw meat hanging red, and something like wet, red string trailing across his shoulder.

Cold terror was allied to purpose now. She was a machine working for survival, an organism dedicated to flight. The bunker entrance lid was open as she had left it, and Flavor hauled herself out.

Her vision was tunnelled, as though everything peripheral was excluded as irrelevant. She dashed through the gap between the vehicles, and half-stopped, slithering to a halt, realising she had not closed the bunker lid.

She turned, only to see Gregory emerging, grievously wounded and bloodied. Flavor gave a half-choked cry of fear, as she saw him blinking like a new-born white rat in the glare of the garage neon.

She blundered on, and gave a short cry of breath-catching agony, as in her haste she caught her knee with a sickening crack on the metal upright of a workbench.

Her leg buckled under her, but she staggered on, putting all the weight on her right leg, dragging the left, until she was back in the corridor.

Her mind went blank. Where was the door?

In blind panic, hopping on one leg, she inadvertently passed the front door without being aware of it, reached the stairs, and half crawled onto the first step, before something rational stopped her. She was about to climb into a self-made trap.

She lifted herself, turned, the pain in her knee agonising now, located the front door, moved towards it, and as she did, Gregory came out of the utility room, clawing blindly with his free hand, the sword a locating cane, tapping out a path with the point like a deadly Blind Pew.

The realisation stunned her. His eyes were like slits and it was clear he was virtually blind in the daylight. Nielsen said Sarah Ziegal had always taken him out in the van, and the van had smoked windows.

The murders had been at night – night was Gregory's country – and when she had led him into the homes of the unwitting victims she must have guided him, or let him adjust to the artificial light.

Flavor stopped, but Gregory had already located her by sound, and his face sniffed the air like an animal. He moved confidently towards her, rocking on the bowed legs, the sword like a water diviner, waving from side to side in front of him.

Flavor abandoned caution. She hopped, backwards, favouring her agonising leg, never taking her eyes off Gregory, found the study, opened the door, slammed it shut behind her, felt frantically for a key, located it, and locked the door.

She listened, terrified, as the pad-pad sound of Gregory's bare footsteps reached the door, and then stopped. His evil essence leaked through the door like ectoplasm.

Flavor waited, her heart pounding, her lungs heaving against her ribs. There was just silence. Silence. More silence.

She hobbled closer to the door, and as quietly as she could pressed her ear to the woodwork.

She could hear nothing, no movement, no breathing. She knew the bullet had wounded Gregory, perhaps fatally. He was losing blood, and soon he must –

The blade came through the door with the force of an arrow shaft, as though the wood was paper. The point missed her waist by just a couple of inches. Flavor thrust herself one-legged from the door, and fell heavily.

The pain was agonising, and to quell it she bit at her torn lip, lighting another cruel fire to distract herself from the furnace that was consuming her leg.

Through the blinds she could see the foetid swimming pool. If she could get outside and reach the wall, even with her injured leg, she could perhaps clamber over it and reach her car.

In whatever corner of her brain that still worked normally she doubted if the stunted Gregory could follow her.

She gripped at Ziegal's desk, clambered to her feet, and clawed at the blinds, yanking them from their mounts. Two sliding bolts secured the French windows top and bottom, and she reached up, tottering on her good leg, and freed one bolt.

She then lowered herself, lost her balance and fell over. Her knee flared with agony, but lying on her side she clawed at the remaining bolt. It stuck. She pulled at it, felt a nail tear like some distant event, tried again, felt skin rip like fabric, but at last the bolt slid free of its housing.

She pulled herself up on the door frame, turned the handle, and pushed at the doors. Nothing.

Flavor gave a small sob of panic, then saw the silver protrusion of the floor lock, at one corner of the doors, the key – mercifully – still in it.

She knelt again, went off balance, unwittingly put weight

on her injured leg and heard the knee give a sickening crack.

The pain was like a giant wave breaking over her. It threatened to drown her. Sweat broke out on her forehead. The kneecap was fractured, she knew it.

She regained her balance on the good leg, found the key with her clumsy, bleeding fingers, turned it, and slid out the lock.

The French windows opened, and she felt the wave of heat on her skin as she emerged into the yard. The fence – and safety – was just twenty yards away.

She hopped from the shelter of the house into the open space between herself and the wall.

At that moment a strong arm encircled her, and smothered the scream that was forming in her mouth. Flavor blacked out.

The swoon lasted just a few seconds and then she was pulled like a cork onto the surface of consciousness, to see a face inches from hers. She was about to scream, when realisation dawned.

"McCall!"

"Flavor, what the hell is going on?"

He saw her face, the expression of horror etched into it, realised she was not looking at him, but over his shoulder, and McCall turned.

It was as though someone had plunged the sun into a glacier and trapped it in the ice. His blood chilled.

Gregory stood there in the hot, bright sunlight, like an alien who has wandered into a different and hostile environment. He had an expression of agony on his face as the sun blinded him.

His left hand held the sword's handle across his eyes, trying to blot out the light, while his right gripped at the chopped butcher's meat of his wounded neck.

McCall gave an exclamation of horror.

Gregory heard the sound, swivelling like a blind man, centreing on its location.

"Flavor, what is it?"

She was trying in vain to rise to her feet.

"What in God's name is it, Flavor?"

She couldn't answer, the pain was choking her.

McCall raised the automatic. He was scared; more deeply scared than he had ever been in his life. It was hardly human.

She found the words, steeled herself, shouted them, and accepted the stab of vicious pain that was her reward.

"Don't kill it, McCall, don't kill it. It can't see, it's blind. In the light it's blind."

But McCall's eyes and mind were on Gregory, on this naked monster and this vicious blade that glinted in the sun. He screamed an order: "Put it down, put the weapon down."

McCall half-turned as he heard the cry of pain as Flavor tried to rise. She said through the mist of pain:

"I don't know if it can understand."

Gregory's head came up, the eyes closed against the light, the sword arm raised, and McCall saw properly for the first time the horrific wound, and the blood that poured in a steady funnel from the raw meat.

"Put-the-weapon-down!"

Gregory said one more, sibilant word: "Play."

McCall centred the foresight of the Colt on the strange dwarf-like body.

"I'm a police officer. Put down the weapon, NOW!"

Flavor screamed it: "He doesn't understand. Gregory, put it down, put the sword down." Her words trailed off in a cry of pain from the knee fracture.

Gregory charged.

McCall would remember it as a dream sequence. It was as though a statue on a plinth had suddenly taken life. The creature came towards him in its trundling, crab-like gait.

Then the dream speeded up and the creature was almost upon him, the sword raised, its blade glinting in the sun. For a nano-second – no more – McCall saw upon the head of Gregory the face of the youth in the riots. The youth he had shot. Then it was gone, and there was just the white skull head, the red sucking hole, the white red-rimmed eyes, as they would be for ever imprinted on his mind.

McCall fired.

The automatic bucked, there was a tremendous spout of red and blue flame and a crack-slap of percussion as the gun went off. The heavy bullet hit Gregory in the upper left torso, shattered two ribs, tore open his heart and exploded out of his back in a widening hole, carrying fragments of rib cage, flesh and heart muscle.

The force stopped him dead – literally. Death was instantaneous from the moment the heart ruptured. Then the opposite impact combined with his forward motion, spun Gregory in a full circle, and threw him into the pool.

McCall stepped backwards, incredulous and frightened.

Gregory floated sideways in the pool, the scabrous water darkening with blood around him. The sword had disappeared, there was a long and narrow break in a distant patch of the scum-covered water where the blade had gone through.

McCall turned to where Flavor lay. He was shaking. Carefully he put the automatic down on the weed-infested paving, and with one hand, tried to still the other.

She was looking up at him through gritted teeth and pain-filled eyes. He cradled her head in his arms, stroking her forehead, and spoke fearfully, terrified now of losing her love.

He didn't know, couldn't possibly understand yet, the complex truth of what had happened here, but he knew the creature would have killed them both.

Yet he knew he had ignored her pleas, and now he wished to explain:

"I had to do it, Flavor. I had to shoot. I had no choice. You have to understand, I HAD to."

Everything was becoming distant, as the ringing in her ears turned to the distant sound of police sirens.

Then she heard the woman who had escaped from the cellar begin to speak. No, she corrected herself, it was not a cellar, it was a bunker, a nuclear bunker. Ah well, her hallucinating, pain-filled brain argued with her, it was a cellar too. You said yourself the cellar was just a metaphor.

Yes, a metaphor, she argued, but it was a real metaphor. And don't forget, she told the wicked, hurting pain that argued with her, I've beaten the cellar too.

She heard that woman, who she knew was herself, Flavor Cartouche, who had stopped arguing with the pain now, because that pain was hurting her so badly she just wanted to weep with it; she heard that woman say to the man she loved, who was surely real:

"He was born to die, McCall. Gregory was born to die. Kathleen said so, only I didn't know it was Kathleen. She said he was born to die."

And she realised, before the fog took her, that he didn't understand. He didn't understand at all. But she had for ever to tell him.

Flavor lay with her plastered leg up on the edge of the sofa, a balloon glass of brandy in her hand, occasionally easing sips over her sore and stitched lip. Madonna lay across Flavor's stomach, purring contentedly.

McCall sat with his back up against the sofa, his drink-free hand alternately stroking both the cat and its mistress. Apart from the deep, throaty purr there had been silence like that for long minutes.

At last he turned and looked up at Flavor. She was crying silently. He raised himself, hugged her and brought her wet face into his. Madonna shifted with a tsk of annoyance at the disturbance.

"Don't say it, I know." Flavor brought her face out of the embrace and looked at McCall. "I should be happy."

He kissed the side of her mouth: "No, not happy. Just satisfied, it's over now." She shook her head: "I feel – CHEATED. It's like some party, or movie, or something, and it doesn't end the way it should end."

"The Angel is dead, and we know why it all happened, and who."

"Poor Gregory."

"How can you SAY that?"

"Yeah, it's crazy," she wiped away some tears with the back of her hand, "it's just the thought of him being locked away down there all those years by those two monsters."

"Remember what he did, Flave."

"I know that. They made him, they turned him into that. If he'd led some kind of life . . ." she began to cry again. He held her for a long time. "You know, McCall, the worst thing of it is, it seems like Ziegal gets away with it."

McCall managed a grin: "If you call ending as a victim of your own murderer getting away with it."

Flavor grimaced as her lip suddenly stung painfully:

"Oh, shit, I don't even know what the hell I mean. I wish she could face what she's done, face the evil of what she was." Flavor took an awkward drink of cognac, dribbled a little of it because of her injured lip, and McCall licked the brandy off, kissing her at the same time.

"Remember what you said about this one, way back? This was a shrinks-fest, psychiatrists wall-to-wall. If we'd brought her to trial she'd end up in a hospital someplace. Isn't it better that she's dead? Poetic justice? The person who creates the Angel killed by the Angel?"

"I guess so. Come up here properly," she squeezed up, and he lay next to her on the sofa.

"It's just – Jack, all the others . . . I would have liked to have seen her, told her, God, I know it's crazy . . ."

"Hey, come on." He stroked her and soothed her, and they fell silent again. As if sensing some need, Madonna crawled up and ran a rough, rasping tongue over her chin. McCall broke the silence:

"You say something earlier about the Q and A, on this?"

"Yeah," Flavor answered drowsily, "Internal Affairs called the hospital this morning, they want to get it over as soon as possible."

"I didn't get MY call yet, and I was the one who shot him?"

"Well, maybe it's all that suspension stuff, maybe it's the Press, I dunno."

"Who's doing the Q and A?"

"Kirkpatrick, a prelim session here, then with the lawyers and stuff downtown."

"Kirkpatrick? She's a sonofabitch."

"Not technically possible."

"You know what I mean. Why's she coming here, never known that woman give a concession in her life?"

Flavor reached down and patted the cast: "This, I guess. It's not a problem, everyone knows what they found down there. Gregory had the sword, he attacked you, you didn't have a choice."

He gently turned her head to him: "You believe that, don't you?"

"Sure."

"I *didn't* have a choice."

Her hand cupped his chin: "I know, honey. Really."

"If I were you I'd have a lawyer here, Kirkpatrick takes no prisoners. Don't forget, it was an illegal entry."

"Bit late, she's coming tonight."

"Tonight? When?" He looked at his watch, it was six: thirty.

"Eight."

"I can't believe that woman. Jesus, you're still in shock, you only got out of the hospital five hours ago, I told you she was a sonofabitch."

Flavor soothed him: "Hey, come on McCall. A half hour, that's all."

"And I can't be here, right? In my own home."

"You can't be present, that's obvious. She'll send her Q and A report to Bev Hills, you're still under suspension – be reasonable."

"I am being."

"She's due at eight, go down to the Silver Spoon, have

coffee, read the Times, come back. No problem."

McCall moodily gulped some cognac.

"I want out of LA."

"What?"

He turned his head to face her again: "When this is over, the Q and A, the Internal Affairs enquiry, I want out."

"There can't be a charge, you acted in self-defence. I'm your witness."

"And," he said, with sarcasm in his voice, "you're my lover. I'm white, you're black."

"Forget it. We solved the Angel case and we're clean."

McCall looked at the floor: "I still want out. I'm finished as a cop here, you know that. I want out of LA."

He looked back at her: "You're the star. Stay if you want. I'll understand."

"Hey, hey," once again her hand came up and stroked his face, "this is all too heavy. After Kirkpatrick goes I'll cook dinner – "

"Your leg, you can't – "

"I'll cook dinner, you can buy some expensive wine – champagne, why not? – and we'll talk. Deal?"

"Oh, it's just – "

"Deal or not?"

"OK."

She kissed him.

"What I'm saying Flavor is, maybe this changes things, if you want to stay. Christ, you could be chief one day."

She put a finger across his lips.

"We'll talk, OK. And remember what we once said, for ever and ever, until the moment we die."

He looked into her brown eyes and he felt, like an unfamiliar garment, the terrible vulnerability of loving and being in love.

"We'll talk." He kissed her.

Chapter Twenty-One

McCall pulled on his sports jacket and checked his watch:
"She's late."

Flavor looked up from her magazine: "Yeah? What time is it?"

"Ten after," he padded his pockets, checking for his wallet. "Maybe she crashed her car or something because that must be the first time in her career she's even been a SECOND late, from what I heard of her from the guys at Bev Hills."

Flavor pulled a face: "The key word in that sentence, being GUYS. She's a woman in her Fifties, so she's not considered humpable – "

"Come on, Flavor – "

"She's not married, so she's probably a dyke, she has a career, she has power, so she's a martinet, a dragon . . ."

McCall put his hands up in surrender: "Hey, you win, she's a totally misunderstood granny figure, I know. And

363

while she sits in MY apartment with her moustache, and grills the woman I love, I have to walk off and drink coffee I don't need."

Flavor shook her head: "Must be your period, McCall."

He laughed: "Ever tried walking with TWO plaster casts." He went across and kissed her. "She's got 'till nine, then I'm coming back whatever."

"Can you give Madonna the run of the cat-flap, I've got a feeling Kirkpatrick is NOT going to be an animal lover."

"Sure. She can come out with me."

McCall left the apartment building with Madonna in his arms, dropped her out on the front lawn and watched her slide silkily away into some undergrowth, then, turned right and walked towards the lights of Santa Monica Boulevard.

As he did the middle-aged woman sitting in the car parked across the street watched him go, then got out of her car carrying a tennis bag, locked the car and walked across to the apartment block McCall had just left.

The buzzer went.

Flavor got awkwardly to her feet and limped across to the inter-com. "Yes?"

"Kirkpatrick, IA."

"Yes, just a moment. I'll leave the door for you." Flavor pressed the entrance buzzer, then opened the apartment door and left it a couple of inches ajar.

She hobbled back to the sofa and lay down again.

Despite herself she felt a slight wave of apprehension. This was a Q and A, and Kirkpatrick was Internal Affairs. In the LAPD they called them the Gestapo. A force within a force, dedicated to rooting out corruption and wrongdoing.

When an officer fired a weapon – and particularly when someone was killed, and an LAPD officer was involved – IA gave them a thorough grilling.

Flavor, despite what she had said in feminine defence to McCall, had heard of Kirkpatrick's reputation. Everyone called her a dragon, even the women.

Flavor knew she had nothing to fear, and nothing of which to be ashamed. Her lover had pulled the trigger, she had made an illegal entry into a home – but what was that against what had been achieved in the end?

There was no trial at which some accused could be acquitted on a technicality because of what she had done, and the public would never blame her or McCall.

But something still quivered in her at the sound of Kirkpatrick's footsteps in the stone corridor outside the apartment door.

Something strangely resembling fear.

McCall didn't order coffee; he ordered a Scotch rocks, sat at a table on the patio under the canopy, said he'd look at the menu later and unfolded the Times.

Thank God HE wouldn't get Kirkpatrick for the Q and A, because the woman was a sumbitcher of the first order. He knew of two cops who'd lost their careers quite unfairly through her.

Word was she was no lover of blacks either. She had until nine and then McCall was going in, and if Kirkpatrick objected he might just break her neck.

Impressions of a severely-cut suit, auburn curls, a wig surely? Incongruous Slazenger tennis bag, Flavor had only time for that, and the momentary thought that Kirkpatrick looked slightly younger than expected, when the woman faced her, closing the door behind her.

"Hello Lieutenant."

It was Sarah Ziegal. It was Ziegal, Kathleen, Heather O'Malley, that terrible triumvirate of identities that had combined to cause so much agony, pain and death over the years.

Flavor felt some wave pass over her, as though she was not present, and the event was not actually occurring.

It could not be Sarah Ziegal because Sarah Ziegal was dead. Flavor had seen it with her own eyes, seen the unspeakable sight of the woman's severed head toppling from its torso.

So it could not be Sarah Ziegal. And yet, it was clearly Sarah Ziegal. Flavor found she could not speak. The two irreconcilable facts seemed to balance equally on her mind with unbearable weight, suppressing speech.

Then she sensed the poisoned scent of Gregory, and she KNEW, not how, but that it was so.

The woman took off her wig, and the suit jacket.

"Yes," the woman said. "You are not mad. Yes, is the answer your tiny brain is struggling for, Lieutenant. You are right. I am dead, but I am also alive. And that cannot be. And yet it is."

She smiled, cruelly.

Flavor said: "I SAW you . . . I SAW . . ."

"Don't believe everything you see in the movies, Flavor, didn't Jack teach you that? It's reel life, not real life."

"I SAW you dead. I . . ."

"And you saw King Kong climb the Empire State building, Lieutenant, but it didn't happen. This is Hollywood. Nothing is real, all is illusion. It is the land of make-believe."

Flavor was transfixed.

"But this," Ziegal lifted a long-bladed Samurai sword from the tennis bag, "is very real. Ask your late friend Jack."

Flavor came out of her trance, glanced across the room to where her Smith and Wesson hung from a chair in its shoulder holster, and tried to struggle to her feet.

Ziegal was like lightning, and in a second Flavor was sent reeling from a blow from Ziegel's fist that knocked her backwards onto the sofa and split her stitched lip.

"Remember Jane?" Sarah asked the question.

Flavor shook her head.

"Jane was my face double, silly girl, arrogant beyond belief. At times she thought she WAS me."

A flare went off in Flavor's mind. The name she had seen in the diary, when she had first entered the empty house. Jane. A telephone number next to it. Everything had been planned. She had lured Jane to the house on some excuse, persuaded her to be made up as her face double, then had Gregory kill her.

Such a fake body and head would pass cursory examination, then it would be sealed in a body bag until the autopsy, or an initial post-mortem examination.

Ziegal must have known it could only give a day, perhaps two, of breathing space, so she must have planned to flee the country and adopt a new identity.

"That day wasn't an accident."

Ziegal shook her head, then cut a swathe through the air with the sword, making a swoosh of noise that trembled the senses with its implications.

"It was becoming too much. Gregory was increasingly difficult, Kirk wanted to kill him, I knew that. It was all coming to an end. Kirk had another woman – did he tell you that? – yes, after all those years, just me and his pitiable wife, and then – well, this is Hollywood – younger flesh. But as he was the only man I've ever loved, I couldn't go on, knowing that he was seeing someone else. And suppose he had confided in HER?"

Flavor could see the possibilities for slaughter, the ever widening network of the implicated who would have to feel the horror of being visited by Gregory.

She tried to move and the blade came around, flat, the point levelled towards her.

"If you attempt to leave the couch I'll cut off one of your hands. You know how sharp this blade can be."

Flavor sank back.

"He felt you were going to find out, you and the other detective, he felt you were CLEVER." She bit into the word. "I did not place such faith in your abilities, but I knew it was time to bring it all to an end. I chose a date – Gregory's birthday. Somehow it seemed fitting. I telephoned Jane and offered to pay her $2,000 to be made up as me for a celebrity function at my house. She agreed, readily. Money buys so much, don't you find?"

"You got Gregory to kill her?"

"Yes, my little sick boy. It was a birthday present for him."

"Wishaw?"

"Where else would he have come?" She looked off, as if at the far wall, but in reality at something only she could see in her mind: "I was just a child when I married him. Then I met Kirk, and of course it was no contest. But it was touching to think he wished to avenge my death like that."

Flavor regarded her:

"You're evil Ziegal. Sick beyond redemption. The minute they take a serious look at those bodies they'll know it's not you, they'll see the mask, everything. They'll talk to the make-up artist, they'll know what you've planned, that you're still alive. Where can you run to?"

She shook her head: "I had planned Mexico, I have a house there not even Kirk knew about – "

"He's dead, did you know that?" Flavor jabbed with the only weapon she possessed, knowledge, words.

"I read the newspaper this morning," Ziegal replied calmly.

"Gregory did it – he learned Kirk was his father."

"Ah, life," Ziegal said, and continued as though nothing had been said: "I have the ticket, a different passport, I could have left this morning."

"But when you read about Kirk – "

"No, Lieutenant, I TOLD Gregory Kirk was his father. I told Gregory that it was KIRK who had killed his mother. I WANTED him to kill Kirk."

"Then, why stay?"

"You. YOU!"

"I can't believe I was ever that important."

Ziegal swirled the blade in a kind of figure of eight with the point.

"After you came to see us, we talked about you. About black people, black officers, black women, their attractiveness or otherwise."

Flavor took a deep breath. At some point she would have launch herself off the couch and rush Ziegal, there was no other way.

"He said . . ." she paused, "he said that he would like to sleep with you. He said that when the investigation was over, he would pursue you – through your friend the screenwriter. He would seduce you, with his money and power – it's done all the time Flavor, don't look so shocked or repelled, you would have given in eventually, they all do."

"When the Grand Canyon fills in."

"You underestimate him. A man of great charm, of lust and charisma. But he said that to me; to ME, Lieutenant. Can you imagine the man you love, to whom you have dedicated your life, for whom you have killed your own sister, speaking to you calmly of seducing another woman – a BLACK woman?"

"So by killing Jack you thought you'd cut off the conduit to me? It wasn't just me you wanted."

"Oh, I would have had Gregory kill you too, if you'd been there. But it seemed logical to dispose of Jacqueline. I was protecting my assets, you can see that."

"You're insane. You don't realise what you're saying or doing."

She nodded: "Well, you may have a point, there used to be a song with a line in it, 'and you never, never know when you're insane,' do you remember it?"

Flavor didn't answer.

"But insanity, you will find, has its own logic."

"How did you know that Gregory would understand when you told him about Kirk?"

"The idiot child knew far more, understood far more, than Kirk ever realised. I lived with Gregory, I was his mentor, I knew that."

Flavor clenched her teeth.

"Have you no conscience? Does nothing in your heart tell you that doing what you did is wrong?"

Ziegal looked as if she was seriously contemplating the

question: "Consciences are for the likes of you, Lieutenant. I am afraid for me the world just became a battlefield. Did you know why I killed my sister?"

Flavor nodded, and Ziegal said:

"She threatened my Kirk's love for me. So what could impinge on a conscience after that? Killing you will be almost a nothing, but at least a revenge, and revenge, as I have learned, can be very satisfying."

McCall took another sip of the Scotch, and flicked aimlessly through the Times. Yeah, he felt like breaking someone's neck, preferably someone in the Beverly Hills Police Department, but Kirkpatrick would do. How could she do the Q and A, or the prelim for it, NOW? Flavor was traumatised and physically injured. Was there no mercy?

He stopped. Break Kirkpatrick's neck. His fingertips touched the Times. Metro section. Break a neck. Break. The fingertips went icy. Elvira Kirkpatrick of IA broke her hip in a car crash two weeks ago and was in Cedars-Sinai, he had read it in the Times, Metro section. The crash was deliberate, an aggrieved ex-cop was under arrest.

McCall jumped onto the chair, grabbed a canopy stanchion and vaulted the wall, scattering his Scotch, the plates, the tablecloth and an oblong tub of ornamental shrubs. He landed on the hood of a parked car, and it dented under his weight.

He heard shouts, cries of protest, but he leapt off and ran, arms going like pistons, jacket tails flap-flapping behind him, sprinting like a twenty year old. Running like a demon to try to save the life of the woman he loved.

Ziegal took a step forward.

"Get off the couch slowly, and kneel in front of me."

"Fuck you, Ziegal, fuck you."

"I can cut you in pieces if I wish, believe me, it's light, it's tough, and it's razor sharp." She smiled: "It's also – tested."

"You think I'm going to kneel, so you can do what

Gregory did?"

"You would be amazed at how quick it is."

Flavor met the vacant, insane eyes.

"You like it, honey, that's why you do it. Revenge because Nielsen wanted to hump me isn't in it. You LIKE it, don't you?"

"Kneel at my feet."

Ziegal had moved closer now. It would take one angry thrust and the blade would go right through Flavor, and she knew it.

"OK, but you're gonna have to step back."

Ziegal eased back a pace, and Flavor swung her bad leg off the couch.

They heard the click of the door together. Ziegal swung round, the blade trailing, into the whirlwind that was McCall, a blur of charging man.

Then the blade zipped through the space between she and McCall, and Flavor cried out as the tip of the blade sliced across McCall's torso, shredding his jacket, slicing flesh.

McCall gave a breathless gasp as a beaded curtain of blood arced from his chest and hung motionless for seconds like some evil rainbow.

McCall toppled, the apartment shaking as he hit the carpet, and Ziegal raised the sword for the final, killing blow.

Desperately Flavor swung her injured, plastered leg, crashing the weight into Ziegal's legs, felling her with a sharp cry of pain.

The sword spun off, crashed into the wall, and landed harmlessly on the carpet. Ziegal grabbed for it, and Flavor brought the heel of her naked foot down with all her might on the stretched, defenceless fingers.

Ziegal screamed as two of the fingers broke.

When next she looked up Flavor was standing over her with the Smith and Wesson.

"Move to one side motherfucker, NOW!"

Ziegal crabbed sideways, away from the sword, away

from the prostrate McCall. He was looking up, eyes unfocused, a welt of blood across his body, but Flavor could see that there was no pump of the stuff, just a steady drip-drip through his sliced shirt.

"Hang on there McCall, you're going to be OK, she didn't get an artery."

He looked up, focused, found her, and gave a white-faced parody grin of re-assurance. Then he dragged himself backwards, and propped himself against the wall, feeling for a handkerchief, balling it and thrusting it against his slashed chest.

Ziegal had managed to prop herself up and was holding her smashed fingers protectively in to her body. Bizarrely, like an injured child, she looked up at Flavor and said petulantly: "You hurt me."

Flavor regarded at her with astonishment: "WHAT!?"

The woman thrust her good hand out, like a child does, as if to strike, but to indicate hurt and abandonment: "You HURT me. You have to take me to the hospital, I need a doctor." She started to cry: "My fingers hurt, I need a doctor."

McCall said, his voice slurred with pain: "Call 911, get the boys over here, and get an ambulance."

Flavor had her mouth open. It was not – not RIGHT. This woman, this EVIL woman, who had killed her friend Jack, who had killed – or been responsible for – the killing of so many people. And now SHE pleaded for a doctor.

They would set her broken fingers, give her antibiotics, and probably a calming sedative. Then would come the shrinks, and the counselling, and the evaluations, and the hospital, and – even if there WAS a trial – some hospital for ever, with regular food and recreation. Sarah Ziegal would see sunlight and rain, Winters and Summers. Unlike Jack or any of the others. It wasn't FAIR!

Flavor felt shutters coming down all over her mind, like someone closing up a house when the Summer is over. It was like a farewell of youth, like no-one was ever coming back to that house, or to the memories of rooms that have echoed with laugher. It was as though its very beliefs were being covered in dust sheets for ever.

She looked at McCall.

"You want her to learn Spanish, McCall?"

"What?" He groaned.

"You want her to learn Spanish, like the man who killed your daughter?"

Ziegal wailed like a smacked child: "I need a doctor – I have my RIGHTS."

Flavor thumbed the hammer back on the Smith and Wesson, McCall heard the noise and opened his eyes: "Don't Flavor!"

"Keep out of this McCall. Listen, Ziegal, I want to ask you something. What do you think they felt, Jack, and the rest of them, at that moment, that precise goddamn moment when your monster creation stood over them? What?"

Ziegal was crying, an insane, regressed wail, like a smacked toddler in grown-up clothes:

"I don't know, I didn't do anything, it was Gregory, not me. I want a doctor, I want my RIGHTS!"

Flavor looked at Ziegal in new horror.

"Well, you know what I think? I think they probably felt the most awful cold fear of eternity. Say hello to it."

Ziegal looked up, very sane, very rational terror now in her eyes.

"You CAN'T, you're a police officer. You CAN'T . . . I have constitutional rights."

All the darkness of the years flooded in, all the frustration and the misery and the heartache of walking in the gutter and sewer of life.

Everything now, every wrong, every injustice seen or personally experienced, flooded into Flavor like she was a vessel for all the unrevenged sins committed against the innocent for centuries.

She looked at McCall: "Close your eyes."

"Flavor, please, don't. This isn't you. Me, maybe, in the

days before I met you, but not you."

She bit on the newly injured lip and felt the sudden start of pain like a kick of alcohol or cocaine, as the boost she needed for her task.

"I'm different now, McCall. Different."

She levelled the gun at Ziegal and the woman wailed.

"You can't SHOOT me!" The face was stark and terrified, wild-eyed in its frightened madness.

Flavor looked at her for three lifetime-long seconds. Then she spoke:

"The world has closed for today, Ziegal. The courts are empty, constitution suspended. The system will be back tomorrow. As for now, we've got this thing called justice. Special offer. Just for today. And you're my only customer."

Ziegal's face changed from childish spite to adult menace.

"Nigger bitch."

Flavor ignored her: "Know what you smell of Ziegal? Not just Gregory. You smell of evil, pure evil. I didn't think it really existed until I met you. Now I know it does, and you can't talk to evil. I've learned that. You can only kill it."

McCall looked into Flavor's eyes, then closed his.

Two shots, close together, deafening in the enclosed space, and a gasp – almost of surprise – from Sarah Ziegal.

Flavor looked a long time at the body, then let the gun fall from her fingers.

McCall opened his eyes, saw the body, saw the motionless figure of Flavor standing, her own eyes closed now, and said gently:

"Flavor?"

Slowly she eased herself down next to him where he sat, propped against the wall, clutching his bloodied chest, and she laid her head on his shoulder.

They sat like that for a long time, oblivious to the noise of the shouting voices from the other apartments, to the scared but inquisitive faces that peered in through the open door, to the eventual distant wailing of a police siren.

When eventually McCall lifted his head, the first thing he saw was his daughter's photograph.

And her eyes were watching him.

EPILOGUE

It rains a lot in the Pacific Northwest, but Flavor doesn't mind. Sometimes she takes their daughter out into the rain, just the two of them, and they stand in the paddock behind the house just splashing and laughing.

Rain seems so pure to her now, compared with sunshine, and it can wash away so many things.

Flavor and McCall moved here after she got out of the hospital. They got married and had Sophie a year later.

The hospital helped a lot, but occasionally the nightmares still come. She's resigned to them, like a cripple his limp. They're a legacy of her injuries.

But at least now when she wakes, she can reach out and feel the strong body of McCall next to her. Or go into the next room and see Sophie sleeping, the covers up under her chin. That makes it better.

He's in the local Sheriff's office, and covers a 300 square mile area, so his day is long. But he never works the night shift, and he's there next to her every night.

She's taking law classes at home, and hopes to go into law school next year when Sophie starts her school.

The studio took the bones of Jack's unfinished screenplay and made the movie. Flavor was flattered they chose Whitney Houston to play her. McCall was even more flattered. He got Nick Nolte.

They got an agent, were paid story rights and consultancy fees, and Flavor got a chunk of the money Jack left too, so cash is not a problem now.

McCall only works because he can't kick the habit. No charges were ever brought, and King Leonard dropped his lawsuit when the juicy bits of the Angel story became known. The Angellis stayed in Europe.

Flavor and McCall declined an all-expenses trip to LA to see the premiere, and missed the movie when it came to the local cinema complex because Sophie had the measles.

But eventually they got it out on video. In the end they only watched 20 minutes, fact being – especially when you were there – far more enthralling than fiction.

Sometimes, when McCall is out in the patrol car, Sophie is taking her afternoon nap, and Flavor is hitting the law books, the rain drumming on the roof, she finds it hard to believe any of it ever happened.

Then she goes to the chest of drawers, opens one, takes out the piece of carved, varnished wood, and turns it over in her hand. It is her only memento of what happened. The black angel.

She looks for a while, remembers, then replaces it, goes back upstairs, checks on Sophie, and continues her studies.

The house she and McCall bought has a cellar. The old chest of drawers in which she keeps the black carved angel is in that cellar.